STAND UP VIRGIN SOLDIERS

rn in Newport, Monmouthshire, in 1931, Leslie Thomas
he son of a sailor who was lost at sea in 1943. His boyhood
an orphanage is evoked in *This Time Next Week*, published
1964. At sixteen, he became a reporter before going on to
his national service. He won worldwide acclaim with his
stselling novel *The Virgin Soldiers*, which has achieved inter-
tional sales of over four million copies. His most recent
vel, *Dover Beach*, is available now in William Heinemann
rdback. In 2005, Leslie Thomas was awarded an OBE for
rvices to literature.

STAND UP VIRGIN SOLDIERS

Leslie Thomas

arrow books

Published by Arrow Books in 2005

3 5 7 9 10 8 6 4 2

Copyright © Leslie Thomas 1975

Leslie Thomas has asserted his right under the Copyright, Designs and
Patents Act 1988 to be identified as the author of this work

First published in the United Kingdom in 1975 by Methuen

Arrow Books
The Random House Group Limited
20 Vauxhall Bridge Road, London SW1V 2SA

Random House Australia (Pty) Limited
20 Alfred Street, Milsons Point, Sydney,
New South Wales 2061, Australia

Random House New Zealand Limited
18 Poland Road, Glenfield,
Auckland 10, New Zealand

Random House (Pty) Limited
Isle of Houghton, Corner of Boundary Road & Carse O'Gowrie,
Houghton 2198, South Africa

The Random House Group Limited Reg. No. 954009

www.randomhouse.co.uk

A CIP catalogue record for this book is available from the British Library

Papers used by Random House are natural, recyclable products
made from wood grown in sustainable forests. The manufacturing
processes conform to the environmental regulations of the country of origin

ISBN 9780099490043

Typeset by SX Composing DTP, Rayleigh, Essex
Printed and bound in Great Britain by
CPI Antony Rowe, Chippenham, Wiltshire

To Ralph Vernon-Hunt

1

*Drastic cuts in Britain's defence
budget, announced by the Government,
will mean the reduction of the armed
services and the withdrawal of forces
from many overseas stations.*

News item, March 1975

There is a bar in Panglin village, on the island of Singapore, wedged between the main monsoon drain and the premises of a purveyor of dubious cures. In the old days, when Brigg knew it, the bar was called The Heaven-on-Earth Snack Bar and Cabaret, where girls, if not always beautiful, were ever available.

Now it is called the Moonshot Café and the girls, and probably their daughters too, are long retired. The village street has three Datsun and Toyota dealers (the Japanese always promised they would be back); the cinema has proper walls *and* a roof; the laundry, so popular with army customers, where a serene Chinese girl used to feed a baby from her breast as she served behind the counter, has become one of the village's fourteen dentists, gold teeth still being in demand.

1

The beer tasted the same, thought Brigg, as he sat on the balcony of the café and watched the street and the people. He had gone in casually, as though twenty-five hours not twenty-five years separated him from the time when he was last there, and said 'Tiger please' to the lemon-faced Chinese barmaid. The words were still sufficient. She poured the pale pool into a glass and he took it outside and sat at a creaky wicker table to drink it. The thick feel of the sun was familiar on his face. Come you back, you British soldier. Didn't the song say that? It was odd to think he would be one of the last here.

One sip of the beer, cold and sharp on his tongue, brought it all back. The place, the soldiers, the days that seemed, then, to have no end. And yet how brief it had all been. The garrison remained sitting blankly on the hill, virtually unchanged also, except there were Australian troops in the barrack blocks now. He doubted if any of them were so young and unknowing as he and his friends had been. It was a changed world. Men would never be as young as that again. The Virgin Digger did not sound right somehow. That afternoon he had walked the hot, flat square, remembering every pace of it. He had banged his boots on the surface. It sounded the same and felt the same through the soles of his feet. They had built a better canteen and garrison theatre and there was a car park for the soldiers' vehicles. But in the distance, on the other side of the ravine that divided the garrison, he could see them and hear them shouting at the swimming pool, diving from

2

the high board. He stood as though trying to recognize the voices.

The wooden bridge was intact too, hanging just as precariously across the the divisional dip, with its notice: TROOPS MUST BREAK STEP WHEN CROSSING THIS BRIDGE. Tasker had once got seven days for substituting the word WIND for STEP. Brigg smiled at the thought of Tasker. Where was he now? And Lantry and Jacobs and Clay the Yank, and dear Juicy Lucy? She must be the nearest of all. Was she still in Singapore? Was she still alive?

Brigg only knew where Brigg was. He was back where he had started, still a soldier; a less-than-sensational rise had brought him to staff-sergeant from private in a quarter of a century. He was older but how much wiser he could not guess. All he knew was that he was in the same army. He had rejoined after life had promised him nothing better, and he was still there letting it look after him, waiting, like those regulars he had so mocked in the old days, for his pension. And it was the same place. The British were getting out and he was one who had been sent to see that the doors were locked and the lights extinguished. It was poetic that he should have been sent, for he was the ghost of other days. The army he had so despised had returned him once more to the scenes of his happy, sad and fearful youth. He was back in Panglin.

2

Tasker, naked as an onion, sat on his bed in the
barrack room. He was crying. On the adjacent beds
the other young soldiers crouched, leaning towards
him with morose interest and understanding.
Lantry, Sandy Jacobs, Gravy Browning, a ball
bouncing minutely on his table-tennis bat, Foster
and Villiers, their young faces creased with concern,
their hands just touching.

Despite his year in Singapore, Tasker had never
been one for taking off his shirt. His face was the
same iodine colour as the others, so were his arms to
above the elbows. But the rest was bald white skin,
his chest sown with a few poorly nourished ginger
hairs, his loins sprouting a slightly better yield. His
eyes were red. His penis hung like a limp lighthouse.
He was a poor sight.

Brigg's boots sounded up the concrete stairs and

scraped along the balcony. He came at a slouch through the door and stopped. He regarded the weeping Tasker for a while. The other heads turned.

'What's up with him?' asked Brigg.

'He's crying,' shrugged Lantry.

'Jesus wept,' sighed Brigg. 'I can *see* that. *What's* he crying for?'

'He wants to go home,' answered Lantry hopelessly.

'He's had a few drinks, Briggsy,' put in Villiers with his lisp.

Brigg screwed up his face. 'Roll on,' he muttered wearily, walking towards the sniffling Tasker. 'Wants to go home? If that's the case let's *all* have a bleeding boo.'

He took his friend's shoulder quietly. Tasker looked up like a bereaved dog. 'Come on, mate,' said Brigg. 'We all wanted to go home, but now we're not going.' He tried to sound convincing 'It's only an extra six months.'

The very naming of the period set Tasker off on another drunken moan that lengthened to a howl. Brigg backed away from the beery cloud he emitted. 'Pack it up, son, or you'll have us all at it,' he pleaded. 'We're lumbered just like you.' He moved forward again and attempted almost fatherly encouragement. 'Come on, buck up. Be a man. You're a soldier.'

At this Tasker looked up, very slowly like the minute hand of a clock, tear-stained astonishment spreading over his face. 'A soldier?' he croaked. 'I

5

know I'm a soldier. That's why I'm crying, you born bloody loony.'

Brigg, knowing there was no answer, sat heavily on the nearest bed and regarded the white and weeping youth.

Dejection filled his heart and drained into his boots. Around him the other conscripts sat with their abandoned faces. The customary heat pressed in from the barrack square, and above them, on the ceiling, the big fans circled on their endless journey. Home was very far away; beyond dog-eared coasts, upturned mountains and the enormous alien sea; over the last horizon of the world. Brigg had dreamed a dream where he crossed each succeeding skyline, jumping them like hurdles, only to find that, at the last leap, he was back where he had begun: Panglin Barracks, Singapore.

Girls – real, clean, understandable, understanding girls – were there at home in England, waiting. Girls with eyes wide open, clear – not looking at you through slits so you couldn't tell what they were thinking. And the other things. Oh God, the Saturday nights, wet pavements smeared with street lights, football matches seen from smoky terraces, beer, the Sunday newspapers piled on the bed. The old man and the old lady. Each glaring day had been crossed from the demobilization calendars, weeks and months of the little grinning bastards, one by one wiped out, like an enemy force. But after all the promises and the saving up for civilian suits, the buying of presents, the expectation unequalled since childhood – after all that the home-going had been snatched away at the final moment. They had been cheated.

'They bloody promised,' grunted Lantry eventually. 'I wouldn't mind, but they *promised*. The *King* promised.'

Tasker lifted his sodden face. 'I'll never believe any bugger again,' he vowed. 'Just let them try and short-change Harold Tasker again, that's all.'

'Ah, I was already seeing the green fields in my mind's eye,' sighed Sandy Jacobs.

Brigg glanced at him truculently. 'Roll on,' he said. 'Since when did you have any green fields in Glasgow?'

'The parks,' replied Jacobs logically. 'There's fine green in the parks.'

'Oh, get knotted,' grunted Brigg getting up from the bed. 'I'm not sitting around here sobbing my fucking heart out for months. They've done us and that's that.'

'Six months? I reckon it'll be more than six months.' Gravy Browning did not look up from his table-tennis bat upon which the ball still bounced minutely.

Brigg stopped as he made to move off. He and the others looked at Browning in horror and astonishment. Tasker, as though the matter had already occurred to him, was the last to raise his creased face.

'What's that mean?' demanded Brigg.

'What I say,' said Browning, giving the ball an extra flip. 'I reckon this bloody bust-up in Korea is just the start of another big war. We'll be in for years.'

'Oh, Christ,' snarled Brigg moving angrily away and pulling his shirt from his back. 'I can't listen to any more of this cobblers. I think I'll go and enjoy myself – maybe I'll cut my throat.'

He strode across the barrack room towards the entrance to the shower block at the rear. Beyond the middle rank of beds and lockers he was confronted by the gross, naked and prostrate figure of Corporal Eggington, a regular soldier, who lay on his bed anointed with powders and ointments, hair redolent with Brylcreem, flabby-faced, swollen-bellied. He was one of those men who make a prolonged ritual of cleaning themselves and never fail to look unwholesome.

'Blimey, the reclining Buddha,' grunted Brigg.

'Watchit, Brigg, or I'll pull rank on you,' sniffed Eggington, his eyes black-edged and dull.

Brigg was not worried. 'The only thing you've ever pulled is your plonker, Eggie,' he replied easily, going to his own bed and taking off his trousers. He put a towel around his waist and approached Eggington's bed again on his way to the shower.

'Pulling your plonker's better than crying like that load of ninnies over there,' Eggington remarked, jerking his greasy head on his greasier pillow. 'They want to get a bit of service in. Their bleeding knees ain't brown yet.' He selected a stained pot from a small pyramid of lotions and potions on his bedside locker. Brigg watched with disgust while he unscrewed the lid and dipped his middle finger into the pink substance. He began to apply it to his groin.

'What you got there, then?' inquired Brigg.

'Ointment.'

'*Not* the stuff. Where you're putting it, I mean. What's up?'

'A few spots,' answered Eggington. 'I've learned a bit during my years of service in foreign parts. I look after myself I do.' He glanced up at Brigg as though an idea had just come to him. He held out the horrific ointment pot. 'You wouldn't like to put some of this on for me, would you? Some places I can't reach.'

Brigg backed quickly away. 'No, I wouldn't!' he glared.

Eggington put the ointment down and picked up a pornographic magazine; his other fascination. 'All right then,' he said to Brigg. 'Bugger off then.'

'I was just going, thanks,' returned Brigg. He went across the open terrace at the back. It was late Saturday afternoon and the Singapore sun was trapped in a cage of palm trees lining a low hill beyond the camp. He went to the urinal, and was joined by Lantry.

'What was the Calamine Kid going on about?' asked Lantry.

'Wanted me to put some of his horrible bloody ointment on for him,' said Brigg. 'He'd be lucky.'

'I've never seen anybody with so much muck all over them,' said Lantry. 'Where he's not pasted he's powdered. Lying there reading *Girls and Whips*. Horrible bastard.'

'We ought to nick some of his dirty books,' suggested Brigg, finishing and going towards the shower. 'I wouldn't mind having a decko at them.'

9

'Keeps them locked up like gold, dirty sod,' grunted Lantry. He went to the mirror and regarded himself sombrely as though he grew visibly older each moment. 'Do you reckon we'll be here for years, Briggsy?'

'Gravy could be right,' admitted Brigg. 'This Korea lark might be the start of a real war. In which case, mate, we might think ourselves lucky to stay here. We *could* get sent to where there's fighting.'

'Christ,' breathed Lantry. 'I bloody well hope not.'

'So do I,' grunted Brigg. 'I've had enough of this game of soldiers as it is, without them expecting me to fight.'

There were forty beds in the barrack room, the middle floor of the three-storey block – one of half a dozen blocks squatting around the parade ground, built to house Indian troops at the start of the Second World War and conveniently completed in time for the same soldiers, and many others, to occupy them as prisoners of the Japanese.

Now, five years after those prisoners were freed, the new generation of British troops, conscripts most of them, with a remnant of the regular army, slept in four rows to a barrack room, two at the sides and two in the middle of the concrete-floored area. There was a balcony hanging over the parade ground at the front, another adjoining the ablutions at the back. Eight big-handed fans curved incessantly on the ceiling like clocks gone mad.

'I reckon,' said Tasker, still morose but now dry-eyed, lying as if pole-axed on his mattress. 'I reckon that this bloody fan over my head will go around twenty-eight million eight hundred pissing thousand times before I go home. I've just worked it out.' He was lying bare on the narrow bed. His previous audience had dispersed but he continued with his theme for the benefit of anyone who cared to listen. 'Look at this,' he invited. He lifted his wan penis indelicately between a finger and a thumb and demanded: 'When, may I ask His Majesty's Government, am I going to get my rights of using this in a proper manner? Like it was meant – with a girl. For nothing.'

Private Fundrum, who was said to be too intelligent to be an officer, was passing and stopped at Tasker's bed-rail. He was like an unkempt, ill-planted tree. The officers' trade union, it was rumoured, had blacklisted him because he had so many brains he would have shown the others up. His brains were apparent all over his face. He regarded Tasker's poor member, with its shrub of ginger hairs.

'O, withered is the garland of the war,' he recited, 'The soldier's pole is fallen.' He blinked like a professor at Tasker. 'That, Tasker,' he said, 'is a quotation from *Antony and Cleopatra*.'

He strolled on.

'Balls,' Tasker called unhurriedly after him. 'That's a quotation from *Fanny Hill*.'

There were the average number of oddities in the barrack room. Apart from Eggington and his ointments, Browning and his unending game of phantom table-tennis, and Fundrum and his overloaded brain, there was Private Conway, from Belfast, who spent his entire off-duty time in the painful construction of giant jig-saws, Lance-Corporal Williams who was equally slowly reading through a complete set of pocket encyclopedias, and Corporal Field, a man of almost legendary inactivity, who dreamed dreams of fox-hunting and action on the Western front in the tradition of Siegfried Sassoon. The others had their quirks and quaintness, their many social backgrounds miraculously merged so that there were few fights on account of class or status, their periods of youthful joy and teenage despair. They were joined in a loose comradeship by the accident of having been born within the same two-year span and being of reasonably sound mind and body sent to defend the interests of their country in this far, inert place. Their one dreamed-of horizon was that which was shaped with the landscape of home. The anticipation of it was like the anticipation of a thousand childhood Christmases. Brigg and some of the others had almost reached it. Their ship had come in, but had gone out again, leaving them on the jetty. Some wondered if it would ever call again.

Panglin Barracks, Singapore – where they would be required to serve another six months in sweaty boredom as their contribution to a medium-sized but bloody war being held in Korea a few thousand miles away – was a sort of timeless army suburb; but very safe. The blessed strait that severed Singapore

Island from the long land of Malaya kept it, in the main, immune from the sunlit fear and death of the communist guerrilla war which had been fought for four years in the jungles of the peninsula. Singapore was attached to that bitter land by the thin thread of a causeway, so that the island hung like a pendulum into the South China sea.

At Panglin the reluctant National Servicemen kept the ledgers of the war, the records, the pay charts, the marching columns of debit and credit. They clanked to their offices each steaming morning, tin mugs drummed with knife-fork-and-spoon like some robot advance. Busy Chinese, quiet Malays and clever Indians, who had seen the fathers of these boy soldiers surrender without a fight to a small, pleasantly surprised Japanese army, regarded them with introspective interest. They remained expressionless for much of the time they were in contact with the British soldiers, except perhaps for a polite and wispy smile as they took the money for laundry, tailoring, ice cream, cameras, Coca Cola or girls.

Each week-day the youthful soldiers would drum their enamel march to the offices from the squared barrack blocks, crossing the narrow wooden footbridge over a minor ravine. Wednesday afternoons were free of the drooping boredom of the office routine, being designated as recreation periods, which meant most of the soldiers lay sweating on their beds. Saturday mornings were devoted to a charade of military tactical training, marksmanship, bayonet practice, camouflage and cover, riot drill

13

and a mysterious, almost pagan ritual involving the boiling out and pulling through of rifle barrels around a steaming cauldron.

On Saturday nights the awkward young men danced the tango, foxtrot and waltz in the arms of VOGs – Volunteer Oriental Girls – at the official Services Club. More dangerously, expensively and enjoyably a young man could be clutched by a dark dancer in a dark place, who, with only brief encouragement, would slip her hand right down the front of his trousers. If sufficient funds were available sexual intercourse could be negotiated, although this needed to be speedy because the last bus left the city for the barracks at three minutes past midnight and it was a long walk in the darkness, particularly after a furgle.

As for the regular soldiers at Panglin, it was something of a tradition that the majority of them were fit for service nowhere else in the British Army. The Colonel had one eye and occasionally cried from it, his adjutant stammered and was afraid of the dark, and a newly-arrived Regimental Sergeant-Major, Warrant Officer Woods, suffered agonies with his feet; the only RSM in the service to stamp softly.

Other, more lowly ranked, regulars lived out their military exiles at a dreamlike rate, pacing their promised lives out over the months and years, knowing the dodges, streamlining the routine until it slowed to somnolism, knowing that at the conclusion of their term they would return to Britain, or some other place, to perform another gradual circle, until at the end came the day of discharge when many of them signed on again for a further eternity.

Some had acquired wives, British and alien, and fathered children during their military travels, and these followed wherever the soldier went, settling in a perplexed caravanserai called Married Families Quarters on the rim of the garrison.

It was ironic that into this static garrison, with its regulated suburban life, should also come at intervals units of fighting regiments bound for the stealthy conflicts up-country in Malaya, or, after the start of the Korean war, en route for the bald hills and battles of that unknown place. Infantry and armoured units, odds and ends attached to all manner of mysterious military connivance, arrived at Panglin and encamped for the next move. National Servicemen from the same towns, the same streets, as the deskbound soldiers sat mute, holding guns, in the backs of trucks taking them to the jungle and watched while the office soldiers played their march on their enamel mugs as they went to work. The young men going to fight possibly wondered what chance fated one youth to blood-stains and another to ink-stains. The resentment showed in their faces and the embarrassment in the furtive return looks of the Panglin brigade. The desk soldiers would walk almost shamefaced past the armoured cars, but once over the little wooden bridge they would cheer themselves with their marching song:

'We're a shower of bastards,
Bastards are we.
We'd rather fuck than fight,
We're the pen-pushers' cavalry.'

It made them feel better.

If anyone was truly and universally hated at Panglin
Barracks, then it was Sergeant Wellbeloved. The
squad, drawn up at the fore of the battalion's
Monday-morning parade, observed his strutting
progress across the sun-streaked square with
sagging misgiving. They had not expected to see
him again.

'Here comes the Shitehawk,' grunted Brigg to
Tasker.

'I see him,' replied Tasker. 'Look at the sparks
flying from the bastard's boots.'

'Pack it up ! Quiet!' squeaked Corporal Field of
the Quorn Hunt and Ypres dreams. Tasker and
Brigg each glanced accusingly at the silent men on
their other flanks.

Wellbeloved approached like a moving parcel, all
wrapped and sealed, his little pot-belly held up and
in by his webbing belt, his shorts keenly creased, his
gaiters clipped tight to his boots by a private and
concealed device of elastic bands, his face beaming
with malice.

He halted a few paces short of the three ranks and
regarded them with pretended surprise. Then he
performed a clockwork strut along the front row,

16

peering at each soldier so closely that the noses almost touched.

''Ave I not seen these faces before?' he inquired with theatrical astonishment. ''Ave I not seen these bright and soldierly expressions? I am sure I 'ave.' He marched to within a bristle of Brigg's nose.

'Now, *surely*,' he mocked, 'we have a familiar sight 'ere. Name and number, lad.'

'Two-two-one-five-seven-seven-four-one Private Brigg, Sergeant,' muttered Brigg.

'Brigg? . . . Brigg?' mused Wellbeloved, his hand rubbing along his chin. 'Now let me see. I must be getting confused in my old age. We *did* have a Private Brigg. But he went home to Blighty only last week. I *know* he did because as he was going off in the truck he put up *two fingers* to *me*, dear old Sergeant Wellbeloved!'

Wellbeloved's eyes narrowed to spikes and he pushed his face to within one inch of Brigg's face before moving menacingly along the line. He stopped before Lantry. 'Name and number!'

Lantry mumbled the recitation. Wellbeloved smirked. '*What* a coincidence! We *had* a Private Lantry! But he went home last week too! Still owing two dollars to the ice cream wallah and four to the bearer who used to clean his boots and blanco his belt for him – and who has complained to the amenities officer.' He eyed Lantry intently and then moved on to Tasker. 'Tasker, Private Tasker!' he exclaimed. 'But it must be! Are old Sergeant Wellbeloved's eyes deceiving him?'

'No, Sarge, it's me,' returned Tasker weakly.

'I *know* it's you!' bawled Wellbeloved in his face. Tasker blinked with the shock and the fetid breath. 'Nobody could look as 'orrible as you, lad!' He swung round on the rest of the squad. 'Or any of you! 'orrible, that's what you are! When I came on parade this morning and saw you, I said to myself "What is that 'orrible squad over there?" And it's *you*. All back again!'

He strode before them smiling meanly. 'I'll show you the army's not done with you yet. Your little feet won't touch the ground for the next six months. At least. Well, take it from me, you're going to be here for years! Until 1960 I reckon, at least. So, let's start off with some good drill. You always was a shower, but now we've got ten years to get you straight.'

He backed away and bawled the orders that brought them to attention, turning and finally marching through the hated morning sun across the hated barrack square where the military voices howled and wheeled as the other squads of the battalion went through their early formations.

Brigg marched as a man in an endless tunnel, his eyes focused on a fly which was endeavouring to ride bareback on the shaven neck of the soldier in front. He was like a returned prisoner.

'Hift, hite, hift, hite,' bawled Wellbeloved as they marched. 'Hift, hite . . . Hite wheel! Open those legs, let it dangle! Hift, hite . . . Come on, Jacobs, you're not walking to the Labour Exchange.'

He had them whirling around the square for ten minutes and then brought them sweating to a halt on the same spot from which they had started. He regarded them churlishly.

'Oh, diddums,' he mocked. 'Did we want to go home to our mummies and daddies? And the nasty government wouldn't let us. Never mind, then.'

From the edge of his eye he saw the approach of an officer, a young, straight, sniffing officer. 'Officer on parade!' he howled, his voice whirring to a falsetto. 'Squad . . . squaaaaaa . . . atten . . . shun!'

The young man, younger than the youths in the squad, approached easily, flopping his feet in a casual manner across the concrete. He had careful fair hair and a short smile that fitted exactly beneath his moustache. Brigg didn't like the look of him.

'Good morning, Sergeant,' the officer said after an exchange of salutes, Wellbeloved's as stiff as a railway signal, the officer's almost a casual wave.

'Morning, sir. Sergeant Wellbeloved, sir.'

'Ah, yes. Good morning, Sergeant Wellbeloved. I'm Lieutenant Grainger. Just posted.'

'Yes, sir.'

Grainger swung on one foot to the squad, shoulders gently hunched, as though performing a sophisticated ballroom dance step. 'And these are the men.' He stared at them sardonically as though trying to verify the statement. 'Yes, yes,' he nodded. 'The men.'

Some officers had the affectation of slapping their thighs with their canes as they walked about in front of their platoons. In the distance Lieutenant Wilson, a short stodgy officer from the pay department wheeled and whirled, turned and pirouetted in front of his men in an engaging and extraordinary fashion like a mechanical toy. But Grainger, facing the three ranks now, almost lounged, and rubbed the point of his cane down the inside of his leg as though trying to scratch a bite. His voice was odd too.

'Our armed presence abroad, is it?' he said eventually. 'England's might overseas. Hmm.'

It was not the frequently affected, upper-crust voice of the usual young officer, huffing and puffing, trying to sound like the last Sandhurst prize cadet. It was a nasal Cockney tone, undisguised, far more assured than the modulated stammering of so many second lieutenants – and much nastier.

He smiled without feeling. 'I've just come out on the boat that was going to take you away,' he said. 'We would have just missed each other. A bit like boats that pass in the night, don't they say. Well you got stopped. And now we're here, all together.'

Wellbeloved was watching Grainger, and listening to that accent with an uncertain expression, wondering, like the rest, if it was an act.

'Right,' sniffed Grainger. 'Now the first thing I want to tell you is that I'm not your usual sort of push-over platoon officer. I've come from the ranks, I'm ambitious, and I'm a bastard. I'm a real 'undred per cent bastard. So if we all understand that right at the beginning we'll all know where we stand . . . squad!' The order came out in a nasty bark that caused even Wellbeloved to jerk in surprise. 'Squ . . . ad! Att . . . ention!'

Grainger had seen something Wellbeloved had not. The sergeant's eyes swivelled. A gnomish car was shuddering along the perimeter of the parade ground.

'The Commanding Officer, sir,' Wellbeloved said.

'I know, Sergeant,' answered Grainger easily. 'I saw him a long way off.'

The car came to a slipshod halt and Lt Colonel Bromley Pickering stumbled out, closely followed by a cascade of golf clubs. They slid and bounced on the parade ground. The Colonel blinked his lone eye in disappointment, surveyed the spreadeagled clubs and muttered: 'Oh, dear.'

He approached Grainger, Wellbeloved and the squad in almost shamefaced fashion, saluted, and then inquired apologetically if the sergeant thought anyone might like to pick up his clubs.

'Sir!' responded Wellbeloved. He spun on the front rank. 'Lantry, you're a sportsman. Pick up the Colonel's clubs.'

'Yes, Sergeant,' responded Lantry, falling out of the rank.

'Thank you, thank you,' murmured Colonel Bromley Pickering. 'How kind.'

He appeared to see Grainger for the first time and emitted a backward smile like a father too shy to converse with his son. 'Getting to know the men?' he ventured after the pause.

'Yes sir,' acknowledged Grainger. He had abandoned his slouch and was standing as upright as Wellbeloved. 'Fine chaps, sir.' Brigg felt his inside curdle.

'Yes, yes,' mused the Commanding Officer with elderly sadness. 'Yes. Such a pity.' His eye revolved

21

from the ranks to Wellbeloved like a goldfish cruising around a bowl. 'Stand them at ease, Sergeant, will you, please. I'd like to say a few words.'

'Sir!' responded Wellbeloved. Lantry having garnered the Colonel's golf clubs and restored them to the car rejoined the squad and was treated to a grateful and genuine smile from the CO.

Wellbeloved ordered the platoon at ease and they stood, gloomy to a man, while Colonel Bromley Pickering wrung his hands and wrestled for words.

'Chaps,' he said eventually. 'Lads.' There came a pause so protracted that it seemed that the promised discourse might end there. The fatherly man had apparently drifted off into some other dimension, his eye was dimmed, his expression vague.

'Fellows,' he re-started eventually jolting over the obstacle. 'What *can* I say? It's just *damned* hard luck. Off home to England, Blighty as it were, and stopped at the very moment of embarkation. I'm jolly sorry about it but what the government says we must do, we must do. That's all part of the military life, I'm afraid.'

He stopped again and regarded them, solo-eyed, inquiringly, as though trying to gauge if his remarks had cheered them no matter how little. Their ranked faces remained dented with despondency. 'All I can say, chaps, is to keep the recommended stiff upper. People scoff at it these days, I know, but it's always been part of our national make-up and I can recall a good many times when it has helped me.' He lapsed once more, as if trying to remember when it had helped him. Then with a beam of encouragement he grinned raggedly at them. 'Cheer up!' he enthused. 'After all, it's only six months more. And you'll be getting extra pay – a few shillings a week more in your pockets.' He rummaged around, trying to find some last encouragement.

His chin dropped in thought, but eventually he looked up again and he was smiling that damaged smile. 'And just think,' he encouraged, 'you'll be home in time for the cricket season.'

He departed then to brisk salutes from Grainger and Wellbeloved and a strong stamp of boots from the soldiers. He gave them a wave as he opened the door of his little car, and simultaneously his golf clubs once more cascaded on to the barrack square.

'Fuck me gently,' said Wellbeloved below his breath. 'Lantry!' he shouted.

'Sir!' answered Lantry moving out of the squad. He gathered the clubs like a harvester lifting a stook of corn and replaced them in the vehicle while the Colonel murmured helplessly: 'Very kind, very kind.'

Once the implements were inside Lantry retained them cautiously with his hands, a hint to the Colonel that he should get into the car quickly to prevent a further avalanche. The Colonel did. The small vehicle spat and started and then swung erratically around the square, evading by only inches squads of parading troops.

They all watched him go. Everyone knew that at his next call the clubs would tumble out again. The benevolent man in his apologetic yet jaunty car scattered a group of Malay laundrymen at the parade ground entrance and turned out of sight. Brigg and the others returned their eyes to meet the malice aforethought in the face of Lieutenant Grainger. They exchanged stares for a full minute. Then Grainger said to Wellbeloved: 'Carry on, Sergeant.' They saluted and he turned sharply away before pausing, looking back and remarking spitefully: 'And make sure they get home for the cricket season.'

3

They sprawled like stricken men, transfixed on their lined beds in the barrack room, faces immobilized staring at some apparent fascination concealed in the ceiling. The light had gone by seven o'clock and the hot padded night was outside with its noises, metallic boots, voices and the thread of a tuneless whistle. Inside the lights were stark, the fans revolved ceaselessly and carelessly on the high ceiling, and the radio set was broken again. Gravy Browning tapped his table-tennis ball against the stony wall.

The balding Corporal Field lay at the far end reading *Country Life*. He had a flat Midlands voice, which he frequently pointed out was the accent peculiar to the hunting country of Rutland, and he looked up at them now and spoke over the despondent breathing.

'Why don't you lot cheer up?' he suggested with long-drawn patience. 'Why don't you have a nice singsong?' He meant it.

Lantry turned his head slowly, first towards Field and then back to Brigg. 'What did he say?' he asked.

'He said why don't we have a singsong,' replied Brigg helplessly.

'He would,' grunted Tasker on the bed the other

side of Brigg. 'That's just about his mark, a singsong.'

'Yes, I would,' responded Field. He remained peering over the rim of his rural magazine as though viewing a fox across a ridge of a hill. 'It's not going to be much fun in 'ere if you lot are going to lie moping on your chariots for the next six months. For goodness' sake, 'ave a singsong or play Monopoly or something.'

Brigg sat up suddenly. 'He's right,' he said. He called up the room to Field. 'You're right, Corp,' he repeated.

'Ah know I am,' responded Field. 'Start a singsong, Briggsy.'

'Sod the singsong,' grunted Brigg. 'I'm not hanging around. I'm getting out.' He pulled his towel around his waist. It was strange that they lay naked on their beds, of habit, but put a towel around themselves the moment they stood up. It was a barrack-room ritual. He walked determinedly along the bed towards the ablutions at the rear. After a few moments Jacobs went out to the urinal.

'He means it,' he announced when he returned. 'He's having a shit, shave, shower and shampoo. He says he's going out.'

'Out?' Tasker looked up. 'Out? But it's Monday.'

'He says he knows what day it is,' continued Jacobs. 'But he says he's going down to Singapore. To see that Chinese bird of his. What's she called?'

'Juicy Lucy,' sighed Lantry. 'She thinks he's gone home. I bet she's got a royal flush from the dockyard since then.'

They agreed glumly and fell to lounging silence again. Abruptly Tasker sat up. 'Bugger it,' he said. 'I think I'll go with him.'

The others gazed at him with double astonishment. Foster and Villiers, who had been to rug-making classes, came in upon a scene like a Greek tragedy, naked and semi-naked torsos arranged about in a surprised circle.

'Whatever's happening?' inquired Patsy Foster.

'Brigg's going to town,' shrugged Jacobs, 'and Tasker's going with him.'

'On a Monday?' exclaimed Villiers. 'Oh, I say, Patsy.'

'This barrack room gets like a bloody mum's club,' retorted Tasker pulling his towel about his waist. 'What's the matter with going out on Monday anyway? It's not wash-day or anything is it?'

'I always press my things on a Monday,' sniffed Villiers.

'Not just on a Monday from what I hear, mate,' muttered Tasker. 'Anyway I'm going with Briggsy. This place is driving me spare.'

He went to the ablutions and returned with Brigg. They began to get dressed in their civilian shirts and trousers with exaggerated cheerfulness and vigour. They ignored the other inmates of the barrack room who, in turn, regarded them in silence.

'It'll be great,' enthused Brigg. 'Great.'

'Bloody great,' echoed Tasker. 'No Saturday night crush. Plenty of room at the bar. All the birds sitting around hungering for us.'

'Cheaper on a Monday, too,' affirmed Brigg.

'Course it will,' gloated Tasker. 'Miles cheaper.'

'Roll up, roll up,' snorted Sandy Jacobs from his prostrate bed. 'Bargain week for pox.'

'Better than lying here dying of wanker's doom,' taunted Brigg. He jerked his head from Tasker towards the door. 'Come on mate, we'll get the eight o'clock bus. Leave this lot to press their little things.'

In the bus their mood dwindled. The vehicle jolted the ten miles to Singapore city, throwing them about on its wooden seats. There were no glass windows, merely barred openings as though they were encased in some travelling prison. Outside, the night was low and black, with palms and other jungle trees moving about in the void as though trying to clasp each other for reassurance. At intervals they passed small villages, illuminated and noisy, each like a fairground, full of glistening faces, tangled music and voices echoing from open-mouthed shops. Their travelling companions were meagre. A Medical Corps sergeant who looked as though he might die on the journey. Two Chinese men and two fragile old women, a Malay who was fat and rolled about his hard seat as the bus bounced, and a contemplative Sikh, his massive arms knotted, his head hanging below a big turban. He sat imperiously, immediately behind the tiny Chinese driver as though he were being privately driven in some opulent conveyance.

'What are you going to say to her?' asked Tasker.

'Lucy? Well, she's bound to be glad to see me,'

said Brigg without conviction. 'Stands to reason. It'll be a bit of a surprise, though. Like coming back from the dead.'

'She did that once, remember,' Tasker pointed out.

'As though I'll ever forget that,' nodded Brigg. He thought about it again. They said she had been killed by a drunken soldier, kicked to death according to the manager of the club where she had worked. But it was another club girl. Lucy had merely gone off on some spontaneous flit with a British businessman who had enjoyed her so much he had taken her to Penang in the north with him. She had reappeared, unconcerned at the shock of her reincarnation, and Brigg had burst into tears when he saw her again. It was strange how attached a young man could become to a prostitute.

'In a way, I'll be getting my own back,' he said eventually. 'She'll think I've gone off for ever and I'll walk straight across the floor to her and give her a bookful of dance tickets.'

'Do you think she'll still let you have your end away for nothing?' inquired Tasker.

'I expect so,' replied Brigg smugly. 'See, there's a difference between what she does with me and what she does with other blokes.'

'Ten dollars difference,' sniffed Tasker.

'Not just that,' said Brigg ignoring the sarcasm. 'She really *likes* having it with me. I can tell.'

'How?'

'How? Oh blimey. By the way she acts, of course, you twerp. By the way she moves her bits and pieces . . .' He held out his hands as though fondling a pair of buttocks. 'By the way she smiles.'

Tasker regarded him cynically. 'Maybe she's having a laugh. Ever thought of that?'

'Bollocks. Listen, Task, I know.'

'Once a pro, always a pro, I say,' said Tasker relentlessly. 'If you think she's so good why don't you marry her and take her home to show your mum?'

Brigg swallowed at the momentary vision. 'Well, because . . .'

'Because what? If it's love, I can't see what's stopping you.'

Brigg glared at him. They were like two school-boys having a dispute about some game. 'Because she wouldn't fit in our 'ouse, that's why,' he said vehemently. Then, dropping his tone: 'I just can't see her walking down our street.'

'Ha,' said Tasker. 'I wouldn't half like to be there to watch if you *did* take her home. I bet you'd soon know you'd dropped a clanger.'

'You're right,' nodded Brigg. 'I expect I would. After all, here's here and there's there. It's different.'

'Yeah, it is,' agreed Tasker. 'Bloody different.'

'I couldn't see me walking her to the pub, that's all,' continued Brigg defensively. 'And I don't think my mum would take to it all that much either.'

The bus was in the city now, wallowing slowly among the cars and bicycles and tri-shas of the aromatic streets. Washing hung like liberation flags across alleys, children played in monsoon drain-water by the fierce spluttering of carbide lamps, open-fronted shops and gaping living-places were crowded against each other like some haphazard exhibition of vivid pictures. People were thick in the shadows and everywhere was the mangled music and strangled songs of oriental radio stations. Above it all the Cathay Cinema shone like an exotic lighthouse. It was the only building of any height in the city and its programmes were advertised far out to sea. Cabaret girls and prostitutes took their aliases from its neon-named stars. If Rita Hayworth were the attraction of the week, then hundreds of Ritas would walk the streets and dance the floors; if it were Doris Day then they would, at a stroke, all be called Doris.

Brigg and Tasker left the bus at the corner of Serangoon Road. The evening was heavy and sweet. The Padang was on one side, sacred grass where the British and selected Indians played cricket, with the Law Courts large at one boundary like a spectator grown old and fat and knowing. On the far side of the road behind the fanned silhouettes of manicured palms, washed with coloured lights, was the Raffles Hotel, its megaphoned car-index numbers, summonses for the chauffeurs of the wealthy, sounding like God counting in Malay.

'Sounds like wog tombola, calling out the numbers like that,' said Tasker in a dull voice.

'Never thought I'd be walking down here again,' grumbled Brigg, putting disconsolate hands in his pockets. 'I thought the next time I had a night out it would be down Kilburn High Road.'

'Soldier!' The voice came from the shadows. 'Soldier!'

Brigg and Tasker stopped and two regimental policemen emerged on to the pavement. Brigg sighed and kept his hands in his pockets. The pair were fresh-faced, shiny, their green uniforms new and stiff.

'Are you army?' inquired the first with a nasal northern accent.

'That's why we stopped when you called "Soldier",' replied Brigg. 'If we'd been sailors we'd have walked on.'

'Rank?'

'Sergeant, to you,' lied Brigg easily. 'Intelligence Corps. That's why we put our hands in our pockets. We're *thinking*, see? And *we've* been out here two years. How long have you been out here – soldier?'

'Two weeks,' replied the MP uncertainly. 'We're supposed to stop service people with their hands in their pockets. That's what we've been told, anyway, haven't we, Brian?'

'Yes,' confirmed Brian. 'We have that.'

'But *not* Intelligence Corps,' put in Tasker. 'We *march* with our hands in our pockets – and smoking pipes. Came out on the *Orbita*, did you?'

'Yes. Yes, Sergeant,' replied the second police-man, impressed that the name of the ship should be known.

'Thought so,' said Brigg as though he had a full dossier on both men. 'You'll need to get a bit of service in then, won't you?'

'Yes, Sergeant.' He paused and backed away. 'We'll be off then.'

'Yes, why don't you.'

The pair moved off hesitantly. 'Don't go anywhere that's dark,' Brigg called after them.

As they had forecast, Monday nights were always quiet at the Liberty Club. They pushed aside the rattling curtain at the entrance and entered on a scene of slow and dim despondency. The women who worked there, Chinese and Eurasians, dance-hostesses and sleeping partners, sat on uncomfortable wooden chairs around the rim of the floor, curiously like the most abandoned of wallflowers at an English suburban dance.

A few customers were hunched against the bar, surveying the available talent with the curled lips of buyers in a loaded market. The band were in a shadowy clutch on a dais at the distant end of the room, grouped close like tired shipwrecked men crowded on to a raft. There was a general moroseness about the scene which suggested that all in the room had recently witnessed some numbing tragedy.

Brigg and Tasker remained at the door surveying the sombre place. The band began to play two different tunes, stopped unembarrassed, and began again on two others. An overgrown soldier in uniform, with a dull and sweat-coated face, presented a forty-cent dance ticket to a minute Eurasian redhead and held out his beefy arms for the eventual tango upon which the band had compromised. The girl pushed the ticket down the front of her dress and Brigg watched it flutter to the dance floor as it fell out at the bottom. She was new to the business. The huge soldier and the small slave began to tango. His arm went out like the bowsprit of a ship but her short white arm would not extend that far and he had to bend at the elbow. Two Chinese girls began to dance together out of the sheer need to stretch their bored limbs, and another pair began playing pontoon on the wicker table between them. It was not a romantic place.

'Jesus,' murmured Tasker. 'The Naafi's livelier than this.'

'Sod it,' swore Brigg quietly. 'Lucy's not here.' He scrutinized the room in the half-light. A waiter was eyeing them challengingly, waiting for them to sit and order a drink.

'Maybe she's gone out for a crap,' suggested Tasker unfeelingly.

'Gone for a crap,' repeated Brigg still searching the room. 'Sometimes, mate, I wonder why I go around with such a perfect gentleman as you.'

'Sorry,' returned Tasker casually. 'I meant a shit.'

'She's not here, that's for certain,' went on Brigg giving up the argument. 'She must have taken the night off. Probably pining after me.'

'On her chariot with a big black stoker, more like it.'

'You always think the worst of people, you do,' said Brigg. 'You're the sort who'd give a whore a bad name.' He moved towards the table. The waiter looked relieved that they had made up their minds, and made a place ready for them. They sat at the bamboo table and stared unhappily into the blighted room.

34

'Two Tigers, John,' said Brigg to the waiter. 'In the bottles. Don't pour them at the bar. They're half bloody water when you do.'

'Two Tigers,' repeated the waiter unruffled. 'You want tickets, to dance with girls. We got great girls.'

'We're surveying the scene, mate,' sniffed Tasker. 'See if we fancy anything. Up to now it looks like remnant week.'

'You can say that for sure,' agreed Brigg. His attention was taken by a girl at the other end of the room, near the musicians, who was somehow summoning the energy to sway to the uncertain rhythm. 'That's the bird you've been with,' he said to Tasker. 'What she call herself? Nancy Nightmare or something.'

'Dolly Daydream,' corrected Tasker evenly. 'Yes, I've given her the benefit of my fine body.'

'Any good?'

'No good at all. All the time I was prodding her with my one-and-only she was reading a comic.'

Brigg laughed. 'Get away! Reading a comic?'

'Straight she was. I'm doing my stuff like a good 'un and she's reading Korky the Cat or some stuff. I packed it in for a while and waited for her to do something, but she didn't even notice. I gave her a bit of a jog and then I asked her what the 'ell she thought she was at.'

'And what did she say?'

'Well she carried on reading for a bit and then she looked up at me. She seemed a bit surprised I was still there. Then she more or less told me to carry on by myself and bugger off quick. Foul cow.'

'Reading a comic,' mused Brigg. 'That's something I've never heard.'

'I doubt if she was *reading* it, not her. Just looking at the pictures more like. But it hurts a bloke's pride.'

'I suppose it would really,' agreed Brigg. 'But I reckon she knows Lucy. I've seen them sharing a Coke. I'll ask her.'

'She'll want a ticket,' forecast Tasker confidently. 'She won't just have a natter with you. You'll have to dance.'

Brigg glanced hopefully at the polished floor to where the Eurasian girl had dropped her ticket, but it was no longer there. 'Blimey, surely she'll just tell me about Lucy without a ticket,' he said. 'She can't be that hard.'

'Any woman who reads the *Dandy* while Harold Tasker is plonking her is very hard,' assessed Tasker shaking his head. Brigg got up nevertheless; his departure coincided with the arrival of the waiter with their beers. Tasker sighed and paid patiently. He watched Brigg cross the floor. The girl saw him doing so, too, but pretended not to notice. She was giggling with an albino trombonist in the band.

'Excuse me, miss,' began Brigg.

'Ticket,' said the girl briefly holding out her hand but hardly looking round.

'No, no,' pressed Brigg. 'It's Lucy. Do you know where . . .?'

'Ticket,' replied the girl tonelessly.

'Christ, you sound like a bus conductor,' grumbled Brigg. 'I only want to ask you something.'

The girl turned. She had a large dimpled face painted with sad beauty-spots and almost surrealistic curves. She was about seventeen and her eyes were fifty. 'Listen, Johnny, you want to talk, we dance. No dance, no talk. No ticket, no dance. No ticket, no talk. So you fuck off.'

'You've got charm as well,' observed Brigg. He turned and walked towards the waiter who had served their drinks. 'Give us a ticket, mate.'

'No one ticket by self,' cautioned the waiter. 'Only book of tickets. Two dollars.'

'A racket,' protested Brigg, 'that's what it is.' He paid up nevertheless, and caught Tasker's knowing smirk as he turned back to Dolly Daydream. He handed her the ticket, which she nudged expertly into her brassiere. She looked up, her face broke into a remarkable smile composed entirely of golden false teeth, and she held out her puffy arms ready to embrace him. They began to dance; the spicy tang of her black hair shot up his nostrils and her notable breasts pummelled into him like two soft fists. She lifted her face and kissed him erotically on the neck. 'Hello,' she murmured endearingly. 'You want to buy nice pussy cat.'

'I'm in the army,' said Brigg with grim primness. 'No pets allowed.'

She giggled, 'Jig-a-jig many ways, plenty time,' she promised. 'I very clean girl, too. Very clean. But I do dirty girl's things.'

'I do believe you,' agreed Brigg sincerely. 'But listen, love, I want to know where Lucy is. Is she coming here tonight?'

37

'Lucy?' grimaced Dolly as though she did not understand. 'I don't know Lucy.'

'You do,' insisted Brigg. 'She usually sits in the corner over there . . . waiting for me.'

'Ah, Lucy,' sighed Dolly enviously. 'She get lot business. She stay home tonight. Rest pussy cat.'

Brigg left her at the end of the dance and she went sulkily back to the Albino. The other cabaret girls watched Brigg's trousers closely to see if Dolly had given him an erection, for to do so was a matter of professional standing and a topic for considered conversation. Brigg pretended his comb was wedged across his trouser pocket and pulled it out with some show to comb his hair as he walked from the floor.

'You've got to admit she moves beautifully,' said Tasker, as Brigg sat next to him and drank the surface from his beer. 'From where you were you couldn't see her bum. It was worth sitting it out just for an eyeful of that.'

'You didn't mention she'd got fifty gold teeth, though, did you?' accused Brigg. 'Shagging that must be like shagging King Solomon's Mines.'

'They are a bit dazzling if you get her bed-light reflecting in them,' admitted Tasker. 'But she can certainly move. Did she say about Lucy?'

'She's at home,' replied Brigg. 'Broken-hearted apparently. I'll pop round and cheer her up.'

'All right. You do that. I think I'll stop here for a bit. If she's finished her week's comics I might have another rumble with that. See you at the bus.'

'Right you are,' agreed Brigg finishing his beer.

He put a dollar down for Tasker to have one on him. 'See you at the bus.' He paused and grinned. 'If she reads the comic, why don't you read the other side too. Make the best of a bad job.'

'Get stuffed,' said Tasker amiably.

'I'm hoping to,' said Brigg.

In a city of strange buildings, Juicy Lucy lived in one of the strangest. It was a mangy mansion riven by corridors, corners, rooms, cellars and sly attics reached by an amazing series of delicately spiralled but rusty iron staircases.

Brigg ascended the curves he had believed he would never climb again, to the third floor where he could see there was a light at her window. She had warned him never to come to her place unexpectedly because she was sometimes with a private client. Once he had done this, causing the panicked exit of an army padre who was supposed to be out visiting service families in a near-by military compound. Brigg had not realized the rank and calling of the disturbed customer until he found a clerical collar and bib abandoned by Lucy's steaming bed. Lucy had been very angry.

This time he cautiously opened the outside door that led from the curling staircase to a narrow passage outside her room. He pushed the doorbell and heard the childish chimes ringing 'Should Auld Acquaintance Be Forgot'. This had been a present from some well-satisfied members of the Highland Light Infantry. He heard her padding towards the door and smiled as he knew she was looking at him through her security peep-hole.

She cried: 'Bligg!'

'Yes love, it's Bligg. Big Bligg. Let me in.'

'But you gone home,' she said in a crushed voice against the letter-box.

'Blimey. It *is* me. I didn't go.'

'How I know it, Bligg?' she asked, her Chinese suspicion asserting itself.

'God 'elp us. I'll put my plonker through the letter-box if you like.'

Her tone dropped to a whisper. 'No do that. I know it you.'

Protractedly the chain on the door was released and she opened it. He stepped forward into the room and embraced her heavily, looking up a moment later with innate caution and curiosity to see if anyone else had been in the room. She had been lying on her sleeping bed – as she called it, to distinguish it from her business bed – and reading a magazine. The radio was singing a chiming Chinese song. His mouth went down to the instantly recalled scent of her hair and her neck. She seemed to shrivel as she pushed against his chest, but a moment later she pulled herself away and ran back into the room, her face in her small and elegant hands.

'Lucy,' he pleaded, following her and shutting the door behind him. 'What's up?'

'Nothing up, Bligg,' she sniffled through her fingers. She examined him between her knuckles as though to have a final check. 'It is you,' she concluded.

'Of course it's me,' he argued. 'I thought you'd be chuffed to see me.'

'Chuffed?' she inquired, coming out from behind her hands, her eyes miniature flooded boats. 'What chuffed?'

'Oh, Christ, you and your English. It means happy, pleased.'

She sat on the bed and surveyed him with an expression of infinite misery. She was wearing a loose white robe with a blue Star of David on the pocket, and he could see the top swellings of her honey-coloured breasts resting idly against the flowing silk of the garment. She had good legs for a Chinese girl, not splayed or muscular, and they now slid lazily from beneath the robe as she sat. He regarded them with some sense of anticipation. 'You a ghost now,' she said accusingly. 'You say "Bye-bye, Lucy" and you go away for ever. I bruddy cly for you.'

'Now I'm back you're still bruddy clying,' retorted Brigg.

'You not understand,' she replied just as sharply. 'I cly but I tough. I working girl. I say you dead for Lucy. Never no more see you. So I forget. I only have one Number One man at a time. Only one who not pay.'

'I see,' nodded Brigg. He was still standing looking down at her. 'I've mucked it up. Confucius, he say "Man who goes and comes back not welcome".'

'No Confucius – Lucy,' said Lucy.

He went, familiarly, and sat beside her on her sleeping bed. He put his hand on the inviting knee and regarded her soft profile. He had never been

41

able to understand how any woman who did sex for a living could look so tender. 'But you *are* glad to see me, Lucy?'

She nodded her head briskly. 'Chuffed,' she confirmed. 'But all change now. You pay.'

'Bloody 'ell, life gets worse.'

'And we have on working bed,' she nodded to the substantial divan across the room. 'Not on sleeping bed like before. You pay me ten dollars, short time.'

'There goes my extra few bob a week,' he groaned.

They sat in silence for some time, as though trying to think of a joint answer to some memorable problem.

'You want me now?' asked Lucy more softly.

Brigg nodded. 'Yes, Lucy. More or less. That's what I come around for . . . and to see you were all right, of course.'

'Ten dollars,' she said, holding out her small hand determinedly.

'All right,' he sighed. 'Here you are.' He handed her the red note and she made it vanish with the casual air of a professional conjuror. 'Business bed,' she added firmly.

They walked across to the other bed against the wall and she turned away from him and began pulling her jet hair through her hands. 'Take off trousers,' she said with studied coolness. 'And boots. Lucy not allow boots in bed.'

'Nice bloody clientele you must have,' grunted Brigg taking off his shoes, 'if they get on the job wearing their boots.'

'Some people in hurry,' she replied in her business-like tone. He knew she was pouting even though she had her back to him. He had taken off his trousers and army drawers cellular and he craftily moved forward until the helmet of his penis just touched the silk curve of her robe as it descended across her small backside. He felt her stiffen and then relax and then, to his relief, her hands came around behind and gently held his stem, rubbing it into her buttocks like a painter wiping a good brush.

'Oh, Bligg,' she wept, still with her face away from him. 'I think I never see you again.' He turned and clasped her to him: his special prostitute. She was the one who had taken him when he was a virgin. She had taught him, and in her way she loved him, as he too loved her in his way. Some things could only be accomplished to a degree.

'Lucy, love,' he murmured, kissing her miniature face, his hands thankfully travelling up her slim ribs to the soft pads of her breasts. 'Dear Juicy Lucy.'

'I very Juicy Lucy for you, Bligg,' she replied sincerely. She seemed to come to a difficult decision. She said, 'Come, we will go to the sleeping bed.' They stumbled across the room, still knotted in each other. He picked up the magazine which she had been reading and saw it was an American do-it-yourself journal open at a page giving instructions on building a birdcage.

Tenderly he put her on the counterpane. His stomach and his loins were sweating. His member stretched like a giraffe's neck. Her robe slid aside obligingly and he kneeled, looked down, and grinned at her face regarding him so seriously.

The robe had been caught in its descent by the modest rising of her breasts, crumpling the Star of David. He quietly eased it away each side and revealed them, little light brown hills each with a round-roofed hut on its summit. He was very glad to see them again.

'Come in me, Bligg,' she whispered. 'I no find anybody else forever.'

'Nor me, Lucy,' he lied. 'I didn't want to go. It was the government. I missed you like anything.'

He hovered above her and then sank with a thankful sigh on to her and into her. They made the quietest love, moving only sedately until the end. When it was over they lay against each other on her sleeping bed. Brigg let his eyes close with peace and satisfaction.

'To hell with the bloody cricket season,' he said to himself.

4

Dim-eyed, Brigg woke the next day in the barrack room and began moving domestically about his bed-space. He saw only that which was immediately before him, his boots, his blankets, his mosquito net, his razor and toothbrush. Excursions into Singapore were the usual preserve of Saturday nights for, on Sunday, they could lie in bed. But Monday was irrevocably followed by Tuesday.

It was Tasker, moving like a twin ghost about his neighbouring bed-space, who leaned over and touched his arm. Brigg looked up tiredly and then followed Tasker's disbelieving gaze across the room to where a man with a woman's bosom sat on a bed. Brigg screwed up his eyes and opened them again but it was no trick of vision. The man, in his thirties, with thick black hair and jowl, powerful shoulders and an outstanding and pugnacious nose, had two breasts as fruity and round as any of them had imagined in their most ambitious dreams. He was sitting sadly, wearing green-striped pyjama trousers, looking into the toecap of his boot as though trying to foresee the future.

Brigg leaned over to Lantry on the other side. 'Who's the bloke with the tits?' he whispered.

'Keep your voice down for Christ sake,' hissed Lantry. 'He might look like a woman but I bet he's the hardest bugger we've ever had around these parts. He moved in here last night, came in *carrying his bed and bedding under one arm* and all the rest of his kit under the other. He didn't say much to anybody but one of the bed legs wasn't straight so he sat there and straightened it out with his hands! Never saw anything like it.'

'You're kidding! Where's he from, anyway?'

Lantry glanced across as though still fearful that the man might hear. 'He's a reservist, called up because of Korea. He's Welsh and he's been shipped out here with a whole lot of odds-and-sods.'

'He's an odd-and-sod?' put in Tasker.

'Shush!' implored Lantry. 'He'll hear you.'

'They usually send odds-and-sods to the transit wing,' pointed out Brigg. 'Are *we* going to get them now?'

'Seems like it. The transit camp's bunged full, they reckon, because of Korea and all that. So they're being pushed in where they can.'

'I've never seen a man with tits like that,' whispered Tasker. 'Never. He makes me feel quite fruity.'

'He'll kill you, I promise you, he'll kill you,' muttered Lantry fearfully. 'I reckon he's really pissed off with being called back into the cake anyway, and more than ever being sent out to this hole.' His voice took on a tone of wonder. 'Last night, he got up out of bed and went to the bog. There's a bloody great dent in the plaster on the wall there this morning. I reckon he did it with his fist.'

The object of the discussion suddenly discarded his boot and with abrupt decision threw a towel across his shoulder and began to make for the toilet block. It was like a mountain standing up. He was tall as well as fleshy. He walked towards the space between their beds with his breasts, red-nippled, bouncing as he strode.

'Morning,' muttered Brigg respectfully.

'Morning,' nodded Tasker.

'Morning,' smiled Lantry nervously. 'Sleep well?'

'Ah lads,' breathed the huge soldier, stopping and looking down at them. 'Lads, good morning to you, also. That's the first decent civilized word I've had in my ears for a long time. I'm Morris Morris from Caerphilly, South Wales – lovely part of the country.'

'You a reservist?' inquired Brigg cautiously.

'Aye, boy. The bastards called me up. Took me away from the loving comfort of home and family because of SOME FUCKING WAR!'

The violence of the final words, flung out with all the fruity force of an operatic tenor, shocked them. The three young soldiers backed away, for he not only shouted but spread his arms like tree branches to add power and emphasis. Then he strode on to the toilet block. From there they heard him bellowing: 'Terrible! Terrible! These ABLUTIONS are like a SHITHOUSE!'

They returned from the offices in the early evening to find him sitting crumpled on the side of his bed, his massive head in his hands, his breasts hanging pendulously. He refused to go to the cookhouse with them, but Jacobs brought him back a mug of tea and a slice of meat pie which he accepted gratefully and devoured in one swallow followed by a single gulp.

'You're good boys,' he said in his deep Welsh voice. 'Decent lads.'

They sat around and regarded him with junior curiosity. 'You must be really fed up with getting lugged into the army again,' suggested Brigg, 'and brought out to this dump.'

His arms extended slowly like a Shakespearean actor. 'When they call you, they call you,' said Morris softly. 'They come in the cold eye of the early morning and knock on your door where you are sleeping in the peaceful arms of your wife, and the next thing you know you're on an alien barrack square. Back in where you left off five years before.'

'It's a bit of a bloody nerve,' agreed Jacobs. 'Especially when you've actually been in during the war. Done your service.'

'Aye, I saw enough,' agreed Morris, his black hair nodding slowly. 'Blood and battles, you know. The usual nonsense. Prisoner-of-war camp.' He paused and brightened. 'I was in much demand in the camp,' he reminisced. 'On account of my unusually well-developed mammary glands.' He spread out his arms and displayed the voluptuous bosom as though it might have gone unnoticed by them.

'I expect it was hard to get any women in a prison camp,' remarked Longley, a slow-thinking soldier with vicious acne and a tendency to lean to one side

48

owing to a weak hip bone. Brigg and the others stared in disbelief at the tactlessness of the remark.

But it brought only an ingenuous smile from Morris Morris. 'Right you are, boy,' he nodded pleasantly. 'Always in demand for camp concert parties. Gentlemen, the stripper! You know the sort of stuff. Some of it wasn't too bad at all. But this . . . oh, this, lads, is too much for a man.'

Brigg nodded his head sagely. 'You're right, Taffy,' he said. 'It's bad enough trying to get *out* of this bloody mob. Getting out and then being dragged back in again is beyond a joke. Terrible.'

'I'm a strong man,' said Morris, looking up at the ceiling as though wondering whether to lift it. 'Very strong. But it was too much even for me. I've got three little children . . . Davie, Dilwyn and Doris.' His voice died and the young soldiers sat in embarrassment. Then Longley tried one of his dim jokes. 'Three little children?' he repeated. Then he nodded at Morris's breasts. 'Did you feed them all yourself?'

Every face turned to Longley and then, at once, back to Morris. They knew immediately that something terrible was about to take place. The great man stared at the stupid soldier for the whole of one minute while Longley blushed, picked at his pimples and assayed a half-witted grin.

'I threw a man clean over the barbed wire in the prison camp for saying less than that,' said Morris in a voice low, boiling. 'And he was the only one who didn't want to escape either . . . Over the wire he went.'

49

'He was just joking, Taff,' tried Jacobs, putting out his hands hopelessly. 'He's the barrack-room twit . . .'

But the huge Welshman had risen to his feet and now towered above them all like some cartoon ogre, his eyes afire, his black jowl working, his breasts projecting like shining hubs. His arms, white and hairy, went forward in the manner of a mechanical grab. He moved towards the stultified Longley.

'Oh, Christ,' said Brigg.

With the most outrageous roar, Morris flung himself towards Longley, who squealed like a piglet and rushed off down the centre aisle of the barrack room with the great legs pounding behind him.

There was a point, a moment, when the squeaking conscript might have escaped. He reached the door to the front balcony – his one exit route – a few seconds ahead of Morris, but he panicked and missed the chance. Instead he mounted the left-hand line of beds and bounced along them like a crazed antelope pursued by a gorilla.

'He'll kill him,' forecast Corporal Field sitting up in bed with sudden interest.

'Do something then,' muttered Brigg slowly, entranced by the chase. 'Stop it.'

'Why?' inquired Field. 'I like it.'

At that moment, Longley missed his footing and plunged surrealistically between two beds. The gigantic man was immediately towering above him and then, growling with furious satisfaction, reaching down to grasp the lad.

'Oh, Christ,' whispered Tasker. 'Somebody ought to get the guard.'

'That's right,' Brigg nodded in slow motion. 'Get the guard.'

But no one moved. They stood transfixed, mouths limp, while the mighty hands grasped Longley and drew him up from the space between the beds. He was a frail soldier and he seemed weightless in the grip of Morris. The Welshman performed a quick let-go-and-grab movement and there was Longley hanging head down. Morris held him out in the manner of an angler displaying a prize fish, massive hands around the ankles, head two inches from the concrete of the barrack-room floor. Oddments fell from Longley's pockets: coins, a scattering of paper and, to everyone's surprise, a packet of contraceptives.

Morris held him out with no effort. He made a brief movement and Longley's thin head scraped the floor. The young private was emitting minor moans and his eyes were tightly shut.

'Good trick this, init?' said Morris beaming around for approval.

'His blood will run to his head, Taff,' Brigg pointed out deferentially.

'Aye, that is a possibility,' agreed the Welshman, looking down at Longley's head. 'There must be plenty of room for it in there.'

'What are you going to do?' inquired Tasker. They were all standing around like interested spectators of a fisherman's catch.

'Oh, I don't know, boy,' said Morris Morris

slowly. 'I thought I might drop him on his napper.'

'Don't do that, Taff,' put in Jacobs hurriedly. 'It's a concrete floor.'

'Aye, I can see that,' agreed Morris. 'I still reckon he'd make a dent in it.' Then suddenly, as though wearying of the performance, he let the stiffened Longley gently down to the floor and let him lie there trembling.

He trundled towards his bed. 'And don't anybody else take the mickey out of my titties,' he called back over his shoulder. 'It upsets me.'

On Friday evening, after the first week of the new six months' service, Lieutenant Grainger came into the barrack room with Wellbeloved sniffing like a nervous whippet at his heels. The soldiers were distributed around their beds, reading, writing letters, or lying prone and gazing at the ceiling.

'Stand by your beds!' squeaked Wellbeloved almost in Grainger's ear. The officer grimaced and strode into the room.

'Right,' he ordered. 'All come over to this side of the room where you can hear me.'

They padded round in bare feet and towels about their waists. Morris Morris had obtained an oriental dressing-gown from the village and stood with his full feminine torso draped modestly in this.

Grainger pointed his cane at him. 'Who are you?' he asked.

Morris's large bare feet flopped to attention.

'Three-One-O-Five Morris M., sir, Royal Signals detached, sir.'

The young lieutenant grinned patronizingly at the man old enough to be his father. 'Ah, one of the reservists, eh. A *real* soldier. Nice to have a *real* soldier in the vicinity.'

He said it in a normal officer's tone, but then dropped into his strange confiding Cockney accent. 'Righto, I've got to tell you lot about a little operation that's on the go tonight. In two hours. It's not an exercise; it's the proper job.' He looked around greedily. 'Some of you might even get shot.'

He grinned at the shocked reactions and then glanced at a piece of paper in his hand. 'This platoon will be ready at twenty-one hundred hours in field-service marching order; rifles to be drawn, each with ten rounds, at twenty-thirty. Got that? You will assemble here on this floor and await further orders. Any questions?'

'Yes, sir,' asked Lantry, nervously. 'Are they sending us to Korea?'

'Could be, sonny,' replied Grainger maliciously. 'And Gawd help you if you are.' He emphasized the 'Gawd'. 'By my reckoning, you ought to sit down now and write your last letters home to your mums.'

'The village, Reggie?' questioned the Commanding Officer, his face immediately folding with worry. '*Our* village?'

'That's c-correct, sir, the village. It's got to be s-s-s-s-surrounded, sir. Coffee, sir?'

'Please, Reggie. I feel I need a sip. But the village . . .' He read the order in his hand again in disbelief. 'But they are all our chums down there. The laundry and the little cafés and the tailors and the camera shop. *They* can't be Communist agents.'

'I think headquarters have got w-wind that C-Communist agents are in hiding there, sir. Waiting for a chance to slip across the Causeway and go up country to join their pals, sir.'

'Dear, dear, dear,' muttered Colonel Bromley Pickering. 'It all gets *so* involved, doesn't it. Friday evening as well. After all, it's the beginning of the chaps' week-end. We've got two football teams to field tomorrow, quite apart from anything else. You'd think GHQ could have waited until Monday.'

'Perhaps they felt that by Monday the Communist agents might be gone, sir,' suggested the adjutant.

'Communist agents, my eye!' exclaimed the Colonel. Then, remembering his dumb eye, he amended: 'My foot. You know as well as I do, Reggie, that it's merely some damned fool at GHQ with nothing better to do than to think up silly scares like this. Surrounding the village, searching premises! Honestly. I dread to think what the folks down there will think. It won't do anything for our good relations with them. It's so damned ill-mannered.'

'Ah, sir, they'll soon g-g-get over it,' comforted the adjutant. 'Once the troops are back they are buying cameras and suits and shirts, and all that sort of thing. They'll soon forget.'

'Well I jolly well hope you're right, Reggie,' said the Colonel. 'Dash it, I've half a mind to send someone down to put the word around so that they won't be too upset.'

'I d-d-don't think GHQ would ap-ap-ap-appreciate that, sir,' said the adjutant hurriedly. 'Even our own chaps don't know what's on yet.'

'Agents,' repeated the Colonel sulkily. 'Some people have simply got nasty suspicious minds.'

'Villiers,' gritted Wellbeloved, stalking along the first rank, 'you're a shower.'

'Yes, Sergeant.'

'Call yourself a soldier? How the hell do you think you could actually kill a man?'

'Depends how strong he was, Sarge,' replied Villiers sweetly.

'You're a shower,' Wellbeloved sneered again. It was as if he were compelled to use the phrase by some regulation. It was always used. Nothing, in military parlance, had bettered it as a meaningless insult. A shower. A shower of shit; a rank cliché that dragged itself like some dreary old trooper accompanying the squads and echelons of the army paraded throughout the earth. Each time the utterance fell from some sergeant's mouth it dropped dead on to some parade ground. And yet it was used as though it were freshly coined each day. It would be shouted and said for many more years and wars. It took a long time to change a saying in the British army.

The squad had deduced that they were not going to Korea, because they had not been told to roll up their bedding or pack their kitbags. Their sheets were open and those who used mosquito-nets had hung them ready for when they would return to go to bed that night. The operation was not to be far away.

'It's the village,' Wellbeloved informed them. 'We're going to turn over the village.'

Lieutenant Grainger moved stiffly towards them across the square. He looked like a genuine soldier in his battle kit, his revolver holster straight, his sten-gun easily held, his ammunition pouches well squared. Most of the officers were ill suited to military equipment; it hung and sagged on them like leaves on a dead shrub. Their webbing belts girdled their waists in embarrassing loops, their pouches were dented like cardboard boxes, and their service revolvers were jammed in stiff and uncomfortable holsters at dangerous angles.

Grainger, aware of his own sharpness, strutted by the other squads and surveyed his platoon. He suddenly lounged as though the strings of his body had been slackened.

'Kids,' he said airily, 'we are mounting an operation in the local village. Intelligence has got wind that there's a couple of Chink agents hiding out down there and it's our job to root them out. Okay?'

It was not a question and none of the squad answered. 'They'll be armed, of course,' he went on. 'And they'll fire.'

He paused and scanned them, savouring the drop-ping expressions as they digested the information. 'Oh yes, they'll certainly fire,' he nodded sagely.

'Can we shoot back, sir?' inquired Lantry.

Grainger took two swift strides and confronted him with feigned amazement. 'Shoot back?' he whispered. 'Are you mad, lad? You may not fire – and you certainly may not *shoot*. Cowboys shoot, Lantry. Soldiers fire.' He stepped back and stared at the squad. 'You must await the order to open fire at all times,' he said. 'Is that understood?'

They nodded. Lantry said: 'It just seems to put us at a sort of disadvantage, that's all, sir.'

The officer regarded him maliciously, then extended the expression to the whole squad. 'Yes, it certainly does,' he agreed. 'A decided disadvantage, especially when they are known killers. But we can't have you loosing off your rifles all over the shop, can we now? From reports I hear you can't shoot your rifles very well, can you? These Communist chaps at least know what they're doing with a gun.' His voice and his eyelids dropped. 'They *shoot* to kill,' he said.

Brigg swallowed and sensed the same swallow undulating along the rank. He was a pace from Villiers but he could feel the young man's nervousness. Around them other squads were formed on the square; wooden figures like clothes-pegs on long washing lines. The moon was hanging about the Naafi and the eternal noise of the crickets rattled the night.

Eventually each line turned and the whole battalion snaked down the steady hill towards the glowing village. They were formed in two long lines trudging alongside the monsoon drain. One youth actually put his leg into the deep open drain and remained there, trapped, with his other leg stuck out in front of him like a one-limbed pavement beggar. His comrades hauled him clear and a medical corporal, looking for action, rubbed the boy's knee. Otherwise all was sombre movement and deep apprehension.

Their entry into the village was strange. To them it was a familiar place of open shops and rattan houses, squabbling children and flaring lights; to each one as recognizable as their home town. They went there on many evenings, drinking in the three bars, eating steak and chips in the eating shop, and eagerly collecting their civilian shirts from the laundry where the young Chinese mother forever had her baby at her teat while she served at the counter. But now, with studied abruptness, they entered as strangers, invaders. Children playing in the pools of abandoned rain stopped and looked up, oval-eyed, with the orange light of the kerosene shop lamps rounding their countenances. There was a kerbside healer cutting his neck with a great knife and then treating it with some ointment that made the skin balloon. He did that every Friday and Saturday, without fail.

Of necessity, for he had already inflicted the wound, he continued with his miracle-cure demonstration as the soldiers emerged from the shadows of the garrison hill and fanned out along the flanks of the street. The villagers had seen his performance many times, but its fascination hardly dwindled and there were always some to watch. They saw the soldiers but at once returned their attention to the

Chinese quack, indicating that they were not surprised by the invasion and equally that they wanted nothing to do with it. A man swollen with elephantiasis, his arm like a big joke, was at the corner by the camera shop, and he glanced at the moving soldiers and then looked away again as though he had sufficient trouble. The other Chinese, Malays and Indians in the shops, conversing, eating, sitting about with exotic jangling music flying all around, looked briefly at the troops and also went carefully about their business. On this evening they had expected this because everyone knew that no soldier had been down to do his shopping, have a drink or collect his laundry.

Only the group of Chinese girls who solicited in the Heaven-On-Earth Snack Bar and Cabaret showed any reaction. They came like coloured birds to the balcony at the front of the establishment and chorused shrilly at the curious sight of their familiar and vulnerable customers in the paraphernalia of combat. Mucky Meg, the plump and motherly Eurasian who did midweek masturbations for impoverished soldiers at a dollar a time, missed the serious importance of the invasion altogether.

'You like dollar wank, Johnny?' she inquired politely of Brigg as he stood stiffly at a street corner.

'Bugger off, Meg,' whispered Brigg. He had never availed himself of her delights, for she seemed very elderly to him and the proffered hands, one holding the invitation of a piece of rag, repelled him. But she was an economical, safe, and popular attraction with some.

'Dollar wank,' she insisted. 'All good. Take long time.'

'Go and ask him,' grunted Brigg, nodding at Wellbeloved fussing around at the other corner of the street. 'He will.'

'God bless,' remarked Mucky Meg religiously and rolled with chubby confidence towards Wellbeloved.

'Nice dollar wank? You like?' she inquired.

Brigg felt the delight gurgle within him as he saw Wellbeloved stiffen. The other men, drawn up in warlike order along the monsoon ditch, grinned in the village lights.

'Nice, very nice,' encouraged Meg. She held out her plump hand and her square of material.

Wellbeloved's mouth worked up and down on its hinges but no sound came from it. His mean face expanded, his eyes bulged and a pelican pouch swelled from under his chin.

'Go away!' he eventually managed to squeak. 'Get out! Sod off at once.'

Meg remained. 'You like last time,' she assured him maliciously. The soldiers turned away in their unconcealable mirth. Wellbeloved's eyes were all white. Grainger came stalking along the street, full of juvenile importance. He saw the woman and Wellbeloved and lengthened his stride to them.

'What's going on, Sergeant?' he asked.

'A suspect, sir,' said Wellbeloved quickly.

'A suspect?' queried the officer screwing up his face and regarding Meg with distaste.

'You want dollar wank?' Meg asked him.

Grainger's eyeballs went up into his head. 'What?'

60

he snorted. 'What!'

'Importuning, s-sir,' stammered Wellbeloved. 'Soliciting.'

'Get rid of her for Christ's sake!' Grainger snarled. 'You and you.' His finger lunged at Brigg and Corporal Eggington. 'Get her out of here.'

'Sir!' responded Eggington. He and Brigg moved forward and firmly grasped the matronly Meg. Brigg was surprised how warm and full her upper arm felt. Like his mother's. They led her away from the street. As they took her she shouted defiantly her slogan and trade mark: 'Dollar wank! Dollar wank!' All along the street, before the populace and the grinning troops, she bellowed while Brigg and Eggington tried to shush her. But she did not struggle. She was enjoying the experience and the opportunity for advertising it presented. 'Dollar wank! Dollar wank!'

They reached the end of the street, where the light of the village suddenly fell flat against the roadside jungle and all was dark. There they left her mockingly calling her invitation after them.

As they walked back towards the squad Eggington said: 'It might have done that sod well if he'd gone off with her. The officer, I mean. That Grainger. He looks as though he could do with a bit of that.'

Eggington's smells, calamine, talc and unidentifiable lotions were wafting to Brigg. 'You're right,' he agreed blandly. 'I've heard she does it with feeling.'

5

The village was cut through by short dark alleys, dirty lanes between the houses, full of the conglomerated smells of the place and the surrounding vegetation. Cooking fires glowed vaguely, half-dead flowers in the dimness of the living-places. The soldiers had never been into the back alleys before, only at their entrances with one of the Heaven-On-Earth girls, but now the warlike patrols went from the main street into the openings between the shops and houses. The populace, after their first silent reaction, went on with their evening business as though the soldiers were not there.

Corporal Field, his equipment hanging about him like the accoutrements of a beggar, led his squad around some yards where people were squatting and cooking in the smoke-lined shadows. Considering he boasted of his hunting background the corporal was far from eager. He trod cautiously and jumped at each flicker of light or blot of darkness, at each unexpected corner, as though he had run into the first bullet of an ambush. The patrol behind him jumped in reaction to his jumps, giving the effect of an apprehensive caterpillar. Field's water-bottle had somehow detached itself and hung between his legs like a bulbous tail. Brigg, just behind him, had a moment to wonder why they had been required to bring their water-bottles at all, particularly as they were empty.

Although they knew every shop and eating house and bar in the village, the backyards and hidden corridors of the place confused them. Field led them straight through a collection of tethered goats and then plunged blindly into a cesspit serving half the street. He was reluctantly rescued by the men behind him. Then, as they advanced in the dark, a burst of automatic gunfire sounded some distance ahead. There were no flashes but they heard it ripping out and the shouts that followed it.

Without embarrassment the squad flung themselves flat against walls and the warm muddy earth. Brigg could feel his whole body vibrating. They waited for the next gunfire. Two village boys, miniature Chinese wearing white singlets and shorts, arrived and surveyed the prostrate Englishmen with interest. One moved forward, called to the other, and the second boy left his inspection of the rear part of the squad to come and observe the spectacle of Corporal Field with his face pressed close to the village mud, the back of his fruity neck pulsating. Field, and immediately, Brigg, who was lying behind him, looked up timidly and saw the thin legs of the two boys. Their expressions met blankly. Then, ahead, a door opened casually and two Malay customers emerged from the village cinema. A further fusillade of shots sounded as they left.

'Right, men,' ordered Field, pulling himself slowly

and muddily to his feet. 'Up we get . . .' He glanced shamefacedly at the Chinese boys and added: 'Practice is finished. Forward.'

They trooped into the cinema, where a drama of Chicago in the gangster days was being shown. A shoot-out was still in progress on the screen and Brigg and the others regarded it sheepishly. Their entry by the side door was complemented at once by the fortuitous appearance of Grainger, Wellbeloved and attendant soldiers from the main entrance.

'Stop! Cut!' shouted Wellbeloved importantly. He strode forward down the central aisle between the rough wooden benches, his arms held out in the beam of the film so that his shadow was thrown on to the screen.

'That bastard's never looked so big,' muttered Brigg to Lantry.

'Stop! Pack it in!' ordered Wellbeloved again and the image of Edward G. Robinson faded obediently behind him. The lights of the bare enclosure came on reluctantly, as though they had been roused early from sleep. The place was roofless and from above the palm trees peered down with apparent curiosity.

The audience numbered about a hundred, depleted because of the absence of the usual soldiers. They sat stoically while the troops formed up around the outer gangways. Sergeants gave orders, but the Chinese, Malays and Indians remained unmoved. They would wait patiently for the return of Edward G. Robinson in Chicago.

A bucolic Military Police sergeant was ushered to the front of the audience and in tortuous Malay told the people that the soldiers would want to see their identification papers. No one could speak Chinese or Indian so the sergeant asked optimistically if the Malays would kindly pass on the information to their neighbours.

'Brigg,' ordered Wellbeloved, 'you come with me.' Brigg followed him to the back row. 'Look at their papers,' said Wellbeloved. 'Make sure they're all right. I can't stand the smell in this bloody place.'

Brigg glanced at him with distaste. Then he moved along the row, each person obediently producing an identity card which he checked and then returned with the professional smile of an usherette. It was strange to realize how quickly he could feel important. His rifle felt heavy and warm against his shoulder. Along the other rows other soldiers were making similar examinations.

At the end of Brigg's row sat two Chinese men, flat-faced, holding their identification cards before them, but close to their chests as though each held a good poker hand. Brigg approached and then the first winked slowly as he showed the card. Brigg saw the words SINGAPORE CID, and half glanced at the second man, who winked also. Brigg winked back, pleased with the contact, and then walked down the aisle to rejoin the rest of the squad. The soldiers left by the main exit, and Brigg and the Chinese detectives exchanged a knowing grin as he passed. He felt full of secrets and importance.

*

Lt Colonel Bromley Pickering, his eye like a lamp, arrived at the centre of the village while his soldiers searched.

His face was pained. 'Reggie,' he said to his adjutant. 'I wonder if these people would mind turning down their wireless sets a trifle. It's quite deafening.'

The Colonel had located a new aspect of the operation. Touch by touch the villagers had been turning up the volumes of their many radio sets. Gradually the cacophony of half a dozen oriental stations had increased until the lit streets were hideous with discord and the soldiers were pressing their ears and shouting at householders and shopkeepers to turn the noise down. Each Chinese, each Malay, each Indian did so with an obliging smile, but immediately turned the sound to its highest again once the British soldier had moved on.

'Stop them! Stop them!' implored the Commanding Officer, his hands over his ears. 'Ask them, please. They must be stone deaf, every one.'

But a hundred and fifty radio sets were difficult to silence. As troops managed to tame the sound in one part of the street, it swelled in another. It was not an anti-British demonstration nor a protection for the Communists hiding in the settlement; it was a protest against loss of trade. The people standing in the lights behind the open counters of the shops and in the vacant bars and cafés had scarcely taken a dollar all evening. No one had bought a tube of toothpaste or a shirt. The beer, the food and the prostitutes had not been touched. It was a bad state of affairs. Only the young breast-feeding mother at the laundry remained bowed and unmoved by it all. Soldiers' washing could be exchanged at any time.

Lieutenant Grainger and Sergeant Wellbeloved were leading their squad from the extreme end of the village towards the centre, searching alleys and inlets as they progressed. Grainger pressed each search eagerly, patently hoping at every turn to discover some enemy on which he could turn his gun. Observing him, Brigg knew he was watching an odd and ruthless man. A man who would eagerly take gratuitous risks for himself and those under his command. And, when a soldier has only five months and three weeks' service left, such men are dangerous. Wellbeloved, as apprehensive as Brigg but unable to show it, followed Grainger at as great a distance as he dared, sniffing into what appeared to be the less likely hiding places for a terrorist.

Apart from the officer and the sergeant there were six soldiers in the patrol. They had poked through a number of cuttings at a place where the tail of the village spread out into rubbish dumps and yards stacked with empty oil-drums and where two old lorries, relics of the Japanese occupation, had been left to collapse. Beyond these were some more huts, closer together and more squalid than the rest, which occupied the uncertain ground right to the edge of some swampy secondary jungle. It was quieter and darker there, although the raucous protest of the native radios was filling the streets beyond the rough rooftops.

'We'll have a dekko over there,' decided Grainger

in his cockney voice. 'Split into twos. Sergeant, you take the left bit. I'll take the right with Brigg. Corporal Field and Corporal Eggington down the middle bits, each with one man. We'll meet round the back. It looks to me like a bit of an arsehole of a place.'

The men stood uncertainly in a group, like loungers at a street corner. Wellbeloved licked his lips. There was no movement among the low houses – a few cooking fires and three lying dogs but no people. Brigg swallowed uncomfortably. Grainger said, 'Come on, then. Move.' They moved.

The young officer went ahead. Apart from his holstered service revolver he carried a sten-gun, and Brigg's sweaty hands were gripping his rifle. They crossed the rubbish area and skirted the two scrap trucks before making for the dark access to the huts. Grainger was like a snake, eager for a strike. Brigg cursed him silently, his apprehension increasing to flapping fear at each successive pace. He followed the officer quickly, less through devotion than the terror of being left behind. He had a quick thought of his bed, his belongings, his civilian suits bought for his triumphant return home, all only ten minutes' walk from this unholy, dark and risky place.

They saw immediately that there were people in the huts. Some had gone to the street to see what was taking place but the majority stayed within their weak walls, crouching in the gloom. They were squatters and poor people. They wanted no dealings with the soldiers. Grainger briskly went into several houses and Brigg timidly followed him. There was scarcely room for two laden men with guns in the space available. Brigg remained by the door in each case, trying to look stern and businesslike, his jaw set tight to stop it trembling. The people in the houses, Chinese people, creased faces in the dim lamplight, regarded them with overwhelming apathy, slow looks and slow movements, as though they had spent half their lives being searched by soldiers. Only the children, like bundles with eyes, regarded them with surprise and curiosity. As they left each of the three houses they investigated, Grainger said cheerfully and patronizingly 'Thank you, folks' and ducked through the door. But his expression did not change. He would have liked someone to capture or, if possible, to kill.

The muddy ground took on a decided slope as it reached the end of the street of hovels. The final house was on the brink of the swamp, and the jungled growth that reached from the mud clutched at its roof. Brigg was beginning to feel relieved that the search was almost over. But abruptly Grainger pushed him back against a wall made from the beaten tin of a purloined advertisement hoarding. The officer was bent like a bow against the wall; Brigg's nerves were vibrating. Just behind his shoulder a slant-eyed version of the Ovaltine girl, especially adapted for the Chinese market, carried her healthy armful of alien corn.

Brigg heard Grainger slip the safety catch of his sten. The young officer's face, set hard with excitement, turned to him. 'Put one up the spout,' he murmured. 'Catch off. I think we've got them.'

Fumbling with his rifle, Brigg only succeeded in jamming the round of ammunition in the breech. His fingers went to jelly as he tried to release it. It stuck grimly. His chin felt wet. Bloody thing! Oh Christ, fancy it sticking now. Grainger still had his face looking towards something only he could see in the ground before them. Brigg tugged at the bolt again. Fucking thing! Come out. Oh, please come out. It would not. He pictured them coming at him in the dark, not two hiding bandits but dozens. Grainger shot down, and he with his rifle-bolt stuck. He imagined how he would look with his hands raised above his head. Move, you bastard, move!

'What's the matter?' demanded Grainger whispering over his shoulder.

'Stuck, sir. The round's jammed.'

He saw Grainger's neck stiffen. Slowly he turned. 'Twerp,' he said bitterly into Brigg's frightened face. 'Twerp.'

'Are they still there, sir?' whispered Brigg.

'Who?'

'I thought you'd seen something ahead, sir.'

'Just a couple of mangy dogs,' replied Grainger. He took the rifle from Brigg and handed his sten over. 'Good bloody job it *wasn't* anything,' he cried. 'You'd have been right up the creek.'

'Yes sir,' agreed Brigg hugely relieved that there were no enemies ahead. He watched Grainger unlock the rifle. Then the officer, as though by some aberration, closed the bolt again and pulled the trigger. The weapon exploded almost beneath Brigg's chin, throwing him back against the tin wall.

His mouth opened in a wordless cry. Grainger stood before him. A grin dawned on his mouth. A bullet hole had appeared right between the oriental eyes of the Ovaltine girl, a foot above Brigg's grey face. Deliberately Grainger put the rifle back into Brigg's hands and took his own sten. Some chickens in a coop had been disturbed by the report and a clutch of dogs set up a barking in the hot darkness. But there were no human movements. The rowdy radios of the village continued to sound over the roofs.

'Court martial offence,' said Grainger briskly.

'Sir?'

'Letting off your rifle negligently,' said Grainger. 'Particularly under active service conditions.'

'But . . . it was you . . .' Brigg's words came out slowly, unbelievingly.

'That's a serious accusation to make against an officer, Brigg,' said Grainger calmly. 'It's *your* rifle, sonny, and you fired it. Do you want me to take the matter further?'

'But I didn't . . .'

'Court martial offence,' repeated Grainger smugly. 'Very nasty. Just missed my napper that did, Brigg.'

Brigg opened his mouth again, but said nothing. His face became taut as Grainger's grin of assurance widened. Brigg deflated and turned the weapon over in his hands. 'What about the bullet, sir? They count the bullets at the armoury when we hand the rifles in.'

Grainger patted him protectively on the shoulder. 'I happen to have the odd rifle round in my billet,' he said. 'Luckily for you. I'll get it to you before you check in at the armoury. I'd hate one of my chaps to be in trouble.'

'Yes sir.'

'Shall we go?'

'Yes sir.'

As Grainger moved forward all the radios in the village stopped at once. It was as though some signal had been arranged. Silence dropped across the whole area. The soldiers returned from the hidden places behind the houses and shops and formed up in the street. At once all the shopkeepers doused their kerosene lamps and the village was in darkness, the troops fumbling shadows.

'Put those lights on,' pleaded Colonel Bromley Pickering through the darkness. 'Play the game.' In reply a solitary Indian stall-holder at the far end of the street lit a dim carbide lamp.

'Damned unsporting,' said the Commanding Officer to his adjutant. 'Let's clear out of here. The whole thing's been a farce, Reggie. An absolute farce.'

The platoons of the garrison moved away up the hill towards their barracks. As the final rank left the edge of the village, all the lamps were lit again and the radios began to sound, as though power had been restored to the entire neighbourhood at once.

Brigg marched with Grainger's strange grin filling his imagination. The explosion and the heat and smell of the discharged rifle were still with him. He could see the bullet hole in Miss Ovaltine.

'Mad,' Brigg told himself. 'Bloody mad.'

*

'I think the bugger did it on purpose. Honest.'

Tried to shoot you? What's he want to do that for?'

Brigg again imagined the heat of the rifle in his face. 'No,' he said after considering, 'I reckon he just wanted to scare the shit out of me.'

'Well he obviously did that all right,' observed Tasker. He sat on his bed and looked towards Lantry.

Lantry said, 'I still can't see why.'

'Because he's a crazy sod, that's why,' said Brigg fiercely. 'He just did it for a laugh. He couldn't resist the chance to frighten me. When I got the round jammed up the spout he decided to do it. He had me scared enough thinking there was some wogs with guns just down the bloody street.'

'We'll have to watch that Grainger,' nodded Lantry sagely. 'He's a bloke that could be dangerous.'

Brigg stared at him: 'What do you mean? Could be? He *is* bleeding dangerous. You should have him part *your* hair with a bullet'

Tasker nodded: 'And then make out it was you that let it off.'

'That's just it. He's dotty *and* dangerous with it.' Brigg thought about the words. 'And crafty too. I thought he was going to stick me on a charge. Imagine me trying to talk my bloody way out of that. My word against his. Who'd believe me?'

'Nobody,' forecast Tasker accurately. 'You'd get six months for letting off your gun and another six months for perjury. He's a strange bugger all right.

73

All this Cockney-talk stuff of his I don't understand. It's like he's taking the piss out of us.'

'He changes his voice when he talks to the Colonel,' said Lantry. 'He speaks like the rest of the officers then.'

Brigg said, 'But have you noticed when he salutes the Old Man. He *shuts* his eye. Screws it right up tight. Just like the Colonel's. He's taking the piss out of him too.' He stretched out on his bed. The final troops had returned from the operation on the village and were dispersing down below on the square. They had found nothing.

'Listen,' said Brigg. 'Don't let the rifle business get around. Keep it to us three, all right? I don't want any more bother with Grainger.' He leaned out and touched his new blue heavyweight civilian suit hanging in the wardrobe by his bed. It had been specially made for his arrival at home. He sighed sincerely: 'I want to stay alive to wear this. Tonight I was wondering if I'd ever get home to put it on.'

Foster and Villiers, lagging behind on their own devices, were last into the barrack room. They dragged their webbing and equipment on the floor after them.

'I bet you two sweethearts are tired,' commented Lantry from his bed. 'All that nasty soldiering.'

They were never put out. 'On the contrary,' said Patsy Foster. 'We rather enjoyed it, didn't we, Sidney?'

'Yes it was smashing,' responded Villiers flashing his eyes at his friend. 'Charging about with bang-bangs. Ordering people around. I thought it was really lovely. In fact it made me think that when I get out of this mob I wouldn't mind joining the police force.'

'You'll have to get rid of that lisp first, Sidney,' Brigg pointed out from his bed. 'You'd never arrest anybody with a lisp like that.'

'Thod off, Brigg,' returned Villiers emphasizing the impediment. 'We'd be in the plain-clothes branch, wouldn't we, Patsy?'

'I bet,' returned Brigg. 'High heels and handbags.'

They had no opportunity to pursue the exchange, for Grainger and Wellbeloved, followed by a Military Police major, strode into the barrack room.

'Stand by your beds,' bellowed Wellbeloved.

The young men sighed and scrambled up, hung mostly in towels. Grainger waved his arms impatiently at them. 'Come around here,' he ordered. 'At this end of the room.' Three or four draped recruits came from the showers, and joined the strangely biblical gathering.

Grainger spoke. 'During the village operation tonight, did anyone here check the papers of two men who were supposed to be members of the Singapore CID?'

Brigg opened his mouth but the word 'supposed' made him shut it again.

'Anyone?' repeated Grainger. 'Two Chinese with identification papers with "Singapore CID" on the top?' He looked around, his twenty-year-old face seeming older. 'Nobody?'

They shook their heads and mumbled noes. Grainger turned to the Military Police major and said something quietly. The senior officer said, 'Two Chinese detectives were found murdered on the outskirts of the village tonight. The Communist agents escaped by using their papers. But they were undoubtedly still in the village when we were down there. A glance at the photographs would have given them away, even to anyone who can't tell one Chinese from another. Now did anyone see those papers or those men?'

Brigg shut his eyes hoping no one would notice his shaking. They didn't. Wellbeloved dismissed them and they returned to their beds. Brigg lay down. What a bloody night it had been.

6

Wads of grubby rainclouds lay over the palm trees in the initial light of Monday. Rain had fallen on the camp in the night in its customary tepid torrent and there was another downpour just as the night guard sleepily quit the offices and went across the bridge against the tide of disgruntled soldiers trudging, hunched beneath their rain-capes, in the other direction. Some may have wondered why they had imagined the East was perpetual sunshine.

Beneath the capes the knives, forks and spoons drummed their habitual march, slowed to a dirge. All day they would be scratching pens on the hundreds of forms which the British army had evolved over generations of trying to keep track of itself; forms of many rulings, colours and numbers covering eventualities as diversified as illnesses to mules and retirement to the Chelsea Pensioners. All day they added and subtracted the pay and allowances of soldiers encamped that very morning in the risky jungles to the north.

As they trooped by, the soldiers collected their mail from a window of the orderly room. It was distributed by a gull-faced Chinese woman clerk, rumoured to be the discreet but frantic lover of Regimental Sergeant-Major Woods of the aching feet. She, it was said, had introduced him to Tiger Balm, a Chinese preparation which cooled and eased the pain that was throbbing within his socks. He, in turn, had purchased a new gold tooth for her as a birthday present, but few had seen evidence of this because she never smiled for private soldiers.

Tasker had a letter and so did Brigg. Lantry pretended not to care that no one had written to him and he whistled drearily as they sat down at their wooden desks in the office. Rain was jumping on the corrugated-iron roof. Brigg and Tasker read their letters below the level of the tables because they were supposed to begin work at eight-thirty.

'My old man's got an ingrowing toenail,' murmured Brigg over his letter.

'That's nasty,' nodded the unoccupied Lantry knowingly. 'I knew a bloke once who had to have his leg off because of an ingrowing toenail.'

'You're kidding.'

'No, straight, he did. It spread all over his leg.'

'I bet my dad won't go to the hospital,' forecast Brigg. 'He won't take any notice of the old lady. If I was home, I'd make him go.' He read on, 'Stone me,' he said. 'My dad's mate is taking his missis abroad. They're going on holiday to *Spain*. Christ knows how they can manage that.'

Tasker said, 'Lily's all upset because I'm not on the way home.'

'Lily's not half so upset as I am,' returned Lantry glumly.

'There's tears on the page,' Tasker's voice became awed. 'Look, tears.'

Lantry glanced over and sniffed: 'She's let the tap drip on that.'

'Bollocks. Just because yours don't write to you.'

'Keep them at a distance, I say,' shrugged Lantry, not put out by the remark. 'I mean, your lark looks like it's getting too serious. You're going to be lumbered with her when you get home, you see. And you've hardly laid a hand on her yet.'

Tasker dropped into deep thought. 'Ah, but the times I've had it with her in my mind, mate, I'll *have* to marry her to make her an honest woman.'

'God,' muttered Brigg dismally. 'Fancy sitting in this dump on Monday morning in the rain when we could be sitting in England in the rain. Sometimes I think I'll never see it again. Fuck it all.'

Dismally he folded his letter away and carefully crossed off another day on his desk calendar. To cheer himself he crossed off two more and then another and then, at an abandoned dash, recklessly crossed off the remainder of the week. Even such extravagance took only a small segment out of the great mocking battalion of numbered spaces defending the next six months; a few casualties inflicted on the vanguard. And now he would not be able to cross out any more before the following Monday. He regarded what he had done guiltily.

The section's officer and NCO, Lieutenant Perkins and Sergeant Bass, entered together through the door at the end of the office. They were like Laurel and Hardy, the officer thin, the sergeant fat,

79

and both glum, but exchanging, always, prim little jokes and remarks. The officer knocked the Monday rain from his hat and Bass stamped his treetrunk legs on the wooden floor, presumably to get his clothing hanging correctly about his body.

The sergeant waited pedantically until the officer was seated and then sat down himself with caution reminiscent of an elephant squatting on a tub. Each then privily crossed off a day on his desk calendar. From the back of the section, Brigg watched them do it and grinned sardonically. When their days were all gone and they had finished here they would go on somewhere else, for they were regulars. For them there would forever be days to cross off.

'Everybody here?' rumbled Sergeant Bass. 'Nobody on sick parade?' His large head moved pendulously from one side of the office to the other. Everybody was there. Ten soldier clerks and one ambitious young Chinese, stiff in starched whites, lifted their heads and looked towards Bass. The Chinese, Mr B. Wee, his black hair rigid with Brylcreem, smiled with servility.

'Right then,' boomed Sergeant Bass. 'Let's get on with it then. Nothing like transferring ration allowances to cheer up a dull morning.'

Perkins, who was weak and dawdled through the office hours doing the minimal portion of work, permitted himself a grin as thin as a piece of fuse-wire and said: 'Quite right, Sergeant Bass, quite right.'

During their interminable months under the tin roof of that army office, Brigg, Tasker and Lantry had evolved a system of secret activity below the level of their work tables. Each held their pen in the left hand, apparently writing; while the right hand, using a book or blotter as a rest, performed some activity below the level of the table. They wrote all their letters home in this way; wrote heroic poems, drew indecent pictures, and played noughts and crosses and battleships. It required skill and ingenuity. Sometimes its surreptitious nature made them feel romantically like prisoners tunnelling from a camp under the very eyes of the guards.

The day's work began. At ten-thirty the tea wagon would arrive from the Naafi with its steaming urn and sticky cakes. That was one event, anyway, to which they could look forward. The arrival of the tea meant another quarter day had gone in the army. That was something. Small, but something.

At twelve-thirty, they would all clank across the bridge again, cutlery and mugs drumming, to line up at the cookhouse for the predictable offerings of the Army Catering Corps, whose troops stood like glistening gods behind their hot pans as the first soldiers burst through the door, and halted crest-fallen as they were transfixed by the same old odours.

The early rush was not, in any case, occasioned by a desire to get at the food, but because it meant longer stretched out on the barrack-room bed before returning to the office at one-thirty. Afternoon tea arrived at three; they were in the cookhouse again at five-thirty, and flat out on their beds again by six-fifteen. Wednesday afternoon was designated as a recreational period, so they could get their feet up as soon as they returned from the midday meal, with only the interruption of a quick call at the Indian ice-cream seller's on the way back. Soldiering for them was not a violent existence.

On the evenings at the beginning of the week, few of the men moved from the barrack room. It was dark by seven and it often rained when the sun dropped. The bed, the charpoy, the pit or the chariot, as it was variously called, was the domestic place for each soldier. It was where he lived. It was his island. His possessions were either beneath it or in the wardrobe-locker at its side. It was his sitting-room as well as his sleeping place; it was there he received visitors, read and wrote letters, performed his domestic tasks; and the mosquito net, if he chose to rig it up like a green sail, gave him privacy in the event of his wanting, in a barrack room of forty men, to spend a night with himself.

Lance-Corporal Williams had made a bookshelf which hung like a guillotine over his prone head, and on it had ranged his set of encyclopedias which he was reading through from A to Z, educating himself for a better life thereafter. Sometimes another inmate would shout across the beds to him: 'How far have you got, Willy?' Williams, a thick, slow man, would report his progress. 'I'm up to the Dodo. D-O-D-O, Latin *Didus ineptus*. Extinct bird with massive clumsy body and small wings.' He looked up laboriously from the book. 'I wonder what it looked like?'

'Bit like you, I reckon, Willy.'

Lance-Corporal Williams could not be offended. He solidly returned to his self-instruction.

Another man had kept a small, secret monkey under his bed until his neighbours, wearying of its smell and spiteful spasms cut its retaining string and sent it into the surrounding trees. The lost creature returned every night for a week and sat pitifully on the barrack room balcony, wanting to come in, but had been finally driven away to the alien jungles by the missiles and insults thrown at it from its hostile liberators. Private Conway, the quiet, inward youth from Belfast who spent his free hours making complex jigsaws, sometimes life-sized, on a board set across his bed, had annoyances to swallow. It was a favourite game to upset Conway's jigsaw just as, after weeks of labour (for his was also a slow process), he was about to fit the final piece into place. He always made great ceremony of moving the bits about the board to assess their fitting, and he did this even when there was only one space and one piece left. They watched him secretly, night after night, and always endeavoured to tip the board just before he dropped it into place. But he was of a placid nature and merely set about reconstructing his puzzle on the following night.

Gravy Browning was eternally playing table-tennis against the wall of his bed-space. He was highly skilled and could even play when he was lying in bed. The click-click of his activity irritated newcomers but quickly became a mere background to their existence, like the ticking of a clock.

The advent of Morris Morris, the big-breasted

Welshman, into the monastic life of the barrack room had changed it a little. He was the first manic-depressive that Brigg had ever encountered. He would be bright and soldierly at times, apparently forgiving the army for calling him back from peace and wife and family, and then would descend hideously into the hole of despair, crying out from its depths with loneliness and anxiety. More to cheer him up than anything, he was invited to play in an unofficial Sunday football match, Skins versus Vests, on the hockey pitch parked out for the garrison Gurkhas on the side of the barrack square. He was goalkeeper for the Skins team and he stood, stripped to his PT shorts and frighteningly large boots, as the final line of his team's defence. He had been loudly enjoying himself bellowing encouragement to his forwards as they played the coloured toy ball towards the opposite goal, then barring the way ferociously to the Vested forwards who invested him. Then two conscript cooks, who had come from their duties for some Sunday-morning air and were watching the game, began to laugh at Morris's bouncing breasts. Their ribald comments floated across the game despite worried warnings from players of both teams. Eventually the Vests got a penalty kick, and as their captain lined up to strike the ball towards Morris, spread like some pale pagan god across the goal-line, one of the two cooks hooted: 'Give him time to put his brassiere on, mate!'

Morris Morris, with only a little change of expression, held up his hand quietly but imperiously for the taking of the penalty to be suspended. Then teams and spectators solidified in the sun as the large man walked like an executioner towards the cooks. Men watching from the barrack block balconies called urgently to their friends within to come and see. The cooks, abruptly aware that something spectacular was about to occur to them, shuffled closer together and, with concern accumulating on their faces, waited for the terrible arrival of Morris Morris.

What happened was quick and violent. Morris said nothing, but caught the heads of the aproned youths, like coconuts, one in each of his widespread hands, and crashed them fiercely together. The pair sank with neither a word nor a cry to the hard square and lay sagging against each other like two bundles of dirty washing. Morris turned briskly, in the manner of a man who has completed one task and now gives his attention to another. He marched back to the goal, where he easily saved the weakly-kicked penalty shot of the Vests' captain.

Nobody really knew what to do about Morris. The soldier in transit, the attached man, the odd-and-sod, was not an unfamiliar figure at Panglin; like wraiths they wandered and wafted around, doing nothing in particular, waiting for orders or destiny. But Morris was the first odd-and-sod, and certainly the first recalled reservist, to be put among the young men of the office corps. He was given no particular duties. Oversized and eye-catching though he was, officers and NCOs somehow overlooked him as though hoping he might go away. He clattered about the camp, always appearing to be going somewhere or just returning from there. An old soldier, he knew the value of the useless piece of paper in the hand and the expression of the dedicated message-carrier on the face. He appeared early in the queue at Naafi break, and was always first in the cookhouse line. Most nights he would lie like a great pie on his bed as it bowed spectacularly under his weight, his brassy nipples pointing directly to the ceiling. Sometimes he would sing in a huge, sweet voice, and at others would lie silent and wrecked. One night he tumbled into the barrack room heavily drunk just as the lights were going out. He swung ponderously towards his bed. When he reached it he paused, emitted a giant sob and then crumpled to his knees and began to pray loudly for his wife, his home and his little children. The prayer went on for several minutes, and all around him the young conscripts lay stiff with apprehension, embarrassment and sorrow for his predicament.

In one corner of the barrack room stood a large wooden radio set, struck dumb by successive and ever-clumsier attempts by various incumbents to repair a minor fault. Whenever it was touched, it discharged a shower of wires and bits from its back on to the floor.

The radio had given them some pleasure: records of Doris Day, Nat King Cole, the Andrews Sisters; commentaries from the Bukit Temah race-course in Singapore, which none of them had ever been rich enough to visit; and news from home. It was that which was difficult to suffer. They would sit hunched on their beds listening to reports of snow in the Pennines, Attlee and Churchill in Parliament, labour disputes at the docks, and HM the King visiting the Festival of Britain in London. Homely, familiar things, now far removed and nostalgic. Rumours from a strange land. Their spirits would fall lower. They were not entirely sorry when the radio set became a speechless junk box.

Some occupants received regular copies of the *Overseas Daily Mirror*, a week's issues bound in lurid yellow covers, and these would be read and passed on until they were in tatters. Pin-up girls would be measured by many hopeless eyes; the sports news provided pointless arguments; the names of places in the columns read with sad nostalgia because they were the sounds of home: Manchester, Dundee, Worksop, Saltburn-by-the-sea, Southampton and Pontypool. Magic places.

The regular pattern of their military domesticity continued like this, enclosed, exiled, elongated in time. There were occasional excitements and odd novelties. One of these occurred on a mid-week evening when into the lamplit life of the barrack room appeared a strange, foreign soldier.

'An American, Reggie? An *American*?'

'Y-yes, sir, I'm afraid s . . . s . . . so.'

Lt Colonel Bromley Pickering sat stunned at his desk, looking from the posting order in his grasp to his adjutant and back to the order again.

'It's preposterous, quite preposterous. Whatever

will they think of next? Foisting an *American* on us. We don't know what to *do* with an American. Have you rung Postings at GHQ?'

'Yes, sir,' the adjutant sighed. 'They s-say there's no mistake. We've got to have him. He's become detached. It's only temporary. Are you ready for some coffee, sir?'

'Yes, Reggie, I jolly well am after this. Why do they have to attach every detached soldier to us? Anyone they don't know where to place they send here. It's getting like a bottom drawer. We'll have the Camel Corps next.' He seemed to reach a decision and looked fiercely at his adjutant. 'I'll have a slice of bread and butter too,' he said. 'Marjorie's sent me some plum jam from the garden at home. I might as well open the pot now.'

'P-p-plum jam. That's very nice, sir. Is she an expert jam-jam-jam-maker, your wife?'

'Southern Counties Women's League Champion,' replied the Colonel, his voice suddenly sadder. 'That's one reason why she stays in England. Has to defend her title you see. There's no jam-making to speak of out here.'

The adjutant moved towards the coffee-pot. He took a ready-cut slice of bread and carefully spread it with butter from a dish shaped like a rabbit. 'You have the p-pot with you, sir?'

'The jam? Oh, yes, Reggie. It's here in the desk. If you ever feel like a spoonful, help yourself. Third drawer down, with my revolver. You'll like it.'

'Thank you, sir, I'm sure I will.' He took the miniature pot from the Colonel and carefully distributed the plum jam across the bread and butter. He then placed it on a tea-plate and handed it to the Commanding Officer with the cup of coffee.

The Colonel sampled the jam and cheered a little at the taste of sweet home. But then he returned to the posting order. His face creased. 'It really is too damned much,' he complained. 'Why do we have to have an American? Somebody not even in *our* army. Why can't he go to the transit camp?'

The adjutant shrugged. 'Full, sir, crammed to the b-b-brim. It's the Korea business. It's all these new units passing through on the way there.'

'But this chap's not a unit. He's just one soldier.'

'He belongs to a unit, sir, but I gather they've got lost somewhere en-en-en-en route.'

'Lost? Lost?'

'They've been misrouted, so GHQ think, sir. The intention was that they were to come to Singapore to work with a British unit before going off to Korea. They've got to get to know each other's m-m-methods and that s-sort of thing, sir, seeing, as our chaps are fighting in Korea with the Americans.' He hesitated, then added: 'On the same side.'

'What methods?' asked the Colonel. 'What do these people actually do?'

The adjutant glanced at the paper. 'Logistics, sir, it says here.'

A further cloud settled on the Commanding Officer's eyebrows. 'Logistics, eh?' he muttered. 'Yes, of course, it would be. Logistics.' He looked up at the lost face of his adjutant. 'Right Reggie,' he said firmly, 'perhaps we'd better see this chap.' He glanced again at the posting order. 'Clay. William. Private First Class. First Class? My goodness, don't they give themselves fancy airs these Americans? It's just like the films.'

Private First Class William Clay entered the Colonel's office. Colonel Bromley Pickering looked up nervously into the face of a tall, puzzled youth. The salute was slow and thoughtful. 'Clay, sir,' he announced briefly.

'Ah, Clay, yes, Clay,' mumbled the Commanding Officer as though he had some difficulty in recalling the circumstances. He wondered whether, out of sheer hospitality to a foreigner, he ought to offer the soldier a chair. But he resisted and said instead: 'Er . . . make yourself comfortable.' Clay glanced at the armchair by the desk. 'Stand easy,' put in the Colonel hurriedly.

'Sir.'

'Now, Clay.'

'Sir?'

'You are a First Class Private, I see,' he stared at the posting order as though it had to be decoded. 'Yes, well, that's jolly good.'

Clay was looking intently at the Colonel. A blob of plum jam was hanging to the corner of the officer's mouth. The Colonel noted the direction of his stare, removed the jam with his finger and after regarding it on his fingertip for a moment, popped it into his mouth. 'Plum jam,' he explained. 'My wife makes it.'

'Sir,' agreed Clay.

The Commanding Officer seemed suddenly to make up his mind about something. 'Where are you from, Clay?'

'Benstown, Colorado, sir.'

'Ah yes, Benstown,' said the Colonel as though he went there every week-end.

'And Japan.'

'Oh, Japan as well?'

'My unit is in Japan, sir. We were detached to join up with a British unit here, but the rest of my group, another six, sir, seem to have gotten side-tracked to Korea.'

'Yes,' nodded the Colonel co-operatively. 'I heard they had, er, become side-tracked. So you're here and they are not. Ah well, that happens in the best of armies, Clay – even ours.'

'Yes sir, the army guys at the airport told me to report here.'

'And it's logistics, is it?'

'Right, sir. We are going to work with a British unit so that when it comes to operating in Korea, we will have familiarized ourselves with each other's methods.'

'Of course. Can't have two opposing lots of logistics working at the same time. That would never do.'

'No sir.'

The Colonel's chest gave a little jump as he sighed. 'Well, Clay, if you've been posted here in transit, then this is where you're posted.' He paused to consider the sentence, shrugged to himself and continued. 'You have been fixed up with a barrack room and all that. I don't suppose they're as luxurious as you're used to in the American army, but, er, we don't have as much money as America.'

'It's fine, sir. The guys have been great.'

'Good chaps,' agreed the Colonel. He seemed reluctant to continue, but then he asked: 'You've no idea how long you'll be here, then?'

'No sir,' replied Clay. 'I thought maybe you would know.'

'Me? No, I don't. I'll ask though, higher up. I'll try and find out.'

'Yes sir, thank you sir. I'd like to get back with my buddies as soon as possible.'

'Of course you would. Very natural. We'll try and see that you're back with your buddies very soon. In the meantime, Clay, make yourself at home. It's always a job to find duties to give to people in transit, but I expect we'll find something to occupy you.' He glanced at the American's thin frame. 'Stop you running to fat.'

'Yes sir.'

'Well, I think that's all, Clay. Dismiss.'

Clay's loose limbs came together as though someone had pulled a lever. He saluted, American fashion, edge-on as though he were trying to shield his eyes, and left the room.

'Reggie,' called the Colonel.

The adjutant came obediently from the outer office. 'I was just 1-1-looking it up, sir,' he said.

'Looking up what, Reggie?'

'L-1-logistics, sir.'

The Colonel's glance sharpened, but dropped again at once. 'Yes, logistics. I suppose we'd better have a proper definition. I'll have another cup of coffee then, Reggie, if you please. And I'll jolly well have another slice of bread, butter and jam. Damn it.'

7

They lay like a child's cut-out paper pattern: a string of men, legs wide apart, bellies down, squinting along the sights of their rifles. Brigg's elbows felt raw against the earth. His right boot was touching Clay's left boot, but there was no contact with Tasker's on the other side. For some reason Tasker could not open his legs as wide as the rest.

'The legion of the ruddy lost,' complained Wellbeloved in his whine. He would have said 'bloody' but he could see Grainger standing sniffing across the prone backs at the other end of the firing line, and he did not yet know how to take Grainger. The sergeant fussed up and down behind the boots. 'Shooting,' he muttered, keeping his voice low. 'I've shit better.' He stopped behind Tasker and raised his binoculars towards the target three hundreds yards distant. 'You haven't marked it yet, Private Tasker,' he snorted. 'You haven't even chipped the woodwork.' He strode on.

Tasker half turned to Brigg. 'The bastard bullets are leaving this end all right,' he said.

Brigg grinned. He revolved his head half a turn and whispered to Clay. 'Listen, Yank, don't be so bloody keen. You're showing the rest of us up. We don't *want* to be too good at this lark. They might send us somewhere where we have to use these bleeding things.'

'Stop talking!' Lieutenant Grainger came springing along the line like a lean and eager hunting dog. 'Who was it?' He reached Brigg's feet. 'Come on, who was chattering?' There was no response. The men lay unmoved.

'Up! Up!' hooted Grainger suddenly. 'On your feet.'

'Unload first, sir?' inquired Brigg over his shoulder.

Grainger's face ran scarlet to the neck. 'Party! Party!' he squeaked. 'Un-load!'

The bolts of the rifles were rattled to and fro and the unspent rounds cascaded to the earth. 'Party!' squeaked Grainger again. 'Party! Att-ention!'

They scrambled to their feet and stood, backs to the officer until he ordered them to about-turn. He stalked along the line nastily. 'I will not . . .' he began. He got no further because his stride took him abreast of Private Fundrum, standing awkwardly with a folded white handkerchief hanging from the edge of his beret and down his face.

'Oh . . . oh . . . now what's this? A new fashion?' inquired Grainger, his voice descending 'Or are you waiting to be wounded?'

Wellbeloved, hovering behind, opened his mouth as though he had never before seen Fundrum firing with a handkerchief hanging from his beret. But Fundrum answered in his modulated, learned voice. 'I am unable to close the left eye, sir.

An unco-ordinated muscle, I am informed. It is not uncommon.'

'Name and number?' Grainger snapped.

'221987384 Fundrum Q., sir.'

'Ah,' Grainger creased his arms. 'The famous Fundrum. The brains of the battalion. What's the Q. stand for?'

'Quentin, sir.'

Grainger stared as though he suspected Fundrum of making a fool of him. Wellbeloved, a pace away, interrupted: 'It was the Commanding Officer's idea, sir. I think that's one of the Colonel's hankies. He gave it to this man, sir.'

Grainger closed his eyes. 'So, if you're ever ambushed you have to ask for a truce until you've fixed your handkerchief over your eye.'

'That's the only way I can look down the sight, sir,' replied Fundrum quietly. 'Sergeant Driscoll, who has been posted now, had the same trouble.'

'My God, what a shower,' said Grainger as though to himself. He directed his face at Fundrum again. 'I hope to God you're never called into action, that's all,' he sneered.

'I sincerely hope not, sir,' replied Fundrum.

Grainger opened his mouth, then shut it, and stepped towards the centre of the squad again. Each step was like a bite. 'Right,' he said. 'I've told you before that I'm not one of your airy-bloody-fairy officers. I'm a bastard, and I don't care who knows it. I'm a working-class bastard, what's more, so I know exactly the way you people operate. Apart from our friend with the hankie, of course, who seems to be a class above us all. So let's have no more chit-chat, answering back, or poncing around. We came here to hit those targets, in the middle, and we're going to do it, and do it my way, or we stay here all day, Saturday or no Saturday. Right, Sergeant Wellbeloved.'

'Sir.'

Wellbeloved, his expression that of a rat who has just met a stoat, stood nervously and ordered the squad to take up their firing position once more. Brigg imagined that the bull's-eye was Grainger's eye. His hands turned minutely against each other to keep the rifle in a firm vice, the stock felt warm against his cheek and the butt sank into his shoulder.

'Five rounds, application,' bawled Wellbeloved. 'Squad. Fire!'

Brigg stopped his breath for a fraction, squeezed the trigger tenderly and felt the weapon jerk against his face. The smell of the shot steamed through his nostrils. He pulled the bolt and reloaded. The others were doing the same. They always said the rifle was the soldier's best friend. Nasty bloody thing.

Corporal Field, the man who spent much of his life in lethargic dreams about being a man of action, liked to be part of the butt party on the Panglin firing range. As far as he could be stimulated, he had been stimulated by films about the Western Front in the First War, with erupting shells and deep holes, outposts and earthworks; and being in the safety trench behind the targets, walking the wooden duckboards and hearing the bullets smacking above gave his dream the only reality he would ever require. He was a truncated, balding, blustering man who liked puffing out his cheeks in the way he imagined a hunting squire might do. He was aggressive, too, in a miniature way, seeming to imagine that anyone over his five feet two inches was a threat to his manhood.

The butt party, sixteen men, were marking the shots fired from the other extreme of the three-hundred-yard strip of red earth. With their disc markers attached to long poles they reached up and indicated an occasional bull's-eye, a magpie, demonstrated by twirling the banner so that the black and white faces of the disc showed alternately, an inner and an outer, and a sad wave, like a goodbye, if the shot was a wash-out and had not blemished the target at all.

Villiers and Foster, also members of the entrenched party, played a simple and familiar game of their own. Foster held the marker pole towards his friend.

'Sister Anna . . .'

'Yes, dear?'

'Carry the banner.'

'I carried it last week.'

'You'll carry it this week!'

'But I want to go to the pictures . . .'

'There's pictures on the wall!'

'But they don't move.'

'Move the buggers then!'

Their play was interrupted by a bullet, fired low,

hitting the bank three feet above their heads and peppering them with red earth. They looked up like startled children.

Foster, the stronger of the pair, wiped the debris from his shirt with a grimace. But Villiers was more alarmed.

'I don't like it, Patsy,' he said. 'It's dangerous and it's dirty.'

'Some things are, love,' replied Foster enigmatically. 'Stick your pole up and give it a waggle.'

Villiers came out in a smile. 'You are a laugh, you know, mate,' he said appreciatively. He pushed the marker pole up to ground level and decorously waved it. On its third wave it was struck and split dramatically by a bullet. The shock numbed Villiers at the bottom end of the pole. He let it drop with a frightened cry and followed its descent to the bottom of the trench.

'Sidney, Sidney, what's the matter?' howled Foster bending over his friend.

'I'm shot in the arm, Patsy!'

'No, you're not,' replied Foster. 'It's just the marker pole. Somebody hit the marker pole by mistake.'

Corporal Field edged his way with lightweight importance along the trench. 'What's going on?' he demanded. He looked down at Villiers. 'Why are you lying down there?'

'A bullet hit the marker pole, Corporal,' replied Foster speaking for his friend. 'It gave him ever such a nasty shock.'

'Get up, Villiers,' ordered Field unfeelingly. 'Stop

poncing about and get on marking those targets.'

Villiers picked himself up from the foundations of the trench, glanced at Foster, and then, with hurt, at Field. The blunt sound of a shot going through the target above them made all three look up.

'Come on then,' ordered the stumpy Field. 'Mark it. Magpie.'

'Yes, Corporal,' replied Foster. 'Give me the stick, Sidney.'

Villiers readily handed over the marker pole, its wooden staff split by the first shot but remaining serviceable. Suddenly apprehensive and with his friend smiling and Corporal Field watching him impatiently, Foster pushed the marker up above the earthworks. It was immediately blasted from his thin hands by a bullet which severed the disc from the pole. Foster cried out and tumbled backwards in his shock, while the disc fell and struck Field on the forehead.

'Bastard!' bellowed Field in his loud, small way. 'Whoever it is, he's doing it on purpose!' He made a grab for the field telephone and wound the handle frantically. 'I'll nail him,' he promised. 'I'll nail that clever swine. We'll soon find out. There's not many of the twerps who can shoot like that.'

Lieutenant Grainger, a patient sneer hanging on his face, walked along the drawn-up firing party. 'It was target four,' he repeated. 'And since Tasker is on target four and couldn't hit an elephant at the end of an alley, I'm inclined to think it was somebody fooling around. Now who was it? We'll hang around here until night-time if you like. It's Saturday afternoon that's sacrificed. Who was it? Own up.'

Clay stepped forward. 'I guess it could have been me, sir.'

'Ah, Mister America,' breathed Grainger. 'The hot shot from the hills. So it was you.'

'Accidental, sir,' said Clay. 'It was just coincidence I hit the pole twice. I was aiming for the next target.'

Grainger looked at him between the eyes. 'An accident,' he repeated. 'Just bad shooting.'

'Yes, sir.'

'Get this, sonny, Private First Class Clay. Just because your army managed to mislay you, don't get away with any idea that you can play the fool with me. We have an expression – "Watch it" – and that's what I'm saying to you now – watch it. Okay?'

The 'Okay' was drawled like a taunt. Clay stood to attention, expressionless. Grainger's nose was so close that he had a good view up his nostrils.

Each Tuesday, Lt Colonel Bromley Pickering had what he enjoyed calling, in his gentle way, an officers' coffee morning. He did not go to his office that day but waited for them at his house, where they were expected at eleven. They would sit drinking coffee and eating slices of bread and butter and homemade jam from England and discuss the problems and events of the battalion.

The officers realized that the roots of these gatherings were in some distant, probably dead, headmaster's weekly meeting with his staff in the Commanding Officer's schooldays. The corporate, often juvenile life of the soldiers was recognizable in the same boarding-school context, but not by them since few of them had ever been away from home before the army called them. Their schools were normally at the bottom of the street. Few complaints about the young soldiers ever provoked much agreement or action from the Colonel. 'Yes, yes, yes,' he would nod into his coffee. 'But they're only lads. They're only lads.'

'Clay,' began Lieutenant Grainger at the Tuesday meeting. 'Private First Class Clay.'

'Our American,' nodded the Colonel.

'Becoming a nuisance,' said Grainger. 'Fooling about on the firing range. Throwing his weight about. He seems to think he's something special because he's American.'

'And so he should,' observed the Colonel mildly. 'He would not be much of an American soldier otherwise. It would be a sorry day when soldiers cease to love their country, don't you think?'

Grainger, as politely as he could, grunted. 'I don't think his presence is doing the chaps much good, sir,' he pressed.

'Well,' shrugged the Colonel. 'It's not his fault he's here. He's been mislaid, so to speak. And we can't find anyone who owns him. Can we, Reggie?'

'We k-k-keep t-t-trying, sir,' stumbled the adjutant. 'But there seems to be a c-c-c-complete break-down somewhere.'

'He wants to get back to his buddies,' said the

102

Colonel. 'He himself keeps reminding me of that. But we can't *find* his buddies at the moment. The least we can do is to extend some friendship to him. He's only a lad. Anything else?'

'Another attached man, sir,' said Lieutenant Perkins. 'Morris. The big chap.'

'Yes, Perkins, what about him?'

'Could he be ordered to wear a jacket at all times, sir?' Perkins dropped his eyes to the plum jam.

The Colonel was genuinely amazed. 'Whatever for?' he inquired. 'The chaps are allowed to strip to the waist. It gets horribly sweaty for them.'

Perkins sighed. 'Yes, sir. Normally it's all right. But there would seem to be medical reasons.'

The Colonel looked nonplussed. He glanced at the medical officer. 'What reasons, Bilking?'

Major Bilking tugged at his moustache ends. 'He appears to have breasts, sir.'

'Breasts! Good heavens. I thought everybody had br . . .'

'Like a woman's,' continued the medical officer. 'I've never seen anything like it. If you'll excuse the expression, sir, he's got real tits.'

The Colonel blushed immediately. 'I'm not sure I *can* forgive that expression, Major,' he said. 'The whole business sounds most distressing. Poor fellow.'

'It's causing bother, sir,' interpolated Grainger. 'He really does look a bit freakish. He's got nipples like a woman . . .'

'Oh my God, Grainger. Please stop.' The Colonel was so shocked his coffee-cup shook.

'I'm sorry, Colonel,' said Grainger. 'But it is a matter of discipline.'

'Good gracious, man, you can't discipline a man because he's got . . . er . . . breasts.'

'The men make fun, sir,' sighed the medical officer. 'I had two unconscious cooks in my sick-bay the other Sunday. He'd banged their heads together because they'd been poking fun at him.'

'Oh dear, oh dear,' swallowed the Colonel. 'I must confess I've never noticed. It must be dreadfully embarrassing.' He paused and took an absent-minded bite from his bread, butter and jam. Then he looked up. 'All right then. Suppose, in the interests of discipline, we order him to wear a jacket. Who is going to tell him? You can't write a thing like that into orders.'

They drank their coffee and thought. Then Bilking said slowly, 'Staff Sergeant Ambrose, sir. He's applied for a compassionate posting to Hong Kong. He's got a Chinese wife and she won't come down to Singapore. He thinks she's started running around.'

'Yes,' nodded the Colonel. 'I know about that. I've sent the request to GHQ.'

'I suggest, sir,' said Bilking, 'that we make sure he's given the okay – but tell him it's on the condition he gives Morris the written order before he goes. Once he's done that we could rush him to the plane and get him out of the place quick.'

The Colonel looked about him. The Officers were all nodding agreement as they munched.

*

The rhymes the young soldiers said and the songs they sang were all part of their locked lives. There were sayings and slogans, too, some quite meaningless, which were the small props of their existence. 'Old boot!' one would abruptly yell to another across the cookhouse. 'Old boot!' would come the absurd reply until the air was full of the cries of 'Old boot!' and the orderly sergeant, like some harassed schoolmaster, would whinny about trying to quell the idiocy, silencing it in one place only for it to break out in another. It was a manner of rebellion.

In the days when they had expected to go home at the end of their eighteen months, a soldier would proclaim that he was 'Peachy', meaning that the troopship was already sailing out from England to fetch him.

Their anthem was 'We're A Shower Of Bastards', and odd exchanges, like well-acknowledged catechisms, would be chanted in the barrack room in the empty boring hours. Some were established and handed down from earlier soldiers and times.

'They're building a house!' the cry would be, for no particular reason.

'Booooooo,' the response would sound from some soldier unseen, perhaps astride a thunderbox, in the ablutions.

'A public house!' the chanter would call.

'Hooray!'

'Only one bar!'

'Booooooo.' This time from everyone in the barrack room, some standing, some sitting, some flat on their beds, some darning holes in socks, some reading or writing, some dreaming improbable dreams. But, as though it were an ordained service, they would reply, mostly absentmindedly, continuing to do whatever they were about. It was like the chorus of bored monks.

'The bar's a mile long!' the originator would cry, still continuing with some other occupation or duty, even if it were only staring at the electric fans revolving their lives away on the ceiling.

'Hooray!' A dull cheer.

'The barmaid's having a baby!'

'Boooooooo.'

'A baby Guinness!'

'Hooray.'

Clay, the American, listened to these descants with wonder, and then gradually and carefully learned the words.

'To the woods!' Again a cry for no reason.

'Not the woods!' A concerted high-pitched squeak.

'To the woods!'

'I'm only thirteen!' The same squeak.

'To hell with superstition!'

'I'll tell the vicar!'

'I *am* the vicar!'

Clay said to Brigg, who was in the next bedspace, 'Say, Briggsy, why do they suddenly start calling like that?'

Brigg looked up from the local newspaper his mother had sent. He seemed surprised that the question should have been asked but he was short of an answer. 'I don't know,' he shrugged. 'I suppose it's just something to do.'

It was Morris Morris, now condemned to wear a jacket, an order which he accepted with no apparent surprise or reprisal, who had the idea of the concert. He had frequently joined in the fragmentary entertainments in the barrack room, although he disliked what he called indecent ribaldry. He would squat like Buddha and groan 'The Minstrel Boy' and 'Flow Gently Sweet Afton' in a voice that swooped from strangled tenor to throttled bass, and the younger men would sit and listen to him as though he were their father.

He was the master of ceremonies at the concert and he spent a week nervously rehearsing his jokes aloud in bed, so that every one of his neighbours knew his act by heart before it had ever reached the stage of the garrison theatre. He pressed his uniform three nights in succession until it was as stiff as a pea-pod, and polished his off-duty brown Oxford shoes until the footlights glowed in their toecaps.

On the night of the concert he stood before them, his chin decimated by over-enthusiastic shaving, his hair so gross with retaining oil that it stuck to his head like a poultice, his face alight with a holy joy and enthusiasm that touched the audience and aroused their response not because they themselves felt the same joy, but because they did not want to hurt him. They cheered, laughed at his old jokes, and sang with him:

'There were rats, rats,
Big as pussy cats,
In the Quartermaster's stores.'

It was a chorus that had been sung through all the battles, and all the days and hours of waiting for battles, in the war that Morris Morris remembered. Now these new soldiers chanted it into the sticky Singapore night just as others had a few years before on the eve of defeat and death. But for these new men it was nothing but another song.

'Tonight, boys,' announced Morris Morris when they had finished, 'we've got a lovely bill of fare for you.' He paused, indicating an imminent wonder. Brigg found himself nodding amiably at the stage as though encouraging the fiction. Morris was cascading with sweat caused by the heat of the lights and the effort of the singing. His jacket has turned deep olive under the armpits and down his bosom.

'And to start us off,' panted Morris, 'we have a delightful young lady who will do a tap-dance. She is the little daughter of Cook-Sergeant Gilchrist, known and loved by you all as the man who provides our daily bread and whatever else he's thought up! But seriously, boys, give a big hand to little Dawn Gilchrist, who is only ten years old.'

There was obedient applause and the piano and drums which comprised the irregular camp orchestra clattered into an appropriate Shirley Temple dance. From the wings, like a pot of jam draped in satin, came a thick-set child, strawberry-faced, white-socked, patent-leather-shoed, who fell to rapping her toes and heels on the stage with utter disregard to the time and rhythm strenuously supplied by the musicians. It was a brief performance, a fusillade from each hefty young hoof, a running-on-the-spot-step, each foot flying backwards while the podgy pink arms swung across the body like the efforts of a small washer-woman over a tub, and then Dawn Gilchrist flew off as though catapulted from the opposite side of the stage. In all she was not in the limelight for more than thirty seconds.

Morris Morris, apparently taken by surprise at the swiftness of the act, was back in front of the audience before he was prepared. He called for more applause and then encouraged the little girl to return for an encore.

'That kid will burst,' forecast Clay confidently in Brigg's ear.

'You can see where all the *good* cookhouse grub goes,' nodded Brigg. 'If she blows up, the whole place will be splattered with sausage and chips.'

Dawn gave a short, cutting nod to the pianist in a precociously professional manner, indicating that she was not altogether satisfied with the previous accompaniment. Then she put her head down and did her running-on-the-spot routine again, changing to her frenzied tap-dancing, and then inexorably slowing and dragging the piano and drums with her until she sank to the stage like a plump, exhausted goose. She was helped off by her father and mother who leapt the footlights to her aid and exited to great applause.

'Christ almighty,' complained Lantry from the other side of Brigg. 'If this is meant to cheer us up, I'd rather be fucking miserable.'

The others gloomily ratified the comment and their darkness deepened with the announcement of the next act: monologues by an aircraftman from RAF Saletar, a neighbouring camp. He was a wispy man, pale-haired, tight-faced, who stood, uniformed, with his hands clasped as though for protection in front of his trousers, and reverently recited a 1940 poem by A. P. Herbert. Physically and spiritually the British soldiers slumped lower as the stanzas went on. Clay, who had a sensation of being caught in some strange pagan rite beyond his understanding, stared dumbly at the stage. The performer lifted his tone to a squeak at the final dramatic line, bowed like a broken matchstick, and marched stiffly off to clapping tempered with relief.

He was followed by Panglin's own Regimental Sergeant-Major Woods, whose bad feet sometimes had him in tears and caused him to wear furry bedroom slippers during all his off-duty moments. These peered like timid pets from beneath the trousers of his tailed suit while he performed some mildly amazing conjuring tricks and essayed a juggling act with a tea-cup and two saucers. His entertainment completed he shuffled away, dropping the tea-cup and saucers as he reached the wings, an unrehearsed finale which evoked twice as much audience appreciation as the act itself. The RSM scraped the shattered china off-stage with one of his slippered feet and left moodily. The evening was not going well.

110

Morris Morris then told some jokes in the desperate manner of someone determined to enjoy a funeral. They were old and poor, but the reaction from the audience was appropriately charitable. His barrack room friends hooted obligingly and shouted hollow encouragement. When he had finished, Brigg said, 'I don't think I can stand this much longer. If it wasn't for old Titty Taff up there I'd have gone long ago.'

They were prevented from leaving by the sudden promise of the next announcement. 'Gentlemen,' intoned Morris – his face was like pulp, the comedian's grin riddled with perspiration. 'We now have a magnificent treat for you. Four glamorous misses, nurses from the British Military Hospital, ah, lovely girls they are, who have volunteered to take their lives in their hands and dance the cancan!'

Gigantic enthusiasm greeted this news. Some men who were making for the door, bent almost double so they wouldn't be seen, swivelled and at the same crouch retraced their paths to their seats. 'Boys!' exclaimed Morris. 'We proudly present the Four Glams!'

Only one Glam trotted on at first, as the drum and the piano played an entrance.

'Christ, what a mug,' groaned Brigg.

The woman hoofed her way to the footlights, her powerful square countenance severed by a thick fixed smile, her golden curls bouncing like carpenter's shavings. Another Glam joined her and the moan from the denied soldiers was audible, for she was sharp and stringy, her bony knees going like metal

111

pistons alongside the large padded joints of her partner.

But then all was transformed, for the following pair, arms linked, entered together, and a howl of appreciation went up throughout the theatre. They were young and smiling, fresh hair flowing, legs incisive and enticing. There was a blind rush by the audience to get to the front of the theatre, a charge over the top of seats and down the aisles, like a mass attack by intrepid infantry. They crammed directly below the stage, jostling to get a better view up the kicking legs.

It was an inexpert cancan, but at its conclusion the soldiers went wild for more.

'All right,' announced the big boxy lady in a deep voice. 'More you shall have.' They whistled at her and applauded and she blushed over her round cracked cheeks. 'But!' They were stunned to obedient silence by a single warning hand from her. 'But we need some help. Four volunteers . . .'

In the ensuing madness to get on to the stage she was lifted bodily towards the backdrop. The soldiers mounted the footlights like lemmings in reverse; there were sixty men on the stage, pushing and complaining and trying to get near the girls. Morris Morris appeared from the wings and like a bulldozer swept them back into the auditorium. It took several minutes before they were restored, and in order, below the footlights. His great palms still spread out like a restraining barrier he stood grinning and sweating in front of the anxiously reunited ladies.

'Boys, boys,' appealed Morris Morris. 'That's no

way to behave, now is it?' He beamed, glad at last for the enthusiasm. 'Now here is what we'll do. A little competition, it is.' He whispered to the pretty dark-haired girl at the end of the short line. She smiled and whispered back, provoking a storm of hoots, innuendoes and anguished frustration. Morris revolved towards the audience again, face beaming with pleasure.

'All right, all right,' he announced holding up his wide, wet hand for order. His tunic had come undone and his deep chesty valley was exposed. 'He's still got the biggest knockers on the stage,' observed Tasker.

'Now then,' announced Morris. 'The man who can guess the first name of this young lady on my right can choose three more blokes to come up here and do a dance. Hands up. No shouting! No shouted bets will be accepted.'

The hands went up like an eager assembly of clever children.

'Ann.'

'Betty.'

'Lorna.'

Morris suddenly pointed to Brigg. 'Bernice,' Brigg said casually.

'Right!' exclaimed Morris in amazement. 'You're dead right.'

There was a further storm of cheers and booing. Tasker and Lantry banged the grinning Brigg on the back, and Clay, whooping, shook his hand. The four then mounted the stage, Brigg first to make sure that he was the one dancing next to Bernice. It was wonderful, marvellous, to feel again a girl's hand in his – an amateur hand, soft and empty. He could feel his own palm throbbing against hers. She smiled at him and said: ''Ow the 'ell did you know?'

He blinked in surprise at her cockney voice, the aitches brutally dropping from those beautiful lips. 'I heard . . .' he stumbled. 'I heard your friend. When we were all on the stage, you know. I was right next to you and I heard her say something about "Are you all right, Bernice?"'

'Bernie she said,' corrected the girl confidently. 'Everybody calls me Bernie. It's just as well you didn't hear properly.'

Morris was trying to give his instructions on the technique of the cancan, but he had not finished when the Panglin drums and piano collapsed into the music and they were in the lights kicking their legs. Clay was hanging enjoyably on to Bernice's other flank and had his arm around the other, slim, girl. Tasker and Lantry had been left to sort out what was left. Tasker clung on to the outside, his arm trying to hold on the thick column of the tall square woman with the golden curls, while Lantry found himself clutched to the same lady's left side and leaning over like a cripple to remain attached to the wispy woman on his other hip. It was a ragged line and it plunged through the dance with great difficulty. The audience shouted taunts and ribald encouragement, the juvenile soldiers' faces shining up with envy at their comrades dancing with real girls.

Brigg could see his feet flying out in front of him

and the sweat was spouting down his forehead into his eyes. But he shook it away and kept looking to his right and down to where the white bosom of Bernice jogged exquisitely under the frilly bodice of her cancan dress. His mind jangled with memories and hopes. Chinese girls – not even Juicy Lucy – did not have breasts like that: white, unused, unprofessional breasts. The dance went on madly. He could feel her heart hammering against her ribs, and against his. God, please make her slip and drag him down too.

Then it was over. He held on to her for a few seconds more and she kissed his cheek. 'Give them a kiss!' somebody inspired advised from the audience. Brigg's throat filled as he half turned and saw her still there, smiling a beckoning smile, waiting to be kissed. Clay was closing in on his partner, Lantry timidly backing away from the thin lady, and Tasker was caught in the massive hug of the one with curls. Brigg took a pace and kissed Bernice on the lips.

'Sorry, I'm sweating,' he mumbled.

'Me too,' she said.

Then they kissed again, tenderly, considering it was in such public view. But Morris Morris, the old Welsh fool, spoiled it by making comedy from it and pulling them apart. He sent Brigg after Clay who was reluctantly leaving the stage to join Tasker and Lantry already back in their seats.

They sat down, both limp with happiness and perspiration.

'Did you date her?' asked Clay.

'N . . . no,' admitted Brigg. 'I didn't get a bloody chance, did I? Are you fixed up?'

'No,' admitted the American gloomily. 'I was kinda leaving it to you.'

'Oh, bugger,' muttered Brigg. He looked up at Morris preparing to throw himself into an announcement. 'It's all right, though,' he added. 'It's the interval in a minute. We'll go and give them some chat.'

'You're joking,' put in the disgruntled Tasker. 'You don't think you'll get anywhere near them, do you? They'll have the garrison police outside their dressing-room.'

'How you going to see yours, then, Task?' asked Brigg maliciously. 'You're not going to let a gorgeous bit of crumpet like that get away, are you, mate?'

'Get stuffed,' muttered Tasker. 'Trust me to get landed with King Kong.'

'What about me, then,' put in Lantry grumpily. 'King Kong on one side and Minnie Mouse on the other.'

Clay said, 'Well I don't think we should throw this. Maybe we could see them some way.'

'You're right, Yank,' agreed Brigg. He glanced at the stage. Morris Morris was telling some more groaning jokes. 'We'll skid out,' Brigg said to Tasker. 'Since you don't want to see your woman you'd better stay here, because it'll be too obvious if we all creep out together. All right?'

'Oh, all right,' sighed Lantry. 'We'll hang on.' He glanced at Tasker. 'I wish I was pretty like old Briggsy, don't you, Task?'

'Ugly bastard,' said Tasker unfeelingly as Brigg

and Clay crouched away. 'Still, let them try. They won't get anywhere. Can you imagine those two girls going out with a couple of squaddies, even if one of them's a Yank squaddie.' Brigg and Clay were already bending towards the door.

'I don't care,' affirmed Lantry unconvincingly. 'I can wait until I get home. I reckon it would be terrible getting your hands on a girl for a couple of minutes and then having to get them off again. More than flesh and blood could stand.'

'You're dead right,' agreed Tasker. 'Those two will have their mosquito nets up tonight for sure.'

As forecast, the way to the garrison theatre dressing-room was barred. Sergeant Wellbeloved, who was orderly sergeant that night, was standing, legs and smirk spread out, in the corridor, accompanied by two temporary and puny regimental policemen who regarded Brigg and Clay spottily.

'Cakes and buns that way,' said Wellbeloved pompously pointing towards the NAAFI canteen. 'Nice Naafi tea.'

'Sarge,' Brigg opened defensively, 'we wondered if we could just have a quick word with two of the nurses. The ones we had a dance with.'

Wellbeloved regarded him as though he had asked for compassionate leave. 'A quick word with them?' he echoed. 'A quick word? No, my boy, you can't. Haven't you had enough female enjoyment?'

Brigg had to swallow a comment rising in his throat. 'They asked us to come round,' he lied.

117

'I've received instructions that no Other Ranks are to proceed beyond this point, whether or not they have actually danced with those young ladies,' sniggered Wellbeloved. 'At the moment they are in their dressing-room, being entertained by the orderly officer.'

Brigg said, 'And who is the orderly officer tonight?'

'Lieutenant Grainger,' smirked Wellbeloved.

'I thought it might be,' grunted Brigg. 'I suppose he's filling them up with champagne.'

'I expect so, Brigg,' agreed Wellbeloved amiably, 'One of the privileges of rank, lad.'

'Can't we maybe get a message to them?' asked Clay.

Wellbeloved was not sure about Clay. He could not make up his mind about his authority over the American. 'No messages, Private First Class Clay. Not even for you. We haven't got a despatch rider.'

'Sarge,' pleaded Brigg. He got no further because along the far end of the corridor strode Grainger bearing an ice-bucket from which a napkined bottle protruded and a tray arrayed with bright glasses. He stopped when he saw Wellbeloved talking to them.

'Fan club, Sergeant?' he called with amiable nastiness.

'They want to come through, sir.'

'No question of that, I'm afraid, Sergeant. I'll arrange to get some autographs sent out.'

Brigg felt his face and fists tighten. Grainger opened a door and a girlish chorus floated out. He grinned up the corridor once more and waltzed out of sight.

'Cakes, buns and tea, straight down there,' said Wellbeloved again, pointing firmly to the canteen.

Heavily Brigg and Clay slunk out into the stirring night. An overblown moon was hanging ludicrously over a clump of palms; crickets in the grass rubbed their legs together in love-play; through the open yellow-lit windows of the theatre came Glen Miller's 'Moonlight Serenade', playing on the amplifier during the concert's interval. The scent of eastern flowers was suspended everywhere. It was a very romantic night.

'Oh, bollocks!' howled Brigg. His frustration burst and he flung himself down on the warm, wet grass and beat it with his fists. Clay watched him with surprise and sympathy. 'There ain't no justice,' he nodded.

'Justice?' groaned Brigg looking up starkly. 'I don't *want* justice. I just want that girl! For ten minutes. Five minutes. Is that too much to ask? Just to talk to.'

'Sure, sure,' nodded Clay sagely. There were times when he looked very wise and old for a young man. 'Why don't you get up from that grass? You're going to get wet.'

Brigg sat up, the anger seeping from his face to be replaced by despondency. 'This army is denying me my natural functions,' he said grimly. 'It's stopping my bodily processes.'

'Armies do,' nodded Clay. 'Sometimes they stop them altogether. That's when you get killed.'

Brigg looked at him hollowly for a moment. Slowly he got to his feet. 'That bastard Grainger,' he moaned, 'Champagne, ice, all the bloody caboodle. And he's younger than me! I'd give him three lengths start with any bit of stuff in the dance-hall back home and still get there first. He's got fuck-all.'

'He's got a pip on his shoulder,' grunted Clay practically.

'I knew you'd say that. One bloody pip.' Brigg rose and brushed his trousers and tunic. 'I'm glad I didn't put my civvies on now,' he observed practically, looking at the wet stains. 'Mind, if I'd known Bernice was going to be here I would have worn my suit.' He brightened slightly. 'Then she might have thought *I* was an officer.'

'Look, pal,' said Clay kindly as they began a dis-consolate walk along the path. 'It's no good you going for a commission now just so you can qualify for sexual intercourse. You'll be out of the army while Grainger is still worrying about his next promotion.'

'Will I though?' wondered Brigg grimly. 'I reckon I'll still be a squaddie in twenty years' time, the way things are going in Korea and that. And he'll be a bleeding general. That's the way it all works. No justice.'

His soliloquy was interrupted by the eager advance of a dozen or so soldiers towards the rear of the garrison theatre. They were pursued by a further group.

'Hey,' said Clay, catching Brigg's arm, 'where are they heading?'

'The back!' exclaimed Brigg moving off briskly in the same direction. 'Maybe the girls have opened their dressing-room window.'

They both ran to the corner of the building and then stopped short with dismay. Against one of the curtained windows was a pyramid of young soldiers, piled several layers high, hanging on to each other's backs, falling, grabbing, sliding off and climbing on again, all silent, all frantic, all trying to look through the narrow crack of light between the curtains. Clay and Brigg advanced more slowly and sadly.

'Grainger's collecting the glasses,' whispered the boy pressed nearest the window. 'He's just going.'

'Will they get undressed?' The stifled hope came from a minute private with spectacles crushed almost at the bottom of the pile with no hope of seeing anything.

'I reckon they will,' whispered the commentator. 'I reckon they're going to start stripping off now.'

The entire pyramid wriggled with corporate anticipation. Two men tumbled from the top. Brigg and Clay observed it helplessly. 'The big ugly one's going to unzip,' announced the youth at the window. 'I hope the others get on with it. I can't stand this.'

'I can't either,' called the little glassy soldier from the base. 'I'm getting crushed.'

They hushed him with threats. 'The nice one's doing it now. *And* the other nice one,' came the excited comment from the top of the pile. Clay felt Brigg move forward but restrained him.

'What are you going to try?'

'Those are *our* girls they're looking at,' retorted Brigg. 'Dirty load of bastards.'

'*Our* girls?' smiled Clay shaking his head. 'Come on, leave them to it.' His thin hand was still on Brigg's elbow.

Brigg sulked. 'Well, ours more than theirs.'

'More than Grainger's?'

'Oh, bollocks.'

'If she turns around I'll see them,' the eager lad at the window exulted. 'She's got a terrific back. God, I can see her bum! It was more than the others could tolerate; he was grabbed from behind and pulled back by a stronger rival for the peephole. He shouted with anger and punched the invader in the ear. The whole human structure began to sway and then it toppled spectacularly, dissolving into a confused and fighting pile below the window. The noise attracted a face to the window and the curtains were tugged quickly together.

Brigg rammed his hands in his pockets and with Clay began to walk round the building again, scuffing the path with the toe of his shoe. Light appeared in a room at the end of the block. They looked at each other and hurried hopefully towards it. The curtain was scarcely drawn. Within was the wan airman who had recited the monologues. He was standing in string vest and pants before a mirror, squeezing some facial blemish.

'Sod it! That's the final insult,' spat Brigg.

'Maybe we ought to go back to the show,' suggested Clay. 'The girls will be coming on again. Could be we could get a message to them.'

'No,' said Brigg, firm in his misery. 'It's more than flesh and blood could stand. Sitting there looking up their legs and all that.'

Clay walked with him morosely. 'The Japanese,' he said eventually, 'used to give their soldiers rubber women. Great idea. They used to fill them up with hot water.'

'So I've heard,' grunted Brigg. 'With my luck I'd have one with a leak.'

Clay laughed thoughtfully in the darkness. 'Listen, buddy,' he said. 'I took a couple of days to find Panglin, you know, when I got here first. I had a couple of wild nights down in the city. Okay, so you have to pay . . .'

'I've got a Chinese girl down there, Yank,' interrupted Brigg smugly. 'It didn't used to cost me either, not then anyway.'

'Let's go on downtown tomorrow night.'

'We could,' agreed Brigg with shallow enthusiasm. 'But it's not the same.' He nodded back at the garrison theatre, now only lights screened by trees. 'That's what we *ought* to be doing now. We shouldn't have to go paying for it. You only do that when you're old. But we never get a chance. None of us knows how to go about having a shag with a genuine lady.'

A tiny Chinese girl from the village, brown, calm-faced, walked by them, two thin cans hung from a bamboo pole on her shoulder. Also on the pole was a small lantern to light her path. Both men let her go by and then turned and watched her backside, tidy and tight in her peasant trousers. She walked into the darkness, never having given any sign that she had noticed them.

'Untouchable,' shrugged Brigg.

'Wait a minute!' said Clay before walking on.

'What?'

'Maybe we could get ourselves down to the hospital and contact them.'

'They'd chuck you out if you weren't sick or wounded.'

'Okay, so we'll be sick.'

'Ha! You'll be lucky, mate. You don't know the MO here. Old Bilking. Your heart's got to stop beating before he'll send you to hospital.'

'In my army they've *got* to send you for one thing,' grinned Clay.

'A dose,' murmured Brigg immediately. 'That's right, in ours as well. If you say you think you've got VD he's got to send you for a check-up. We could get up there that way.'

'Tomorrow?' said Clay.

'Right. You're on, Yank.'

Clay stopped walking. 'Maybe we ought to go back, so we'll recognize the girls next time.'

'Jesus, as though I could forget.'

'Coming?'

Brigg grinned. 'Why not? No use mooning around like this.'

In the barrack room they were just putting out the lights. 'Going to put your sail up, Briggsy?' asked Jacobs amiably from his bed.

Brigg tossed his mosquito net under the bed. 'No need to, mate. I've got everything fixed. You ask the Yank.'

'Sure, sure,' yawned Clay from his bed. 'We've got it all right.'

Tasker sat up in his sheets. 'You didn't look all right when we saw you outside when the interval was on,' he said scornfully. 'Old Brigg was rolling around on the grass.'

'I was having it off with a cricket,' replied Brigg calmly. 'Didn't you know it was the cricket season?'

8

An army ritual decreed that when a soldier reported sick he was required to take with him his small pack, containing such oddities as knife, fork and spoon, just as if he were going on a picnic. Thus equipped, Brigg sat guiltily with Clay in the medical officer's waiting-room in line with the bowed heads and pained faces of a further dozen men. From the parade ground had come the halt and the lame to sit in communion with malingerers, rolling dramatically with malingerer's agony, and the shamefaced who suspected unpleasant postscripts from brief encounters in the wicked city. Within his surgery the medical officer prepared with a long sigh for an unappetizing procession ranging from coughs to consciences. There were few words passed in the waiting-room. An atmosphere of guilt and infirmity pervaded the place. It was such that Brigg began to wonder in his idleness if there really *could* be something wrong with him. After all, Juicy Lucy was on the market. Some of the soldiers from other units at Panglin, who had never seen Clay before looked at his American uniform with some curiosity but no one raised enough interest that morning to ask any questions. It was like a Trappist monastery after a wild night of illicit talking. Depression and guilt were everywhere.

While they sat, Regimental Sergeant-Major Woods crept in, straight from the early parade, agony nailed to his face, his barrack-square boots throbbing on his feet. Beyond embarrassment, he sat on one of the benches with the wrecked expression of a torture victim. Pain had vanquished pride, and before the gaze of the sick parade privates he undid his bootlaces and thankfully unhinged the boots. His arrival had apparently been awaited, for Corporal Lunes, the medical orderly who was rumoured to be mad, opened the surgery door and said bleakly, 'Sarn't-Major.' The RSM looked at him in the manner of one about to receive unexpected deliverance. He stumbled to his feet, pushed them gingerly back into the hell of his boots and, laces trailing, hobbled into the inner room.

'I'd say that was real hazardous for a sergeant-major,' suggested Clay.

'Poor bugger,' nodded Brigg. 'He's not a bad sort. My heart bleeds for him on the square. Just to see him trying to stamp his feet gently. The poor sod's a picture. All sort of haggard. It's only at Panglin they'd allow a sergeant-major like him. He ought to be put into a comfortable pair of slippers and sent home.'

'My feet are worse than his any day.' The low complaint came from the back of the doleful room, and Brigg turned to see Corporal Eggington.

'Be strange if they weren't, Eggy,' replied Brigg. 'Your foot-rot's a bit of a hobby with you.'

'Watch it, Brigg. You'll find yourself on a charge.'

'Sorry, Corp. How's the ears, incidentally?' He turned to Clay with pretended concern. 'He suffers,' he confided.

'Getting better,' replied Eggington, always keen to discuss his infirmities. 'But now I've come to see the MO about this rash I've got on my tummy. I'll probably see him about my eyes and feet at the same time.'

'He makes a sort of festival of it,' whispered Brigg to Clay. 'Any time you want to see something nasty, just pop around to his bed-space.'

'He sure looked in a bad way in the barrack room last night,' recalled Clay in a return whisper. 'Jesus, he was covered in dressings and creams. I thought he'd been ambushed.'

In deference to his rank and his feet, Sergeant-Major Woods was let out by the rear door. Then one by one the dismal parade hobbled, slouched or staggered in to see the medical officer. Brigg and Clay were last. Brigg was called, and walked smartly up to the doctor's desk, put up a stiff salute and announced himself: 'Two-two-one-five-seven-seven-four-one Private Brigg, sir.'

Major Bilking, a grim unimaginative man with a moustache like buffalo horns, scarcely levered his eyes up. 'What's the trouble, Brigg?' he asked, his attention on the newspaper spread before him.

'Worried, sir,' replied Brigg.

'If you're worried, go to the padre,' replied the MO monotonously.

'It's not that kind of worry, sir. Not religious. Physical, sir.'

'Have you had a discharge? From your penis? Not from the army.'

'No . . . no, sir.' Brigg was taken by surprise by the short-cut of the discussion.

'What makes you think you've got VD?'

'I went with a woman, sir.'

'I didn't think you'd been with the regimental goat, Brigg,' sighed the doctor.

'No, sir. But I've been worried ever since. I didn't much like the look of her, sir.'

'Why go with her then?'

'Drunk, sir.'

'And you think she may have infected you?'

'Yes, sir.'

'Well, why?'

'Well, sir, I was drunk, like I've just explained and she was the cheaper sort, sir.'

'You usually go for the better stuff, eh?'

'Yes, sir. In a way. But this one only cost five dollars in the Serangoon Road.'

'Five dollars? If you've got it, it's a bargain, Brigg.'

Major Bilking looked wearily down at his paper again. Brigg saw he was surveying the runners for Bukit Temah.

'Well, Brigg,' said the medical officer tiredly, 'I suppose I ought to have a look at it, but quite truthfully I don't want to. It's too bloody early in the morning. I've already seen two scarred and battered monstrosities and I couldn't stand another.'

'No, sir.'

'I do wish you people would be a bit more choosy

about the direction you point your weapons. I can remember the time when contracting syphilis was a chargeable offence. A self-inflicted wound.'

'Yes, sir, like sunstroke,' said Brigg helpfully.

The medical officer sighed. 'Brigg.'

'Sir?'

'Shut up.'

'Sir.'

'I suppose I'd better send you to BMH for an FFI. Go and sit in the ambulance outside with the other rotten Romeos.' He resignedly picked up a form and wrote 'Surveillance' and handed it to Brigg. 'Give that to your section officer when you get back,' he ordered. 'Then he'll know why you were absent.'

Brigg took the form reluctantly. 'He'll know then, won't he, sir,' he pointed out unhappily.

'Of course he will, if he can read,' said Major Bilking.

'It'll be a bit embarrassing for me, sir. Him knowing.'

'That's your fault, Brigg. You shouldn't go looking for cheap thrills. Are you the last in the waiting-room?'

'No, sir. Private First Class Clay, sir.'

'The American? What the hell's the matter with him, I wonder?'

'Same thing, sir.'

'Same thing? God, is there no sense of decency or even hygiene in the world today? How do you know it's the same complaint?'

'He was with me, sir. Drunk, sir.'

'Don't keep telling me you were drunk, Brigg. It's not the absolution of all sins. He availed himself of this lady, too, did he?'

'No, sir. It was a different one. Worse than mine, sir.'

'Send him in,' sighed the medical officer. 'You go and sit in the blunderbus.'

The ambulance journey to the British Military Hospital in Singapore took almost two hours because the vehicle had to make detours to various service establishments to pick up other soldiers, airmen and sailors who had been sent to undergo the mysterious ritual of Surveillance.

They sat like a clutch of unmarried mothers, some ashamed, some in fear, some dull with resignation, some with forced jollity and self-assurance. There were two ostensibly devil-may-care Naval ratings who had apparently made that and similar journeys many times.

'They're sadists, these blokes at BMH,' announced one of the sailors confidently. A dozen concerned faces turned to him. 'Sadists,' he emphasized. 'Ain't they, Nobby?' His comrade nodded with grim wisdom. 'Terrible,' he confirmed. 'Them and their spikes and their hooks.'

'Spikes and hooks!' croaked a trembling air-craftman.

'Spikes and hooks, friend,' confirmed the sailor. 'And don't they just love to use them, too! Eh, Nobby?'

'Not much they don't. You can see them crowding to the windows of the clinic as soon as this pox wagon draws up, rubbing their rubber gloves together, choosing out their victims.'

Faces turned yellow. Brigg looked nervously at Clay. 'I thought all they did was give you a blood test,' Brigg suggested to the sailor.

'Not bloody likely, mate. That's what they're *supposed* to do. But they makes a game of it. They get out all their spikes and hooks and start sticking them in your old man.'

A young soldier in one corner began to sob into his hands. 'They mustn't do that to me. I'm only a kid.'

'Aw,' sympathized Nobby. 'He's only a kid.'

'They'll like that,' forecast his friend with grisly confidence. 'Love it they will. They like the young ones. They're a very queer lot, take it from me.'

'*We* haven't got it,' announced Brigg with old-maid primness. 'Not my mate and me. We're just going up to see some nurses.'

The sailor regarded him with calm scorn. 'Listen, mate, are you on the pox list?'

'Er . . . well, yes, I reckon we must be.'

'In that case you've *got* it. As far as they're concerned at BMH you've *got* it. It's like being guilty until you've been proved innocent. They'll give you the spikes and the hooks.'

'Oh God,' murmured Clay.

'And it ain't no use saying you caught it from the bog seat, either,' continued Nobby indomitably. 'Not unless you're a padre. Because they won't believe you.'

'I've had a hundred and thirty-seven needles, I

have,' said the first sailor. The young soldier began to whimper again.

A shocked quiet settled on them as the ambulance bumped its way along the red mud road out of Singapore city and on to the hospital. It finally swung and stopped and the back doors opened like those of a prison truck. The fierce sun burst in. Dolefully they began to troop out.

'Listen,' said Nobby grimly as they stood outside the hospital. 'Can't you hear them sharpening the spikes and hooks?'

Trembling in the sunlight the grubby parade trooped into the hospital. They sat on scrubbed benches in a waiting annex redolent with disinfectant.

Clay said, 'This is going to be great, buddy. I sure don't like the sound of the hooks and spikes routine.'

Brigg shivered. 'Do you think I do? Especially when we know we haven't got anything.'

'I guess it seemed like a good idea at the time.'

The sailors were immediately recognized as regular customers. The orderly called, 'Nobby first.' Nobby rose and the other sailor put his hand with encouraging sadness on his sleeve, a movement which sent a draught of apprehension through all those sitting on the benches. Nobby hesitated convincingly and then straightened himself and made a reckless plunge through the curtains. Two minutes later a terrible scream came from the examining cubicles. It chalked the faces of the waiting men; knuckles went white to the bones on the edge of the bench. Brigg felt his eyes go cold, Clay's forehead

133

was bubbling with sweat, the young soldier whispered something that could have been a prayer, and Nobby's friend hid his face in his hands as though the sound were too much to suffer.

The dingy curtain through which Nobby had gone was half pulled aside. The untidy red-haired medical orderly peered out. 'He's passed out,' he said to Nobby's comrade.

'Again?'

'Yes, it was the spike. You'd better come and give him a hand.'

Mouselike squeaks were coming from the young soldier; every mouth was dry, every brow was wet. The sailor walked in bravely to his friend.

'For Christ's sake, let's get out of here,' whispered Brigg to Clay. 'We can try and talk our way out of it later.'

Clay nodded a desperate agreement. They rose and crept towards the door, but they were only half-way when the orderly's voice caught them. 'Come on back, you two.' They stopped. 'Which are you, soldier?' he asked pointing at Brigg.

'Private Brigg,' swallowed Brigg. 'But I'm all right. Straight I am.'

Unimpressed the orderly looked at the list. 'Right, you're next. Come on.'

Brigg's knees felt as though they had come out of joint. He stumbled towards the curtain, opened invitingly, took a deep lungful of disinfected air, and went in.

'Cubicle two,' grinned the orderly wickedly.

Brigg went towards the ominous curtain. A young

medical officer sat at the desk. He smiled amicably, then looked up into Brigg's ashen face.

'What's wrong?' he asked.

'No . . . nothing . . . sir,' trembled Brigg. 'Just . . . this.' He waved his hand to encompass the situation.

'Shouldn't do it,' replied the officer affably. 'Even so, I can't see why you're so worried about a blood test. It's only a pin prick.'

'Blood test, sir? What . . . what about the hooks and spikes?'

The doctor smiled wearily. 'Oh, they're working that one again are they? Is that those two sailors?'

Relief flooded through Brigg's body. 'Sailors. Yes, sir.'

'Old lags,' commented the officer. 'They just put on an act. I've only just got in. Did they do the screaming bit?'

'Yes, one of them screamed, sir. And they said about these hooks and spikes.'

'One day they'll have some youngster cutting his throat out in the waiting-room,' forecast the officer.

'I felt like that, sir,' admitted Brigg.

'It's your own fault, anyway,' said the doctor. 'It'll teach you to keep it inside your trousers.'

Brigg lingered in the odorous corridor waiting for Clay, tapping his boots on the bald floor, whistling without a theme, smiling an inch at a time at nurses and orderlies who passed purposefully by, standing up straight when anyone who looked like a doctor approached, and trying to appear as if he had no

135

connection with the VD clinic in the same vicinity. To further this deception he even stood, pain all over his face, holding his elbow as though awaiting some treatment for an injury in that joint.

Eventually a keen young tea orderly appeared, white-coated, his trolley bearing a steaming urn and cakes and pastries properly laid out below white towels. By his devoted expression and the manner in which he propelled the vehicle with careful and dexterous urgency, it obviously represented to him, at any rate, a serious patient being wheeled to the operating theatre. Below those white cloths was a human body, its heart flailing bravely, not Chelsea buns and Eccles cakes and cheese rolls curling their crusty lips. That tea-urn, breathing heat at his hand, was blood transfusion unit pumping life into the heart.

'Excuse. Excuse. Mind your back please,' the orderly requested with quiet medical urgency as he progressed along the corridor. He seemed upset that Brigg should suspend his progress.

'Is this for anybody?' Brigg asked, pointing to the trolley with its precious load.

'What d'you mean by that?' asked the orderly staring down at the imagined patient beneath the cloths.

'Can I have some tea and a cake?'

The young man looked immediately despondent at the realization that a stranger had so easily detected that his business was buns not blood. With ill grace he nodded and served Brigg with two cardboard containers of tea, letting the final drops from the tap go into the cups with the intent eye of a theatre surgeon checking the end of a transfusion drip. Then, with quiet drama, he folded back the hem of his white cloth and revealed the ashen face of a coconut cake.

'I'll have two of those,' said Brigg looking at the young man curiously. 'My mate is coming in a minute.' He added hurriedly. 'Busted his wrist this morning.'

'That's why we're here,' said the tea orderly gallantly. 'Anything else? If not, that's twenty cents.'

Brigg gave him the money. 'Do you know a nurse called Bernice something in the hospital?' he asked casually.

'I know *all* the nurses in BMH,' replied the orderly with the knowing smile of a handsome house doctor. 'Bernice – Nurse Harrison is in Casualty. Nice girl.'

'Casualty,' said Brigg. 'How can I get there?'

'You could always get yourself shot,' said the youth.

'Any other way?'

'Straight along this corridor, turn left at the end. But be a bit careful. They can get dodgy down there if there's a rush on.'

'Right you are. Thanks.'

''S'all right. I must get on.'

He folded the linen over the pastries again, checked minutely the tap of the tea-urn, and continued on his devoted way. 'Excuse. Mind your back please. Excuse . . .'

Clay, smiling like a tall cat, emerged from the

waiting-room of the clinic and together he and Brigg sat on a bench in the corridor, ate their cakes and drank their tea.

'I've found them. They're just down the end of this corridor, turn left,' said Brigg with the studied casualness of a successful detective.

'Great work,' said Clay. 'That's terrific. Let's go get them.'

But, immediately, they glanced at each other uncertainly. 'We'd better go a bit careful,' suggested Brigg. 'I don't reckon they'll like two blokes just wandering about in a hospital. Try not to look suspicious.'

'Check,' agreed Clay.

'If anyone stops us we can always say we'd got lost after coming out of the clinic. Nobody could say that wasn't true.'

'Okay, let's go.'

They brushed the cake crumbs from their laps and put the tea containers in a bin. Then they walked boldly but unhurriedly down the dull green corridor, the fans swishing above their heads, looking left and right into distant wards and rooms full of strange and frightening hospital equipment.

They reached the end of the corridor and then, with more caution, turned left along a shorter arm. A notice in red lettering on the door said baldly: CASUALTY DEPARTMENT. KEEP OUT UNLESS ON BUSINESS.

'That's where she is,' nodded Brigg at the door. 'Right in there. Bernice.'

'How do we get to her? Just walk in?'

138

'You could get yourself shot . . .' joked Brigg. He got no further, because the doors were fiercely opened and Bernice, her face as white as her apron, was standing there. Brigg put on a huge smile and moved forward to do his act. But she did not seem to recognize him. 'Out of the way!' she snapped. 'Clear off!'

Then he saw why. They were bringing through a stretcher on which was a soldier. There was blood all over his face, his mouth sagged, his eyes whirled wildly as though seeking some desperate help. Others were pushing the trolley through the doors, their faces set and urgent. Bernice held the soldier's shaking hand in hers.

Horrified, Brigg and Clay retreated to the wall. Another stretcher followed immediately, carrying another soldier, stark and white against the red blankets, eyes closed. Orderlies and nurses and doctors hurried with him.

There was some trouble with the swing-door and one of the doctors pushed it violently almost into Brigg's face and then snarled: 'Get out of the way, will you. This corridor *must* be kept clear!'

'Sorry. Sorry, sir,' mumbled Brigg. But the procession was already yards down the corridor heading for the operating theatres.

'Jesus Christ,' breathed Brigg, looking after them. 'Poor bastards.'

'Let's go,' said Clay. 'Let's get out. I don't think we should be here.'

*

Brigg surveyed his safe desk, the familiar inky doodlings on the wood and blotting paper – faces, scrolls, maps of home, ships with full sails and girls with similar chests; paper clips sprawled like casualties from some fracas; his calendar, loved and hated; the soporific room, sun seeping under the blinds, the other clerks and the officers moving like librarians, the slow gnawing of pens and the whispering of paper.

Sergeant-Major Woods and a Scots staff-sergeant from GHQ were discussing their futures in the aisle between the desks, like two women who have met in a shopping street.

'I'm having to think hard about what I'll do,' said the staff-sergeant. 'Only two years left to do now.'

'My trouble, of course,' said Woods sadly, 'is my feet. You know about my feet, Robbie?'

Robbie nodded. 'Aye, I've heard tell of them,' he sighed.

'They're no better.' Woods looked down as though hoping to spot some miracle. 'I fancy one of the nationalized industries myself. But I don't know, with these.'

They moved on, two men in middle life, planning careers. 'He'll never make a postman,' said Brigg to himself.

Tonight there was going to be tombola in the Naafi, the football team had reached the final of the Army Cup, another day had gone of his extra service. Only four months, three weeks and five days now. He had checked the tide tables for Singapore and he calculated that his ship would be leaving at three in the afternoon. That was four months, three weeks, four days and six hours.

Today he would be dabbling in the army lexicon, just as he did each day. Post Office Savings Bank – P.O.S.B., Posbee; War Office Selection Board – W.O.S.B., Wasbee; Kings Own Scottish Borderers – K.O.S.B., Kosbee. And, his own addition, for any paper work connected with the Intelligence Corps – L.O.S.B., Losbee, Load of Stupid Bastards. All day he was encompassed with the lexicon – W.R.A.C. ex-A.T.S.; F.S.M.O., Field Service Marching Order; A.W.O.L., Absent Without Leave; R.A., Royal Artillery and Ration Allowance; A.I.A.C.P., Action in Aid of Civil Power, which was the heading for all military operations against the Communist guerrillas in Malaya; up-country – that enormous twenty miles away. B.M.H. was British Military Hospital, and D.O.A. was Dead on Arrival.

Singleton of the K.O.Y.L.I. had been D.O.A. at B.M.H. That was the soldier on the second stretcher. He had looked pretty dead. Very stiff. Brigg was sitting on his morning paper, *The Straits Times*. He secretly shifted it from beneath his backside and read the item again below the level of the desk, with the fascination of someone who has to take another look at a pornographic picture.

'SOLDIER DIES IN JOHORE AMBUSH' the headline said. It was not an important item. He was not the first; not even the first that week.

Bandits in the Bekok region of Johore yesterday ambushed a patrol of the Kings Own Yorkshire Light Infantry killing one soldier and severely wounding another . . .

The dead man was Private John Singleton, aged eighteen, whose home is in Leeds. Private Adrian Phillips was wounded and is reported as being in a serious condition at the British Military Hospital in Singapore.

The ambush took place on the road to the Darah Rubber Estate when the patrol . . .

'Brigg – what are you doing?'

The sergeant's obese voice rolled dolefully up the office. Some clerks looked around at Brigg and grinned like boys in a classroom when the teacher has detected one at some misdemeanour.

'Tax Tables, Sarge,' replied Brigg glibly.

'Watch it,' the sergeant warned turgidly. 'Watch it.'

'Yes, Sarge,' nodded Brigg. 'I'll watch it.'

He folded the obituary of eighteen-year-old John Singleton of Leeds, Yorkshire, England, killed on a rubber estate at Darah, Bekok, Johore, Malaya, putting it beneath his backside again and returned to the safety of numbers and letters.

But the stiff face and the smeared blood of Private Singleton, the frightened eyes of Private Phillips as Bernice held his hand were still imprinted on Brigg's desk. He imagined in *The Straits Times*: 'Private John Brigg, of Kilburn, London, was killed in a bandit ambush on the Kota Tinggi Road in Johore last night. He was twenty years old and would have been

142

demobilized in October but for the additional six months' National Service . . .'

'Brigg.' Sergeant Bass's tired tones rumbled again up the subdued room. 'You're staring into space, lad.'

'Tax Tables, Sarge,' replied Brigg just as wearily. 'Working them out.'

Perkins, the stick-insect officer, took his pipe from the grip of his teeth and said petulantly. 'There's not enough work being done all round. There's too much fussing and time-wasting.'

'It would do some of them good if they got sent up-country with the infantry,' rejoined the sergeant. It was an observation he frequently made.

'Quite right,' agreed the officer. 'That would make them move a bit faster.'

Brigg's head was already low over his work. P.O.S.B., W.O.S.B., K.O.S.B., A.W.O.L. Anything was better than D.O.A. at B.M.H.

9

Clay and Lantry left the guard-house at the office blocks at nine o'clock in the evening to walk to the NAAFI canteen. There had always been an undefined coolness between them. Lantry had inherited from his father an illogical dislike of Americans, based on imagined cowardices and prejudices from the war, and Clay had come to know this. But they were on guard for the night together and when their break-time came they walked across the bridge to the bar. Lantry, as if to show his sporting nature, insisted on buying the first pints of beer, and they sat, an uncomfortable wedge between them. When the others from the barrack room were around it was not so noticeable.

'What's it like in England?' asked Clay eventually.

'Best country in the world,' said Lantry uncompromisingly. 'Castles and fields and all that. And the King. I always reckon it's better to have a King than anything else.'

'We think our system is pretty good,' said Clay. They had drunk the first pint with unusual speed because of their vacuum. Clay stood and bought two more Tiger beers at the bar. He returned and set them down. 'With the presidential system we get the chance of a new face every four years,' he said. He was more intelligent than Lantry and he was aware that it showed.

'Ah,' said Lantry, his face looking into his beer glass as into a mirror. 'But the King don't get bribed like the presidents do.' He squinted into his drink. 'We have bloody good beer in England,' he said. 'Best beer in the world.'

'We have a place called Milwaukee where the whole city is occupied in making beer,' countered Clay. 'Famous all over the world, I guess.'

'We've got Burton,' said Lantry stonily. 'That's where *our* beer comes from. And we don't send it *anywhere*. We drink it all ourselves. You've heard of the saying "Gone for a Burton", I s'pose – even in America. That's *our* beer. Burton. But the pilots in the Battle of Britain used to say that when one of them got shot down by the Germans. I s'pose you read about the Battle of Britain?'

'Sure, sure, we know all about it.'

'Gone for a Burton,' repeated Lantry. 'I've never 'eard any bugger say "Gone for a Milwa . . ." whatever that place is.'

There was a rivalry about their drinking now; they had three further pints each and their chins got lower over the table. 'Yeah,' slurred Clay. 'We've got a great, big, beautiful country. Rich too. Real rich. At home we always felt sorry for you Britishers. My ma used to send you food parcels.'

'Well she didn't send me any,' said Lantry nastily. 'Far as I'm concerned you could 'ave kept them. We was by ourselves against the fucking Germans.'

His head dropped a little further and he added mysteriously: 'The white cliffs of Dover.'

They sat drinking sullenly, cementing their enmity. 'The war was only won because of America,' announced Clay with simple truculence. 'We cleaned it up.'

'Bloody nerve!' exploded Lantry. 'Cheeky bastard.' He leered at Clay. Five pints had taken their toll. 'You never came in until the war's half over. You ought to hear what my old man's got to say about your bloody bunch. In England screwing all the women while their 'usbands was doing the fighting abroad. And you couldn't fight neither. Ran away half the time. Then all we get on the pictures is Errol Flynn winning the sodding war.'

'Errol Flynn is an Australian,' said Clay carefully. He was keeping cool, despite the beer and the insults, but his ire was climbing his throat. 'Which is just the same as a Britisher. Tough luck on Errol Flynn.'

'Listen, big-head Yank . . .' Lantry got shakily to his feet. He was shorter but broader than Clay. Clay stood up also.

The Chinese manager of the canteen, a little bouncing balloon of a man, crossed the floor and put a babyish yellow hand on the British chest and another on the American. 'You two drink too much beer. Go bugger off. I call the guard.'

Abruptly Clay and Lantry realized they *were* the guard. Sulkily they moved away, between the tables of grinning soldiers, and walked silently, Lantry to the front, Clay ten yards behind, over the wooden bridge back to the guard-house.

Unspeaking they went into the shed and lay on their beds until ten o'clock. Lantry dozed off and Clay lay disgruntled and awake. Why the hell couldn't he be found? Stuck here with these foreign fools. At ten the sergeant of the guard told them to get ready for their two hours of duty. Clay had a powerful ache behind his eyes. They stumbled out into the close night and began their patrol around the main office block.

Each had one long length and one short length of wall to walk. Unsteadily they converged at right-angles for the first two occasions and turned away at the corner wordlessly. But at their third meeting Lantry muttered: 'Useless bastards.' And Clay returned: 'Jerks.'

Five pints of Tiger beer was a lot. Their boots refused to keep straight on the concrete path around the building. At their next meeting Lantry said: 'The Yanks could always run. And they did.'

'After the British,' sneered Clay. 'Remember, boy, we only had *one* fight with you and you came second.'

This plainly puzzled Lantry. He turned and retraced his way back along his patrol. Clay was at the corner first when he returned. The young men stared at each other. 'Listen,' said Clay. 'I can't wait to get away from this fucking Limey army. Just take a look at yourselves. Bums!'

In a moment the two sentries were locked in a fight. Their rifles fell to the ground and they wrestled and rolled like two beery schoolboys. Fists and knees went in, wildly, oaths were grunted and threats spat. They rolled over on the concrete pathway, doing little damage, until Clay caught Lantry a sharp punch in the midriff and the English youth curled over slowly and was spectacularly sick.

'What's happening there? What's going on?'

'Jesus, the officer,' said Clay. He pulled Lantry and leaned him back against the wall. 'Wipe your mouth, quick,' he said. He realized they had no rifles. He could hear footsteps on the gravel leading to the office block and a voice called: 'Guard! Where's the guard?' Frantically he scrambled around looking in the shadows for the abandoned rifles. He found them gratefully, thrust one into the tottering Lantry's hand and attempted to stride smartly towards the approaching officer. He met him and the orderly sergeant at the opposite end of the building. It was Lieutenant Wilson, a rosy-faced, bossy man. He blinked at Clay. The sergeant was staring apprehensively.

'What's going on?' asked Wilson again. 'All that row?'

'It's something,' said Clay logically. 'But I couldn't figure out what, sir.'

'Well, where is it? Where's it coming from?'

'Down there, sir,' said Clay pointing through the scrub that climbed the bank. 'On the garrison road. I tried to get a view of it, but I couldn't see a thing.'

Wilson regarded him suspiciously. 'You don't look very spruce, Private First Class Clay,' he said. 'In fact you look very dishevelled.'

'I fell, sir,' said Clay desperately. 'I fell down the bank trying to see what the noise was about.'

'Who's the other sentry?'

'Lantry, sir, Private Lantry,' said the sergeant, indicating that he was in control of the situation.

'Where is he?'

'The other side, sir,' said Clay. 'Kinda guarding.'

Wilson looked at him churlishly. 'Let's go and see,' he said. 'Go ahead, Clay.'

They went along the concrete path and turned the corner. Lantry was standing as stiff as any Buckingham Palace sentry. He whirled about as they turned the corner. 'Halt or I shoot!' he bellowed. 'Who goes there?'

'Guard commander, Lantry,' replied Wilson a little anxiously. 'No need to overdo it.' Clay glanced about for the sick and realized that Lantry was standing on it. He grinned to himself. Wilson sniffed the air and for a moment it seemed that he might have detected the beer. But eventually he turned, said, 'See you keep your wits about you then,' and marched off back to the officers' mess. The sergeant, after a deprecatory look at Clay and Lantry, went back to the guard-house.

'Jesus, that was close,' said Clay.

'You're not kidding. Court martial offence: drunk on guard. Thanks, Yank.'

'That's okay. It was the beer, I guess.'

Solemnly they shook hands. 'Bleeding Chinese beer,' muttered Lantry stepping daintily out of the sick. 'Muck, that's what it is.'

'Sure,' agreed Clay. 'Muck.'

'Nothing like as good as British beer,' said Lantry. He glanced at Clay. 'Or American neither.'

'You're on orders, Briggsy.'

Brigg stopped clanking his cutlery as he entered the barrack room; his webbing belt was thrown like a bandit's bandolier across his shoulder, his green shirt was undone, everyday sweat coated his stomach. It was an exceptionally hot day and he had just come from the cook-house.

'On orders? What now?'

'Special guard duty. You and Tasker.'

Jacobs was running his finger down the list. 'I'm not there, thank God.'

'Why, what's it all about?'

Brigg pushed his way through the schoolish group at the foot of the notice-board in the barrack room. The fans were swishing on the ceiling and the big room was cool. He felt the sweat going cold on his chest and stomach. 'Christ,' he muttered as he read the order:

SPECIAL GUARD DUTY
NO. 8 DEPOT. ROYAL
ORDNANCE CORPS. RAMAH,
JOHORE BAHRU.
*The undermentioned will report at
1600 hours, Thursday 7th December, for
special guard duty at the above Depot.
Troops will be absent from their units
for three days.*

A parade of names followed, unfamiliar most of them for they were from other base units in Singapore. Brigg and Tasker were half-way down.

'Bleeding nerve,' breathed Tasker who had been standing staring at the notice as though hoping his eyes could in some way change it. 'That's what I call it. They've got hundreds of blokes up-country, thousands, whole infantry brigades, for Christ's sake. Why can't they do it? We're supposed to be trying to get on top of the office work and they do this to us. Some of the infantry blokes would be only too glad to do a bit of depot guarding.'

'We're three weeks behind on our section,' agreed Brigg with badly-acted solicitude. 'We'll never catch up if they're going to keep taking us off to play bloody soldiers.' Private Singleton's stark face was all over the white order sheet, staring at him in death. He turned slowly away and sat heavily on his bed. Tasker was still at the notice-board, ''Ere,' he said after a few more minutes. 'Do you see who's the officer coming with us?'

Brigg stared with added concern. 'Not sodding Grainger?' he ventured.

'Sodding Grainger,' confirmed Tasker grimly.

'Oh Jesus, that's just all we need. That bastard will go looking for bloody trouble.'

The waxed wings of the infantry Sergeant-Major's brief but bombastic moustache each caught a splinter of eight-o'clock sun. Before him, drawn up none too straight on the dusty compound of the wire-encased depot at Johore Bahru, were the twenty-eight assorted soldiers, plucked from the static units in safe Singapore to perform depot guard duties.

The Sergeant-Major, a ruddily fierce-looking man, loved to play his part theatrically, as sergeant-majors are intended to perform. Every movement was bone-stiff, every expression accompanied by a scarlet ballooning of the cheeks, every order a hooted cliché. And yet, only fractionally below the military skin, he was a kindly man who dreamed decent dreams and collected beer labels from all over the world.

Small points of light twinkled all over him: his diamond eyes, the whirring feelers of his moustache, his sunny buttons, the brasses of his belt, and the shining windows in the bulging toecaps of his boots. Even the creases of his jungle-green trousers seemed to catch the morning rays.

He had marched them up and down a few desultory times in the red dust, upbraided them for their nondescript appearance, then stood them at ease.

'Right!' he bawled quite unnecessarily, since it was a small parade. 'Is there anybody in this shower, before my eyes, who knows Mrs Ringbold.'

No one did. 'Right!' he bawled again. 'Well I am her only son, Sergeant-Major Ringbold, Royal West Kents, and I am a hard, nasty man!' Grins filtered along the line because they could see he was not.

'This morning,' he continued loudly, 'I am going

to give you a lesson in the Malay lingo followed by a potted course in Chinese. These two languages are for the use of guarding this here depot. If you challenge any person whilst on your duty with the usual smart "Halt – who goes there?" you must follow it with the Malay word "*Beranti*" which means more or less the same thing, in case the person is of wog nationality. *Beranti*. Got it? All repeat it after me – *Beranti*.'

'*Beranti*,' they chanted.

'Very good. Word perfect. Now for the Chinese. *Hueng Fi Hong*. Say it everybody. *Hueng Fi Hong*.'

'*Hueng Fi Hong*,' they repeated raggedly.

'The gift of tongues,' breathed Ringbold. 'I could almost see your eyes slanting as you said it. Very good.'

He strode along the single rank with mock admiration. 'I never thought that one day I, a humble warrant officer, would have the privilege of drilling His Majesty's Household Cavalry,' he beamed. He ceased his promenade. 'Now, jungle craft,' he announced briskly. He waved his hand to where the deep-tangle trees pushed against the barbed wire at the rear of the compound. 'That, out there,' he said, 'that green material. It is not Kew Gardens. It is the Malay jungle. And the jungle is full of nasty things. It is possible that you will be attacked by a snake or a tiger. Now a snake looks very much like a tiger because they both have yellow stripes. The identification trick is that the snake is lower to the ground than the tiger on account of it having no legs. When confronted with one or the other of these wild creatures, the drill, by numbers, is the same. One – face the snake or tiger, feet apart. Two – thrust out the right hand and push it down the enemy's throat. Three – push the arm right down as far as it will go. Four – grasp the inside of the enemy's tail. Five – with a quick withdrawing movement, turn the enemy inside out! Right, have you got that?'

'Yes, sir,' they grinned obediently.

'Good. So today you have learned Malay, Chinese and snake and tiger fighting. Any questions?'

There were none. He dismissed them and they went away smiling. He walked in the other direction, smiling also. He had delivered the lecture a thousand times before and it never failed to amuse him.

'The trouble wiv me, matey, is I ain't got a clue what this lark is all about.'

Brigg looked across the guardroom's cluttered table. Outside, the Malay sky was orange and vermilion. It would drop to darkness in a few minutes. He regarded the small, sticky private on the other side, an ordnance store soldier brought up, like Brigg and Tasker, from Singapore.

'Well, as far as I can make out,' said Brigg, 'they haven't got enough chaps to guard this place, so everybody's got to muck in, including people like my friend and I doing important jobs in Singapore.' He was aware that he had changed his voice, putting it up a grade for the benefit of the ragamuffin private. He had said 'my friend and I' and 'chaps'.

The man looked at him suspiciously. But you're only a squaddie, ain't you?' he inquired. 'What important job 'ave you got?'

'Listen,' interrupted Tasker leaning over the top of a comic paper. 'We've got *specialist* jobs, we have, in our office. An *officer* from your mob couldn't do the jobs we have to do.'

The other man's name was Sparks but everyone called him Sparkles. 'Go on, then,' he argued dolefully. 'Just explain it to me then. This fucking war lark, I mean.' He had a huge enamel mug of tea in front of him on the table, painted with a skull and the words 'Death or Glory'. The same motto was tattooed on his small hairy forearm. He leaned forward to drink, elevating the mug until it covered the entire lower and middle part of his face like a strange armour helmet. From within, like an echo in a drain, came the sounds of his drinking.

He put it down and licked his lips noisily. He had a tea-coloured rim-mark across his forehead where the upper edge of the large mug had rested.

He pursued his point. 'Oh, I know all about the bleeding war,' he said. 'The Germans and the English and the Japs and the Yanks. I *know* all that. My dad's told me about that, even if he was a prisoner most of it.'

'Where was he taken prisoner?' asked Brigg.

'Birmingham,' replied Sparkles as though it were the easiest logic. 'He knocked three buckets of shit out of some Frenchies, so they put him in the nick and he was there for years. He kept getting out. They'd nab him and put him back for a bit longer.

He was in Shepton Mallet glass'ouse nearly all the war.'

Brigg and Tasker grimaced at each other, but Sparkles saw nothing. 'I never even 'eard of this place till I got 'ere.'

'Johore Bahru?'

'Malaya,' corrected Sparkles. 'Never 'eard of it. Can't get it into my 'ead what I'm doin' 'ere. Who am I supposed to be fighting?'

'Communist bandits,' said Tasker simply.

'So they reckon,' replied Sparkles. ' 'Ow did they get 'ere in the first bloody place?'

'Force 136,' replied Brigg.

'Who's that when they're 'ome?'

'Well, they were the resistance against the Japanese.'

'They was fighting the Japs?'

'That's right. From the jungle.'

'And now they're fighting us?'

'Yes.'

'Funny ole world, init?' said Sparkles going back inside his tea-mug so that the end of the comment echoed as though it came from a cave.

'It's six o'clock, nearly,' said Tasker to Brigg. 'Better start moving.'

'Right,' nodded Brigg. He and Tasker fastened on their belts with the bulky oblong ammunition pouches, miniature coffins against their ribs, and their bayonets hanging down like metal tails. They straightened their gaiters, stamped their boots on the wooden floor, and fixed their soft berets at a rakish angle across their foreheads. Sparkles was still wearing his beret at the table. It was hard, unpliable khaki, ribbed and lined stiffly. It sat on his head, above his white, silent-films face, like a halo.

Brigg and Tasker picked up their rifles from the guardroom rack and trudged outside. Sparkles took Tasker's comic and began to read it laboriously.

They were detailed to patrol the eastern perimeter fence flooded by yellow lights that brought squadrons of ecstatic insects in from the edging jungle. Beyond the lights was a trough of darkness and then, three miles away, the innocent illuminations of the town of Johore Bahru sitting pretty by the strait that divided the mainland from the island of Singapore.

'He's a poor ignorant bugger, that Sparkles,' said Tasker.

'He is, right enough,' said Brigg. They walked cautiously, nervous as only those who are unfamiliar with the proximity of a jungle at night can be nervous. Their conversation was more for the comfort of each other's voices than anything, and their eyes moved to and fro along the bright bars of wire against the void beyond.

'Ordnance,' sniffed Tasker as though that explained everything about Sparkles. 'You know that cap badge of theirs.'

'Yes. A field gun is it?'

'And three cannon-balls. And they reckon that the cannon-balls are too big for the gun and this is because the Ordnance Corps supplied the wrong-sized ammunition in some battle or other.'

'That wouldn't surprise me, either. Look at *our*

bloody regimental motto: "Faith in the Future". I've got no bloody faith in the future.'

'No,' agreed Tasker. 'No, I haven't either. Up here in this God-forsaken dump and for what?'

'Because some high-up has got a lot of shares in rubber on the Stock Exchange, I bet,' grunted Brigg.

'I reckon so, too. And we're risking our personal lives for them. Not that we've had a *chance* to live. It's a pity some of those rich bastards don't come out here and do their own shooting.'

'Too old, I expect,' said Brigg.

They continued walking grimly, both thinking of the suddenly revealed injustice of it. The crickets and the other jungle hordes were creaking and buzzing. Mosquitoes milled around the arc-lights, falling away as the great glare dazzled them, but always returning again to try to get even nearer the centre of the great light.

Then there came a sound in the darkness just ahead. Brigg clutched Tasker's arm at the same moment as Tasker caught his. A crunching, stony sound as though a footstep had disturbed the gravel of the path.

'Oh God,' whispered Brigg. 'There's somebody there.'

They closed together, their rifles pointing aimlessly at the general dark. Each was aware of the other's trembles.

Brigg could hardly make his tongue utter the challenge. 'H . . . Halt,' he eventually emitted. 'Who is it?' In this dire moment 'Who goes there?' seemed unnecessarily ceremonial.

'*Beranti*,' added Tasker tremulously. '*Beranti*. Who is it?'

There was no response, only another incisive scrape on the gravel, underscoring the unabated rattling of the crickets. The arc-lights shone dumbly on the fence and made a pool on the path ahead which diminished into void and darkness. And it was from this place that the sound came again. A scraping on the gravel.

'What's the Chinese, for God's sake?' demanded Brigg in an urgent whisper.

'Can't remember,' trembled Tasker. 'Something like *Hueng Fi Hong*, was it?'

'Try it,' suggested Brigg. They had backed into an alcove between two huts. Because of the confined space their rifles were now pointing down at their toes.

'*Hueng Fi Hong*,' attempted Tasker unconvincingly. Then: '*Heung Hi Fong!*'

This time the noise on the gravel was much nearer.

'What d'you reckon?' whispered Tasker.

'Let's creep back and tell somebody.'

Tasker turned in the darkness and nodded grateful agreement. They were about to retreat when a chilly laugh sounded in the near-by dark. They were cold, shivering. Then two hands appeared from the shadow immediately beside them and in a frightful moment their rifles were easily twisted from their hands and thrown on to the gravel. Lieutenant Grainger walked into the light. He was laughing.

'Christ!' he exclaimed. 'What a couple of right cunts you look.'

Their fear evaporated and became misery. They stood like shamefaced small boys caught urinating against the school wall.

'Stand up!' bellowed Grainger abruptly.

Brigg and Tasker came to panicky attention and stood, their faces glistening yellow in the lights. Brigg realized that his lips and chin were wet. He looked at Grainger's grin with contained loathing.

'Sorry,' acknowledged Grainger surprisingly. 'I should not have called you a couple of cunts. That's not the language an officer should use to his men, is it? But since nobody else heard it I don't suppose it matters all that much. We'll just keep it a little secret between us.' He glanced at Brigg. 'I'm very good at making little secrets for us to keep, aren't I, Brigg?'

'Yes, sir,' agreed Brigg. 'You are.'

'I'll amend it to a couple of Charlies,' said Grainger. 'And, by Christ, you *were*. Talk about sending kids to do a man's job.' He suddenly seemed to realize he was younger than they were – 'Allowing for the exceptions to every rule, of course. Pick up those weapons.'

They slouched forward and retrieved their rifles. 'Sam, Sam, pick up thy musket,' smiled Grainger serenely, going through one of his strange immediate changes of mood. 'Did your father ever recite that to you, Tasker?'

'No sir, can't say that he did,' replied Tasker nervously.

'My father did,' recalled Grainger. They were

standing now all at once like three acquaintances having a conversation at a street corner, Grainger as relaxed and easy as they were anxious. He smiled in the arc-lights, a superior, much older smile than they could have managed. His eyes were sharp and deep in his head. Brigg wondered if he really was mad.

'Yes, yes,' the reminiscence continued. He lifted his chin in reverie. 'Sam, Sam, pick up thy musket. My dad loved telling me that. Anything military he liked. He used to sing "Bumpity-bumpity-bumpity-bump, Here Comes The Galloping Major" and bounce me on his knee pretending it was a charger. Anything military. I could recite "Let Me Like A Soldier Fall" by the time I was seven. *And* dance "The Dashing White Sergeant".'

'Very good, sir,' admitted Tasker feeling that one of them ought to contribute something.

Grainger hardly seemed aware of the remark or of them. 'Wanted me to be an officer,' he said. 'The old chap. He never managed it. D'you know how he died, Brigg?'

'No sir,' replied Brigg reasonably. Then he ventured: 'How?'

'Pneumonia. Got drunk at a regimental dance and then got into a bath. Fell asleep in the bath and was in it all night. It was in the winter too. He was a warrant officer. Class one.'

He blinked at them, then suddenly appeared embarrassed by what he had told them. 'Now look, you two,' he confided. 'Get on with it. And keep your wits about you. There's enough guns and ammo in this depot to keep the Communists going for years.'

'Yes, sir,' they agreed together.

'And forget all this rubbish about challenging in Malay and Chinese. Sergeant-Major Ringbold knows as much Chinese as I do Swahili.'

'Yes, sir,' said Brigg. 'We thought he was serious.'

'Listen, Brigg, nobody Chinese, Malay or Indian has got any business inside this wire. If they're in – shoot them. Okay?'

'Shoot them, sir?'

'Yes. Shoot them,' smiled Grainger confidently. Then he did his patronizing wink and added: 'But don't tell anybody I told you, eh?'

Relays of special-duty guards at the depot had bequeathed books and papers to those who followed them on the rota. They included *Blighty* and *Soldier* magazines and Hank Janson paperback novels, and, not so predictably, *How to Grow Succulents*, a dictionary of engineering, and *A Woman Missionary in East Bengal*.

It was the second night of the duty. Brigg lay on his lower bunk looking directly above him to where Tasker's weight swelled the hessian of the berth above like a threatening rain-cloud. 'What you doing, Task?' he called up with no great interest.

'Thinking,' replied Tasker. 'Pondering.'

'What you pondering?'

'Just how I'm wasting my precious life away in this poxy place. And I was thinking of Lily back home, too. I expect she'll want a white wedding.'

'Well you haven't had a chance to touch her yet,'

called up Brigg. 'So that sounds all right.'

'Nor will I,' replied Tasker huffily. 'I'll save it for our honeymoon, mate. I want to start off on the right foot.'

'It's not your foot you're supposed to use.'

'There's no doubt about you, Briggsy,' said Tasker. 'You're a foul-thinking bastard.'

'That I may be, mate,' acknowledged Brigg, 'but when you come to think of it, we're out here in the Far Fucking East, a million miles from home. We could get done by the bandits, we might go mad like Grainger, or we might end up going native with the Bongos. Anything could happen. And all we think about is getting home and carrying on straight where we left off, like nothing's ever happened to us, nothing's changed. That's what's so loony about it. A few pints, a few dances, get a job, get married; here's your sandwiches, off you go dear, see you tonight.'

'How often do you reckon you have a bunk-up each week when you're married?' asked Tasker thoughtfully as if he were, at last, sharing some secret worry. 'I've often wondered, you know.'

'Ask your mum,' replied Brigg. 'But when you do ask her, don't call it a bunk-up.'

'Well, all right. How often do you reckon married people have sex?'

'With each other, you mean? With their own wives and husbands?'

'Of course that's what I mean,' said Tasker indignantly. His face turned over the edge of his bunk to look down at the grinning Brigg. 'Go on,

163

laugh, mate. Go on. I'm serious. You're the sort who'll end up in the divorce court, you watch. You don't take it serious enough.'

'Balls,' said Brigg amiably.

'I'm serious. I want to know how many times a week married people have it. Most of them, around us anyway, have a few pints on a Saturday night and go home and bang away then. You can see them in the pub nudging each other and sniggering. And on Sunday afternoons too. I reckon my old man and my old lady used to do it on Sundays when I was a kid, once I'd gone to Sunday school. They used to make me go and I thought it was because they liked the idea of Jesus and all that stuff. I liked the idea of that – being keen on Jesus, see – because I thought it made me a bit superior to the rest of the kids in the street. Then one afternoon I spewed up and I got sent home. The door was locked and I looked through the kitchen window and saw my dad making a cup of tea and he was wearing my mum's pink silk drawers. Honest.'

'Blimey!' exploded Brigg from below. 'A nice bloody perverted family you come from, I must say.'

'Oh, I don't know. I reckon he'd do something like that just to make my old lady laugh. He was always making her laugh.'

'Maybe if you'd gone upstairs you'd have found your mum with a whip and wearing his garden wellies.'

Brigg knew he'd said the wrong thing. Tasker's face, darkened now, slowly rolled over the top of the bunk again. 'Don't you take the mickey out of my mum,' he said threateningly. 'Or I'll be down there and bash all the wind and piss out of you, son.'

'Sorry, Task,' said Brigg. 'I didn't mean anything.'

'I bloody hope you didn't neither,' said Tasker. He rolled back on to his bunk.

'But I don't know,' returned Brigg after a silence. 'When I think of my dad. He was in the war and he's always saying he was lucky to get out alive. And *what's* his *life?* Just grind and boredom. It's just like he's marking time till he drops dead. Christ, I don't want to be like that.'

'A career,' said Tasker, as though he had just deciphered some wise message on the ceiling. 'That's what you've got to have, mate, a career. Once you've got qualifications you can do anything.'

There was another gap of several minutes. Then Brigg said: 'You know, Task, this might sound mad. In fact it *does* sound mad, after nearly going home and then being pulled back, but . . . You won't believe this, but I don't think it would be too bad living out here, getting a local release from the mob . . .'

He could hear the astounded reaction over his head before he had reached the end of what he had to say. 'You're stark raving potty,' Tasker said, his face again appearing above Brigg like a small moon coming from behind a cloud. 'You're just saying it.'

'No, no,' argued Brigg. 'I *did* really think about it the other day. Straight I did. Not being in the mob, of course. And living in Singapore, in the city, away from all the blood and guts. I reckon you could have a decent life out here. None of your qualifications lark either. Just being white and British. You could have things you could never have at home.'

'You've been with that Juicy Lucy again,' accused Tasker slowly. 'That's where all this has come from. I wondered where you'd gone all Wednesday afternoon.'

'She's terrific, Task,' said Brigg quietly. 'It's bloody marvellous being with her.'

Tasker sighed: 'Haven't I told you before? Once a tart always a tart.'

'I know,' acknowledged Brigg. 'But I can't help it, mate. When she's off-duty and I'm with her, I'm crazy about her. I feel real proud of her. How can you explain that?'

'And you've got the cheek to accuse my dad because he wore my mother's knicks,' sighed Tasker. 'I don't know how you've got the bleeding nerve, straight I don't.'

He *had* been proud of her that day. When he knew that he had to go over the Causeway for the special guard-duty in Johore, and with Private Singleton's dead face still on his mind, he had gone to visit Lucy during the Wednesday afternoon recreation period.

It was necessary to go on chance because some-times she had a daytime customer, or she was attending what she liked to call 'school for working girls' where well-bred and well-meaning English ladies taught prostitutes the charms of basket-weaving and embroidery. The prostitutes attended in masses because, being in the main Chinese and

166

therefore of artistic inclination, a sweet tooth, and a liking for gossip, they enjoyed the occupations, were given free orange juice, cakes and peppermints, and the opportunity for trade talk among themselves. In the evening everyone returned to her own more ancient craft.

He had caught the bus for the city immediately after he returned from the cookhouse in the middle of the day. Others were preparing to sprawl on their beds as they habitually did on Wednesday afternoons, though some were going to play football. Morris Morris was going to a meeting of the Singapore Welsh Association, Gravy Browning was tuning up for the Inter-Services Table Tennis Championships, Corporal Field was in ecstasy as he began reading through a pile of hunting magazines which he had received by sea-mail, and Corporal Eggington was trying out a new armpit ointment. Clay went with Tasker and Lantry to the swimming pool, and Brigg slipped off without informing anyone of his destination. If he had told them he was intending to visit Lucy, Tasker and Lantry would anyway have been primly scornful. To them she was just another Chinese whore.

The bus journey did not seem so protracted by daylight. The heavy afternoon sun seemed, in a strange contrary way, to dull the oriental greenery and diminish the bright tropical flowers. Everywhere seemed to hang with lassitude, and heat. It lay across the land like dust. Few people moved in the shops, as they drove through desultory villages. Human beings were strewn like bundles, sleeping in the shade until the day cooled. The city was heat-hung and quiet too – the traffic sluggish, windows shuttered, people slouched beneath great dull ceiling fans or lying in the dark.

Brigg left the bus, and saw the Malay driver drop his head against the frame of the steering-wheel, and fall at once into sleep. A few dogs scavenged, relieved that there was no one to kick them. The laden smell of the city was in every wall and along every alley. He had not walked a hundred yards from the bus before the back of his olive-green uniform shirt was limp with his sweat.

He reached Lucy's street and cautiously climbed the curious and curling iron staircase at the back. His caution was occasioned not only by the suspicion that Lucy might be occupied but by the unsteadiness of the rusty spiral stairs which he had always thought would one day lean over and unceremoniously topple like a dead giraffe.

There was a small Chinese child sitting cross-legged on the floor of the passage outside Lucy's room. He regarded Brigg's arrival with the huge boat-eyed disinterest of oriental children. Although Brigg nodded and smiled at him with his version of a fatherly manner, there was no other reaction.

'Is she in?' inquired Brigg cheerfully of the boy. The child turned down his eyes shyly. Brigg rang; Lucy opened the door and called the soldier and the little boy into her room.

'Who is he?' inquired Brigg nodding at the boy. It momentarily crossed his mind that, in Chinese, his question might be its own answer.

But Lucy said: 'Wee-Fat he is. He is from my sister for me to take care.'

'Great,' nodded Brigg unconvincingly. 'What was he doing outside in the passage?'

'I had customer. Just gone away,' shrugged Lucy.

'Oh I see,' murmured Brigg, never failing to be surprised by her frankness. 'Well, you couldn't have a kid hanging around, er, seeing, er, that going on, could you.'

Lucy shrugged daintily. 'Kid okay. He don't care. Customer care. He no like little boy.'

'I can understand that too,' nodded Brigg. He looked at the lad, who looked back without faltering; orange-faced, almond-eyed, coconut-haired. Brigg thought: he's going to be in my way too.

'Englishman,' Lucy sneered the word. 'White shirt, white little trousers. Fat. Stinky. I no like him.'

'Why have him then?' inquired Brigg huffily. He had always considered that she should be more selective, preferably pruning her selection down to him and visiting royalty.

'He customer,' she shrugged as though that explained everything. 'He pay.' She suddenly and sharply threw a look at him: 'Why you come here, Bligg?'

'To see you,' he said. He stood two paces from her and saw again how unblemished she was. She was wearing her working robe, a tatty thing of elderly dragons on silk, but her feet projecting at one end and her neck at the other were pale and flawless. Her face looked no older than her true twenty years; her eyes were settled and her smile genuine and pleased.

'So you come see me,' she said with a minute spread of her hands. 'I am here.' Then suspiciously: 'You not go England again?'

'No,' he grinned at her concern. 'Not yet anyway.' He stepped forward and eased her against his chest. The small boy sat heavily on the floor and began to explore his nose. Brigg tried not to look at him. He pushed his cheek against her neck and, like the star of a thousand war films, he muttered: 'But I'm going up-country. To the Ulu. And it's bloody dangerous.'

'What broody dangerous?' she inquired in surprise.

'Up-country. The Ulu. The jungle. Blimey, Lucy, don't you read the papers or listen to the wireless? The Communist bandits.'

'Ah,' she remarked, as though it had slipped her mind. 'Ah yes. Well, I tell Ching Peng to not kill you.'

For a moment he believed her – the way the name Ching Peng, the leader of the jungle Communists, came so readily to her. After all she *was* Chinese. Then she laughed close to his throat and he relaxed and dropped his hands down her slight silken back, over the tatty dragon cloth, until their palms lay on the humps of her backside. He rubbed them enjoyably while he kissed her, smelling the bitter-sweet of her mouth. With the index finger of each hand he massaged the soft ravine between her buttocks, starting at the swelling on the base of her spine and going as far down as he could reach without overbalancing.

'You come for business,' said Lucy.

'Pleasure,' he corrected.

170

'Can no do now,' she said. 'Boy not like to sit outside.'

'I thought that was coming,' sighed Brigg. He looked down at the Chinese infant, who returned the look challengingly. 'And I don't fancy him squatting there watching me on the job. We're a bit shy like that, us English.'

'No fun then,' said Lucy simply.

'Maybe we could get him to shut his eyes and count to a hundred,' said Brigg dolefully.

She laughed and pushed him gently away. 'We all go out,' she decided. She pulled away her robe and stood with her naked back to him. She began to climb into a pair of pants. He went behind her and put his hands around to her modest breasts, tickling the nipples with his palms. She wriggled like the young girl she was into her pants and then reached for a pair of Chinese trousers from her wardrobe. They were splendid peacock blue and she turned and showed them off like an exotic model, bare-bosomed, her hair smoking about her shoulders.

'You're bloody lovely, you are,' said Brigg sincerely. He caught her about her naked waist and gently kissed her right nipple before turning his mouth to the left. The boy watched as though wondering what the man was about. But he was not entranced. His nose, his storehouse of surprises, was still his primary interest.

'How about me coming out with you, then?' asked Brigg. 'Would that be all right?'

'Sure you come,' smiled Lucy, greatly pleased. 'We go take boy.'

'How about going to Changi?' said Brigg on impulse. 'We could show him the prison.'

'He like see prison,' responded Lucy genuinely. She spoke to the boy in their own language, relaying the suggestion, and a large sliced smile travelled around his face. Like a family, they went down the curling outside staircase and took the bus from the end of the road to Changi.

Brigg had found in being with her, and with the boy, a sort of growing pride in ownership. He held her hand in the bus and then, to the child's obvious bemusement, held the little boy's hand too. He enjoyed the stares of the other passengers, mostly Chinese and Malays but including a pair of British service wives who watched him with suburban carefulness all the way. They all left the bus at Changi terminus and the two Englishwomen nodded patronizingly at Brigg, and looked at Lucy and the boy. One of them lied 'Lovely' and the other smiled false agreement.

'Thanks,' replied Brigg, muttering 'Silly mares' as they hunched off with their shopping baskets.

The sea rolled easily up the beach at Changi. There were worn-out bungalows along the untidy sand and an area set off for swimming and diving. Brigg bought them all ice-cream cones and they sat on the hot, grubby beach and licked them. The boy had slipped off his shoes and wandered off, by childish instinct, to sample the shallow margin of the China Sea.

Lucy laughed and went down after him, barefooted, her hair scattered by the coastal wind, her chiming voice returning on the same current. She took the little boy by the hand and splashed with him along the feathered edge of the sea. He jumped and shouted in a surprisingly deep voice for a Chinese child. A serious paternal glow spread throughout Brigg's body as he watched them. Lucy squealed when the boy fell on to his knees and swooped to pick him up before the returning tongue of the tide caught him. Her form was so lithe and young, her face so clear, herself so free. God, thought Brigg, if only she wasn't a Chinese whore.

Eventually she returned alone to where Brigg was watching. The boy continued to dance with the tide. As she came up the beach she was still laughing. She had rolled up the legs of her trousers to below her knees. Her hands went to her cheeks and she split her wandering hair, parting it each side of her face.

'Boy like sea,' she called ahead as she walked. Brigg grinned and nodded. She sat beside him, at first carefully picking any small debris from the place, and he leaned and kissed her ear through strands of black hair. She glanced about her, strangely prim. 'He not come before,' she continued.

'Never been to the seaside?' asked Brigg surprised. 'And he lives in Singapore?'

'Where he live no people go to beach,' she said shortly. 'Too long have to work.'

'I get it. Well I'm glad he's having a good time.'

'You have good time, Bligg?' she asked with concern.

'Oh yes. Of course. I feel sort of odd, that's all, being here with you and the kid . . .'

173

She produced a small smile. 'You only see Lucy in dance-club or bed.'

'I suppose that's it. You look terrific today, love. In the sun and that.'

'Changi very good,' she said decisively. 'Where is prison?'

'Over there,' said Brigg nodding briefly inland. He became thoughtful. 'Funny to think how all those poor bastards were shut up there by the Japs and just spitting distance away was this beach with palm trees, all the issue. I bet sometimes they could see it or hear the waves. I bet that made the poor buggers cry.'

She seemed unimpressed. 'Japanese make babies of English,' she said bluntly. 'I see all English hands-up with little Japanese taking them to Changi.'

Brigg was annoyed but defensive. 'Yes, well,' he started, 'we'd surrendered hadn't we? And if you've surrendered you've got to keep your word. If you're an Englishman, that is, because we always keep our word. Play it straight, see. That's why you saw one little Jap taking them off. A lot of them died in that jail, too. Remember that.'

'I not remember,' she shrugged. 'It only war.'

'Only war?' He was getting angry, the little Englander within him struggling to his feet. 'I like the way you say *only*. The Japs were inhuman bastards. Ask any bloke who was in Changi.'

'Only war,' she repeated firmly. 'My mother, my father killed in street by Japanese. I not remember them now. All gone.'

'Christ, Lucy, I didn't know that,' he said

174

apologetically. 'You didn't tell me.'

'You don't ask me,' she replied logically. 'You know crazy girl outside army club. One who got no tongue.'

'Dumb Doris,' said Brigg. 'I know.'

'She my sister,' said Lucy. 'Japs cut out tongue. Make her crazy.'

'God, that's terrible.'

'God no help her,' shrugged Lucy. 'You not tell anybody Lucy her sister. Very bad for business. She real crazy girl.'

She made her selfish point in a calm manner, the matter-of-fact words level in tone, her eyes watching the boy by the waves. She saw him turn and begin to run up the beach towards them, his face anxious. When he was a yard away, he said something in Chinese and Lucy asked him a question to which he replied in an urgent affirmative.

Brigg grinned knowingly as though he dealt with children his whole life. Lucy said in her everyday way: 'He want to go shit. You take.'

'Me!' exploded Brigg. 'Why me? Can't he go behind a tree like other kids do?'

'No go on tree,' she said reprovingly. 'He think this beach very fine place. No want to spoil it. You take.'

'But where? Where can he go?' demanded Brigg looking wildly about him.

'Soldiers on road,' Lucy pointed out briskly. 'You ask where.'

'Oh God, just my luck,' moaned Brigg. Lucy's expression indicated she expected no further

175

argument and the boy was regarding him with urgent pleading, his orange head on one side. Brigg stood up and took his hot round hand. They staggered through the sand together and reached the road. A hundred yards farther down it Brigg could see a gate with a Royal Air Force flag flying above it.

'Come on, mate,' he said to the boy. 'Maybe the Raf will let you use theirs.' The child nodded, apparently ready to agree to anything, and they trotted towards the flag.

As they approached Brigg saw that it was hung above a guardhouse at a gate, across which was a barrier. An Air Force sentry stood with rifle and fixed bayonet.

'Mate,' began Brigg hopefully as they reached the sentry. 'Do you think . . .'

'Ask inside,' said the sentry out of the edge of his mouth. 'I'm not supposed to talk.'

'Right,' agreed Brigg. He glanced at the infant. The boy's expression was tighter. 'Come on,' Brigg encouraged. 'We won't be long.'

A serious looking corporal came from the guardhouse door. He stared at Brigg and the child. 'What's up?' he asked.

'Corp,' opened Brigg familiarly. 'Do you think this little chap could use your toilet?'

If the request had been for the temporary use of a bomber the reaction could not have been less surprised. 'Our toilet?' he asked. 'Our bog?'

'Whatever you like to call it, Corp. But hurry. He's not going to last long.'

The corporal was not going to let any timetable

panic him. 'Is he yours?' he inquired looking closely at the Chinese boy's face. The child abruptly exploded in huge tears, great pear-drops rolling down his brown cheeks.

'No, he's not mine,' replied Brigg testily. 'I've just borrowed him. And he wants to go urgently. Can he use yours?'

'There's no facilities,' intoned the corporal pedantically.

'Surely you've got a bog?'

'No facilities,' repeated the RAF man in a hurt way. 'No unauthorized Chinese civilians allowed on RAF property.'

'He's *not* an unauthorized Chinese civilian,' protested Brigg. 'He's a little kid. Look!'

The boy, realizing that the request was meeting opposition, howled louder and began to stamp his legs.

'Look,' appealed Brigg again pointing at the lad. 'Can't you see. He's in bother.'

'There's no facilities,' repeated the corporal unmoved. 'Take him somewhere else.' Then he wagged a warning finger: 'But not up against our perimeter fence.'

'Oh, come on, be a pal,' implored Brigg with a final try. 'Is there an orderly officer?'

'I suppose I could ask him,' said the corporal, immediately becoming reasonable at the thought of transferring responsibility. 'I'll get him on the phone. But I can't guarantee he'll get down here right away and he won't give permission just over the blower . . .'

The boy suddenly squatted and let out a frightful

cry. Then looked up with a wet, defeated face at Brigg. 'Forget it,' said Brigg to the corporal. 'It's too late. He's poohed himself.'

'Oh,' said the corporal as though someone he did not know had died. 'Oh well, sorry about that. We haven't got the facilities, you see.'

Brigg took Wee-Fat's hand and walked slowly away from the gate, the child sniffing with each bow-legged step. 'Clowns,' muttered Brigg to himself. The child looked at him piteously. 'How those stupid sods ever won the Battle of Britain I'll never know, mate,' confided the soldier to the boy. 'Never.'

That evening the child curled up like a dog on a rug in the corner of Lucy's room, snoring poetically, while Brigg lay and waited for Lucy in her sleeping bed. The pleasurable sensation of domesticity engulfed him as he lay beneath her sheet watching her move gracefully about the room. He thought she felt the same because she was wearing a long delicate nightdress. He had never thought of her in a nightdress. To him she had either been dressed at the dance-club or naked in the bed.

'You know, it feels like it's been the best day of my life today,' said Brigg as he lifted his hands from beneath the sheet and put them behind his head. He felt his face tight where the sun had been on it, an undemanding tiredness had settled over him. Years ago he had felt happily weary like this after being on a charabanc outing to the seaside.

'Humm, humm,' she agreed. She was brushing

her hair and he caught the delicate carving of her features in the mirror, the sweet skin, the long neck, the extraordinary eyes. What would they think of her in Kilburn?

She turned out the lights except the one at the bedside, walked domestically to the bed, the corners of her body just shining through the nightdress. Brigg stretched in an exaggerated yawn. 'God,' he sighed, 'I could just go off to sleep tonight.'

'Okay with Lucy,' she replied promptly. 'It my night off.'

'You'll be lucky,' he grinned reaching out and gently catching her wrist. She looked solemnly at him and opened the sheet. There were dim noises in the street outside, occasional cars and the chattering of two meandering night-watchmen. She got into bed beside him and for the first time they knew that brief but nightly moment of happiness and reassurance that comes to all married people who love each other.

'I love you,' said Brigg sliding his arms about her. 'Right now.'

'Right now, I love you,' she replied, the import of his words not lost to her.

He felt embarrassed that she should have known so immediately what he meant. 'Did you have a good time today?' he asked, his face wedged between her hair and her pillow, his hand resting on her flat stomach.

'Very good time today,' she confirmed. 'Pity boy shit.'

'Stupid bloody Raf,' muttered Brigg. He

179

mimicked: 'No unauthorized Chinese civilians admitted.'

She had remained lying easily on her back and he had turned on to his side and was lying against her, his knee bent up and its ball rested on the tops of her thighs. He could feel their warmth beneath the nightdress.

'You look terrific in that nightie,' said Brigg.

He felt her giggle. 'Always keep in case my mother come visit,' she said.

'Your mother?' Brigg paused. 'I thought you said the Japanese killed your mother. In the street.'

'I lie,' replied Lucy without concern. 'All time I lie.'

'Stone me,' muttered Brigg. 'And I believed you.'

'Japs shoot my father,' said Lucy simply. 'Miss my mother. She still here.'

'And is Dumb Doris your sister?'

'Sure, she my sister. Don't want to talk about her. You want fuck or talk about family.'

'Sorry, love,' said Brigg chastened. 'It's just I can't get over the easy way you tell fibs.'

'Fibs? What fibs?'

'Tall stories. Lies.'

'Lies all part of business. I make lies. Customers make lies. It don' matter.'

'I see,' he said. 'Yes, I can understand that. Sorry, Lucy.'

He explored and enjoyed the unfamiliar feel of her body below the skin of her nightdress; like that it had a different warmth, a different texture. He thought he had better stop talking and get on with making love to her. His member was hard against her hip. She was still and quiet. He ran it against the bone beneath the material and she caught its end in her fingers and squeezed it rhythmically between her finger and thumb.

'*Him* talking now,' she murmured. Brigg laughed softly and kissed her. He eased himself to his knees and looked down on the serenity of her face, the eyes even closer slits, the lips open to a slit also, the one gold tooth of which she was inordinately proud.

'You'd be a sensation in Kilburn,' said Brigg.

Lucy was unimpressed. 'No more talk,' she said. 'We have bash and then sleep.'

'You do pick up some romantic words,' he sighed. 'All right. Let's have a bash.'

She had spread her legs and he was kneeling between them. The bedside lamp was amber over their bodies. The hem of the nightdress was still hung like a pelmet draping her little pubic rump and across the top of her thighs. He lifted it courteously and laid it back in a fold against her waist so that her navel button peeped out from beneath it like an inquisitive eye.

The lower part of her body was so small that he felt he could span her waist with two hands. Her hip-bones projected mildly and curved down below her small belly to her middle cleft.

'Beautiful,' he said, unable to do anything without a commentary, and added: 'I wish you were mine.'

'I yours, Brigg,' she replied gently, eyes closed. 'You come much come for me.'

He remained with her until the first insipid

daylight was exploring the city. There were noises of early beggers and sweet-sellers in the street below. The boy sat up and rubbed his eyes. Brigg kissed the girl and left to catch the first bus back to Panglin.

Lucy was still in her sleeping bed as he made to leave. 'Today I must do many things,' she said airily. 'My father he come to visit me.'

Her father? thought Brigg as he went down the curly stairs. Her *father?*

10

The Depot Guard, drawn as it was from so many static units from Singapore, remained an odd and ill-formed parade. It seemed that the varying functions of the non-combatant soldiers was not only reflected in their badges but in their posture and demeanour. The mechanics had oil ingrained in them, the cooks were red-faced, the clerks slightly sagging at the shoulders, while the two recruits from the Veterinary Corps had about them the unmistakable waft of livestock.

'Right then, my likely lads,' came the predictable bark from Sergeant-Major Ringbold. 'I want four volunteers.' They sighed and mentally recited the next line: '*You, you, you* and *you*.'

Brigg and Tasker were two of the chosen, Sparkles was another, and the fourth was a limp-looking cook-corporal called Dobbie.

'Volunteers, one pace forward – march!'

They stamped one step from the rank.

'Right, you fine body of British soddjery,' said Ringbold. 'You will take the truck, depot, platoon for the use of, and proceed under the command of Corporal Dobbie, Army Catering Corps, to Rajit village for the collection of mail, flour, tea, and a packet of fags for me.'

There was an acknowledging titter in the ranks. All Brigg could think about was the five miles of road between the safe wire compound in which they now stood and the village of Rajit. Five miles of open, exposed road, with the concealing Johore jungle leering at them from either side.

But he grinned stupidly at the others as they broke away and made towards the five-hundredweight platoon truck. 'Nice little skive,' he pretended. 'Good as a morning off.'

Tasker glanced at him sourly. 'Listen to you,' he grimaced. 'Don't tell me *you* fancy sitting like a bloody duck in the back of that thing. Just time for the morning ambush, I reckon.'

'Oh, shut up, for Christ's sake,' muttered Brigg, his face dropping. 'It'll be all right. I hope.'

'*And* me. I can't say I fancy my chances outside this wire. And they reckon they're always having ambushes on that bit of road.'

'I don't know why four of us have to go,' grumbled Sparkles, his eyes red rings in his pallid face as though he had spent some time weeping. 'Just to do a bit of shopping.'

'It's so we can all look after each other,' replied Corporal Dobbie, the Catering Corps man who was to choose the flour and the tea. Sparkles was to drive the truck and Brigg and Tasker were the escort.

'Come on, lads, move! Sergeant-Major Ringbold was striding exultantly across the square. 'Don't stand around like spare lovers at a wedding. Get a move on.' He sensed their apprehension. 'And don't worry about the bandits, boys. They're all on leave today. Religious holiday.'

They climbed up on the truck. For the first time Brigg realized what a cumbersome weapon the British army rifle was. He and Tasker crouched in the way that they had been taught. Sparkles started the vehicle and Corporal Dobbie sat blankly beside him. They turned on the red dust of the depot square and went out of the barbed-wire gates.

'If it's a religious holiday,' said Tasker thoughtfully, 'how is it the shops and the post-office are open?'

The road went like white tape, at first dividing some unruly jungle trees, then through a regimented rubber plantation, before climbing a short pack of rocky hills and descending to the village of Rajit. It was enclosed, encompassed, through all its five miles until the final few hundred yards when it ran through some open scrub and swamp on the flanks of the village. The small Sparkles drove irresponsibly, hunched down low as he steered, so low that he seemed to be grasping the top rim of the wheel like a chimpanzee hanging on to a hoop. Dobbie sat still and said nothing. The eyes of Brigg and Tasker shuttled to and fro along the trees at the roadside, the warning shout of 'Ambush!' already in their mouths, in company with their hearts.

'Have a guess what we're guarding up along here?' The voice was Dobbie, a slow Dorset drawl.

He did not turn round, but rode upright alongside Sparkles, like a shotgun guard on a covered wagon.

'Guarding?' said Brigg puzzled. 'The depot, I suppose.'

'I know that. But what's *in* the depot?'

'Not the atom bomb?'

'No. Not that.'

'Well, guns and ammo – that sort of stuff.'

'That's what I thought,' said Dobbie. 'But it b'ain't.'

'All right. What then?'

'Nothing.'

Brigg exchanged glances with Tasker. Mad Catering Corps corporals were not unknown. 'Nothing?' replied Brigg. 'Get away.'

'I'll bet you a week's pay,' said Dobbie. He turned in his seat now and regarded their astonishment. He had a coarse face for a young man, a haphazard nose, a turn in one eye, and short, tough piggish hairs sprouting from chin and cheek.

'I went along in there last night,' he said in his rural way. 'In all the underground storehouses. Right through the bloody lot. And that's true. *And there's sod-all in there!* Except a pile of old army boots and some bedding that's gone mouldy. It's the truth.'

'What we doing guarding old boots and bedding?' inquired Sparkles looking away from the wheel. They were going through a village where children stopped playing in the street and stared at them. Brigg, in the middle of the conversation, caught the expressions on their faces, interest and fear, and it occurred to him that the children in Occupied

France must have looked at German soldiers like that.

'Don't ask me,' said Dobbie in answer to Sparkles. 'All I know is the sodding place is empty as a cowshed.'

'How did you get in?' asked Brigg. 'It's all locked and everything.'

'Last night,' confided Dobbie, 'when I was on my stag, a car turns up with an Ordnance Corps major and a sergeant and a couple of other blokes. They had the keys and I had to go down along with them. They'd come to nose about the place. And it was blind empty. Ah, and they *knew* it was empty. It was no surprise to them, I tell you.'

'No guns or anything,' murmured Tasker. 'So we're wasting our time guarding it. Risking our lives.'

'Well, *why* is it empty?' asked Brigg. 'What's the idea? His eyes were still flitting the roadside and he saw that Tasker was still watching too. The warning word was still trapped in their throats.

'Either they haven't put the stuff there yet,' said Dobbie. 'They're just trying out guarding it, like. Or it's a sort of dummy, to make them bandits think it's full of ammo. Or somebody's made a cock-up. And I reckon it's a cock-up.'

'That's my bet, too,' said Brigg. 'Did this major bloke seem very hairy about it?'

'Oh dear, oh lor,' said Dobbie in his rural way. 'He wasn't all that pleased, I can tell you. I reckon it's somebody buggered up the whole thing. We're there standing guard over empty air.'

'Ordnance Corps again,' said Tasker leaning

forward to taunt Sparkles. 'Who brought up the wrong cannon-balls for the cannon, then? Who's got it on their cap badge?'

'I don't bloody well care,' replied Sparkles without annoyance. 'All I know it wasn't me.'

'Your balls are too big for your cannon, Sparkles,' grinned Brigg.

'Better than too small, mate,' came the reply. 'I already told you, I don't care. I don't even know what I'm doing in this poxy army in the first place.'

Once the village was in sight and they were away from the dumb threat of the crowding trees, they relaxed and congratulated themselves on having an easy milk-run like this to do while others were guarding the empty depot or cleaning their equipment.

Rajit was commonplace: a wide dirt-holed street, open-fronted shops and shacks nailed together from tin, haphazard wood and rattan. The familiar smells and the familiar music drifted out into the street to mix with dogs and children.

There were some lorries from the rubber estate coughing their way through the dust. But few inhabitants were out in the blatant sun, now clear of the surrounding palms and striking the middle of the village. The store where they were to get the milk and the flour was at the centre of the settlement, with the post-office conveniently near. On the opposite side of the street was the village cinema displaying across its entrance an advertisement in Chinese, Malay and English for a horror film. The poster was decorated with skulls and blood and concluded with a broken English promise: 'This film will seat you to the edge of your thrill.'

They stood laughing and poking their fingers at the words while Corporal Dobbie went into the store to arrange for the milk and flour. They stood around the truck parked in the middle of the street, feeling like real soldiers for once, in their olive-green and their jungle boots, their rifles held with displayed nonchalance. Village people watched them with anonymous expressions but did not approach them. The dogs kept their distances.

Dobbie came out from the store, which was owned by an Indian. The Indian came to the door to look at the soldiers and the truck and then went inside, into the cool dark again.

'Right,' said Dobbie. 'You three go on along in and start loading the stuff on.'

Brigg said: 'You're not going to carry anything, then?'

'I'm in charge,' Dobbie pointed out. 'I'll stand by the truck.'

Grumpily they walked through the sun towards the shop. 'Blimey,' said Tasker. 'Give a soup-merchant a couple of stripes and he thinks he's a general.'

They stamped up the wooden steps, beneath the sunbent sign PATEL EMPORIUM, and went into the gloom, feeling it close like a relief over their heads and backs. The Indian shop-owner's teeth were distinctive in the half-light. He accorded them a bow, which Brigg acknowledged with a wave of his cap. It was almost as if that were the signal.

A shot sounded from the street, followed by a swift, jagged stream of a dozen, shattering the shop's windows. The dust in the place jumped as everyone, owner, assistants, and soldiers fell to the boarded floor. Brigg had his face pressed so close to the wood that he had splinters in his cheek for a week. He caught Tasker's frozen expression a couple of feet away and realized that they could not stay down there like that.

'Come on, Task,' he shouted, although the other youth was within whispering distance. 'Come on. They'll be coming in here next.'

The prospect made them move. They got up to a crouch. Sparkles was wriggling like a hedgehog on his stomach trying to get to the back of the counter, behind some sacks of meal. Brigg gave him a kick and he turned and sat up. His face was that of a child who has been crying. 'What you doing?' he demanded. 'Fuckin' kickin' me like that?'

'Come on,' said Brigg trying to control his trembling. 'Let's get to the door.'

The Indian shop-owner who had more sense of warfare and self-preservation than the soldiers, appeared, head only, on a neck like a spring, from behind the counter. 'Please, sirs,' he hissed. 'Rear exit best. Thank you.' His head descended again quickly.

'Right,' said Brigg implying that he had always intended getting out that way. 'Round the back.'

They scampered through the shop and went out through a rough storehouse filled with bags of beans and flour and ran into the enclosed yard at the back.

A sharp turn and they were in the narrow divide between the shop and its neighbour. Brigg realized that the opening at the end, where they would emerge into the dangerous sunlight of the street, was two feet wide. It wouldn't need a marksman to get them as they went through there. The same thought occurred to Tasker.

'What we going to do, Briggsy?' he asked.

'We'll go underneath,' decided Brigg, wondering why he had assumed command. Even in all the fear and turmoil he had the passing thought that he might well have made a good military tactician.

'Underneath?' asked Sparkles. 'Under the shop?'

'No, under the sodding ground,' rasped Brigg. 'Of course, under the shop.'

It was a good idea, for the shop was on low stilts to keep it above the monsoon rains, rats and termites. They went down on their bellies and, Brigg in the lead, went painfully forward. It was only twenty feet but it was like advancing through a low, thick and filthy jungle. They emerged clownishly into the street festooned with dry earth, vegetation and cobwebs.

The street was empty of people. Their truck stood in the middle, stark and solitary, abandoned in the heavy sun.

There was no movement, no sign of Corporal Dobbie. Then a pair of mangy dogs cautiously crept from a shadow on the far side and, close to the ground, edged towards the vehicle. Brigg watched them sniffing.

'Dobbie, Dobbie,' he called in a forlorn stage whisper.

There was no sound. There was only silent sunlight in the street.

'He's around the other side of the truck,' he muttered. 'We'll just have to go over there.'

'They could shoot us, just pick us off,' whispered Tasker. 'Can't we get on the phone to somebody?'

'Good idea,' said Sparkles. 'I'll go.'

'Stay here,' grunted Brigg preventing him backing beneath the shop again. 'One of us will have to make a dash across and the other two will have to cover him.' He glanced at Sparkles. 'Any good at running?' he inquired.

'No, not me, mate,' protested Sparkles. 'I'll keep you covered. Won't we, Tasker?'

'Go on, Briggsy,' encouraged Tasker. 'We'll keep you covered.'

'That thought fills me with confidence, I must bleeding well say,' answered Brigg. He felt tight in his lungs. Someone was going to have to run for the truck and it looked like it was him. He came up to the crouch and closed his eyes to blot out his terror. Then along the street came an old, slow man with a bullock cart. He passed the other side of the truck and made no pause. He appeared to see nothing nor find the bleak sunlit silence of the place unusual. Brigg held back. Then two Chinese boys on bicycles rode along the middle of the street, pedalling carefully, then wavering as they saw whatever there was to be seen on the far side of the truck. They dismounted and with fixed faces began to wheel their machines forward. Across the street people were coming out from the rough shadows.

'I can see his boots,' whispered Tasker. He was lying cheek down to the ground, looking across the uneven street surface and beneath the truck. 'He's there, all right. His boots are sticking out.'

'I'm off,' said Brigg. He guessed it was probably safe now. He reasoned that the people would not be emerging if the ambushers were still in the vicinity. He went across the road swiftly, at a Groucho Marx crouch, and still in real fear. He got to the truck and edged around it until he reached the corner. Then he looked round the side and saw Corporal Dobbie.

He was sitting on the running-board of the vehicle. His legs stuck out stiffly in front, wide apart as though he were trying to brace himself. His chest was bloody and caved in by the bullets. The blood splashed up on to his neck. No man from the Army Catering Corps should have died like that. On his face was the hurt, beseeching expression of a cook defending the integrity of his treacle pudding. Brigg turned away and was sick over the mudguard of the truck.

The following day they went back to Panglin. He and Tasker, walking like men who have seen death and action, went along the side of the barrack square towards their block. Sandy Jacobs emerged from the staircase. 'You've missed some excitement here,' he called immediately. 'Somebody's stolen the Colonel's stamp collection!'

*

'We lost a good man, didn't we, Task,' said Brigg wearily.

'Great bloke,' agreed Tasker.

They looked like proper soldiers. Grit was in their eyes, their faces were raw from the Malay sun shining only a few miles away from the pallid overcast heat of Panglin, their uniforms greasy, the strange elongated jungle-boots laced up at the sides like something grandmother wore.

The others in the barrack room came from their beds. It was Sunday morning and Brigg and Tasker were back in their safe place, returned heroes with tired eyes. The other soldiers grouped around them clad in towels and sheets like pale non-combatant Romans.

'Lost?' inquired Sidney Villiers, who had been the first to ask them what it was like in Johore. 'How d'you mean, Briggsy? Lost?'

'Dead, mate. Shot dead,' muttered Brigg.

He and Tasker watched the reaction spreading on the unused faces around them. Everybody would have to take a turn at the depot.

'By the bandits?' whispered Patsy Foster standing next to Sidney.

'It wasn't bleeding Robin Hood,' said Tasker.

'He was with us when he copped it,' said Brigg. 'Great bloke called Dobbie. Right through the guts. In the street.'

'Christ, in the street,' echoed Lantry. 'Not even in the jungle. Was he infantry?'

'Catering Corps,' sniffed Brigg. He dropped his eyes with genuine tiredness, but continued to watch their anxious reactions from beneath his lids. There was grit sticking to his lashes and it was like looking out of a cave protected by boulders. The faces pressed nearer.

Morris Morris's puffed-up head appeared behind the others. He had been drinking the night before but he had risen early to wash himself and he now radiated that faintly artificial pinkness of newly cleansed drinkers. 'A cook,' he mused. 'A cook.'

'It comes to something when bloody cooks get shot,' said Lantry. 'It's not fair.'

'And you were right there?' said Villiers. He leaned forward as though he were going to touch Brigg, who glanced a warning at him.

'On the spot,' said Brigg. 'On supply convoy, Tasker and me.'

'Right there,' affirmed Tasker. 'Poor bastard.'

'Did they fire on you?' asked Lantry.

Brigg opened his eyes to regard him with a veteran look. 'Listen, mate,' he said. 'When these shitehawks start shooting you don't ask who they are bloody well shooting at. You hit the deck. And quick.'

'Did you shoot back, then?' It was Jacobs, his oldish teenage face threaded with concern.

'Couldn't see the bastards,' said Brigg. 'No use letting fly if you can't see them. There were innocent civilians around, Sandy. Kids, women. And they don't let you get a sight of them, not the commies. Like ghosts they are. Out of the jungle, kill, and back again. Christ, I'm tired. Shagged out.'

'So am I,' agreed Tasker. 'I'm not sorry that lot's over, I can tell you.'

'I'm going next,' muttered Jacobs miserably. 'Next week.'

'And me,' said Lantry in a thinning voice.

'Oh, you'll probably be all right,' said Brigg easily. 'Just keep your heads down that's all.'

'Oh hell,' muttered Lantry. 'We've only got four months and thirteen days to do.'

'It's near Christmas,' added Jacobs unnecessarily.

'Ah well,' came Morris's philosophical voice. 'You've learned a little about soldiering.' He nodded at Brigg and Tasker. 'You look like soldiers now, you two.'

'It's all right for you, Taffy,' said Lantry, keeping his voice to the respectful level they always adopted with the large Morris. 'They probably won't send you up there. Being as you're . . .'

'Too old?' suggested Morris.

'I was going to say because you're attached personnel, Taff.'

'Ah, was you? Well then, I'm sorry, son.'

They always spoke to him as though he were their father, and he to them as though they were, indeed, his many sons. They intimated by their very expressions that Morris Morris would never be sent to where he might be shot. He was too old to die.

'Well, I've had my bundle,' said Morris. 'In the flaming war. I've seen dead men lying around like drunks.' He sat heavily on the bed as though the thought had suddenly weighed him down. 'Maybe you're not a soldier until you've seen a man die.'

'I could do without it, thanks,' said Brigg. 'It was

bloody horrible. Getting rubbed out in that shit-heap up there. He looked so surprised, too.'

'Aye, it's a surprising thing, death,' agreed Morris Morris thoughtfully. 'And it messes up your life so, don't it?'

They became silent, grouped around the two beds. Villiers moved forward, his towel bulging large around his little waist. 'Did you hear?' he said bravely. 'The Colonel's stamps have been stolen.'

'I heard,' muttered Brigg from his closed face. 'As soon as we got back to this dump we heard about the Colonel's stamps. We was almost beside ourselves with fucking excitement, wasn't we, Task?'

'Stand by your beds!'

Wellbeloved's professionally demented shriek woke Brigg and Tasker. Brigg scowled at his watch. It was midday, an hour since they had gone to sleep. His weariness hung over him like a heavy net. He glanced at Tasker and saw his own disgusted expression mirrored.

'Not on bloody Sunday,' growled Tasker.

'Come on, look lively!' bleated Wellbeloved. Sergeant-Major Woods was shadowing him, grimacing in tennis shoes. He was in a khaki shirt and civilian trousers. As he walked short, cautious steps, little squeaks came from the canvas shoes as though his feet, tormented and imprisoned, were crying through the lace-holes. Wellbeloved, who was orderly sergeant that day, was in uniform. He primped along the iron bed-ends.

197

'Right, who's missing?' he demanded. 'Everybody's got to be here.' He indicated Field. 'Corporal, round up anybody who's in the Naafi. And there's some men playing football on the waste ground. Get them back.'

'Yes, Sergeant,' responded Field. He went off on his mission with an odd hunting trot, almost like a boy playing at horses. Brigg had once caught him in the act of running and whacking his hand against his own backside to spur himself on.

The Sunday-morning soldiers, in civilian shirts, oddments of uniform, and football shorts, came through the barrack room door. Clay walked in last and looked surprised at the parade. He was wearing a flowered shirt which brought a smirk to Wellbeloved's narrow face. Clay grinned at Brigg as he stood in his bed-space. 'Welcome home,' he whispered.

Wellbeloved was moving down the barrack room, his habitual sniff turning his nose and head one way then the other as though he were being towed behind an erratic vehicle.

'Bloody fine welcome this is,' grunted Brigg.

Clay was going to tell him something but Wellbeloved squawked from the end of the barrack room. 'Everybody here? Right!'

They waited. 'S'arn't-Major?' inquired Wellbeloved with lofty formality, his nose tipping high above the RSM's head.

'Carry on, Sergeant Wellbeloved,' said Woods wearily.

'Right then,' Wellbeloved tipped his chin again.

His thin frame stretched out, with his growing gut bending out like some projectile. He smirked along the bed rows. 'Right, well . . . So sorry to get you out of your pits on Sunday. I know how you young lads need your rest.'

He performed a slow strut down the line. 'But every barrack room is having the same.' He stopped and stared at Villiers wrapped in his huge personal towel, covered with mermaids and sea-horses. He sneered and jerked on. In the centre of the room he halted, his feet sharply striking the floor as if it were the barrack square.

'The Colonel,' he announced, 'has had his stamps lifted.' He twirled around, the faces flitting before him. Seeing no change of expressions, he said: 'As you all know.'

He gave a long thin sniff. 'A theft like this is a very serious matter and the police and the SIB have already begun investigations. That collection is worth quite a few bob. Besides that, it's the Commanding Officer's hobby. So today all lockers will be searched, all personal possessions will be laid out on the beds for inspection.'

The farce then began. Wellbeloved and, unenthusiastically, the Regimental Sergeant-Major went through all the soldiers' possessions, digging in pockets and letters, shaking out books, grubbing in lockers and kitbags. It took two hours and nothing was discovered. Brigg and Tasker had to be searched too.

'Ah, our brave fighting lads,' remarked Wellbeloved. 'Back from the Ulu. Right, let's see what you've got.'

'Nothing, Sergeant,' said Brigg with excessive dignity. 'Tasker and me were up-country when the stamps went.'

'Every locker has got to be searched. That's orders. Jungle fighters included.' He rummaged around in Brigg's kit and other belongings. 'Have a good time up there, did you?' he inquired out of the side of his mouth, his eyes just flicking a moment from his task.

'Not very, Sarge,' said Brigg. 'A chap got killed. By the bandits. Catering Corps bloke.'

'Catering Corps,' commented Wellbeloved straightening up. His small but carnivorous teeth projected from below his drilled moustache. He widened his mouth a trifle until he had achieved his normal unpleasant grin. 'Well, you know what they say – too many cooks.'

To Brigg's amazement he felt sudden tears wash his eyes. His fists clenched behind his back. He gripped his hands together then and the moment went. Wellbeloved, unaware, moved on to Tasker's belongings, picking up a picture of Tasker's girl-friend, Lily, and saying 'Lovely' as he put it down again. Brigg turned to replace his things in the locker and wiped his eyes with the back of his wrists.

The inspection was completed at last. Gratefully the RSM shuffled to the door and went out without a word. Wellbeloved had to say something. 'Right,' he said. 'Carry on playing with whatever you was playing with.'

Brigg descended tiredly to his bed. 'What a

shit-face,' he said. 'Too many cooks. I'd like to tie his knackers around his skinny neck.'

'He's sneaky,' said Clay in his strangely high-school American way. 'A real sneaky guy. In the US Army he would have stepped on an anti-personnel mine by now.'

'No chance of that here,' muttered Brigg. 'Worse luck. Maybe we could stick a pen up his jacksie and hope he snuffs it of blood poisoning.'

'So you had a guy killed,' said Clay.

'Yes, I'll tell you about it later. I'm shagged out, Yank.'

'Sure. That's okay. I've got some news.'

'What is it? You're going back?'

'I'm working on that too. No, buddy . . .' he leaned closer. 'It's about the girls, the nurses.'

Brigg grinned, suddenly awake. 'Get away,' he breathed. 'You're kidding.'

'No kidding. Next Saturday night you and me, boy, are going to the Red Cross Ball.'

Delight spread on Brigg's face. 'Blimey, how did you swing that?'

'I went calling,' said Clay easily. 'Yesterday I took off to the nurses' hostel and walked right up to the door and asked for Bernice, Nurse Harrison. And she came down. Oh, she was real nice. She'd been playing tennis, and, boy, did she look something. Brown legs, white shorts . . .'

'She's mine, don't forget,' said Brigg hurriedly. 'The other one's yours.'

'Well we got ourselves invited to the ball.' Clay turned and went in two long strides to his bed. He returned with a pair of large tickets. 'Your invitation, sir,' he grinned, handing one to Brigg. Brigg read the wonderful words. Then his expression fell. 'But it says "Dress Formal",' he said dismally. 'How are we going to get around that?'

'Relax, you'll be the belle of the ball,' Clay assured him. 'That's where I've been this morning. To the laundry, the dry cleaners. That's where we're getting our evening clothes.'

'Somebody else's?' said Brigg doubtfully.

'Right. We borrow them for the night. The woman, the one who's always feeding the baby, will do it for five bucks as long as we don't let her pop or her husband know.'

'Jesus, you think of some things, Yank,' admitted Brigg. 'You ought to be President.'

'Everything in time,' said Clay. 'Right now we've got to hope that the right sizes arrive for cleaning. She gets a load in there and she says they'll have more next week because it's Christmas coming along.'

'Listen, though,' warned Brigg. 'We can't go in officers' clobber. That's a court bloody martial if we're caught.'

'Sure, I thought of that too. She gets plenty of European civilian stuff in too. We'll get something. Maybe they won't be the perfect fit, but we'll get something.'

'Next Saturday,' breathed Brigg. 'The Red Cross Ball.' He stood up, naked, and pretended to do a waltz with an imaginary partner. 'Oh, Miss Bernice, you look so romantic tonight,' he cooed. He stopped and stared seriously at Clay, 'I wonder if we'll get a shag?' he said.

Abruptly, Wellbeloved came through the door again, a quick emerging jump like a pantomime demon. 'Right!' he bawled. 'All quiet a minute.' He took two paces into the room. 'Can everybody hear me?' he shouted.

The voices replied: 'Yes, Sergeant.'

'Right, Sarge.'

'Yes.'

'We can hear you.'

'Good. Because you're not going to like what I've got to say. The Colonel's stamps have *not* been found. So there's no week-end leave for anybody next Friday, Saturday and Sunday.'

11

The metallic click of Gravy Browning's table-tennis ball striking the barrack-room wall and rebounding to the concrete floor was like the tick of a large clock. Browning had just come off overnight guard duty and was allowed an hour to get showered and changed before going to his desk at the office. Brigg and Tasker, also permitted a late arrival at their desks because their rifles needed to be checked by the armourer after their return from the Johore Depot, sat in the swathe of sun that unrolled like a carpet through the door, and nodded admiringly at the finesse of the ping-pong fanatic.

'Marvellous that,' nodded Brigg. 'You can just about make that ball talk, Gravy. Marvellous don't you reckon, Task?'

'Beautiful to watch,' agreed Tasker. 'Poetry.'

Browning appeared unimpressed by the admiration. He backed away along the wide alley between the beds and sent the ball spinning and skidding from a greater range. Then he advanced until he was delicately patting it within a few inches of the barrier.

'Application, that's what you've got to have,' decided Brigg. 'Dedication too.'

'Application,' echoed Tasker. 'And dedication. Nobody's got it like old Gravy.'

Browning flicked the ball up on his bat and bounced it minutely as though he were carefully frying an egg. He sat down on the bed opposite and regarded them sardonically. 'Funny how every bloke's got keen all of a sudden about my table tennis,' he said in his nasal voice. He flicked the ball into the air, let it bounce on his forehead, and pocketed it with the air of a conjurer who has finished his act. 'Ever since the Old Man says that the only blokes allowed out of camp this Friday and Saturday night are the ones who I pick out to support me at the Championships.'

'It's sod all to do with that,' protested Tasker. 'Is it, Briggsy?'

'Sod all at all,' agreed Brigg. 'We're proud of you, Gravy. *Our* mucker, our mate, in the Army Championships.'

'Inter-Services Championships,' corrected Gravy.

'That's what I meant.'

'But you're the blokes who keep yelling at me to stop the noise when I'm practising,' pointed out Browning archly. '"Shut that row, Gravy, or we'll stuff that ball up your arse". D'you call that encouragement?'

'Aw, come on, Gravy,' pleaded Brigg. 'We all have a go at somebody at some time. We're proud of you, straight up we are.'

'You two,' replied Brown accusingly. 'You two were in on it when all my table-tennis balls got thrown over the balcony and they was bouncing in

205

and out of the pay parade on the square. I always reckoned one of you actually chucked them out.'

'Roll on!' protested Tasker. 'That was nothing to do with us.'

'Nothing,' lied Brigg. 'We've always been your mates.'

'Well,' said Gravy firmly. 'I'm allowed to take a dozen blokes as supporters on Friday and another dozen on Saturday. It'll cost you five dollars a night each.'

Brigg and Tasker looked at him aghast. 'Five bucks?' questioned Brigg. 'Five bloody bucks. Move over! You're not supposed to be *selling* tickets. The Colonel said you've got to pick out a dozen supporters.'

'Listen, I haven't *got* a dozen supporters among the bastards here,' shrugged Browning. 'So I thought I might as well make a profit on it. I know that as soon as they get to the Championships they'll all hare off to do some stuffing or something. Be honest, that's all you two really want.'

Brigg's expression was iron in its sincerity. 'We want to see you win that table-tennis cup, Gravy,' he announced.

'It's a shield,' sniffed Browning. Then after some apparent thought, 'All right then. You can be two of the supporters.'

'And the Yank,' interrupted Brigg. 'He's keen to see you win too.'

'Three then,' said Gravy. 'For your money you get transport and entrance tickets.'

'Both of which you're getting for nothing,' said

Tasker grimly. Brigg nudged him. 'Lay off, Task,' he warned. 'Gravy's entitled to make a couple of bucks out of it. He's a sportsman, after all.'

'Ten dollars each,' said Gravy bluntly.

'Ten!'

'Five for Friday, five for Saturday,' shrugged Browning. 'I want guaranteed support both nights.'

'What if you don't get to the finals on Saturday?' asked Tasker suspiciously. 'What if you're knocked out on Friday night?'

'You'll have to find another way of getting out of Panglin, won't you?' said Browning. 'I'll collect the money first, just to make sure. Then if everybody shouts loud enough to encourage me on Friday night, maybe I'll still be there on Saturday. Get me?'

They nodded in doleful surrender. 'Who else is coming?' asked Brigg, without much interest.

'It's full now,' said Browning smugly. 'The supporters' list is closed. There's you three from this barrack room, and Eggington, and the rest are from . . .'

'Eggy?' asked Brigg. 'What's Eggy paying ten bucks to get out for? He hardly ever leaves his bed-space.'

'He's happy powdering his spots,' agreed Tasker.

'He's wants to come,' said Browning. 'Maybe he's a secret table-tennis fan.'

Browning rose and, taking out his bat and ball, tapped his way towards the ablutions. The others looked after him grimly. 'Money-grubbing bastard,' said Brigg when he had gone. 'Ten bucks.'

'I hope he treads on his own balls,' added Tasker.

The truck taking Gravy Browning and his supporters to Singapore for the Inter-Services Table Tennis Championships left Panglin skirted with a banner which said: 'Up Private Browning!' It had been produced in the garrison paint shop at the request of Colonel Bromley Pickering.

In deference to his status, Gravy was established in the cab beside the driver. His supporters sat bumpily at the back. Eggington was hunched at the tailboard end, his hair plastered down with Vaseline, his acne newly anointed, his armpits powdered. The lights of passing villages glowed yellowy on his face, but those familiar with those pebble-dead eyes would have noticed, in the travelling lights, a restrained glint of anticipation.

'I wonder what Eggy's up to?' asked Tasker.

Brigg shook his head. 'Maybe he's off to collect the money on the Colonel's stamps,' he suggested. 'One thing he ain't doing, mate, and that's paying ten bucks to watch old Gravy play ping-pong.'

'We can use all the support that's around,' commented Clay. 'Gravy's just got to win tonight – or we don't get liberty tomorrow. Right?'

'Right,' they echoed the Americanism.

Brigg looked around at the dozen bumping men in the truck. 'Not that many of this lot will stay to shout,' he forecast. 'They'll piss off as soon as they can.'

Heads and eyes turned to him at the remark. No one argued.

The truck entered the city and turned into the Happy World, a garish concoction of Chinese fairground, dance-hall and indoor sports arena. The Panglin contingent scattered briskly and craftily through the arena crowd so that a complete line of seats would not be vacant when they left. Eggington sidled away by himself, sitting fatly on the end of a row. Tasker, who had promised to stay in the interests of Saturday night, sat with Clay and Brigg. The outer lights dropped and the table-tennis began in the arena.

No contestant had support as vocal as that given to Gravy Browning. The trio were on their feet, cheering every shot and every point, cajoling neutral supporters all around to applaud with them. From the other end of the row Corporal Eggington honked like a seal as he willed Browning on to his first victory. Brigg looked along at him, nudged Clay and Tasker, and they all stared as the gross and greasy Eggington raised his fist in an enthusiastic salute to his barrack-room comrade. He turned and saw them regarding him and the delight fell from his expression. A weak grin tottered across his face and he gave them a thumbs-up sign.

'You don't figure he's going to the Red Cross Ball tomorrow as well, do you?' suggested Clay.

'No,' said Brigg shaking his head. 'Not unless he's the spot prize. He's got enough spots.'

Gravy had a difficult match in the second round. He lost the first set, and his four supporters sank deeper into their seats and gloom as his opponent, a bow-legged sailor, sprayed shots all round the table.

'Those jacks play ping-pong all day,' grumbled Brigg as the contestants changed ends. 'Nothing else to do when they're at sea and they can't play football because there's no room. Come on Gravy, son, don't mess it up for us.'

Browning was a cool strategist. He had learned from the first set and he narrowly won the second before taking the third easily and ensuring that he would return the following night for the finals. Clay, Brigg and Tasker did a dance in their seats and Eggington honked spectacularly. A fatherly officer sitting in the reserved box behind said to his wife: 'Marvellous to see these young chaps taking such a lively interest, don't you think?'

'Lovely, lovely,' breathed Brigg. 'Well done, old Gravy!'

'From now on you're on your own,' sniffed Tasker.

The dinner suits were less than a perfect fit. Brigg's was too broad across the shoulders and the arms hung down like an ape's. Clay's was too tight to allow the button of the white jacket to be done up and the trousers cut him like a knife under the crotch. Sidney Villiers provided a needle and thread and sewed back the cuffs of Brigg's purloined jacket so that his hands at least peeped out, but little further could be done.

'Jeeze,' breathed Clay. 'These pants are going to

be painful. Can't you do anything, Sidney?'

'Short of cutting a hole and letting your testicles hang out, there isn't a thing, dear,' tutted Sidney. 'You'll have to dance with teeny-weeny steps, that's all.'

Gravy Browning was out, track-suited, doing a few warming laps around the sports field, and with him away from view they had tried on the suits and made an entrance into the barrack room, Brigg with the curtseying Villiers on his arm and Clay with Foster on his.

'M'Lords, Ladies and Gentlemen,' intoned Lantry sarcastically. 'Baron and Baroness Danglers. The Honourable and Mrs Honourable Longcock.'

'Lovely,' commented the generous Morris Morris. 'You look a treat, really, boys. Good as officers, any day.'

'What are you going to say you are?' asked Jacobs practically. 'I mean, you can't admit to being just a couple of squaddies. Even if one is a Yank squaddie.'

'That just means more pay, not more class,' agreed Lantry.

'We'll be okay,' said Clay. 'We know not to slurp from a glass, not to wipe our noses on our sleeves. Don't we just.'

'And no calling the head waiter a Fucking Flunkie,' warned Tasker.

'Aw, come on,' protested Brigg. 'We're not all as bloody ignorant as you, you know. There'll be plenty there more ignorant than us, I bet.'

'But they'll have more *class*,' pursued Lantry. 'It don't matter how ignorant you are if you've got *class*.

Don't mind me saying so, mate, but in those duds, the way they fit, you look like the cabaret. Look at the shirts for a kick-off.' He pointed scornfully at Brigg, 'Yours is too big. You can move your head about and not touch the collar. You look like a sodding tortoise.' He transferred his attention to Clay. 'And he looks like a bloke trapped in a bloody gun barrel,' he scoffed. Everybody laughed and Brigg glanced at Clay dubiously.

'And he's got class, he says,' shrugged Lantry. 'All right, all right. Go and have a good time. It's just as well it's a couple of nurses you're going with, because our Yank mate is going to do himself a nasty injury in those trousers before the last waltz.'

They changed in the lavatory at the Happy World and abandoned Gravy Browning intensely returning and receiving the white ball across the green table. Tasker went off to the Liberty Club and Eggington vanished into the Singapore night.

'I feel so excited I feel sick,' said Brigg. 'Just fancy, two beautiful birds, music under the stars!'

'I'd feel better if I could walk in these pants without them circumcising me,' said Clay. He stopped and sighed hopelessly. 'Do I look ridiculous, Brigg?'

'Yank,' said Brigg. 'You look great. As great as any bloke I've ever seen wearing a suit two sizes too small for him.'

'Thanks. You look good, too. Particularly as that coat was made for King Kong.'

They stared at each other dejectedly. 'Aw, bollocks,' said Brigg. 'Do we look that bloody silly?'

'If we do, we do. Maybe, like the man said, we could pass ourselves as the cabaret.'

'Come on,' decided Brigg. 'Let's go. Before I lose my nerve.'

They got a taxi to the nurses' home and stood tremulously outside after they rang the bell. The evening and its attendant crickets were close about them. There was the smell of night flowers at the door. A rancid-faced woman answered their ring and stared as though they had come collecting for charity.

'Nurse Harrison, please,' said Brigg eventually.

'And Nurse Porter,' added Clay.

'Are *you* going to the dance?' asked the woman. She was looking at Brigg's jacket. He shuffled back into a shadow.

'Yes,' he said. 'It's the dance. We're taking them.'

'Wait,' she said suspiciously. She went inside and they heard her retreating down a corridor. 'Didn't know it was fancy dress,' her voice echoed.

'Oh God,' muttered Brigg.

'Sure, oh God,' said Clay.

A young, ugly nurse poked her head round the door and took them in. She withdrew quickly and they could hear her laughing in the corridor.

'Somehow,' said Brigg, 'I don't reckon either of us is going to get a furgle tonight.'

Clay nodded miserable agreement. Then Bernice appeared at the door in a blue dress. Her face was bright and pleased. She motioned them into the hall.

'You'd think the old cow would have asked you in,' she said.

She looked slyly towards a corridor leading dimly from the hall. The place had been an old colonial home and they were caged by classic columns. It was dull and green now, with the smell of soap about it.

'She's the sister-in-charge,' said Bernice. 'The old boot. Last time she had a date I bet the bloke came on horseback.' She giggled. She was rounded and young. Brigg was staring at her. His head moved about freely, inside his big collar.

'Valerie won't be a minute,' she said. 'She didn't get off duty until late.'

'Are we all right?' asked Brigg stupidly.

'All right?'

'For the dance, I mean. Do we look all right?' He caught the force of Clay's patient sigh in his ear.

Bernice laughed. 'I thought it was the lady who was supposed to ask that,' she said. She whirled herself round in her blue dress. 'Do I look beee-utiful tonight?' she mimicked.

'Great,' said Brigg genuinely. 'Thanks for the tickets.'

She grinned at him. 'That's all right. They're free. We'll have a good time. It's all a bit fuddy-duddy they say. You know, the Valeta and the Gay Gordons, and all ancient stuff like that, but I don't care.'

Incisive footsteps sounded in the corridor and Valerie Porter appeared, taller and more slender than Bernice. 'My, my,' she smiled at Clay and Brigg. 'You two are all done up.'

214

'Do we look nice?' inquired Brigg anxiously.

'Handsome. I can't wait for the first foxtrot.'

They took a taxi to St George's Hall in the centre of the city. Cars and taxis were lining up along the palm-treed road outside to unload their decorated occupants at the floodlit steps. Brigg felt himself shaking as he helped Bernice from the cab, and she took his arm as though to steady him. At the summit of the steps, pink diffuse lights and muted music stole out into the close air. Excitement and pride made Brigg feel he was swelling enough to fit his clothes.

They entered the incandescent foyer and found themselves in a scene so strange to Brigg as to be alarming. Nasal ladies humming, whisky-faced men hawing, distinguished people shaking hands, the men bowing so that the medals on their chests played brief tinkling tunes. The ladies, most of them elderly or middle-aged, were swimming in tulle and chiffon; faces creased by years of foreign sun were set in an orgy of organza.

They were shown their table and they sat and watched the novel scene. Couples were already swanning across the polished floor; the orchestra leader high on his stand waggled his baton and peered over the skimming heads as though he were there to see fair play. Brigg held Bernice's fingers as they watched. Then he said: 'I wonder did the Japanese have dances like this?'

The others looked at him in astonishment. 'Excuse my buddy,' said Clay. 'He gets some crazy thoughts at times.'

'No, wait a minute,' said Brigg defensively. 'I meant it. After all it's only five years ago, and they must have had some sort of social life.'

'Somehow,' said Valerie, 'I can't imagine a Japanese doing the quickstep. What would he do with his sword?'

'And who would they dance with?' asked Bernice.

A waiter hovered for their drinks order. Bernice and Valerie would only have orange juice.

'Aw, come on,' encouraged Brigg. 'Get a few gins down you.'

They laughed and refused. 'Whisky for me,' said Brigg bravely. 'How about you, Yank?'

'Whisky too.'

'Doubles, sir?'

'Er . . . well, yes, of course, doubles.'

'You've got a bit of pink cotton hanging down from your sleeve,' observed Bernice. 'Can I pull it off?'

While Brigg was still feigning surprise she took the thread in her fingers and pulled at it. Villiers's sewing had been rudimentary and the stitches wriggled out immediately. Bernice held the freed thread in her fingers and Brigg's tucked-up sleeve came down with it.

'Oh, sorry,' said Bernice genuinely. 'Oh, what have I done?'

'Nothing, nothing,' trembled Brigg. 'It's all right, really.'

'But your sleeve's all flopped out. Oh, I *am* sorry.'

'Look love, it's nothing,' said Brigg patiently. 'Straight it isn't.'

Clay was regarding him with a mixture of amusement and alarm, before rising uncertainly and asked Valerie to dance. They walked on to the ballroom floor leaving Brigg miserably trying to tuck his sleeve back.

'Why don't you ask me to dance?' suggested Bernice kindly.

'Oh yes,' blinked Brigg. 'Will you?'

She rose and he spent a panicky moment trying to get the long sleeve pushed back inside itself. He walked after her like a man with a withered arm. She turned and smiled expectantly and he held her, her cheek near his, his chest brushing her breast, his crippled hand, still clenched, behind her back.

'It's not my jacket, see,' he explained close to her ear. 'I had to borrow it. I got mine mucked up . . . spilled Scotch all down the front of it last week. Regimental booze-up we had.'

He could feel her laughing gently. 'You're ever so strange,' she said. 'You're a bit unusual, really. I can't for the life of me think what made you wonder if the Japanese had dances.'

Brigg began to cheer up. He thought he could feel the soft pimples on the summit of her breasts touching him on the lapels of his purloined jacket. They returned to the table holding hands. The drinks were there and Clay had paid. A short florid man, like a stunted rose, had now cornered Clay and was breathing whisky up at his face. 'Grand job you chaps did, out here,' said the man, adding 'Americans', as though he felt the sentence needed explanation. 'Grand job. Can't see how we could have won it without you. Terrific job.'

'Thank you, sir,' said Clay.

'And you're in rubber now, you say.'

'Yes sir. Rubber exploration.'

'Damn good.' The Englishman fumbled in his jacket. 'My card. Any time, you know, any time.' Clay bowed politely and took the card, shaking the man's trembling hand before returning to the table. He grinned at Brigg.

'Rubbah,' imitated Brigg. 'Damn good to be in rubbah. Dahn hot, but damned good.'

They began to enjoy themselves. Bernice produced a safety-pin and pinned Brigg's sleeve back. The girls each agreed to have a gin and tonic.

'You Americans dance so different,' said Valerie.

'How different?'

'Such tiny steps. You hardly move. I'd like to see you dance a tango.'

'So would I,' grinned Brigg maliciously, glancing at Clay's constricting trousers.

Clay glowered at him. 'I guess I couldn't manage a tango,' he admitted.

'The next dance,' announced the Master of Ceremonies, 'will be a Paul Jones!'

'Oh good, come on,' said Valerie giving Clay a tug. Bernice took Brigg's hand and led him purposefully into the arena. A great turning circle was formed after the initial waltz, and Brigg watched the worried Clay moving sideways with tiny cogged steps, his face wan with anxiety for his trousers. When the music stopped, Brigg found himself opposite a thin, wooden woman with a smile tacked to her jaw. He nodded unsurely and, holding his rogue sleeve between his thumb and first finger, began to dance a foxtrot with her.

'Singapore?' she snapped.

'Er, yes, Singapore,' agreed Brigg nervously.

'Malacca,' she sniffed. 'Hate Singapore. Detest it.'

'No,' swallowed Brigg. 'I don't like it. Too wet.'

That was the sum of their conversation until the circle was formed again and they split to join it. This time he was matched with an elderly lady in a long ice-blue dress which she gathered in one hand. He looked for Bernice and Valerie and saw they were dancing with two young grinning officers, sharp in their dress jackets, while Clay was struggling in the engrossing arms of a fat woman. 'It's a polka!' the Master of Ceremonies exclaimed from the bandstand. Brigg looked with immediate concern towards Clay. As he jogged around sedately with his own frail partner he saw Clay being bounced violently about the floor by the big woman. Then Clay fell down.

A quick ring of spectators formed as he lay prone, his eyes rolling like a felled animal. Brigg said hurriedly, 'Excuse me. My mate,' and abandoned his aged partner. He pushed through and, with the two hearty young officers who were with Bernice and Valerie, he lifted Clay and helped him to the side of the ballroom. 'American', he heard the blahed voice booming somewhere. 'A Yankee. In rubbah. Rubbah.'

The waiter brought a glass of water and Brigg

leaned near his friend. 'I had to do it,' whispered
Clay desperately. 'It's these fucking pants. Another
second and they'd have split.'

Awkwardly Brigg manoeuvred Bernice around one
flank of a hedge outside the nurses' hostel. He could
see Clay steering Valerie through the flitting moonlight at the other end.

'Was it all right?' he asked.

'Oh yes,' she said. 'It was very nice. Those things
are always a bit stuffy. Your friend collapsing like
that brightened it up a bit.'

'Those two chaps, the two officers. Do you know
them?'

'Oh those. Yes, Val and I, we know them.'

'I see.'

Her face was very near him but it was as though it
were behind glass. 'I've got to go in,' she said
decisively. 'I'm on early duty tomorrow.'

'I'm sorry about that day in the hospital,' said
Brigg. 'I meant to say before. When you were
coming out of the Casualty place.'

'Don't talk about it,' she pleaded. 'It wasn't your
fault. It just gets very nasty there sometimes, that's
all.'

He bent forward and kissed her on her soft cheek.
She stiffened a little but she did not pull away. He
moved his mouth two inches to the left and
connected with hers. He kissed her clumsily and she
stirred and responded. His hands went to her waist
and then around her so that he pressed her front

against him. Their faces disengaged and her head lay passively on his shoulder as though she were resting. Anxiously, in case the moment went, he touched the undercurve of her breast.

'Be a good boy,' she admonished. 'Don't spoil the evening.'

'Oh, sorry,' he said his heart sinking. 'Sorry.'

'That's all right.' She paused and then said, 'One more and then I've got to go in. I'll be out on my feet tomorrow.'

'All right,' he said, crushed. They kissed flatly, and as he tried to fully embrace her again she disentangled herself, turned and walked up the steps.

'Goodnight,' she called back from the top. 'And thanks ever so much.'

Brigg, caring nothing now, waved limply at her with his idiotically flapping sleeve until she had gone through the door. 'Thanks ever so much,' he grunted to himself as he turned away. He slouched down the drive; the night was ridiculously full of moonlight and the lulling scent of flowers. Clay was waiting like a disconsolate policeman beneath a street light.

'Nice mess-up that was,' grunted Brigg. 'All of it.' He glanced at Clay. 'I don't suppose you got much either?'

'Nope, nothing,' shrugged Clay.

'In your case, mate, it's just as well,' said Brigg. 'Once you'd got your trousers down you'd never have got them up again. We looked like sodding clowns, the pair of us. That's the last we'll see of them.'

'I guess so,' agreed Clay.

'Did you see those two smarmy bastard officers,' grimaced Brigg. 'I bet they never go away empty-bloody-handed. Christ, I just touched her on the tit, hardly felt it, and she told me to be a good boy. At least if you pay for it you *know* what you're going to get.'

'That's the difference,' said Clay philosophically. 'These are girls, not hustlers. You always have to spend something. Sometimes it's time and some-times it's cash.'

'Did we spend much money tonight?' asked Brigg practically. 'I'd better settle up with you.'

An Indian watchman walked by with his lantern. 'Goodnight, sahib,' he said, and Brigg waved a hand at the words.

'Nice to get some respect from somebody,' he said.

'We spent thirty dollars, including the taxis,' said Clay. 'Then there was ten dollars each to Browning and five for the suits.'

'That was money up the spout for a start,' grumbled Brigg. He sighed: 'All that for nothing. A week's pay. We could never afford to take them out regularly anyway. It's a dead loss. Bugger it.'

They were in time for the last bus to Panglin. It was ready to go and they jumped aboard to be confronted by the face of Corporal Eggington, torn both physically and with anguish. He looked at them with alarm, noting their dinner suits but making no comment. They sat opposite him and stared at him curiously.

'All your face is bleeding, Eggy,' Brigg said eventually. 'All your spots.'

'I know that,' said Eggington irritably. 'I don't need you to tell me, Brigg.'

'All right, all right, don't get shirty. What happened?'

To their astonishment Eggington buried his face in his hands and sobbed. 'I've got a big lump of stuff stuck to the back of my head,' he cried. *I can't get it off!*

'Stuff?' Brigg and Clay advanced across the aisle and looked at the back of the bent head of Eggington. A slab of hard material, like concrete, the size of a bar of chocolate, was stuck fast to the skin and the hair.

'How did you get that fixed to you?' asked Clay.

'A bastard Japanese,' sobbed Eggington. 'Advertised in the paper. Reckoned his treatment would get rid of all spots and blemishes. That's why I had to get out of Panglin, see. He was only here for one night. Twenty-five bucks it was too.'

Clay glanced at Brigg. They retreated to their seats keeping their expressions rigid. 'What kind was it?' asked Clay. 'The treatment?'

'Mud,' sniffed Eggington. 'Bloody mud. Mud bath, and the swine put me into it, all hot. And then he fucked off with my money. When . . . oh, Christ . . . when I got out, it all dried on me. I was like some bloody mummy and I had a terrible time chipping it off. I couldn't get this lump off my head. I couldn't . . .'

His face emerged from his hands, red, bleeding,

tear-ravaged, a bloated old man of thirty. 'You,' he sobbed accusingly; 'you just don't know what it's like . . .' the voice collapsed and his face shook, '. . . to have pimples.'

12

At ten o'clock on a Monday morning the day's first damp sun had steamed the overnight monsoon rain from the roofs and gardens of the St James-the-Less Rest Home for British soldiers.

Brigg was making a telephone call. 'Hello. Is that the nurses' hostel? Good, thanks. Could I have a word with Bernice, please. Nurse Harrison.' He tried to make his voice confident.

'Hold on. I'll get her.'

Brigg heard the female steps clicking down the corridor and a voice calling in an echo. He glanced pessimistically at a picture portraying St James-the-Less regarding him with a holy stare from the wall above the telephone.

'Women,' Brigg shrugged at the picture.

He heard footsteps returning towards the phone at the other end. His hope and confidence evaporated as they got closer.

'Hello,' she said. 'Bernice here.'

'Oh hello, love,' said Brigg, feigning ease. 'Thought I'd call you. It's me, Brigg. Briggsy.'

'Hello, Briggsy,' she answered. She sounded neither encouraging nor discouraging.

'I've taken some leave. Five days.'

'That's nice. Where are you?'

'Little Jim's, Saletar Road.'

'Little Jim's? What's that?'

'The soldiers' rest home,' said Brigg. 'St James-the-Less.'

'Oh, blimey,' she laughed impulsively. 'I've never heard it called that.'

'All the boys call it "Little Jim's",' he said feeling easier because she had laughed. 'It's a bit dull. There's hardly anybody here. But it's cheap.'

'Did you spend a lot of money the other night?' she asked seriously.

'Money? No, it was hardly anything. Peanuts really.'

'Oh, Briggsy,' she said with real concern. 'Did you have a lousy time? I'm sorry. I'm a bit of a misery sometimes.'

'No. No, you're not. I had a terrific time. And the Yank. He did too. The suits didn't belong to us, that's all. They didn't fit all that good, did they?'

He heard her laughing. 'It was ever so funny when the Yank fell down.'

'He *had* to,' grinned Brigg. 'That big woman was barging him all round the floor. His trousers would have split.'

'I just can't forget it,' she giggled. 'Val and I laughed all night. Where did you get them? The suits.'

'Well, to tell you the truth, we sort of borrowed them – from the laundry in the village.'

Her fruity chuckle bubbled over the phone. 'Oh, no! Not really?'

'Straight,' he said. 'That's why my sleeve was yards too long and poor old Clay could hardly walk.'

'You are funny,' she said seriously. 'You really are.'

'Thanks,' he said doubtfully. 'Sometimes I don't feel all that funny. I felt a right twit I can tell you.' He waited. Then he said: 'Any chance of seeing you?'

'If you like . . .'

Brigg's eyes widened. 'You want to? That's great. When are you off duty?'

'Today's my day off,' she said. 'They've got a tennis court there, haven't they? At the St James. Can you play tennis?'

'Er . . . well, yes. I've played on and off in the park at home. I'm not all that good. But there's nobody on the court. I can see it through the window.'

'All right. I'll come up in about an hour.'

'Terrific,' he said. 'I haven't got any gear, but I'll pop out and get some. I'll make sure it fits this time. They've got some sports stuff here. I'll be able to get a bat.'

'A racquet?' she said. 'I'll bring a spare one in case.'

'All right, Bernice. See you then.'

'See you then, Briggsy.'

He bought white shorts, shirt and tennis shoes cheaply at a shop half a mile from the St James's, this being normal everyday wear for many Chinese. An incredibly thin and slow old lady, one of the group of volunteer assistants who helped to run Little Jim's, offered him a sagging tennis racquet from the sports stores. He accepted it out of politeness. She also insisted that he accepted a white eyeshade and that he put it on his forehead at once.

'Are you having a nice time at St James's dear?' she inquired, leaning towards him kindly.

'Well, I've only just arrived,' replied Brigg. 'But I think I will.'

'We haven't many guests at the moment,' she wheezed. 'Would you like *me* to play tennis with you? I was forty years in India, you know.'

Brigg was astounded by the sporting offer. She could hardly creak from one side of the room to the other. 'Lovely India,' she ruminated not looking at him. 'Lovely, lovely India.'

'Yes,' replied Brigg politely. 'I've heard it's lovely. India.'

'Would you like a knock-up with me then?' she inquired again. Her skin was old, brown and crinkled like paper, but her eyes in their sockets were sharp with life.

'Tennis?' he said stupidly. 'It's very nice of you, but I have a friend coming to play.'

'Ah, good,' she sighed as though completely relieved. 'It's nice to have friends. I had many friends in India, many friends.'

'I expect you did,' he said awkwardly. 'Good spot to make friends, I should think.'

'Oh yes, oh yes. Have you ever been?'

'Not in India,' he said. 'This is the only place I've ever been, abroad. And Port Said and Aden, like, calling in on the boat on the way out.'

'You'll like India,' she dreamed. Then she came awake. 'Is your friend coming soon?'

'Any time,' said Brigg. 'She said she'd take an hour. She's a nurse.'

A brief cloud brushed the old woman's face. 'No ladies are allowed in St James's after nine o'clock in the evening,' she warned. 'You will remember that, won't you?'

'We'll pack up the game before then,' he said, intending it as a small joke. But it missed her.

She said: 'Would you mind if I came out in the sunshine and watched? Perhaps I could keep the score for you, I like to see young people enjoying themselves. The world is very short.'

Brigg was nonplussed. 'Well . . . yes, I don't see why not,' he half laughed. 'After all it's your place.'

'No,' she corrected. 'It's your place, young fellow. It's for the soldiers.' She became thoughtful. 'St James-the-Less,' she said. 'Some people say he was the brother of Jesus.'

'Get away,' said Brigg. 'I never realized.' He had been glancing anxiously through the window and now he saw Bernice, beautiful, bouncy, in tennis whites, coming through the flowered entrance on a bicycle. 'Oh, my friend's come,' he said relieved. 'I'd better go and meet her.'

'I can watch, can't I?' asked the old spindly lady. It was a plea.

'Of course you can. You can sit on the bench.'

'Good, good. I'll lock up. I'll come right away. Keep that eyeshade on.'

Bemused, Brigg walked out into the rich morning

229

sunshine. Bernice was walking down a sloping path towards him, ducking beneath leaning flowers, her hair tied behind, her neck descending brown into her swollen shirt. He tried not to look at her legs.

'Oh, Briggsy,' she smiled. 'You look very sporty. I like the eyeshade.'

'It all fits this time,' grinned Brigg. He reached out and touched her tubby fingers. 'The old lady in the sports store gave me the eyeshade and I nicked the rest from a Chinese who's just my size.' They walked down the path towards the court, their elbows touching. 'Listen,' he warned, 'I'm not all that good at this tennis.'

'That's all right,' she said. 'We won't play for money. Who is that old dear sitting in the court?'

She was there already. Placed primly on the bench at the net, staring directly ahead of her as though seeing again a thousand games from the past.

'She's the one from the sports store. She says she wants to watch,' he shrugged. 'So I said it would be all right. She's been in India umpteen years and I reckon she's a bit off her chump. And she's a bit lonely as well.'

Bernice glanced at him so quickly that he did not notice. 'You don't mind, do you?' he asked suddenly.

'Mind? No. How could I mind? I play better with a crowd anyway.'

She had brought the promised racquet and she handed it to him as they entered the court. The lady looked up abruptly from her reverie. 'Good, good, you've come,' she fussed. 'Now I'll sit here and I promise I'll behave. I won't be in the way.'

230

Brigg stood, a shade embarrassed, between the two women.

'This is Miss Harrison,' he said motioning towards Bernice. 'She's a nurse. I'm sorry but I don't really know your . . .'

'Miss Phillimore,' squeaked the lady as though she had just remembered it. 'Rose Phillimore. I'm a bit mad.' She laughed with croaky delight at their discomfiture. 'Don't worry,' she spluttered touching both their arms. 'I'm pretty harmless.'

They had to laugh with her. Brigg rolled his eyes wildly at Bernice as they separated to go to opposite ends of the court. Bernice grinned at him.

He was not a very good player and their game was all stops and starts. In addition he found himself mesmerized by her as she moved on the court: the mobile brown legs, the arms, the rolling of her breasts. The old lady, quiet for a while, her face creased with age and concentration in the sun, soon lapsed into shouting advice and encouragement.

'Go on, laddie! Volley! Volley! Oh dear, hard luck, old chap.'

She heard Bernice call him Briggsy and she cried, 'Rally, Briggsy, rally!'

She kept their score too, in a squeaky official voice as if she were sitting on a referee's ladder, with gestures and flattenings of her hands to keep the sun from her brittle eyes. She was like the ghost of a thousand summer days.

Eventually when Bernice had won conclusively Brigg called to Miss Phillimore. 'Would you like to have a knock, miss?'

'Oh, love to, love to!' She jumped up enthusiastically.

She rushed madly from the court and they could hear her calling 'I'll be back! I'll be back!' over the heads of the shrubs. Brigg and Bernice walked towards the net and faced each other like neighbours over a garden fence. Their faces were sheened with perspiration. He leaned over the net and kissed her, touching her arm just above her warm elbow.

'It's ever so sad, isn't it?' she said to his surprise. 'Being old like that. She makes me want to cry.'

He swallowed heavily and nodded. 'I suppose it is really, when you come to think of it. Mind, it's not as sad as getting killed when you're nineteen.'

Her face clouded even more in the sun. 'Yes, you're right, Briggsy,' she said. 'That's worse.'

Miss Phillimore returned, whooping like a goose through the shrub garden, waving an incredibly ancient tennis racquet above the head-high flowers and emerging wearing a long split skirt which, with her sparse legs, looked like a pair of signal flags. She also had a sailor shirt and white plimsolls. She arrived on the court whirling the racquet like a butterfly net, grinning a gaping grin. Brigg realized that she had removed her false teeth.

Miss Phillimore and Brigg played against Bernice. The old lady was all enthusiasm and shouts, returning the ball quite well when she managed to reach it, and once hitting her partner on the back of the head with a full-volley. But she was soon tired in the increasing sun, and they walked from the court with the game unconcluded.

They sat on a terrace above the tennis court and the wispy lady with a suddenly piercing colonial voice called 'Boy!' and clapped her hands. An Indian appeared and she ordered three glasses of iced orange, dismissing the servant with an impatient flip of her fingers. Immediately he had gone she seemed to crumple. 'India,' she sighed. 'Lovely India.'

'This is where I live,' said Brigg stopping outside the green door of the chalet. He did not look directly at her. 'Want to have anything? A shower or something?' He stumbled on lamely. 'I could go over to the lounge and write some postcards.'

She said nothing but just remained there. Fumbling, he opened the door, and she walked in ahead of him. His heart accelerated. The room closed over them with its drab coolness. Brigg waved his hand. He was aware of its trembling. 'The Maharajah Suite,' he announced trying to keep his voice from squeaking. There was a wicker chair, a boxwood dressing-table and the stiff narrow bed.

He had not closed the door, but now he did so. 'Keep the heat out,' he muttered hollowly. His next pace took him directly to her; they were facing each other, a foot apart.

'You're a very *kind* boy, aren't you, Briggsy,' she said in a low voice. Her hand reached out and lay casually with its own weight against the warmth of his shirt.

'Kind?' he answered in a slow confusion. He could

233

not believe what was going to occur. 'Can't say I've ever thought about being kind.'

'You were very kind with the old dear,' she said.

'India, lovely India,' he said, making a poor job of the mimicry. He moved two inches and kissed her on the cheek, almost at the side of the mouth. Her skin was still glistening from the tennis. His shirt was rubbed by hers.

'Is there anyone around?' she asked, as though she had just made a decision. She gave a mischievous giggle, but looked at him seriously, without mirth. She was nervous.

'Nobody,' he managed to say. 'There's hardly a soul in the place, anyway. The old dear's gone . . .'

'Have a look,' she suggested carefully. 'Take a shufti outside.'

He was loath to go in case she changed her mind or had magically vanished by the time he returned. 'There's no one about,' he repeated. 'Honest.' He seemed remote from his voice, as though someone else were saying the words.

'Just look,' she insisted and, judging his thoughts, 'I won't run off.'

He turned and took two strides to the door, lifted the latch and looked out. It was like a sunlit museum out there, brilliant shrubs standing on the tended grass, flowers and insects, but no people apart from a gardener crouched in the distance against the green. Brigg turned back to her.

'Well?' she inquired. 'Is there?'

He grinned, swallowed and went close. 'Not a sausage,' he said. She laughed at the words and looked into his face. He manoeuvred her to him and felt her plump parts ease to his body.

'I can feel you sort of glowing through your shirt,' she said. 'Can you feel me?'

He nodded, speechless, and bent towards her face. They kissed again, but she terminated it in her strangely practical way. 'I'm ever so hot and sticky,' she said looking down at her brown legs. A trickle of perspiration was indeed travelling towards her knee. On impulse she put her finger down and scooped up the sweat. Then, to his astonishment, she giggled and put it into his mouth as if she were giving him a sweet. He felt the salty taste, the soft finger and the hard, figured fingernail. Words were still beyond him. He put his hands to her waist, took them away, then put them back again.

'I'm really hot,' she said again.

'Tennis,' Brigg muttered, 'makes you.'

'Why don't you take your shirt off then, silly?' she said with deliberate carelessness.

'Never thought of that,' replied Brigg truthfully. He could not take his eyes from her. He forced his fingers to his shirt buttons and began to undo them. When his shirt was open she smiled. 'Ah,' she said, 'you've got a nice chest. I'm glad you've not got a load of hair on it, Briggsy. Sometimes I have to shave hairs off the chests in the hospital, before operations . . .' She began to unbutton her own tennis shirt. 'Have you locked the door?' she asked fearfully.

'It locks itself,' answered Brigg with dreamlike slowness. He watched while her front was shown to him; the white brassiere full of her flesh was released and fell away as an awning. Her breasts hung their heads.

'Jesus, Bernice!' Brigg choked over both Christian names. The young man and the girl fell against each other clumsily, their skins slippery, their mouths gasping, their arms grasping. Blimey, thought Brigg, if the Yank could only see me now!

'I might as well tell you something, Briggsy,' she said, her body glued against him.

Oh God, no, he thought. Just my luck. 'It's all right, love,' he lied. 'What is it?'

'I'm a virgin,' she whispered.

'Oh, that's all right,' he said hoarsely. 'I haven't been doing it all that long myself.'

'I honestly meant to save it,' she mumbled. 'But what with one thing and another, somehow it doesn't seem worth it. I have to cry sometimes in that hospital, Briggsy. It's something terrible.'

'I saw a bloke shot in front of my eyes two weeks ago,' countered Brigg. 'Cruel.'

'All the time,' she said ignoring his contribution. 'They wheel them in. Somehow I don't think I'm cut out for this nursing lark.'

'Forget it now,' he said, anxious that she should not become too introspective. 'Sit yourself down.'

She descended inelegantly on the bed, the slight young fat of her body rolling in small waves around her waist. He saw that she had been crying against his shoulder. She sniffled. 'I'm a bit of an odd one,' she said. 'You'll find that out.'

'You look all right to me,' he said earnestly. He eased her back on to the skimpy bed and manoeuvred himself into a kneeling position beside her. There was little room. They were like two people crouching on a ledge.

He decided to start on her left breast, bent and attached his tongue to the placid nipple, feeling the button tough in his mouth. For some annoying reason it reminded him of trying to blow up a football. She lay still and unrelaxed.

'Nervous?' he inquired lifting his head and seeing her stiff expression.

'Frightened to bloody death,' she nodded.

He unromantically wiped his mouth, still wet from her breast, and placed it chastely on her lips – a reassurance.

'Talk to me a bit, love,' she suggested hopefully. 'About anything you like except what's going on here. It might settle my shivers down. I don't know what to expect.'

Brigg's penis and his confidence were growing apace. 'I'll show you something instead,' he said in the way of a small boy with a secret. 'I'll just show you.'

He undid the tennis shorts and tugged them away. He was still wearing his white shoes and he had to perform several swimmer's kicks before getting the shorts free of his ankles. She was staring at what he had revealed with a mixture of joy, horror and fascination.

'It's all coloured,' she whispered.

'I can't do it in black and white,' said Brigg, unsure whether it was a complaint or a compliment. 'Don't you like the look of it then?'

She hesitated then speedily reached out her girl's hands for the thing. 'Oh no, Briggsy,' she croaked. 'It's very pretty.' The sensation of her fingers and then her palms on its surface produced the feeling of levitation in his body. He felt he could have flown several feet off the bed and remained there, while she held him like a balloon.

'Oh, pet,' he said tipping his face forward on to her vacant, trembling stomach. His passion was genuine, running through him like a current, but he kept enough presence to move his knees sideways so that her access to his addendum was not blocked. He pushed his nose deep into her navel. His left hand wandered blindly until it contacted the catch of her shorts. It was fiddling and difficult and she needed to break off her occupation with his member to unclip it for him before quickly returning her hand.

His clumsiness continued. He tugged at her shorts like a dinghy sailor tugging at a small, jammed sail. Bernice astutely obliged by taking her weight on her heels and her shoulders and curving her back so that he, abandoning her navel, could pull her shorts and the brief pants beneath away. His palms felt the slight wings of her hips and the warm humps of her buttocks as he eased the garments free. She had to give similar kicks to his to get the shorts free of her plimsolls. Brigg helped her and she said: 'Why don't we take the shoes off? We won't be playing any more today.'

He undid the four white laces and pulled the shoes and socks from their feet. Then he began the trembling return journey up her body until he was kneeling beside her again and both were feeling as before. Brigg, his blood bubbling from her stroking, now turned his attention to the artist's beard below her stomach. He gave some of the hairs a gentle tug.

'Is it all right?' she inquired anxiously from the other end, as though fearing it would come away in his hand.

'It's lovely,' Brigg assured her over his shoulder. 'Very nice indeed.'

'Will you move back a bit this way,' she called like a garage mechanic. 'I'm having to stretch too far.'

He wriggled back, crouching alongside her again so that she could reach him. She was much easier now. 'D'you know,' she said conversationally, cupping him in both palms, 'I've never actually seen one of these off-duty. It's an amazing contraption isn't it.'

'Very useful,' said Brigg, his instinctive male timetable saying it was the moment to make further gains. 'I'll show you.' Immediately he sensed her returning anxiety and moved up to kiss her face. His left leg slotted itself between hers. 'Don't hurt me, sweet,' she said quietly. 'Not if you can avoid it.'

'I'll be ever so careful,' he promised.

'What will you do first?' she inquired genuinely.

Brigg blinked. 'There's no fixed method,' he hedged. 'But don't worry, Bernice. It will work out, I promise.'

Trembling with the promise he eased her legs apart and climbed into the crevice between them. He lay on top of her and they embraced while he edged up the uncomfortable bed. An inch at a time, like a tracker, he advanced. They touched.

'It doesn't hurt so far,' whispered Bernice hopefully.

'I haven't put it in yet,' said Brigg leaning up on his elbows and staring at her.

'Sorry, I've got such a mix-up of feelings. I hope you're not going to be disappointed, Briggsy. I hope I'm not either.'

'Please, Bernice, don't worry.'

'Ah! You did it *then*. I felt it.'

'Yes, I did too.'

'It's inside me.'

'Yes more or less.'

'It must be dark in there.'

'And he's only got one eye.'

'You're funny.'

'You are too.'

'I'm only talking because I'm scared.'

'I know. Keep talking for both of us, if you like.'

'There's more of it in now . . . Ah . . . ah . . . Oh Christ, Briggsy, I *felt* that. My God, there's *yards* of it!'

'Sorry, love.'

'And so you should be. Oh . . . again. We'll make a mess on your bed.'

'Oh God, I forgot.'

'Here. Here's a tennis sock. It's yours. Will that do?'

'I don't know. Can you reach the shirt.'

'I'll try. God that thing's like a stake sticking into me. Here it is. The shirt.'

'It will muck it up for tennis.'

'Tennis? I'll be lucky if I can walk again. Oh, Briggsy, take it easy. EEEEEEeeeeesy.'

'Sorry, I'm clumsy.'

'If it's going to be like that I'll go back to being a virgin.'

'I think it's too late.'

'I'm crying. Can you see?'

'Yes I can see.'

'Do you love me?'

'Very much.'

'I love you too, Briggsy.'

'I love this too, Bernice. Doing this to you.'

'It still feels wrong. Are you sure you know what you're doing?'

'Don't be daft. Of course I know.'

'I'll be sore for a week.'

'I'm sorry.'

'Take no notice of me. I'm an old grumpy. It's easier now. Is it easier for you?'

'Yes, I think we're over the hump.'

'I'm not a camel.'

'Oh, Bernice . . . oh love . . . hold on.'

'What's up, Briggsy?'

'It happened.'

'What? The end?'

'We . . . yes, Bernice, I'm afraid so. I couldn't wait.'

'Oh. And I *missed* it! Wasn't I supposed to hear music or flocks of geese flying south or something?'

'Pack it up.'

'Sorry. I *do* love you.'

'Me too. I love you I mean.'

'Your winkle's vanished.'

'He's down there somewhere.'

'Poor thing. Let me try and find him.'

'He's not *that* small.'

'*There* he is. What a tiddler, Briggsy!'

'He enjoys you tugging him. *Not too hard!*'

'I'm mad.'

'That's what Miss Phillimore said.'

'You *haven't* done Miss Phillimore?'

'Oh Jesus, no. She said she was mad. Remember?'

'Yes, isn't it sad. Do you think she's very lonely away from India?'

'We're all a bit lonely.'

'I'm not now. I've got you, Briggsy.'

13

The same Monday morning came to Panglin with the customary yellow heat, steam rising from verges and vegetation, smoke and early cries from the village, pedlars walking, women digging ditches, and then the mug-clanking procession of the office soldiers trooping across the wooden bridge to their desks. The pea-green figures moved reluctantly across the skyline through a bank of palm trees on the far side of the bridge, and were swallowed, until Naafi time, by the low-shedded offices. It was two weeks before Christmas.

Lt Colonel Bromley Pickering, awaking to another Monday without his wife and now without his beloved stamp collection, sank back into his pillow unable, immediately, to face the bleakness of life bereft both of Marjorie and of philately, and then forced himself to get up from the bed. Despite the growing warmth outside, the house seemed cold. His Chinese servant would get his breakfast, and two women would appear after he had left for the office and clean the house and launder his clothes. When he returned at lunchtime his servant would be sitting beneath the bo-tree opposite the front gate, like an impassive and impressive prophet, and would prepare his food. In the evening he had dinner in the officers' mess before returning to his billet. He was a lonely man.

Unless he had to visit GHQ, or go to the city, or had arranged to play golf in the afternoon, the Colonel would leave his modest car beneath the rattan shelter that did as a garage and walk down the baked hill to the offices. His dejection as he left his unfriendly house was pushed professionally aside during this walk so that he appeared to his adjutant, and the rest of his battalion, to be cheerful and alert when he arrived. That, anyway, was his intention.

'Any private mail for me, Reggie?' he inquired as soon as he sat behind his desk, his voice airily covering his anxious hope.

'N-nothing, I'm afraid, sir. Just the usual b-b-business stuff from the War House and GHQ.'

'Oh, well, she can't be writing all the time, not every week, I suppose,' sighed the Commanding Officer. 'After all she's busy, terribly busy.'

'Oh, she m-must be, sir, what with the jam b-b-bottling and one thing and another.'

The Colonel glanced secretly at his aide, but there was no malice in the man's worried face. 'That's exactly it, Reggie,' he continued. 'She'd be lost out here. Life of a lady. Nothing to do.'

'Perhaps you'll get a letter tomorrow, sir,' said the adjutant sympathetically. 'They take ages s-s-sometimes. I f-f-frequently get f-four or f-five at a time. All in a b-bunch. I think they must save them up down at the Postal Unit.'

'Four or five? *Do* you, Reggie? Really?'

244

'Yes, sir . . . s-sometimes.'

'Ah well, as you say, something may turn up tomorrow. Perhaps she's sent some more jam. The last jar's nearly gone, isn't it?'

'Very nearly, sir.' The adjutant took the small pot from the cupboard and held it up to the light as though assessing the result of an experiment. 'We could do with another consignment. Would you like some now?'

'Yes. That's a splendid idea. Start the week off on the right foot. As soon as the coffee's ready, a nice slice of bread, butter and jam. Splendid.' He paused and then, trying again to sound unconcerned, he said: 'Don't suppose the album's turned up, has it?'

'Sorry, s-sir,' said the major returning from the coffee-making. 'Not a s-sign. The whole place has been searched.'

'Oh dear. I rather hoped it would be discovered.'

'You want to lift the leave restrictions I take it, sir.'

'Of course, of course. That was a bad thing anyway. It was that young fellow Grainger's idea. He hasn't got the *feel* of this unit yet. You can't bully these lads. I shouldn't have listened to him . . . It was just that I wanted my stamps returned.'

The coffee was placed on his blotter and a neatly spread slice of bread, butter and jam beside it on a small plate. The Commanding Officer touched with his little finger the jam and tasted it. At once he seemed to smell and taste his Hampshire garden. He sighed for what might just have been.

'The medical officer wants to see you, sir.'

'Oh! What was that about?'

'About the number of men reporting for an F-F-F-F-F-I, sir.'

'FFI? Now what would that be?'

'Examination for venereal disease.'

The Colonel looked genuinely shocked. 'Oh dear, poor fellows. It's very difficult to know *what* to do out here, I suppose. It's no use advising them to take icy cold showers like they tell you at school. To start with, the water's always lukewarm.'

'The MO wonders if you would have a w-word with the chaps, sir.'

'Me! Good heavens, I couldn't do that, Reggie. I mean . . . I wouldn't know what . . . Anyway that's his job.'

'He says the medical aspects are his, but the d-d-disciplinary aspects are yours, sir,' shrugged the major. 'He s-suggests that the efficiency of the unit is being affected.'

'Oh, Reggie, I would die of embarrassment.'

'He's a very difficult chap, sir, the MO. Very blunt, if I may say so. He even suggested tying up an anti-VD Campaign with Christmas, sir, playing on the s-s-sentimental s-side, if you s-see . . .'

'My God, how dreadful.'

'Indeed, I f-f-felt so myself,' sniffed Reggie, 'and I conveyed the feeling to him. He thought you might like to address the men, in a suitably subtle way of course, from the pulpit during the Christmas church parade.'

'No! By heavens, Reggie, I've never heard of a nastier idea. Never. And I shall tell him so.'

'Quite, sir. He is due to call in tomorrow morning after sick parade.'

'Good, I shall be prepared, believe me.'

'There's one other thing, sir. The American. P-P-P-Private F-F-F-irst Class Clay. He wants to see you again. He's coming at nine-thirty.'

'Oh dear. Clay. What can I tell him? We *have* tried, haven't we?'

'We have indeed, sir. But nobody seems to w-want to know anything about him.'

'It's certainly Monday morning,' groaned the Colonel. 'Frankly I can understand the chap wanting to know what's to become of him, but I don't know either. I suppose I'd better see him.'

'It's nine-thirty now, sir.'

The Colonel sighed. 'All right, if he's arrived, send him in.'

Clay had been waiting outside and now marched smartly to the desk and flapped up an American salute. The Commanding Officer, who had never ceased to be confused by the complications of saluting within his own army, attempted to return it with a sort of mid-Atlantic version of the courtesy, realized he was hatless, and substituted for it a friendly wave of the hand.

'Ah now, Clay,' he said, adding hurriedly, 'Private First Class Clay, that is.'

'Sir,' replied Clay.

'Er . . . how are you?'

'Me, sir? Very well, thank you. I was just kinda wondering if I'd been found yet, sir.'

'Found?' ruminated the Colonel. 'Yes, I suppose

one could put it like that.' He looked honestly at the young American. 'No, Clay, I'm afraid the bad news is that you're still lost.'

'Oh heck.'

'Indeed, oh heck. It must be very galling for you to be kicking your heels in a foreign army not knowing what is going to happen to you. We *have* tried, Clay.' He lifted his face and his voice and called into the outer office. 'We have tried, haven't we, Reggie?'

'Y-Yes, sir, w-we've tried,' the adjutant's voice trembled. He poked his head around the door. 'We've telephoned and written and even sent t-t-telegrams.'

'The United States Army doesn't seem to answer letters,' shrugged the Commanding Officer. 'You might mention that, when you do get back. And our own people at GHQ keep fobbing us off with "When we know something we'll tell you". Quite honestly I don't know what to suggest.' He attempted an ill-starred smile. His eye beamed sympathetically. 'I hope you haven't forgotten all your logistics.'

'Well, no. No, sir.'

'You'll be wanting to use them, though, I suppose.'

'I'd just like to know my situation, sir. It's not a nice feeling when your army just forgets you.'

Lt Colonel Bromley Pickering nodded sagely. 'Like being left on the battlefield when the rest of the guys have retreated.'

'Yes, sir, it's a little like that.' He glanced at the CO. 'We don't retreat very much though.'

'No, no, certainly not,' the Colonel apologized

hurriedly. He pushed his face into his hands. 'What do you do to keep occupied?'

'Anything I'm told to do, sir,' responded Clay. 'I pick up trash, help in the armoury, run messages, do guard duty . . .'

'How about some leave, Clay?' suggested the Colonel brightly. 'I'm sure you could do with some leave.'

Clay nodded. 'Furlough? That would be appreciated, sir. I didn't know . . .'

'Reggie,' called the Colonel. The adjutant appeared. 'L-L-Leave is it, sir?'

'Exactly. Give the chap a few days off. Seven days. How would that be? Pay, ration allowance, the whole caboodle.' He hesitated. 'Ration allowance at *our* rate, of course. You Americans eat so much more than we do. Are you paid at US Army rates, by the way?'

'No, sir. Nobody could work it out. I get British pay, and later, when the whole thing is worked out and they catch up with me, I guess I'll get what's owing. Then the US Army will have to reimburse the British Army.'

'It's all become terribly complicated,' mused the Colonel. 'Anyway, Clay, have a jolly good furlough. And we'll make it unofficial so that it's not American leave nor it is British leave.' He brightened. 'It's a kind of French leave.'

To Brigg and to Bernice had come the peculiar ease, the artless familiarity, which blesses those who do not have to pretend any longer, those who delude themselves into believing life holds no remaining mystery. When she was free of hospital duties they explored the city like children, they made love at some juncture every day, improving only a little with practice, and when she was not with him, Brigg lay on his bed at Little Jim's and wondered deeply about her.

Clay arrived for his leave on the Thursday and Brigg boasted the whole afternoon. 'Never known a woman like it, Yank,' he said as they drank Tiger beer on the balcony outside the chalet. 'I'm so bloody happy when I'm with her. And she's potty about me.'

'Great, Briggsy,' acknowledged Clay with his customary generosity. 'Great. I'm sure glad you made the show.'

'I reckon your chances are good,' encouraged Brigg with the air of one completely familiar with the art.

'You do?'

'Listen, *mine* was the tough one. Never been touched, not seriously. Now, I hear that Valerie has actually been *engaged* – twice.'

'Which makes you think the pie's been opened, huh?'

'Wouldn't you reckon so?'

'I guess that's logic.'

Brigg patted him benevolently on the shoulder. 'Listen, Yank,' he confided. 'I think that girl is going to be seeing Old Glory before the night's out.' He spotted Miss Phillimore shuddering in the sun as she locked her lonely sports store. 'And if you don't score,' he went on, 'I'll get you fixed up with that dishy doll down there.'

Clay laughed. 'Briggsy,' he said, 'the way I feel, that don't look too unattractive.' They watched Miss Phillimore totter away and the American emitted a double low whistle and added: 'Not at all.'

'We'll see you do better than that, mate,' promised Brigg with his proprietorial air. 'I reckon you're *on*.'

'What's the plan?' asked Clay leaning forward. Brigg was taken aback.

'Plan? Well there's no actual plan. I mean, I can't fix it *all* along the line until I tuck you into bed.'

'Okay, okay, but just as a matter of general interest, where will the "bed" you just mentioned be? We can't bring them back here. It's against the rules.'

'It's difficult at night,' conceded Brigg. 'I've been having it off in the daytime. They think she comes over to play tennis.'

'Nobody's going to be fooled by white shorts and sneakers at midnight,' said Clay. 'And that's a high wall to climb.'

'I know,' admitted Brigg. 'I've done a good recce all around and there's not many ways you can get in. They surrounded this place to keep the wogs out, and if you can keep a wog out you can keep anybody out. There's only the gate and that's no good because there's a Chinese watchman *and* a military copper on duty all night. If we bribed both of them we'd have no money to go out.'

Clay grinned. 'Okay, so how do we get the dolls in?'

'There's only the wall,' shrugged Brigg. 'But it *could* be done with a rope. Let's hope they can climb.'

'Aw, they'll never do that. There's a limit to even my sex appeal, pal. I can visualize her scrambling over the wall to get *out*, but not *in*.'

'No confidence, that's your bother,' sniffed Brigg. 'I always thought Americans were bunged full of it, if you go by the films that is.'

'I'm not Clarke Gable,' said Clay. 'If I was, I could afford a hotel room for a fuck.'

'We'll get them over the wall, don't worry,' repeated Brigg. 'What I'm wondering is where we take them first. They'll have something to eat at the hostel, thank God, so that won't cost us; and we'll have something here. But where do we go then? The Services Club has got dancing but it's a bit crummy. We can't afford to go anywhere like the Raffles.'

'What about the clubs? I went to some real raunchy clubs when I first got here. When I took my few days unofficial furlough. There was one . . .'

'You're round the bend!' interrupted Brigg rudely. 'You couldn't take these two to clubs like that. With a lot of Chinese knockers! Christ, they'd pass out. They may shag like a pair of rattlesnakes, Yank, but they're *decent* girls.'

There was a volunteer dance band at the Services Club, one which strictly speaking should not have volunteered at all. They struggled to keep rhythm and pace like novice rowers in a heavy boat on a heavy sea. Occasionally their error was compounded by the singing of a suet-faced Eurasian girl who had the extraordinary facility of making a familiar song sound like an entirely new composition.

They sat on wickerwork chairs behind a wickerwork table, faded relics of palmier court days, two glasses of beer and two of lemon juice eyeing them soberly from the surface. The room was wooden and cheerless. By nine-thirty there were only four other couples dancing. One of the fans was clanking rheumatically on the ceiling, keeping better time than the band. Bernice and Valerie had become silent. Clay eyed Brigg apprehensively across their backs.

Brigg asked Bernice to dance a foxtrot, and while the band deciphered 'Some Enchanted Evening', Bernice grimaced and whispered: 'Briggsy, this is terrible. The place is like a shed, and not much of a shed at that. I hope it falls down on the bloody band; that would be two birds with one stone.'

'Where do you want to go, then?' asked Brigg. 'We haven't got jackets so we can't go to the Raffles.'

'Christ, who wants to go to the Raffles?' she replied. 'That's just like this but you pay more for the drinks. Surely you know a club or something?'

Brigg sighed. 'Look, we can't take you two to any of the clubs we know in Singapore.'

'Why not?'

'Well . . . because they're not the sort of places you can take anyone to, that's all. Blimey, the *blokes* have to go in pairs, and they're full of . . . women.'

'*We're* women, Briggsy. You *have* had your eyes shut.'

'I know, Bernice,' he said patiently, 'I know, but they're terrible places. Full of prostitutes and that.' He added hurriedly: 'Mind you, I don't go for anything of that sort.'

'You prissy bugger. Why do you go then? Not to listen to the band.' She released him. 'Come on,' she said briskly. 'Either we go to a club or we go home. I can't abide this place.'

Disconsolately Brigg followed her from the floor. She arrived at the table and announced brightly: 'Briggsy's taking us to a club.'

'Gee, that's great,' said Clay boyishly. 'I was just wondering who would go mad first, me or the band.'

Valerie smiled at him and said: 'Right, let's be off.'

'Listen,' warned Brigg. 'Don't blame me if . . .'

'Nobody will,' said Bernice. 'And if a nasty lady tries to rape you we'll tell her you're under age.'

They went out from the chill of the dance floor and into the warm enclosing night. 'I went to a place,' said Clay reflectively, 'when I first got into town. The name I forgot, but I can show the cab driver where.'

In the taxi Brigg's apprehension increased as he realized the route they were taking, plunging into blind panic when, on Clay's order, they drew up outside the Liberty Club. 'Not this one,' he said desperately. 'There's a better one up the street.'

'No!' announced Bernice determinedly. 'We'll go in here. I trust the Yank's good judgement. Come on.'

254

Brigg prayed that Juicy Lucy had taken the night off. But she had not. The moment they reached their dim table he could see her sitting unaccompanied on the far side of the floor. He hurried and grabbed a chair inside Bernice's position so that she would shelter him from Lucy. But he knew he could not remain unseen for long. The Chinese eye may be narrow but it observes much, especially when it spends so many hours in the rosy darkness of a low-class club.

Fortunately Bernice and Valerie decided to go to the cloakroom. Immediately they had moved out of view, Brigg rushed across the dance floor like a skater. Lucy looked at him coldly. 'Ticket?' she said. 'You want dance, you have ticket.'

'Lucy,' he pleaded. 'Don't frig about, love. Listen, I've had to bring this bird out. She's an officer's daughter, see, and it was a sort of order. Please, love, don't come over and say anything . . .' He looked over his shoulder towards the Ladies Room.

'I don't know you, squaddie,' said Lucy regarding him stonily. 'You get ticket or you fuck off. Okay?'

'Okay,' he acquiesced, backing away. 'I'll come and see you and explain. How's the little boy? Okay?'

'You stay with hofficer's daughter,' she said loftily. 'You no good at bed anyway.'

Brigg got back to the table to see Clay staring at him. 'You know her too, do you?' he said.

'Know her? Of course I do, you nut. That's why I didn't want . . .' He stopped. 'What d'you mean?' he asked suspiciously. 'Have you been having a rumble there as well?'

'Sure,' replied Clay. 'She didn't say she was promised to you, pal. We had a couple of great rolls before I reported to Panglin, and I came down one Sunday afternoon and had me a little light relief. You know . . . at the apartment . . .' He grinned wickedly and whirled his finger like a spiral staircase. Brigg frowned. 'She's not mine,' he shrugged ill-temperedly. 'She's anybody's who's got ten dollars.'

'Five,' corrected Clay, still grinning. 'Five if she likes you a little.'

'Bollocks,' grunted Brigg ungraciously. 'I used to have her for nothing, mate.' Suddenly he looked hurt and his voice dropped. 'Now I'll never be able to see her again,' he complained.

'I thought you didn't need to. I understood you were in love, buddy.'

'Well I am,' muttered Brigg. 'But you never know, do you?'

'What don't you know?' inquired Bernice over his shoulder. The girls were suddenly standing behind them.

'Nothing, nothing,' improvised Brigg standing up. I just said you never know what these places are going to be like until you've tried them.'

'I think it's sensational,' said Valerie. 'Don't you, Bernie?'

'Sensational,' agreed Bernice. 'Those Chinese girls in the toilet were terrific. Ever so funny. Imitating blokes they had been dancing with. I suppose you've got to have a sense of humour to be a whore.'

'You need one to be a nurse,' observed Valerie.

Bernice nodded and her lips tightened. 'It's still bodies, that's for sure,' she said. She turned to Brigg. A waiter was standing behind them. 'We're drinking whisky,' she said blandly. 'Straight.'

Brigg raised his eyebrows at Clay, who nodded and smiled hopefully. 'Four scotches,' said Brigg. 'The big sort.'

The floor had cleared and the band now took up their instruments to play the next tune. Before a note had come from them, however, a fattened figure, sweating in green uniform with shorts and long stockings, was waltzing at the centre of the floor, his back to them.

'Eggy,' said Clay at once.

'It is,' confirmed Brigg. 'Fancy him being here.'

The music began and Corporal Eggington's plump legs parted and came together as though he were performing the waltz by alternately standing at ease and coming to clumsy attention. His back was still to them.

'He's dancing by himself,' observed Valerie slowly. 'There's nobody on the other side of him.'

'Blimey, you're right,' said Brigg as the voluminous soldier revolved. His arms and his expression were equally vacant. He swung his imaginary partner into a wide, cumbersome turn, opened his eyes and saw them watching him. He halted, grimaced drunkenly, and lumbered towards their table.

''Lo, Briggsy, 'lo, Yank, 'lo, girls,' he commenced. 'I've been celebrating . . . really celebrating . . . all by myself.'

257

'We can see that, Eggy,' commented Brigg. 'What are you celebrating?'

'My spots!' exclaimed Eggington with fat delight. He thrust his coarse sweating face close into the light of the small lamp on their table. 'Look – all gone! Every one gone.'

'So the Japanese sandman did the trick after all,' said Clay.

'Mudman,' corrected Eggy. 'Oooooh, it didn't 'arf hurt getting that stuff off. It made me cry, I can tell you. But they're gone, boys. All my spots are gone.'

Suddenly Juicy Lucy materialized at his bulging, shining cheek, her expression sweet and cool. 'You like to dance with me, sir? she inquired of Eggington. Brigg felt his face flame. Clay's astonishment solidified. The girls nodded approvingly like children listening to a happy story.

'Dance? With you?' gasped Eggy unable to credit the words. 'Sure, miss, I will. 'Course I will. For you.'

She held out her slim, creamy arms and the body of Corporal Eggington fell into them like a wet and overloaded sack. He pawed and clutched her. Brigg had to grip himself to his chair. Lucy smiled serenely and put her miniature cheek on Eggy's damp shoulder. She giggled something into his great red ear. He manoeuvred her ponderously so that her back was facing their table. She was wearing a black evening dress open down to the ultimate vertebra of her spine, showing the superb inlet of her finely planed back, sloped and soft in the lights. She swayed in the hapless corporal's grasp, letting her

258

small buttocks flick to and fro within a few inches of Brigg's tormented eyes.

'Steady, boy, you're with me, remember,' Bernice said in his ear. He turned to look at her. She was smiling dumpily, with the shadows being thrown unkindly on to her face from the table-lamp. Bernice returned to her admiration of the long back and revolving bottom. 'She's lovely,' she said. 'Don't you think so, Val?'

'Gorgeous,' agreed Valerie generously. 'Her job seems to suit her.'

'I'd half a mind to take it up myself,' said Bernice dreamily. 'If it only meant I could move like that.'

Brigg felt his stomach contract as Lucy kissed Eggington's raw, wet cheek. 'I yours, lover,' she confirmed loudly.

'No spots, no pimples, see,' bawled Eggy over his shoulder. 'No spots.'

The quartet drank their whiskies, danced, had another round, then the girls paid for a round. The club began to revolve spitefully before Brigg's eyes. Lucy was never out of Eggington's arms. Brigg tried to see if she were collecting tickets from him, but he saw none exchanged. His three companions were laughing and singing while he fell to being morose and withdrawn. None of them seemed to observe his mood. Then, like a huge green jelly, Eggington advanced over the dance floor towards them. 'No spots!' he cried again. 'All bloody gone! Look, Briggsy, look!'

Extravagantly he pulled open his shirt, revealing a puffy white stomach and overhung chest, glistening with his sweat. 'No spots! No pimples!' he roared. Off came his shirt and he whirled before them like some hideous spinning-top. His final turn brought his fleshy rear towards them and he began to swing his lower portions in a heavy impersonation of Lucy's seductive movements. Brigg saw her laughing into her hands on the distant side of the floor. The other dancers had backed away to watch.

'Look!' exclaimed Eggington extravagantly. 'No pimples!'

In one movement he unclipped his webbing belt and had pulled down his jungle shorts and underpants. His buttocks quivered before them like the ears of an African elephant. Screams and cries filled the room. Brigg felt the hysterical Bernice clutch his arm so fiercely he shouted in pain and pulled the arm away. Eggington, apparently thinking the call was to attract his attention, revolved towards them, an enormous grin plastered across his crude face, his chest heaving, his shorts clinging to his boots and his spectacular donkey-cock swinging between his knees like a recently rung bell-rope.

Amid the bedlam of laughter Brigg was conscious of a rush of figures from the darkened back of the room. At first he thought it was the Military Police. But when the first of the men gained the floor he saw they were Chinese. The trouble-handlers were making for Eggington.

'Let's get him out of here,' grunted Clay close to Brigg's ear. He moved forward as he said it, and Brigg reluctantly went to assist him. They arrived a fraction before the first Chinese and each caught the stupidly grinning Eggington by one of his rubbery upper arms. Brigg was conscious of seeing Bernice and Valerie waving hysterically with Eggington's abandoned shirt and shorts, shrieking as they did so. Then he was engulfed in a mess of fighting, clutching arms and legs, shouts, faces and fists.

Fortunately they had immediate allies. It did not take long to pick sides in a fight in the Liberty Club. Brigg felt a flat hand chop sideways across his face. Lights revolved exotically and he found himself sagging against a chair, with Bernice extravagantly pouring somebody's beer over his face. 'We're winning, Briggsy!' she shouted. 'Eggy's getting away!'

Anxiously he caught her hand and fumbled forward through the fighting crowd. Eggington, like some large pallid balloon, was suddenly raised above heads by a dozen pairs of comrades' hands and was carried drunkenly and triumphantly naked above the resisting natives to the main door. His boots kicked as he went. Uproar consumed the place, shouts, screams, fists and boots flying in the semi-light. Above it all Eggington, borne like a fat queen, found time to wave to the crowd.

Brigg and Bernice found themselves wedged against the door. A combined push and a callous trampling over two dormant musicians gained them enough space to escape. Clay and Valerie were sitting on the pavement across the road, weak and weeping with laughter. Eggington was in the custody of the Military Police, who were humping him into a jeep. Bernice rushed forward at the same instant, waving his shirt, and his shorts. Eggy had subsided into the jeep with his socked and booted legs out straight and at a high angle, like naval guns. 'His clothes,' shouted Bernice. 'Here, mate, his pants.' The sergeant, under the red cap, grinned lasciviously at her. 'Stone me,' he said taking the garments, 'what's he got that I ain't got?'

'No spots!' came the exultant howl from Eggington. 'No pimples!'

14

'How do we get over the wall, then?' asked Bernice. She was grinning drunk, leaning against Brigg as he looked up at the unpromising barrier to Little Jim's. Clay and Valerie, uncaring, were dancing close together in the shadow thrown by the same wall. The street was warm and hollow, splashed by random lamps and fingered by oblique moonbeams. On the opposite side of the road an Indian watchman was upon his bench, immersed in snoring sleep.

'We have to climb,' shrugged Brigg. For him the night had taken its emotional and physical toll.

'Climb! Up there? God help us, Briggsy love, I'm not Tarzan.'

'It's the only way in,' argued Brigg dismally. 'It's all very well for you and me, Bernice. I'm thinking of Val and the Yank.'

She regarded him with mixed confusion and curiosity. 'I'm not sure what that means,' she said. 'But whatever it means it's still a hell of a long way up for a wall.'

'There's no other way. They guard the gate like Stalingrad.'

'I'll go,' said Valerie carelessly. She and Clay had

finished their dance and were standing regarding the wall. 'I can get over that.'

'Thatagirl,' enthused Clay. He grinned like a torn cat at Brigg then screwed his eyes and regarded the problem. 'It's got to be Plan X,' he concluded. 'I get up first, then I haul Val up after me. There's that ledge just there. Give me a ride, Briggsy, and I think I can make the top.'

Doubtfully Brigg hoisted Clay up the face of the wall. The whisky affected the balance of both so that they swayed like an inverted pendulum. Brigg sagged at the legs and Clay moved across the face of the wall, first one way, then the other. Brigg's face, already sore from the blow he had taken in the Liberty Club, was rubbed roughly against the stonework. Eventually, however, Clay gained his shoulders, then, unceremoniously using Brigg's head as a one-foot step, he gained first the brief ledge and then the apex of the wall.

'Okay, honey,' he whispered down to the watching faces. 'Come on up. It's a great view.'

'Talking about views – you keep your eyes down,' said Bernice bossily nudging Brigg. 'No peeping up Val's skirt.'

'He won't need to,' said Valerie practically. 'I'm going to take this dress off. I'll mess it up otherwise.'

Brigg blinked and Clay almost tumbled from the wall as she unzipped her dress and caught it as it collapsed about her ankles. She stepped out of it and stood unembarrassed in white brassiere and briefs. 'Hang on to that, Bernie,' she asked. Bernice took the garment and Valerie, kicking away her shoes also, stood in the stirrup which Brigg made with his hands and, with some agility, put her feet on his shoulders so that her ankles were brushing his ears. Clay reached down and with a decisive pull hauled her to the coping of the wall. She sat in front of him so that they were like two people on an elephant.

'I suppose I'd better do a striptease too,' decided Bernice. She flipped off her shoes and wriggled out of her dress, handing the items to the bemused Brigg, together with those of Valerie.

'Christ, I'm getting like an old clothes shop here,' said Brigg. Bernice kissed him in a perfunctory way then, with slightly more difficulty than Valerie, scaled the wall by the same method. When her feet were on Brigg's shoulders he realized how big they were compared to those of Clay's girl.

Gasping and grasping, Bernice reached the top of the wall and sat astride it in front of Valerie. Her arrival had the immediate effect of causing panic. She faltered, slewed over and almost fell. Her wide eyes stared down in instant fright at Brigg on the ground. 'Oh God,' she kept saying. 'Oh God. It's high.' Her terror transmitted itself to Valerie. Both girls whimpered and clung to each other. Then Bernice cried: 'I'm stuck! I can't move! Help me, Briggsy. Please . . . help.'

Her fright and Valerie's attempt to hold her started the other girl swaying too. Clay, like the helmsman in a panicky galley, tried to calm them and hold them straight. 'Quit!' he snapped. 'Quit it. We'll all be off.'

'Get a grip,' Brigg called up hoarsely. 'Get a bloody grip, Bernice.'

The girls froze, their swaying stopping and they remained stiff and nailed with fear on the coping.

A soft Indian voice spoke next to Brigg: 'My goodness, sahib. That is unusual sight.'

Brigg stared around. The watchman had awakened and had padded across the street to witness the scene. 'Bugger off,' said Brigg rudely.

'Gladly I would bugger off,' replied the Indian with soft politeness. 'But also I will stay to help. What is the matter?'

'They're stuck,' said Brigg. 'Can't you see? They're stuck on the bloody wall.'

'And with few clothes,' observed the Indian primly. 'Perhaps, sahib, I could hire ladder for the rescue.'

'Hire a ladder?' snapped Brigg. 'Where the hell are you going to hire one at this hour?'

'From myself,' smiled the man benignly. 'I have charge of many ladders, all sizes and natures, in the compound over the street. I could hire one from myself.'

Brigg glanced up at the three figures frozen like a frieze above him. Bernice rolled her eyes, clutching the curved stone between her bare thighs. 'Oh all right,' muttered Brigg. 'It had better be cheap.'

'Most cheap, sir. I will hire cheapest ladder for you. Five dollars.'

'Five dollars! Bugger off,' returned Brigg. 'I could *buy* a ladder for five dollars.'

'There are no ladder shops open to buy,' pointed

out the Indian logically. 'But I have ladder to hire. Five dollars.'

'Thieving sod,' grumbled Brigg. He took five dollars from his pocket and said: 'Get the ladder first.'

'Five dollars first, please, sahib,' responded the Indian with a minor bow. 'You can trust *me.*'

The innuendo was followed by a tight cry from Bernice. 'Give it to him for God's sake. I'm going to fall in a minute.'

Brigg thrust the money ungraciously into the Indian's thin waiting palm and he faded into the shadow across the street, returning quickly with a bamboo ladder. 'You can now get back your friends,' he smiled placing it against the wall.

'We want them inside not out,' muttered Brigg. 'I'll chuck the ladder back across in a minute.' He mounted it at once, gained the summit of the wall, where Bernice clutched him as though he were a fireman. He pulled the ladder up swinging it like a see-saw over the wall and into the grounds of Little Jim's.

'Cool, cool,' commented Clay appreciatively from his tandem seat on the wall.

Brigg went down into the garden first and held the bamboo steps while the others descended gratefully. He handed Bernice and Valerie their dresses and shoes. Without her shoes Bernice looked squat beside the other girl. Then he and Clay heaved the ladder over the wall again to the Indian awaiting its return. The cry 'God help the King' came faintly back to them.

They looked about them. The moon lay folded across the gardens and grounds of Little Jim's, night birds fidgeted and conversed in the leaves, but apart from the light at the distant gatehouse everywhere was serene and undisturbed. Brigg led the way, like the leader of a commando party, and they followed linking hands. Clay and Valerie slipped into Clay's chalet, Valerie throwing them a brief kiss and Clay despatching a quick pleased wink in Brigg's direction. Brigg opened his own door for Bernice. They went in slowly. He felt deflated.

'Valerie didn't mind, then,' he said, a trifle parsimoniously, 'coming in here?'

'No, why should she? She likes him a lot. And once that girl's got her mind made up, that's it. It's made up for good.'

'I feel terrible,' complained Brigg. 'Christ, what a night.'

They undressed with hardly a glance at each other and climbed in opposite sides of the bed. It's narrowness meant that they collided immediately and lay alongside each other. Brigg thought he could hear creaking from the other room. 'Shall we do it?' he said to Bernice.

'If you like,' she answered. 'After all, we climbed the wall.'

He sighed and rolled on top of her, his face wedging between her head and her left shoulder. Her hand moved about his groin. 'Where's my wandering boy tonight?' she said.

'He's there,' answered Brigg huffily. 'If you look.'

'I'll get a torch,' she returned. She caught his flaccid penis in her fingers. 'Now there's a thing,' she said sarcastically. 'He's gone and died.'

'I feel terribly rough,' complained Brigg. 'Can you sort of play about with him a bit?'

'Play about with him? If I'd known, I'd have brought my bat and ball. Why don't *you* do something. Go on, think of something *sexy*. Like the Chinese girl's arse. That ought to start you off.'

'Lay off, Bernice!' he snapped, rolling off her and almost over the side of the bed on to the floor. They lay stiff and unhappy. 'Look,' said Brigg eventually, 'I'm sorry. I just feel tired out, that's all. And we had all that whisky. Do you mind if we just sleep?'

'I don't mind at all.'

'All right then, give us a kiss.'

They kissed with some summoned warmth. 'Goodnight, love,' he mumbled.

'Goodnight, soldier,' she sighed.

Their night was uncomfortable through clinging to each other from the sheer necessity of support to prevent them tipping from the bed. There was broad bright light at the flowered curtains when they were awakened by the sound of frail female singing outside the chalet door:

> 'All things bright and beautiful,
> All creatures great and small.'

'Jesus,' said Brigg appropriately. 'Sunday, I forgot, they bring you tea on Sunday!'

'Put some clothes on and go and get it,' whispered Bernice. 'Just keep the door closed behind you.' She glanced at his startled face. 'God, Briggsy,' she said, 'you've got a huge black eye.'

The teetering singing continued and there was a modest knock on the door. Brigg looked around wildly. 'Put this on,' said Bernice firmly. She handed him the tennis eye-shade. 'They'll think you're just going to play.'

Brigg plunged into his tennis shirt and shorts. He took the eyeshade from her and put it on his forehead, cocking it slightly over his sore eye. Then he opened the door and smiled an uncertain smile at three ladies; Miss Phillimore and two others, strangers, stood there with a tea-trolley.

'Ah,' exclaimed Miss Phillimore. 'Mr Brigg. All ready for the court, I see.' She beamed at the other ladies then said to him: 'This is Mrs Fernley and Mrs Mason, who assist us on Sundays.'

Brigg nodded and mumbled a greeting to the pair of prim women from beneath his eyeshade. Miss Phillimore went on: 'A cheerful cup of tea, and a lively chorus. We think they start a Sunday so well. Here's your cup . . . sugar? Yes, of course . . . there. Now . . .' she hesitated. 'Would you perhaps like to sing just a couple of verses with us?'

Brigg swallowed heavily. At that moment, the neighbouring door opened and Clay came out, clean and cool, and accepted a cup of tea. They stood there with the three ladies and sang:

> 'All things bright and beautiful,
> All creatures great and small,
> All things wise and wonderful,
> The Lord God made them all.'

When the chorus had finished, not risking a glance towards Clay, Brigg gave a short bow and backed through the door with his tea balanced in front of his nose. The trolley, with the chorusing voices, trundled on its journey.

Bernice was lying concealed on the floor at the far side of the bed. He saw her hand groping up and then her face tight with scarcely repressed mirth. She buried it in the bedclothes and emitted a muffled howl.

'Oh, Briggsy, darling, I would have given a year of my life to have seen that. You . . . you . . . singing. "All things bright and beautiful" . . . And with that shiner . . . I was in stitches.'

Brigg had collapsed, laughing also, across the foot of the bed. 'You ought . . . you ought to have seen the Yank out there too . . . singing.'

'Oh no! Him as well!' She began to tweet softly,

> 'All things bright and beautiful,
> All creatures great and small.'

Brigg leaned over and grasped her in his arms. 'I could show you something bright and beautiful,' he beamed.

'A creature great *and* small,' she returned mischievously. 'Are you feeling better this morning?'

271

'Sorry, love. Honest,' he said. He leaned her backwards so that her plump naked breasts were stretched taut, their nipples pointing like blunt arrows.

'Take your eyeshade off then,' she giggled. 'You look like somebody trying to peep under a door.'

He laughed and pushed the shade from his forehead. She undid the tennis shirt and shorts, undressing him professionally while he was arched above her.

'My God, that's better,' she smiled when he was bare. 'Come to nurse.' She addressed the remark to his member which she cosseted in her palms and massaged with a rolling motion. He kissed her and while he did so he lowered himself against her body, the sensation of her enveloping him. They slipped together easily, joined and rocked unhurriedly in each other's cradled arms. He watched her face and saw it change like a season before his gaze. Her mouth was open, gasping with each movement as if she were attempting a commentary, her eyes clenched, her forehead rutted; then as they reached the pitch she cried out as though in hurt before a clearness moved across her features and she lay perspiring, serene, and with a knowing grin, below him.

'So *that's* what it's like,' she whispered. 'Oh, Briggsy, the geese certainly went south that time. Didn't you hear them quacking?'

'Geese don't quack,' mentioned Brigg quietly. 'They honk. I wasn't so clumsy that time, was I?'

'And I wasn't so scared. It was lovely, Briggsy, honest. I really enjoyed it.'

272

They lay, letting their sweat cool, for a long time. Then they sat up and shared the now luke-warm tea and then embraced again and lay motionless.

'It *was* a bit of a laugh last night, wasn't it really?' remembered Brigg eventually. 'Poor old Eggy, carried starkers out of the Liberty. And you getting stuck on top of the wall.'

She nodded and smiled: 'It was some night, all right,' she said.

'It'll be Christmas in ten days,' said Brigg. 'We must do something at Christmas.'

Her expression changed. She regarded him sorrowfully. 'I won't be able to, Briggsy, darling,' she said.

Brigg drew a fraction away from her. 'Why not?' he said. 'Surely you're not on duty all the time.'

'It's worse than that, love,' she said. 'I didn't tell you before, but I've got to now. A month ago Val and I put in for a transfer to Colombo hospital. We . . . we decided we weren't tough enough for this place.'

'Oh God, no. You're *not* going to Colombo?'

She turned her head from him. 'Posting came through yesterday,' she mumbled. 'We're flying out on Christmas Eve.'

Stunned, he lay against her. 'Colombo,' he muttered. 'I won't see you.'

'It's a long walk,' she agreed sadly.

'How long?' he asked. 'How long will you be there?'

'Until the end of my tour. End of next year. Then I'll go home. You'll be home then.'

'I hope,' muttered Brigg. He examined her. Her face was pretty but podgy. 'We'll meet up then.'

'Yes,' she said. 'Make sure we keep in touch.'

15

Christmas came with tropical thunderstorms beating flamboyantly through the sky, pouring noisy rain on the Panglin garrison. The monsoon drains gargled through the darkness like the sound of a prolonged strangulation.

Midnight lightning flapped about the barrack room walls; the soldiers groaned under the hammer of the thunder. Only Corporal Field, the imaginary adventurer, enjoyed it, sitting tight in his bed, a sheet across his shoulders, pretending he was under gunfire in a trench on the Western Front.

Then the storm stalked away, leaving an hour's calm before a raiding wind arrived, bending palm trees like bows and sweeping along the barrack blocks, banging the doors as though it were searching for fugitives.

The wind's din awoke most of the soldiers, and while some rolled with grumbles to pull a single blanket over their sheet, others remained awake for a while listening to the fury of the night weather. Brigg sat up, motionless in the dark; Tasker in the next bed did the same and lit a cigarette. It was three o'clock on Christmas morning.

'I wonder has Santa come yet?' said Brigg.

'If he has, he's missed me again. Rotten old sod,' muttered Tasker.

Brigg grimaced in the dark. He said slowly: 'I don't reckon Christmas was meant for hot countries somehow. It won't fit.'

'Palestine's a hot country,' replied Tasker. 'That's where it began, so it must fit. The babe in a manger and all that. Shepherds.'

'True enough,' Briggs conceded solemnly. 'But that's a *dry*, hot country for a kick-off. Desert and stuff. It's not a sticky wet dump like this, is it?'

'Palestine's cold in the winter.' Lantry sat up in his bed. 'My old man was in the Palestine Police and he's got pictures of Jerusalem with snow up to your armpits.'

'Get away,' said Brigg.

'Snow,' murmured Tasker nostalgically. 'Just think of it. All white and terrific over everything.'

'Boy, you should see the snow we get in Colorado,' came Clay's voice in the dark. He remained lying beneath his sheet. 'Eight, ten feet.'

'You always reckon you have something better than us,' sniffed Lantry.

'Most of the time we do,' answered Clay coolly. 'Great deep snow. The ski-ing's great, and mountains with fir trees, and the greatest sunsets . . .'

'I wouldn't mind making a snowman,' sighed Tasker to stop him.

'It's always so quiet,' remembered Brigg. 'Dead quiet everything gets after snow.'

'We should have been home by now,' contributed Lantry. 'A few brown ales in the boozer on

276

Christmas Eve. Sneaking in with the little kids' presents and dropping them because you're half pissed.' His voice sank. 'The last year I was home I had our Billy's train-set tearing around the bloody house at three o'clock in the morning.'

'There's a bloke in our street who's got a television set,' boasted Tasker. 'My mum and dad are going to watch it after their Christmas Dinner.'

'Makes you sick don't it?' said Lantry.

'Stuck here,' agreed Tasker. 'Brigg's right, really. Christmas don't seem right in these parts.'

'I don't know how you make that out,' said Sandy Jacobs joining in through the darkness. He sat up and took a light from Tasker's cigarette. 'The star was in the East wasn't it? Right. Well this *is* the bleeding East.'

'Not the *Far* East, though, was it?' argued Brigg. 'Anyway I don't know what it's got to do with you, mate. It's not even your bloody religion.'

'Piss off,' responded Jacobs without heat. 'It's just a yarn, that's all. At least *my* religion is based on *history*, with everything written down. Not some fairy story.'

'It's *not*,' argued Brigg. 'It *happened* all right, matey. And right in your mob's back garden too. And *you* can't see it. Just because it's a bit dodgy from the facts getting passed down over donkey's years, you don't believe it. Disbelieving bloody Jew.'

The remark was without animosity and Jacobs remained unstirred, blowing smoke into the barrack-room dark.

'Stars in the East,' he murmured. 'Shepherds seeing angels. Wise men. Virgin birth. It's just like Cinderella. Make a good pantomime.'

'Flaming cheek,' returned Brigg. 'Don't you take the piss out of our Christianity, mucker. What about Moses going up the mountain to get the so-called commandments, then? That's a load of old shit.'

'And Moses in the bullrushes?' added Lantry loyally. 'That's another yarn.'

'It's more believable than your virgin birth,' observed Jacobs, still unruffled. 'How d'you explain that then, archbishop?'

The remark was directed towards Brigg. 'How do I know?' returned Brigg. 'But it *could* happen. You don't have to have a *reason* for everything. Where did that wind come from just now? Go on, explain that.'

'Let's be honest,' interrupted Tasker. 'The Virgin Mary bit *is* a bit hard to swallow. That's what's so worrying about all this religious stuff. You've got to take everything on *trust*. Nobody comes up with any *evidence*. I'd like to have a bit of proof now and again. I'd like just to meet one bloke what's actually come back after being dead. Just one. I'd have a bit more confidence in the future, then.'

The grim logic depressed them. 'Some of it can be explained,' said Brigg eventually but with no sureness. 'People with brains can explain it. Here – ask old Fundrum. He'll know. Give him a shove.'

Lantry got up from his bed and padded across to the long pile that was Private Fundrum. 'Brainy,' he whispered, giving the form a modest push. 'Brainy, wake up.'

The strained face of Fundrum manoeuvred itself free of the sheet. 'Brainy,' asked Lantry at the first blink, 'what do you reckon about the virgin birth?'

Fundrum stared at him and then looked slowly around at the dim forms sitting in their beds. 'Fantasy,' he yawned. 'Pure undiluted fantasy.'

'Knackers,' Brigg said stoutly in the dark.

The sun looked as though it had been up all night. By mid-morning on Christmas Day it appeared heavy-lidded through the low swollen clouds, and by its turgid, steamy light the soldiers, arrayed in impromptu fancy-dress, paraded around the barrack square to the beat of half a dozen enamel mugs struck rhythmically with eating-irons. The idea had begun spontaneously in one barrack room and had spread eagerly through each of the three floors in that block. Oddments were found from many places; sheets, mosquito nets, buckets, pails and brooms were used. A trio of youths marched abreast, their heads projecting through the holes of a line of three joined thunderboxes which normally squatted above the open lavatory holes in the ablutions.

As the strange and enthusiastic procession progressed around the perimeter of the square, more soldiers tumbled from the barrack blocks wearing their hasty and fancy costumes. They were mostly the young National Servicemen, although Morris Morris featured splendidly as a large green mermaid with a great tail made from a mosquito net. Most of the older soldiers, however, lined the balconies of the blocks and clapped and cheered as the parade performed another circuit, like fathers applauding the fun and initiative of their sons.

Brigg, clad in a pair of leopard-skin swimming trunks, and carrying a broomstick handle with a cardboard spearpoint, walked with Clay as a tall angel in a long sheet, and Tasker, with pillows up his back, as an over-acted Quasimodo. Lantry, in towels and brown-polished face, was an Indian prince. Patsy Foster and Sidney Villiers were appropriately fairies, and Sandy Jacobs, less aptly, a dog-collared vicar.

Spontaneously they carolled 'Good King Wenceslas Looked Out' to a marching beat sounded by the tappers of the enamel mugs. They marched from the square up the garrison road. Some Chinese women, bearing loads on their heads to the village, regarded them with no amazement whatever, but merely paused in their walk to let the procession go by, then continued on the journey. Another group of village people were descending the road farther on, and these too watched the march with the blank faces of those who have long ceased to be amazed at the antics of the British soldier. A child on the back of one of the women cried briefly, but that was all.

Past the cookhouse, where the Catering Corps men came out in clouds of yuletide steam to wave ladles and shout and receive insults; past the sergeants' mess, where the senior NCOs like deacons, decorously emerged, drinks in hands, to nod approval of the unofficial parade.

Then along the row of houses that accommodated what the army quaintly called Married Families, and here the wives and children of the garrison came to the gates and laughed and called as though relieved that someone had done something for Christmas. Amahs, the Chinese servants that the army provided, waved their dusters and brooms from upper windows.

Although nothing had been planned, the ebullient column knew where it was going. Led by the large mermaid Morris Morris, it took the curve in the road from the Married Families' quarters and marched, singing bravely, up the incline to the solitary house of the Commanding Officer. There on his lawn and the gravel drive they stood singing carols. Lt Colonel Bromley Pickering appeared at a bedroom window, wearing a tartan towel, and stood still, listening to them.

Raggedly they clattered to the conclusion of 'Noel! Noel!', having plunged through its strong melody and its descants with abandon. An uneasy silence dropped over them, a hundred men all in ridiculous costumes. The window opened and the Commanding Officer stood there, his good eye blinking, his blank one shining steadily. Neither he nor the young soldiers seemed to know what was expected of them next. Then into the vacuum the thick, theatrical Welsh voice of Morris Morris rose like a fine but heavy bird in the close air. Mermaid tail across his shoulder, silver paper crown and trident amiss, eyes closed, and with no embarrassment, he sang:

> 'See amid the winter snow,
> Bom for us on earth below.
> See the Tender Lamb appears,
> Promised from eternal years.'

Some of them knew the chorus. Morris Morris led those who almost did. The others sang anything that fitted:

> 'Hail, thou ever blessed morn,
> Hail Redemption's happy dawn.
> Sing through all Jerusalem
> Christ is born in Bethlehem!'

When they had finished, almost choked with shyness and pleasure, the Colonel waved his hand and called throatily: 'Merry Christmas, chaps. All of you.'

He almost staggered back into the room while they cheered him madly and then set off down the path again towards the barracks and their Christmas dinner. It was several minutes before the Colonel could bring himself to go to the window again. He looked out. Their strident voices floated up the valley to him. The drive and the lawn were empty. Sitting on the sundial on the edge of the lawn was his stamp album.

*

By tradition the officers served the other ranks at Christmas Dinner. A few performed the annual chore sour-faced, as though it were spoiling their day; but others took it with a good nature and an unhearing ear, or a ready return to sporadic ribaldry, circling the tables of waiting men clad in white aprons and cook's lofty hats. The Commanding Officer presided at the carving of the many turkeys.

Sergeants sat at a special table, decent with a white cloth, and above them on a raised section, looking out over the five hundred munching men, was a further table for the warrant officers and most senior NCOs. At its centre, his face a compendium of suffering despite the wearing of yuletide slippers below the cloth, sat RSM Woods. It was like a vignette of the Last Supper.

'Wonder where they got the turkeys?' observed Brigg, watching his knife grind against the baked flesh.

'Australia,' grunted Lantry through his chewing. 'They flew them up specially. Sergeant-cook told me.'

'The flying's exhausted this poor bastard,' commented Tasker gnawing at the unyielding flesh.

There was free beer, or wine for the senior NCOs if they preferred, which most of them did not. Coloured and funny hats emerged with their Christmas pudding, and the great mess-hall, drooping with greenery, became the enclosure for the strangely empty noise of men attempting to enjoy an occasion without the presence of women.

'Old Boot!' some squaddie bellowed from one side of the huge place. 'Old Boot!' rose the dutiful reply from the middle. 'Old Boot' shouted someone from the far end. It could have referred to the turkey, but it did not. It was the meaningless shout, the spirit-raiser, the failed battle cry.

'Wonder where we'll be this time next year?' ventured Brigg.

'Still here,' said Tasker solemnly. 'Same bleeding turkey too, I wouldn't wonder.'

'Korea,' suggested Jacobs. 'I reckon. Mud and bullets.'

'Home,' said Clay optimistically. He raised his beer. 'I think we'll all be home.' He took on a thoughtful face. 'Mountain turkey, sweet potatoes, candied carrots, venison . . .'

'Oh Christ, there he goes again,' mumbled Tasker. He grimaced at Clay. 'You go back to your bloody hilly-billies, mate. Give me Canterbury any time.'

There was a small silence. Then Brigg said: 'What d'you mean, Task, Canterbury? You come from Shoreditch.'

'All right, all right,' conceded Tasker, swigging into his beer as he said it. 'So I do. I just thought Canterbury sounded better that's all. If the Yank's always boasting, why can't I?'

'I bet the kids have hardly slept a wink,' said Morris Morris, his rubber face folded in thought. 'It won't be light yet and I bet they're all awake, all over the country. I hardly ever got any kip on Christmas Eve. Hardly ever.'

The young men looked at each other in embarrassment. Then Jacobs said: 'You had a nice Christmas card from your kids, didn't you, Taff? The one pinned on your locker.'

'Ah, you had a dekko at it, did you?' acknowledged Morris Morris, his face close to his pudding.

'Yes, I had a look.'

'Drew that themselves,' nodded Morris.

'Say,' said Clay. 'I saw it too, I thought it was great. Reindeer and Santa Claus. Real good.'

'Thank you, Yank,' mumbled Morris politely. 'Very nice of you to mention it. Lovely kids they are.'

'What I want to know,' put in Brigg strenuously – the subject needed changing before Morris Morris, and possibly the rest of them, burst into tears in the middle of Christmas Dinner. 'What I want to know is how Sandy Jacobs here gets all the Christmas cards he gets?'

'My dad's shop,' explained Jacobs with a dark grin. 'He sells cards, and every October he has a clear-out of all the old and damaged stock and he sends it off to me. When I was a kid I used to keep a scrap-book and stick things in, and I think he believes I still do.'

'You ought to write home and tell him that what you've been sticking in out here is different,' commented Brigg chewing.

Morris Morris looked up, his sadness suddenly vanished. He had thought of something funny to say. 'And that's not been stuck in a book either!' he exploded.

They all laughed wildly, the beer and the urgent requirement to enjoy Christmas overcoming everything else. Morris Morris thumped his flabby fist like a gavel on the table, making the plates chatter and the beer swish around the glasses like a captured storm. Then Brigg looked round, across the hundreds of sweating heads, and saw Grainger coming towards them.

'Here's Uncle Holly,' he muttered.

'Maybe he wants to play Russian roulette,' suggested Clay looking over the eating heads too. 'Or shoot an apple from some guy's nut.'

Grainger neared them with his assembled smile. He stood behind Morris Morris and put his hands familiarly on the older man's puffy shoulders. 'Hello, Taffy,' he said confidingly. 'How's it going?'

The thick eyebrows were raised. 'All right, thank you, sir. Lovely.'

'Merry Christmas, lads,' said Grainger beaming around. They returned the greeting with a fraudulent friendliness and temporary familiarity. He was like a schoolmaster patronizing his pupils. And yet they could never forget that he was younger than they were.

'What did you think of the turkey?' he inquired.

'All right, sir.'

'Nice.'

'Not bad.'

'Not too bad.'

He leaned over, stiffly from the waist, so that his head was just above them. 'I thought it was fucking awful, lads,' he said in his confiding way. 'I think the sergeant-cook ought to have been stuffed, not the turkeys.'

They laughed dutifully but shortly. They knew him. 'I tell you what,' he said with boyish enthusiasm. He leaned between Lantry and Tasker, his slim fists on the table. 'When we next get a guard duty up at the depot we'll make up for it.'

Brigg suddenly saw Corporal Dobbie lying dead against the truck in the village street. His mouth dropped open.

'Another one, sir? We'll be going up there again?'

'I expect so. Some of you chaps will,' said Grainger as though it were a sought-after promise. 'And what I propose to do is to take a party shooting. Hunting wild pig. I've been told there have been one or two officers who've taken their lads out into the jungle there and come back with a nice piece of pork. We could get it stuffed and have a feast. How does that sound?' He beamed like a suspect scoutmaster.

They nodded dumbly, a group of seated puppets. Brigg swallowed. 'I didn't realize we'd be going again, sir,' he said.

'Oh yes, I reckon we'll get you another stint up there before you're due home – if you go home that is.' He patted Morris Morris on the shoulder. 'I bet I could fix it so you could come this time, Taffy.' He laughed loudly. 'You could carry the pig back.'

'Oh yes, oh yes, sir,' nodded Morris with wan enthusiasm. He smiled an empty smile up at the young officer. 'I like a bit of fresh pork myself. The crackling I like.'

287

'Good, well I'll see if I can fix it.' He stood upright. 'Fine, fine,' he said beaming around. His gaze went to the sergeants' table and an eager grin filled his narrow boyish face. 'Listen, chaps,' he said leaning over again secretively. 'I must serve Sergeant Wellbeloved with some Christmas pudding.'

He walked away from them. They watched him go, dumbly. He strode to where a cook was doling out bowls of custard and Christmas pudding to the serving officers, took a bowl in each hand, and swung towards the sergeants' table. He leaned over Wellbeloved and let one bowl slip so that the hot custard dropped into the sergeant's lap. Wellbeloved's frenzied howl was heard high over the din of the hundreds. He leapt up, knocking one of his neighbours backwards and danced away from the table, in pain, the yellow substance thick on his shorts and naked knees. Grainger stood back in assumed horror. Wellbeloved ran out, his face scarlet. All the other sergeants, and the senior NCOs on their table, everyone else who had seen it, burst out laughing. Except Brigg's table. They looked at each other in amazement.

'He's mad, that bastard,' muttered Brigg. 'He's stark raving mad.'

On the following day there was a five-a-side football tournament and a comic swimming gala. By six in the evening almost everyone in the barrack room was flat out on their beds in their pre-Christmas position, staring once again at the swishing ceiling fans. Tomorrow they would be back in the military offices. Another year beckoned.

Gravy Browning's table-tennis ball clipped icily against the wall. Conway hovered over a new giant jig-saw, every piece a pleasure. Foster and Villiers were heads together admiring excitedly the houses-for-sale in an elderly copy of *Country Life* lent to them by Corporal Field. Lance-Corporal Williams exhaled deeply as he settled down, puzzlement rammed into every concentrated line of his face, to begin a new volume of *Everyman's Encyclopaedia*, section G to K. Clay was counting the revolutions of the same fan as Brigg. It was a sum with no total.

'Gravy!' shouted Tasker. 'Shut that everlasting bloody row for a bit, can't you.'

'Yes, pack it up,' agreed Lantry. It was the exasperation of idleness towards activity.

The clipping sound continued. Browning called back: 'It were different when I was in the championships, weren't it? Oh yes, it were bloody different then.'

'Well, you're not in the championships now!' shouted Tasker over the top of the lockers. 'And you lost anyway. Lot of good it was us coming to support you.'

'I like bloody that!' The ball clicked and then stopped and Browning's face appeared over the top of a locker. He had jumped on the bed on the far side and now looked directly down on to Tasker's prone head. 'Lot of support I got from you,' he called down. 'You lot pissed off as soon as the bars and the knocking shops were open.'

'Get stuffed,' sniffed Tasker. He would not make anything further of it because Browning was taller and quicker.

'It's a pity *you* don't take up some sport that's nothing to do with what's between your legs,' continued Browning.

'One ball instead of two,' grinned Brigg looking across at Tasker.

'Listen,' said Tasker pushing up on his elbow. 'All I'm asking is just to have a couple of minutes in this bleeding barrack room without that ping-pong ball. It spoils my train of thought.'

'And mine,' said the lugubrious Williams. 'I'm trying to study my encyclopaedia.'

Browning gazed around angrily. 'I never knew so many people *had* bloody thoughts, let alone *trains* of them,' he said. 'Not in this hole.'

'Listen, Gravy,' said Sandy Jacobs reasonably. 'Why don't you go over to the table-tennis room and practise there?'

'There's never anybody over there,' said Browning suddenly vulnerable. 'No one to play with. It's always empty.'

'Well, for Christ's sake, you don't play *against* anybody here in the barrack room,' pointed out Tasker. 'Except the wall.'

Browning's expression descended: 'I just don't like it in the table-tennis room.'

The astonishment that this confession evoked was for some reason never translated into the almost inevitable laughter. Clay nodded seriously. 'I can understand that, Gravy,' he said. 'Playing that game in an empty room must be kinda solitary.'

'It's not like readin' or thinkin' or tossin' yourself off,' agreed Longley, pallid on his distant bed. He spoke as though conversing with himself, for he never expected anyone to listen. 'Ping-pong really *needs* two.'

'Why don't you practise *without* the ball,' suggested Clay kindly. 'Just go through the routine. *Imagine* the ball is there. After all, buddy, when you play against the wall, you have to make-believe there's some guy at the other end of the table, don't you?'

'It wouldn't be the same, Yank,' said Browning seriously. 'I'd look a bit daft playing without a ball anyway.'

'Listen,' put in Brigg, 'why don't you go and play in the ablutions. There's that wall between the thunderboxes. If you can keep it from going into the urinal it would be all right.'

Browning considered the possibility and brightened. 'You know, Briggsy, I might try that. There's just about room there for a tight left-hand spin. Thanks, mate, I'll have a go.'

His head vanished from the top of the locker and they heard him going across the floor on the far side.

'Sit on one of the thunderboxes,' Tasker called derisively after him. 'You can have a crap at the same time.'

'This unit's full of old women and little kids!' Corporal Field suddenly sat up and shouted from his bed at the end. 'Table tennis!'

'Don't shout like that, old dear,' returned Brigg

still flat on his back. 'You'll wake your grandchildren.'

'Wrap up, Brigg,' retorted Field. 'Don't forget I've got two tapes on my arm.' He snarled silently to himself before shutting his eyes tight on the barrack room. He would be a soldier lying on his bed for another twenty years.

Clay stretched and sat up. 'Yuk,' he said, half to himself. He took a quick glance at the torpid Brigg, which Brigg nevertheless noticed. 'I think I'll take me for a walk,' he said. 'I guess the environment in here gets a little claustrophobic.' He stood up and sauntered towards the toilets. Brigg opened his eyes a fraction and watched him go.

'Do you reckon that in America they learn the kids the big words first?' asked Tasker.

Brigg took a half-turn towards Tasker. 'Here, Task,' he said quietly. 'Do you reckon the Chinese have Boxing Day off?'

'Blimey, I don't know. Not while there's a few bob going around, I don't suppose. The village is open tonight. Why?'

'Do you reckon the Liberty will be open?'

'You're a shitehawk,' sighed Tasker. 'No sooner your loving nurse has gone off and you're after Juicy Lucy again.'

'And I'm not the only one,' whispered Brigg. 'I bet that's where the Yank's going.'

'Oh yes? The Yank's been there as well, has he?'

Brigg shrugged. 'Just a sort of casual pick-up,' he said.

'Not the real big-love stuff like you?'

'Shut up. Here he comes.'

He smiled like a false brother at Clay, who had returned from the ablutions with his towel across his shoulder. 'Going somewhere nice?' asked Brigg.

'Just thought I'd take a stroll,' said Clay. 'Get some air. I thought you had dozed off.'

'No, no, I'm wide awake. Wait for me. I'll come too.' Brigg made to get up from his bed. Clay took two urgent strides and stopped him.

'No, Briggsy,' he said persuasively. 'You just relax.'

'I've relaxed,' argued Brigg. 'I'll take a walk with you. Maybe we'll have a quiet beer. Nothing too exciting after Christmas.'

'Do you mind if I go alone?' said Clay. 'You're a great pal, but there are times when, well . . . when I like to be by myself.'

'Thinking about the mountains and the turkeys and that,' suggested Brigg artlessly.

'Sure, sure. Just thinking about home and the folks. Christmas kinda depresses me.'

'All right with me,' sighed Brigg dropping back on to his bed again. 'I don't want to go anywhere I'm not welcome.'

He watched Clay get hurriedly dressed, pretending to doze but observing him under his eyelids; watching the quick guilty glances which Clay sent his way. In a few minutes the American was in civilian clothes and making for the barrack-room door. 'Bye,' called Brigg. 'Have a nice think.'

'The bastard!' he exclaimed as soon as Clay had

gone. 'The thieving bastard. Going off to try and get his leg across Lucy.'

Tasker regarded him sardonically from his bed. 'You ought to tell her not to go with other blokes,' he said. 'Be faithful – like you.'

Brigg returned an obscenity, ran for the ablutions, and in three minutes was dressed and in pursuit of Clay.

The city bus had gone from the village. Brigg guessed that Clay had joined a group of waiting servicemen and shared a taxi into Singapore. He must have been lucky and got one immediately. Brigg cursed, but fortunately there were three airmen waiting at the acknowledged spot and a Chinese taxi-driver just pulling his car to the kerb. In half an hour Brigg was walking up the smoky stairs of the Liberty Club. Wounded music and reflected coloured lights issued from within.

There was a hollow atmosphere about the club that he sensed even before he entered, the music and the lights both seeming to echo it. There were human shadows at the top of the stairs, and Brigg saw that one of them was Clay.

He watched Clay walk into the main room, waited a minute, then continued up the stairs. When he got to the door Clay was sitting on the opposite side of the empty dance floor at one of the few tables which boasted a cloth and a lamp. Brigg strolled across the floor. Clay saw him coming at a sufficient distance to overcome his surprise and compose his features.

'Yank!' exclaimed Brigg as he neared the far side of the dance floor. 'Goodness, fancy seeing you here.'

'Came out for a breath of fresh air,' said Clay acknowledging defeat right away.

'Good place to get it,' commented Brigg looking about him. 'Mind it's fresher than usual in here. Not exactly jumping is it?'

'I guess nobody realizes it's open tonight. They forget that it's Chinese and the Chinese don't have Christmas.'

'Anybody here we know?' asked Brigg archly, looking from Lucy's accustomed chair, now vacant, and around the room.

'No familiar faces,' answered Clay. He rose and stretched. 'I think I'll be on my way, Briggsy,' he sighed. 'Continue my walk.'

Brigg looked at him stonily. Then with his little finger he performed the spiral twirl that he knew Clay would recognize as depicting the iron staircase to Lucy's flat. Clay grinned sheepishly, then turned and made a dash for the door.

'Rotten bastard,' said Brigg to the waiter, who, having only that moment appeared, took it as a personal affront. Brigg pushed the man aside and went after Clay. The American was at the club door. 'Rotten bastard!' Brigg called after him. He heard Clay shout a laugh as he went out into the street.

Outside it had abruptly begun to rain, great opaline drops falling into the streets and gurgling into the deep drains. Brigg saw the American climbing into a tri-sha, still projecting halfway from the sidecar as the coolie began pedalling off, the rain water falling from his wide straw hat. There were several tri-shas waiting at the pavement and Brigg clambered into one and, crouching, curiously like a large baby in a perambulator, he shouted to the bicyclist to follow the man in front.

'Buckshee dollar, John, if you race him,' promised Brigg.

The coolie, thin as a stick and soaked by the downpour, began pedalling faster, raising himself from his seat for the extra leverage. 'Come on, mate,' Brigg shouted at him from beneath his canopy. 'You can beat that merchant.'

They gained, street by street, until, in the Serangoon Road, Clay's tri-sha was held up by a truck backing from an alley, and Brigg's man sailed triumphantly by on a bow-wave of thin spray. Brigg's hand emerged from the shelter of the sidecar as they went by, and two mocking fingers were thrown up to Clay. Clay yelled back like an alley kid and shouted at his saturated driver.

They reached the bottom of the curly iron stairs with Clay twenty seconds behind Brigg. Rain-water was swilling down the ironwork as though it were a huge drainpipe. Brigg ran up the clattering stairs, reached Lucy's floor, turned and bellowed: 'Bugger off. You Yanks think you own everything.'

He went through the outer door and saw with delight that there was a bolt inside. He bolted it and had the joy of looking through the single-paned window and seeing the drowning face of his rival glaring through at him. He did a two-fingered encore and then with cautious glee turned to Lucy's door. He experienced the usual hesitation before pressing her chimes. Their tune sounded within but there was no other sound. He rang again, his hope dropping, and this time he heard a small sound: not a word, more a cry. There followed several bumps and he heard a scraping sound on the other side of the door. The next moment her key was pushed out from beneath the frame.

Brigg looked around immediately for Clay. His soaking face was still framed angrily in the outer door. Brigg moved and unbolted it. Before Clay had stumbled in Brigg said: 'I reckon there's something wrong, Yank. She pushed her key under the door.'

'Better open it,' said Clay wiping the rain from his face. Brigg put the key into the hole, turned it, and pushed the door open. Lucy, in her dragon robe, was lying just inside the door. Clay needed to kneel and gently push away her light form so that they could open the door sufficiently to get in.

Brigg had immediately feared that she had been attacked – the memory of when he once imagined her dead returning quickly – but the room was in no more than its normal disarray. Her business bed was open, the top sheet and the quilt trailing on the floor as though she had been in it. By the side of the bed was an island of dried vomit, and another in the middle of the Chinese rug which occupied the main part of the room.

'She's been throwing up,' said Brigg as Clay bent by the girl. Her face was skeletal, her eyes peacefully closed, her mouth broken and dry. Her head hung by a neck so thin it seemed it might topple off. Clay quickly lifted her. He could have done so with one hand. There was vomit on her robe too. He walked quickly to the bed with her, with Brigg fussing alongside like an anxious aunt. 'What is it, d'you reckon, Yank? What's up with her?'

'Some sort of poisoning, I'd guess,' said Clay putting Lucy gently on the bed and arranging her robe. She was bare beneath it; thin and pale and bare. The two boys looked at the woman's quiet, tired face.

'Better get a doctor, I suppose,' said Clay. 'God knows how. I'll go. You stay with her.'

'All right, Yank,' said Brigg doubtfully. 'Don't be too long. She don't look all that good to me.'

Clay looked apprehensive. He backed away towards the door then went out quickly. As he opened the outer door Brigg briefly heard the rain hammering down. Then it was closed and Brigg was left with Lucy.

He looked about him, empty, helpless. He put his hand on her hard clay-coloured forehead and then went to the sink which he knew to be concealed behind a screen in the corner. There was a silk slip hanging to dry behind the screen. He took it, soaked it under the single green tap, and went back to the bed to gently mop her face. She remained still as death, her breathing hardly discernible. He wiped the vomit traces from around her mouth but her face did not stir. He called quietly near to her face, 'Lucy, Lucy,' but there came no response. He wasn't sure how to feel a pulse, or what to expect when he felt it, but he held her wrist and eventually detected her subdued heartbeat. Her fingers moved, trembling to his hand and she said something in Chinese.

'Lucy, Lucy,' he said urgently. 'It's Briggsy. Bligg.'

But her eyes did not move. Her fingers relaxed on his hand. Frightened he felt her pulse again and watched carefully for her breathing. Chastely he pulled her robe close around her body. She seemed, all at once, very old, like a collection of bones. He wondered how long she had been there and why no one had come to see her.

He left the bed and found another piece of cloth behind the screen, with which he cleared up the vomit at the side of the bed and on the floor. There was a small high window, which he had never noticed before, and standing on a chair he attempted to open it, with a vague idea of getting some air into the place. It was tight with rust and refused to move. It must have looked in on some inner well of the building because he could hear the rain gurgling down the opening. Climbing down from the chair he went around the room, tidying up. He remembered, years before, returning from school and finding his mother ill in bed and awaiting the doctor. She had made him go around the house dusting and picking things up, imagining that the doctor, who saw many worse things, would be offended by that.

There was not much to tidy in Lucy's room. For the first time it occurred to him that she could not have been spending the money she earned, apparently so readily, on herself. Finished with the housework he sat again at her bedside and looked at the dun face, scarcely able to credit that she was the same person who sat in the sun that day on Changi beach, or who, only two weeks before, had looked so entrancing in the fumbling grasp of Corporal Eggington.

'Lucy, Lucy,' he whispered, trying again. 'Lucy, it's me, Brigg.' It occurred to him that he had heard the lines many times in this familiar scene in the films, but there seemed no other way of saying it. She did not respond. He sat hunched with helplessness and feeling strangely lonely; a world away from Kilburn, sitting in an oriental slum by the form of a Chinese girl who might be dying. And knowing, now he considered it, nothing of her. He glanced around the room as if wondering how he got there.

Then his eyes went back to her face as her lips moved a fraction. They were like two dried twigs rubbing together in a touch of breeze. 'Lucy, Lucy,' he bent close to her. 'Water,' he instructed himself. 'Water, you twit.' He rushed to the sink behind the screen, took a beaker from a small shelf and filled it from the tap. 'Hope this stuff won't poison her more,' he muttered to himself, smelling it. Hurrying back to the bed he spilt some of it, but arrived at her side just as her lips began to move again. He put the beaker to her mouth. It brought another memory, himself as a child attempting to revive a dying bird in the street. The cast-down eyelids, almost transparent, the peaceful, uncaring face. She took some of the water, he believed, but the rest dribbled down on to her chin and her neck. 'Oh Christ,' he moaned to himself. 'Oh Jesus.' He took her thin wrist, then dropping it leaned across her to put his ear where he calculated her heart might be. The lobe of his ear touched the silk of the robe and there came to him a faint musky smell that was an abrupt memory of the times they had spent together. 'Please, Lucy,' he begged her. 'Please don't . . .' He could not make himself say the word so he finished, '. . . do anything silly.'

To his huge relief he heard the outer door open, and Clay returned. Behind him came two dark stretcher-bearers and a Chinese policeman.

'I called the hospital,' Clay shrugged. 'I couldn't make any sense to anybody else. How is she?'

The two men, expressionless, were lifting Lucy on to the stretcher. 'She don't look too good to me,' said Brigg solemnly. 'What's the copper for?'

Clay raised his eyebrows. The policeman was nosing about at the far end of the room. He walked back to the bed and smelled at the beaker in which Brigg had brought the water. 'He came with them,' said Clay. 'I guess it's routine. I hung around at the street corner for them in case they couldn't find the place.'

The policeman approached. He was a round-faced Chinese. He produced his notebook and licked his pencil. The British had trained him.

The fact was astonishingly confirmed a moment later. They were taking Lucy through the door when the policeman drew in a momentous breath and in a Chinese voice like a badly played piano said: 'What goes on 'ere?' He said it carefully, as though he had rehearsed it many times and did not want to muff it

301

now. He was obviously confident that it was the way every investigation should and did commence.

Brigg looked towards the vacant door. 'Can't we go with her and see she's all right?'

'Arr Light,' said the policeman shutting his book, apparently relieved at not having to take a statement there. 'I come with you, Jimmy, in the ambruance.'

Three hours later Brigg and Clay walked, hands in pockets, through the damp and dead city. They had left Lucy alive and with her eyes open. 'Fancy her trying that,' said Brigg. He glanced at Clay anxiously. 'You don't reckon it was because she was upset about me, do you?'

'You, Briggsy? Why you?'

'Well, you know, being in the Liberty with the girls that night.'

'Aw, come on, grow up, Briggsy,' said Clay with long-drawn impatience. 'I can't think of any smaller reason for a doll trying to kill herself than that.'

'Oh, all right,' said Brigg a little hurt. 'It just crossed my mind, that's all.'

'Maybe you should think she tried to do it because she has a shit-awful life, eh? Young girl getting stuffed by all the crummy bastards in Singapore – present company excluded of course.'

'Stow it, will you.'

'Sorry, buddy, but what do you want me to say? She tried to end it because of thwarted desire?'

'No.'

'You bet it wasn't. She's had all the desire and all the love knocked out of her, every time some greasy guy she's never seen in her life climbed on her bed.'

'It *was* a bit different with us, straight it was, Yank. Honest. I took her to Changi beach one day, with a little Chinese kid.'

'Okay, okay. So you did.'

'I just couldn't believe it when they said what she gone and done,' muttered Brigg shaking his head. 'I thought it was just something she'd eaten. She was always cheerful and funny . . .'

'Sure, sure. Maybe she was okay while she was with you. What was that? An hour every two weeks. How do you know what her life was like the rest of the time?'

'Yes, you're right. I wonder what she did with the money she earned? She didn't spend it on her room, that's for sure.'

'Family or a pimp,' suggested Clay. 'Maybe both. Maybe they're one and the same. And when she gets out of hospital she'll be doing it again.'

'That's all she's got,' said Brigg sadly. They walked towards the vacuum centre of the city, skirting the silent grass of the Padang. Out on the near-by sea a ship called farewell.

'Funny that doctor saying that they always have a lot of suicides and attempted suicides over Christmas,' said Brigg.

'It's always been the open season for cutting your throat in the States,' said Clay. 'Christmas, New Year, Thanksgiving. People get lonely.'

'But the *Chinese* doing it,' said Brigg. 'At Christmas. They're not even Christians. You'd think they'd do it at Chinese New Year.'

'Maybe it's something they picked up from the British,' shrugged Clay. 'Like the cop.'

16

Brigg was operating his ambidextrous avoidance of work; left hand apparently conscientiously writing on the office folder spread in front of him, right hand beneath the desk writing a letter to his parents, the paper fixed to an army field clipboard. Every now and then he gave his left hand a brief wiggle to indicate, at least to the officer and the section sergeant, that he was working out some figures. He was almost at the back of the section – only Private Fundrum, unofficially studying Greek – sat behind him, so that his hidden work had never been detected. If the florid Sergeant Bass or the stem-like Lieutenant Perkins rose, or stretched to peer suspiciously, he had time to cover up his operations. Unfortunately, in military terms, his rear was exposed, and he had to keep an ear and occasionally an eye turned in that direction in case an officer or a senior NGO should creep up on him from some other part of the office.

The rest of the section, a dozen men, were spread out on the tables and desks before him, crouching like snipers over their interminable writing and calculations. The demob calendars had been marked for the day; Naafi break, the second excitement, was yet to come. Brigg still had exactly three months to do. By his calculations, the troopship which would take him home would be leaving England on her outward voyage in three weeks. He could almost hear the rattle of the anchor chain. The thought cheered him. In those terms it did not sound too long.

He performed a familiar reverie. The first sight of England above the sea: a smudge, then a shadow, then the growing forms of cliffs and hills. And then Southampton, sailing in on a summer-morning sea, the prospect of the train journey through green English fields, cricket matches, church spires, villages, pubs, towns, then London and home. He imagined what the smell of England might be. It was strange that before being sent away as a soldier he had scarcely noticed the place.

A marble-eyed Chinese clerk, clean as a cricketer in his white shirt and trousers, came into the section from the door at the distant end. Any interruption, no matter how mundane, was a good excuse for a minute's cessation of work, sixty seconds eaten away. The soldiers and the civilian clerks in the rows stopped and observed him. He gave a slip of paper to Sergeant Bass who, after conferring with Lieutenant Perkins and receiving a nod to his inquiry, looked up and called: 'Brigg.'

'Sarn't?' Brigg deftly slid his clipboard and his letter into his desk drawer and stood up.

Sergeant Bass blinked down the tables. 'Come here, Brigg,' he said. 'Tear yourself away from your work, lad.'

'Yes, Sarge,' responded Brigg coolly. He closed the folder on which his left hand had been imitating work all the morning and marched to the top of the section. Bass had watery eyes, like a hippo. It seemed that he might have secret sorrows.

'Brigg,' he said sombrely, 'report to Lieutenant Grainger. Special guard duty, Johore Depot.'

Brigg felt his heart tread on his stomach. 'Not again, Sarge!' he protested. 'It's the second time.'

'They must think you're good at it. Guarding,' sniffed Bass.

'What about my work?' asked Brigg, attempting to sound convincing.

'We'll just have to stagger on without you,' replied Bass calmly. 'I don't know how, but we will. That's war.'

Brigg regarded him with a mixture of disparagement and despair. 'All right, Sarge,' he said. 'I'd better go, then.'

'Yes,' agreed the sergeant. 'You'd better go.'

Lieutenant Perkins leaned across like a piece of elastic. 'Nobody else on this section, thank goodness. Not now we've transferred Tasker,' he commented looking at the order. 'Sergeant Wellbeloved, Tasker, Morris – my God, Morris! – and Clay. That's the American, isn't it? We must be short of men.' He smiled a brown-toothed smile towards Brigg, and Brigg suddenly thought: You'll never get a girl, sir.

'Bye-bye, Brigg,' said the officer. 'Have a nice time and don't get shot or anything. We'd miss you. Wouldn't we, Sergeant?'

'I'll try not to, sir,' said Brigg truthfully. He came briefly to attention, but waited until he was outside the door before putting his cap on. It saved him having to salute the fool.

Anyway, it *couldn't* happen again. Lightning didn't strike twice, he told himself as he walked in the bare sunshine along the concrete paths between the office huts. Not another thing like poor old Dobbie. Christ, this time he would report sick if they detailed him to go on errands outside that compound. He couldn't risk it. Not with his boat leaving England in three weeks.

It was Grainger of course, that shithawk. He had fixed this. He could not wait to get up there again, across the Causeway, into that uncertain country. And pig hunting. He had probably meant that too.

He turned the orderly room corner and saw Tasker, Clay and Morris Morris all standing outside. Morris was sweating so much in his compulsory shirt that it was stained three shades of green, like camouflage.

'Ah, here he is, then,' said Morris smiling gallantly. 'Last again.'

'And this is a bloody good lark to be last for, take it from me,' said Brigg. 'God, fancy landing it *again*. Grainger must really have it in for me. He's trying to stop me getting home.'

'It's disgusting, that's what,' grumbled Tasker. 'Why can't they spread it around a bit. Twice in a few weeks is ridiculous.'

'Aw, maybe it will be okay,' suggested Clay with his customary slow voice. 'For me it's *got* to be better

308

than cleaning and painting fire points, which I've been doing all goddam week. It must be an improvement on that.'

'I wouldn't count on it,' sniffed Brigg. 'I bet the poor bugger who copped his lot last time would have preferred to be painting fire points.'

'Here's Grainger,' warned Tasker. 'He's coming through the orderly room. He's laughing.'

'That bugger always is,' said Brigg. 'If anyone gets a bullet in the guts you can bet it won't be Mister Bleeding Grainger. He'll duck in time.'

'Wellbeloved's coming too,' said Morris. 'I saw his name.'

'That'll please him,' said Tasker with some small satisfaction. 'He's more shit scared than any of us.'

Lieutenant Grainger had paused within the door to talk with someone out of their sight. His top half was framed in the panel and they could see him through the glass. 'That's how I'd like to see Mr Grainger,' muttered Tasker. 'Stuffed in a glass case.'

He came out breezily into the sticky sunshine. 'Lads, lads,' he said with spurious warmth. 'It's terribly good of you to turn up. Terribly good. As you know, we're going over to the depot at Johore. It's not our turn really, but the unit which is supposed to do it has an outbreak of dysentery or beriberi or something, and we've been asked to stand in. Sorry about the short notice but' – he lowered his voice melodramatically – 'I thought we might enjoy that wild pig hunting we were discussing at Christmas.' He beamed around at their various faces: Brigg and Tasker void with lack of enthusiasm, Clay composed, Morris Morris grinning unsurely.

Grainger continued: 'Whip back to the barrack room now and get your stuff. Field Service Marching Order, of course. Then we've fixed an early lunch, draw rifles and ammo at fourteen hundred hours – that's if the armourers can be roused from sleep – and off we go. We'll be up there four days, so take plenty of good books. Any questions?'

Brigg said cautiously: 'Is there actually anything to *guard* in the depot now, sir?'

'What does that mean, Brigg?'

'Well last time, sir,' said Brigg, 'there was nothing in the place. It was empty. That chap who got killed, Dobbie, told me. We were guarding nothing.'

'That, Brigg old chap, is none of our concern,' said Grainger confidingly. 'Ours not to reason why. Ours but to do or die . . . Off you run now.'

They trudged across the bridge in the bright noon. 'Ours but to do or die,' echoed Brigg. 'That's a fine fucking choice, I must say.'

Brigg groaned. 'This dump,' he said, 'gives me the willies.'

He dropped his kit on the bottom bunk and looked about the bare room. The pile of books and magazines left, now by established tradition, by succeeding groups of guards brought from Singapore, had become a small mountain. It was as though pilgrims had come to the place and each had left a memento – *How to Build Your Own Radio, Batman and Robin Extra, Three Men in a Boat, Amateur Beekeeping,* and *Slippery Blondes* by Hank Janson.

'Not much of a place to call 'ome,' agreed Morris Morris. The afternoon journey in the exposed truck had made him sweat all down his front. He divested himself of his webbing equipment, including his pack, ammunition pouches and bayonet, and dangled them heavily from two fingers.

Clay sniffed around and then grimaced up at the bare light bulb. 'Maybe it would be brighter around here if we got some of the wild life away from the light,' he said. They looked up without great interest at the squadrons of small insects fascinated by the illumination, circling about those who had already gladly given their lives for that fascination.

'Get on my shoulders, lad,' said Morris unexpectedly. 'Get rid of them. Let's see the place anyway.' He knelt like a dromedary and Clay sat astride his shoulders. Morris stood easily and Clay, with a piece of newspaper, cleaned the dead insects from the bulb. The light increased slightly.

'As long as that's the only dead bodies we have to deal with,' said Tasker mournfully. He glanced at Brigg. 'I remember old Dobbie sitting in that chair, reading that very Hank Janson, just before he had his lot. With old Sparkles. Remember, Briggsy?'

'Listen, butty,' said Morris Morris with sudden and surprising truculence. 'Would you just mind being a good boy and forgetting the funeral talk? You'll put the heebie-jeebies on us.' He glanced at Clay, as though he wanted confirmation of the

Americanism. 'The heebie-jeebies,' he repeated.

'Sorry, Taff,' blinked Tasker, prudently backing away. 'It's just Dobbie was here with us, that's all. And he got killed.'

'Son,' said Morris sombrely, 'one death is not a bloody massacre. Excuse my swearing. When you've seen your butties killed all around you, like I did in the war, all laid out in rows, you have to think a bit different about it. You just have to imagine they're still people but they're not saying very much. Otherwise it gets on your nerves, see. And you never talk about them afterwards. Never. That's bad luck too.' He descended clumsily on to the bottom bunk and it creaked with his weight. 'Ever such bad luck.' His expression wandered away, as it did on occasions, then gradually came back to them. 'I had a pal once, a good man, who got blown up in front of my own eyes. Stepped on a mine. I picked him up in two buckets. I went back to the unit looking like a bloodstained milkman.' He regarded the sallow faces about him. 'But after that, mind, I never mentioned him. Not even in the prison camp, where you always had plenty of time to think and talk. Never. You don't.'

Having closed the subject he stood, to the apparent relief of the bunksprings, and went towards the door. His large form filled the frame, shutting out the rays of a crimson sunset. 'Ah, now that's lovely,' he sighed to the outside. 'Lovely.'

Grainger, marching across the earthen compound towards the hut, disturbed his admiration.

'Evening, sir,' said Morris when he noticed him.

'Good evening, Taff,' said Lieutenant Grainger with his studied easiness. 'That sunset looks impressive shining on your face.'

'It would look nice shining on anything, sir,' replied Morris.

He stepped aside and Grainger snapped smartly into the room. 'Well, well. All settled then? Good.' He glanced around and his expression lighted on Brigg. 'I've asked about the contents of the depot, Brigg,' he said, 'on your behalf. But nobody knows or they won't tell. But I have an assurance that if there's only emptiness in there, then it's a special emptiness. So it's worth guarding. Tactical see?'

'Yes, sir,' mumbled Brigg.

'So if you get shot, then it's not for nothing,' smiled Grainger. 'I've been assured that it would be worthwhile; you would not die in vain. Does that answer your question?'

'Yes, sir.'

'It must come as a bit of a relief to you.'

'Yes, sir.'

'Not very conversational today, Brigg.'

'No, sir. Sorry sir.'

Grainger grinned and patted him paternally on the shoulder. 'Well, cheer up, lad. I've got some news about our wild pig hunt. This will be something to look foward to.'

He could hardly have failed to notice that his eagerness was unmatched by their expression. 'Tomorrow,' he said. 'At dawn.'

He paused awaiting a reaction that did not arrive. 'We leave about five,' he said. 'I've arranged it so that none of you are on guard duty. It means you'll have to do an extra couple of shifts later, but that will be all right, won't it? It's not often you'll get the chance of an outing like this. I've fixed it with the CO here, who's not a bad chap. We'll officially be an anti-bandit patrol, but once we're in the jungle it's the porkers we'll be hunting. Okay?'

'Yes, sir,' they all nodded.

'Five tomorrow morning, then,' said Grainger. 'We'll have some real fun. Get some sleep in tonight.' He strode out of the door in his stiff, boyish way, surrounded by the sunset.

They sat down on their bunks.

'Can't say I ever thought I'd go hunting wild pig with the British Army,' observed Clay.

'What I would like to know,' said Tasker slowly, 'is what's the difference between an anti-bandit patrol and a pig hunt?'

'You mean,' nodded Brigg. 'How will the *bandits* know that it's just a bit of sporting fun?'

'Too bloody right,' said Tasker. 'Can't stand pork anyway. It sticks in my gullet.'

17

Dawn arrived cautiously, half an inch at a time, as though none too sure what the day would be like. Then, apparently reassured, it accelerated and jumped up into the sky, spreading cinnamon and blue and cream along the rim of the earth. The soldiers were not in the mood to appreciate its widespread artistry.

The orderly sergeant had aroused them at four-thirty with a cry of: 'Hands off cocks – on with socks!' They had staggered about in the fumbling pre-dawn, clammy and sleepy, cursing Grainger and his wild pigs. It was a bad time of day, anyway, the air fetid after the tropical night, waiting for the clean wind that arrived with the full light to blow it out into the Johore Straits. They washed and shaved grumpily, barging into each other in the confined hut, struggling into their long-laced jungle boots and putting anti-insect ointment on their cheeks and noses, like some weary early-morning chorus making up for the opening of a show, an illusion reinforced by their floppy feminine jungle hats.

Breakfast cheered them a little, and by the time they stamped out of the mess hut the sky was limp and newly washed and the earth felt cool for once.

Lieutenant Grainger appeared, striding like a young horse, from his quarters. The cloche-shaped jungle hat looked right on him. From the other direction, with a yellowy smile that only just reached the surface of his face, came Sergeant Wellbeloved.

'Morning, sir,' he said after saluting. He merely blinked sourly at the four soldiers drawn up on the cool compound. His hat was low over his eyes, like a bell that had fallen accidentally and heavily on to his head.

'Good morning, Sergeant,' beamed Grainger in his hearty metallic way. 'Good morning, chaps.'

The squad mumbled their return greetings. He stepped to Tasker and rearranged his flopping hat. 'My, my, don't we all look like Jolly Jungle Jims then,' he said. 'I wouldn't be a bit surprised if we came back with two large porkers and half a dozen Communist bandits.'

Brigg wasn't sure if it was cold early sweat that wriggled down his spine or a wet shiver. His eyes felt red and sore. Morris Morris standing next to him looked as though he were made from plasticine. Clay looked gaunt and Tasker pale with apprehension.

'Sorry it's so early,' breezed the young officer. 'Got to make a sharp start or it's no damn good. When we get into the bush a mile or so we'll have a bit of practice in fanning out and tactics in general. But I want to make one thing very clear, right at the start – no one is to fire a shot without my personal orders.' He glanced at Wellbeloved. 'Sorry, Sergeant,' he added insincerely, 'but it has to be strictly that. We can't have idiots firing at each other.'

316

Tasker lifted his lids. 'What if a wild pig charges at us, sir,' he inquired, 'and we're not allowed to shoot?'

Grainger surveyed him with mock patience. 'If a wild pig charges at you, Private Tasker, get out of the way – quickly,' he said sardonically. 'They're covered with bristles like steel and they travel like an express train.'

'Yes, sir,' nodded Tasker, 'I'll make sure to dodge them.'

'You'll 'ave to move a bit more smartish than you usually do, Tasker,' added Wellbeloved, apparently feeling it was time he added something. 'Them things can give you a nasty knock.'

Grainger regarded Wellbeloved with thinly hidden scorn. He coughed. 'Yes,' he agreed coolly. 'A nasty knock indeed.'

He turned to the small squad again. 'Any more questions?'

'Yes, sir.'

'Brigg?'

'What if we meet up with the bandits, sir?'

Grainger sniffed. 'If we meet the enemy we will engage and destroy him,' he said dramatically.

'Oh God,' breathed Brigg.

'What was that, Brigg?'

'Nothing, nothing, sir. Just checking, sir.'

'Right then, let's be off,' said Grainger.

'Single file, sir?' inquired Wellbeloved.

Grainger appeared to be turning this suggestion through his mind. Then he said: 'It's difficult to do otherwise, Sergeant Wellbeloved, with only four men.'

'Yes, sir, of course it is, sir,' muttered Wellbeloved. He turned his bitterness on the squad: 'Squad! Squad, a-ten-shun. Right turn! Quick march.'

They strode to the compound gate, where the tired night sentry summoned a grin as he unlocked it and let them out. 'Have a nice piggy hunt,' he whispered to Brigg as he went by – then, in a sigh to himself as he closed the big gate behind them, 'And fuck your luck.'

Grainger, Wellbeloved, Tasker, Brigg, Morris, Clay – in that order they went for three hundred yards along the white road outside the depot. The sun seemed to have been lying in wait for them, for immediately they stepped on to the road it raised itself on its elbows above the line of the trees and shone fiercely at them. Its heat went straight through their shirts and burned in their early eyes. But when they turned off the highway, down a track that rolled into the jungle, they were immediately enclosed by the dankness of the place.

There was a small kampong a quarter of a mile from the road, and the village was stirring itself. Morning fires were curling and dogs echoed as the soldiers approached down the thin path. Through the trees they could see people moving about. Grainger held up his hand in the silent halt-sign. They stopped and dropped to an obedient crouch. Grainger whispered to Wellbeloved: 'I think we'll skirt the village, Sergeant. No sense in letting these people know that we're in the vicinity. Sometimes they tell tales.'

Wellbeloved nodded sharply, the movement

sending a shower of sweat from his face. Some of the drops fell on Grainger's sleeve. 'S-sorry, sir,' said Wellbeloved.

Grainger did not bother to reply but cupped his hand and motioned the men to filter right, where they followed a secondary path that went off at a wide angle. The undergrowth was at once closer and clung to their equipment, but it was not difficult. Under their rubber shoes the ground softened and then became soggy. Ahead they could hear the liquid jogging of a stream. They came upon it quite abruptly, the jungle standing back and the earth descending to a crossing place. There among the stones were four Malay women washing themselves.

The soldiers stood nonplussed on the bank. The women looked up and saw them and their guns and remained still also. The morning sounds of the village and the insect voices in the undergrowth suddenly seemed louder. Two of the women were middle-aged and they had coloured sarongs about their breasts while they poured water over their brown loins. The other two were young girls, standing naked in the stream, slim as deer, round breasts and curved waists, their legs wet from their ablutions. Their faces and eyes were those of disturbed deer also, pointed and pretty, with the eyes round and dark-bright.

Brigg heard Tasker repeat his own quickly drawn-in breath. They were staring at the dark nipples and the navels and the bushy hairs between the young legs. The girls did not seem frightened. Casually they turned their small buttocks to the soldiers and waded to the stream bank, reaching over for coloured sarongs which they put in front of their bodies before gracefully following the stumbling older women away from the place. No word had been said on either side.

Grainger seemed annoyed at the encounter, or embarrassed, and his hand movement to call the squad forward was sharp and impatient. There were some stepping-stones, and he led them across that way.

'Gee,' whispered Clay. 'What about that?'

'Lovely,' grunted Brigg. 'Bloody lovely.'

'Better than pork,' added Tasker. 'Any day.'

They moved forward for an hour, still along miraculous tracks that needled their way through jungle that was as thick as a wall only a few inches on either side. Grainger had a map and a compass. Wellbeloved looked anxiously over his shoulder while he checked the position, 'All right, sir?' he inquired.

'Still in Malaya,' mentioned Grainger.

'Yes, sir,' said Wellbeloved.

The sun was gone now, obliterated by the thick and lofty trees. It was as though the men were walking beneath the belly of some monstrous centipede, threading their way through its many legs. Undergrowth pressed in closer the farther they went, and monkeys screamed the bad news of their advance from the most distant vantage points. They saw painted birds hovering and hooting high above, and at their low level insects thrummed like an eternal electric motor.

They rested in a clearing for twenty minutes, then pushed on for another hour. It was slow and tiring. By the middle of the day the jungle had become stuffed with compressed heat. Their shirts were soaked against their backs. Grainger called another halt and they sat, curtained by insects, and ate the mess-tin rations prepared for them by the depot cooks.

'Jungle-bashing,' complained Tasker. 'You can keep it.'

'Give me a man's life – behind a desk,' agreed Brigg. He was stretched back uncomfortably, with his hat covering his face. Some insects found their way beneath it and began attacking his face.

'All these insects,' tutted Morris Morris. 'Like Barry Island on August Bank Holiday.'

Clay had been left as a look-out during the break. He was called back to eat his food and Brigg went, grumbling privately, to replace him. He walked in a patrolling circle around the area where they were established, looking at the jungle and seeing nothing but jungle. It seemed all-consuming, all-covering. It was as though they were in the middle of a tightly wrapped parcel.

At two-thirty, without having seen anything but monkeys, birds and insects, they turned and began to retrace their journey of the morning. There were some places, hardly landmarks, which they recognized, but for the most part it was the all-green sameness, like an unending film unrolling before them.

The fearful thought of ambush was never far from

their minds, although in Brigg it receded a little as they journeyed. The jungle growth that pressed against them so insistently was logically a protection, as well as a concealment for an enemy. It was so tight for much of the way that he persuaded himself that an ambush by bandits would have been impossible. There was no space.

In another hour, after miles of green sameness, they could see there was a clearer country ahead. The sun was filtering through the higher trees, transforming their branches into cathedral tracery. The howls of the monkeys and the screeching of the birds seemed to sound more freely too. On some stretches of their way there had hardly seemed room for an echo.

Grainger called a quiet halt. He nodded at the monkeys, redoubling their swinging now, like frenzied acrobats, through the most distant trees they could see. 'That's a sign that there might be something ahead, so I'm told,' he whispered to Wellbeloved. The sergeant's Adam's apple moved up and down. 'Something's upset them,' went on Grainger.

'Could be us,' pointed out Wellbeloved hopefully. Grainger grimaced to himself but did not reply. He called them on with his hand.

Two minutes later they reached a clearing, one of the unexpected oases that give respite in the thickness. It was columned with sunlight that seemed to rise up rather than fall through the big spaced trees. High above it was filtered by branches and leaves, glistening as if it were reflected on water.

Over them, the monkeys continued their unruly performance and the birds were shrill, their cries rebounding from the jungle roof to the soldiers below. Brigg suddenly saw a small monkey sitting only a few yards away, on a low branch, covering its face with its paws.

'Look at that, Taff,' he nudged Morris Morris. 'They call that a croucher.'

'There's funny,' murmured Morris Morris. 'Just sitting and putting his hands over his eyes, so he don't see us. The poor thing must be frightened.'

'I know how he feels,' muttered Tasker.

'They reckon if you shoot a croucher you never leave Malaya alive,' Brigg went on. Grainger half turned at the front of the file. 'Shut up back there,' he snapped. 'It's like a mothers' meeting.'

He had just finished the sentence when a huge tusked boar burst from the trees on their right. Snout down it rushed over the scrubby space, snorting and trumpeting, its bristles rampant. With a speed they would never have attained on an exercise area the soldiers scattered. Some flew to the right of the path, some to the left. Brigg's initial fright caused him to fall over a buried log and tumble comically ten feet down a hidden slope. He lay on his back, his legs awry in the air like a fallen skier. He could hear Grainger's shouts from above, and he rolled over on to his hands and knees and slung his rifle over his shoulder before climbing back to the clearing. When he got there other heads and bodies were emerging from their refuges. Grainger, scarlet-faced, was standing out in the clearing, and the boar was at its extreme end, turning and snorting in the way of a bull turning to begin its run on a matador.

'Keep back,' snarled Grainger. 'Keep out of the bloody way.'

They were grateful for that. They crouched in their hiding places at the clearing's edge and watched in a sweat as the boar angrily tipped its snout and dug its feet and its tusks into the soft earth.

Grainger stood still, tight and enjoying the sensation. 'Come on then, Porky,' he called to the pig. 'Come on.'

The boar stared at him, sizing up the chances. 'Right,' said Grainger decisively, 'so you don't fancy it.' Each of the soldiers, relegated to spectators, knew that the words were for their benefit. The officer was loving it: the showing off, the danger, the decision. And yet they sensed that, had he been alone with that wild animal in that remote place, without a single watcher, Grainger would have stood there in the same way, throwing out the same challenge.

The lieutenant waited another twenty seconds. The boar did not move. Its snorting had diminished. It was eyeing the man with ill-will but with a certain new caution. Then the officer walked briskly towards it. One, two, three, four, five paces. That was too much for the beast. Its spiked head went down and with a great bellow it rushed through the trees, straight at him.

A shout throttled itself in Brigg's throat. His hands went out helplessly. Tasker, standing behind the next tree, said weakly, 'Oh, blimey.'

But Grainger was not going to let the theatrical

moment go. He remained firm, legs apart like some hunter-hero in a lad's book. There came the moment when the animal, half-way on its course to him, cleared all the trees. Grainger fired his sten-gun from the shoulder, a brief, cool, knowing burst.

The boar skidded spectacularly, like a heavy motor-cycle out of control, dipping violently to the left, its nose and tusks ploughing into the ground. The momentum of its body was arrested by the thrust of the tusks, and its powerful, bristled back arched through the air in an outsized somersault, before hitting the earth.

Delighted, the soldiers came out of their refuges, laughing and calling familiarities towards Grainger. He turned towards them, his superior smile already fixed in place. With casual efficiency he pushed down the safety-catch of the sten. 'It's going to take a bit of carrying,' he smirked. 'Maybe we ought to find a kampong and get some natives.'

At that moment Brigg looked up. There were some men standing in the trees at the far end of the clearing. 'Here's some now, sir. They must have heard the shots.'

'Down!' screamed Grainger. 'Flat!'

He was almost as quick as the first burst of shooting. It was high, sawing through the trees over their heads. Blindly the soldiers scattered and tumbled into the hiding places they had just vacated. Brigg rolled into the depression where he had previously fallen, his throat cluttered with fear, his eyes scarcely able to focus, his hands trembling, madly attempting to bring his rifle around to his front.

There was an immediate second sequence of firing, and at once a heavy green figure collided with the ground a foot above Brigg's head. It rolled and then was caught by some roots.

'T-Taffy,' stammered Brigg. 'Oh, Christ, Taffy.'

Morris's large boot was standing up like a stone. The firing ceased briefly, then came more bursts. Scarcely able to control his hands, Brigg reached up, grasped the boot around the ankle and heaved. The big man's weight seemed to make it impossible, but then Brigg heard him crying 'Quick! Quick!' and make some movement to aid himself. Brigg gave another desperate pull and like an avalanche Morris Morris tipped over the lip of the descent and rolled down through the debris of the jungle. His force took Brigg with him and they rolled madly on to a long steep slope, completely concealed in the undergrowth, rolling and letting themselves roll a hundred feet or more, until they ended in the mud of a thick stream.

They lay, faces in the mud, all the breath, and any courage that they may have had, gone from them. Brigg looked up to see the stream water coloured with blood.

'Taff, Taff,' he whispered, shaking Morris as though trying to wake him. 'Where did they get you?'

'Side,' spluttered Morris. 'In my side.'

A new scattering of shots came from high above them. They heard a grenade explode and somebody shouting above the outraged screams of the monkeys and frenzied birds.

'I ought to go back,' said Brigg tremulously. 'I'll have to give a hand.'

Morris slapped a large paw on his wrist. 'You stay here, kid,' he said with difficulty. 'With Taffy. If you go up there, there's nothing you can do. You'll have your lot.'

Brigg's face tightened. 'But I can't just stay down here,' he stammered. 'I've got . . .'

'What can you do?' said Morris. He began to cough, pushing his face forward. Brigg lifted his head clear of the water. There was more blood in the stream water. 'You'd be no good, son. They'd just kill you. Wipe you out.' The young man and the older man remained there another minute.

Then there was another shattering of automatic firing above them, like a power-saw sounding through the trees. 'It's no good,' stammered Brigg. 'Honest, Taff, I'll have to go up. I can't just stay here.'

Morris Morris had his face laid sideways in the brief brown water of the stream. There was a curious moment when he squinted as he followed the progress of a twig past his eyes. He lifted his mouth clear and said: 'They'll get you, boy. They'll get you.'

With a sob Brigg pulled himself away and crawled up the steep incline, under the threaded growth, until he fearfully reached the lip of the crater. The red earth crumbled in his fingers. The clearing was silent. A single monkey had begun to swing aimlessly through the top trees. For some reason Brigg looked at the tree upon which the croucher had been squatting. He was still there, unscarred, his paws still covering his eyes.

Brigg eased himself up the final six inches so that he could look fully into the clearing. His rifle was tight in his left hand, but uselessly pinned below his chest, its working parts covered with slime from the stream. He twisted it around, released the safety-catch, and then realized he was looking ominously down at the cornet-shaped snout, open like a mouth about to shout something. Prudently he put the safety-catch back on.

When his vision cleared the ground level he could see that the clearing was empty. A skirt of blue smoke was caught two-thirds of the way up the legs of the trees, just before the branches began. The air smelled sharp. He eased himself around the perimeter, crawling like a novice spider, until he came in view of the dead pig. It was lying where Grainger had shot it, humped almost at the foot of a tree. And beside it was the equally unmoving form of Grainger. The officer was lying parallel to the dead animal, stomach down, face towards Brigg. His floppy jungle hat was a few feet away, in front of the pig's nose.

Brigg raised himself another inch and surveyed the clearing. 'Sir,' he whispered hopelessly. 'Sir . . .'

He would have been amazed at a reply. Grainger and the pig were in almost identical attitudes, chins against the ground, on each face a fixed grin, the open eyes of animal and man glistening with the frost of death. 'Sir,' he ventured again.

'Oh, Jesus Christ,' he muttered pushing his face

against the burned earth. 'Oh, God help me.' He edged his way back to the place where he had climbed from the stream, and backed down again. Morris was humped like a hippo in the middle of the stream. He whispered 'Hello, son' when he saw that Brigg was back.

'Grainger's dead,' said Brigg bleakly. 'He's lying next to the pig. God, Taff, I hope the others didn't get it – Tasker and Clay. 'Everybody's just gone.'

'Everybody?' said Morris. 'Them as well?'

'The place is empty except for Grainger and the pig. How's the side?'

'I can't feel much,' said Morris. He had put a field dressing against the wound and he took it away to look. 'It's funny though,' he said, 'where this blood is coming from. It's not from my side. It's in the stream, see. I feel sort of frozen down below. I don't suppose I got another packet did I, Briggsy?'

He eased himself with difficulty slightly to the side, and Brigg, horrified, saw the wound across the groin and the lower part of the big stomach. 'Oh dear, mother,' breathed Morris, 'there goes my knackers.'

'Oh, Taffy,' said Brigg. 'Oh, bloody hell. I haven't got a field dressing. I lost mine at Panglin and I didn't report it. You know they take it out of your pay.'

To his amazement he saw that Morris had begun to cry. Great tears were rolling down his rubber cheeks. 'It . . . it'll take more than a field dressing to stop that,' he said truthfully. 'You need a load of fucking cement.' He lay forward on his elbow in the shallow stream and cried softly into the crook of his

329

elbow. Brigg regarded him helplessly. There was no reason to be surprised at a man weeping at impending death, but it was embarrassing just the same.

'Turn over again, Taff,' he said quietly. 'Let's see if there's something I can do.'

With a groan the big man did as he said. Brigg tried not to be sick. The stream water was washing the wound and taking the blood away but it gaped like the mouth of a goldfish. Then he remembered Grainger. 'I'll go and get Grainger's field dressing,' he said. 'Maybe the officers have a better one than ours.'

'Aye, that's a good idea, boy,' whispered Morris. 'You run up and get it.' It was the tone of a parent sending a lad on an errand to a shop.

Brigg scrambled up the bank again, slowing cautiously as he neared the top. He realized that everywhere was dimmer now. The sun had gone lower. He could see Grainger, a mound alongside the mound of the pig. The birds and their neighbouring monkeys had returned, and while the birds were subdued by the day's subsidence the monkeys screamed in their customary alarm as they swooped and swung, as though they were terrified each time they launched themselves through the air on a creeper.

Brigg surveyed the clearing shakily. It remained dim and still. He had reached the point of the depression nearest Grainger. His limbs seemed unwilling to move but, holding his breath, he made himself tremble forward until he was clear of his cover. Then, on his hands and knees, he scampered like a baby across to the elongated officer. Just to be sure, Brigg touched his shoulder. It was lifeless as putty beneath the shirt. Grainger's sten gun was trapped under his stomach and Brigg, at first, thought he should take it. But, prudently, he changed his mind. If they returned and discovered it was gone they might begin a search.

He shrank from touching the dead man again, but located the field dressing pack and returned to the margin of the clearing and down again to Morris. Morris looked at him with dull eyes in the dimness. 'Is it the daylight going or me?' he inquired almost academically.

'It's the daylight, Taff,' said Brigg more briskly. 'You're not going.'

'I wish I could share your confidence, butty,' mused Morris. 'I'm bleeding to death.'

'We'll stem that, don't worry,' said Brigg, wondering how he could do it. 'They'll find us soon. Our blokes, I mean. The Yank and Tasker and Wellbeloved must have got clear. They *must* have. There'll be some gurkhas here in no bloody time, you wait.'

'Wait?' queried Morris. 'Wait, you say? There's no option is there?'

Brigg, gritting his teeth, turned him over again and dressed the wound as well as he could.

'Turn upwards, Taff,' he said. 'Keep it dry for a bit.'

'I'm comfortable like this,' said Morris Morris. 'I can open my eyes and see the ripples going past my nose. Lovely.'

331

Brigg sat down by him. There was no room in the mud on the bank. It was easier to sit in the stream. The big man, lying like a felled log in the water, closed his eyes and seemed to fall into a half-sleep. He muttered a few words and Brigg watched him anxiously.

'Missus Harris,' recited Morris as if dreaming. 'Missus 'arris, your orifice – hif you please.' A smile tried to break against the man's pallor. 'Missus 'arris, your h'orifice, your h'aperture, if you please. Your h'opening.'

He lifted his eyes and stared at the puzzled Brigg. 'Funny that used to be, son. In the prison camp's concert. Missus 'arris. Aye, that was funny.'

Brigg laid his hand on that of the Welshman with an odd, improvised bedside manner. 'I'm sorry, Taff,' he said inadequately.

'Don't pat my hand, son,' warned Morris in a murmur. 'I might take a mean advantage of you.'

Brigg laughed dryly but Morris Morris said, 'I'm serious. Do you know, boy, if somebody don't come and find us, then you'll be sharing the final night of his life with an old poof.' Brigg still thought he was joking. 'I'm telling you the truth,' said Morris rationally quiet. 'Just a poor old worn-out poof.'

'Who's got a wife and three kids,' grinned Brigg.

'No. No wife and no kids,' confessed the man. 'Just figments of a Welsh imagination. Just ghosts.' He recited the names, affectionately: 'Davie, Dilwyn and little Doris. I got very fond of them, you know, Briggsy. And the wife. Very fond. But I made them all up. I'm just a poor old Cardiff Docks poof.'

'Christ,' said Brigg hollowly.

'Don't worry, boy,' said Morris assuringly. 'And there's no need to shift away.'

'I wasn't shifting away,' said Brigg defensively.

'I'm not in a fit state to take advantage of you now, anyway. Not with my balls missing. Anyway I'd retired from it, more or less.'

Brigg shook his head: 'Well, you fooled me, mate,' he said uneasily. 'I never guessed. You used to say your prayers for your children.'

Morris tried a laugh and it became a cackle in his throat. 'Aye, I enjoyed doing that. They got quite real to me, see? I even used to write letters and do the little drawings I made out they did. And I don't suppose the prayers were wasted. After all, to God one Dilwyn or Doris must be very much like another one.'

'You poor bugger,' said Brigg. 'You should have said. You wouldn't be the only one.'

'I thought somebody would twig,' admitted Morris dolefully. 'Well, I mean . . .' He opened the top button of his jacket and produced his wondrous female right breast. 'Look at that,' he suggested. 'Did you ever see a titty like that on a real man?'

'No, no,' admitted Brigg overcome with embarrassment. 'Put it away, Taff.'

Morris obliged. His head fell into the stream again and he spat the water out. It was almost dark now. It was like being imprisoned in a hole in the centre of the earth. 'And I'm a bit of a tea-leaf, too,' added Morris abruptly.

'A tea-leaf? A thief?'

'Aye, that's what you say in London, don't you? Tea-leaf? It's something else I can't help. I've often thought one thing might be the cause of the other. I once nicked a regimental drum, when I was first in during the war, and rolled it down a hill into a river by Salisbury. I've lifted all sorts of things in my life. And I've never been nabbed.' He paused, then said simply: 'It was me who pinched the Colonel's stamps.'

'Taffy!' Brigg was so astounded he almost shouted. Then he realized what he had done, and said 'Taffy' more quietly as though that would repair any error. 'You don't know what you're yapping about.'

'I do,' said Morris confidently. 'I lifted the old boy's stamps. I did it because I was upset, because they made me wear a shirt. They hurt me, so I thought, so when I saw the stamps on the Colonel's window-sill, I stole them. I had them hid for weeks. Then I put them in his garden when we was singing those carols.'

Brigg shook his head in the dark.

'I might just as well tell you now, boy,' pointed out Morris. 'You're supposed to have somebody to talk to when you're dying. To get it off your chest. A confessor.'

'You're *not* dying,' muttered Brigg pushing his face close to the Welshman in the dark. The big nose seemed to travel to meet him. 'You're *not*.'

'Ah, come on,' said Morris, becalmed now. 'Nobody bleeds like this without dying. I reckon the level of this stream has gone up a couple of inches since I've been lying here.'

As he came to the end of the words, Brigg heard

334

voices from the clearing above. He put his arm on Morris's wrist. Morris smiled and patted his hand. 'Shush,' pleaded Brigg. 'It could be our blokes.'

'Or it could be theirs,' suggested Morris.

'I'll go,' Brigg said. He realized he was trembling again. The water felt cold. 'I'll have to go up and have a dekko.'

'Don't be long,' said Morris. 'I might get tired of waiting and piss off.'

'Just shut up, please,' said Brigg. 'I'll go now.'

A few inches at a time, he made again the journey to the top of the bank. Less than an inch at a time his forehead lifted above the rim. Then, with only the top half of his eyes exposed, he halted, his misgivings solidifying to fear.

He pulled his head away and pressed his features into the crumbling mud bank. Then he looked again. A gang of men, twenty at least, were standing around the bodies of Grainger and the wild pig. They had lanterns and electric torches and he could see rifles. At first he hoped they might be villagers from somewhere, but they did not look like villagers. He shivered, as on a freezing night. He remained watching.

Their voices were subdued from long habit of living in a jungle. But a quick sharp order rose above them and Brigg saw what they were doing. They had tied the pig's feet around a stout pole and they now lifted it and began to carry it forward. Then a second group lifted another pole and Brigg saw that Lieutenant Grainger was hanging in the same manner as the wild animal he had shot. Mesmerized he watched them march towards him. One instinct told him to roll down the bank, another to remain rigid where he was. He stayed.

His head descended below the level of the clearing and he lay flat against the slope in the dark, his eyes elevated so that he saw their boots a few inches away, and Grainger's head, hung back, mouth gaping and eyes blankly aglow in the light of their lanterns. Brigg felt sure they would hear his rattling body.

He lay there for five minutes after they had gone along the track and vanished into the trees and the night. No one returned. Then he carefully lowered himself back into the long crevice until he was beside Morris Morris and the stream. Morris had his eyes closed. Brigg looked at him anxiously and he obligingly opened them. 'Don't worry, boy,' he said. 'I'm still here. Was it the foe?'

'It was them,' confirmed Brigg. 'A gang. They'd slung the pig and Grainger on poles and carted them off.' He shook his head. 'Bloody horrible.'

'Ah, I don't suppose the lieutenant minded,' remarked Morris conversationally. 'It makes no difference to him now. And it's a good way of transport through country like this.'

Brigg nodded: 'I suppose so. It just didn't look very nice, that's all.'

'No, a bit offensive to the eye, I admit, but it's a sensible way,' sighed Morris. 'If young Tasker or the Yankee boy was here they could help you sling me on a pole. I wouldn't care.'

'I wonder what's happened,' said Brigg. 'God, I hope they're all right.'

As he completed the sentence there came the amazing sound of a gramophone record playing through the trees. A treacly voice sang a popular song 'Moon Above Malaya' in English, with violins in the background. Had Santa Claus trundled through the jungle trees, they could hardly have been more astonished.

'Oh dear, dear,' said Morris opening his eyes. 'For a minute I thought I was dead. I thought it was an angel.'

'It's near,' whispered Brigg. 'It must be just downstream. Look, there's a sort of glow in the trees there. It's a village, Taff, it's a village!' He stopped suddenly. 'Or the bloody bandit camp.'

'Oh, they'd hardly have bright lights and gramophone records playing in a bandit camp, now would they boy?' Morris pointed out patiently. 'Not unless it's ladies' night.'

'You're right,' agreed Brigg. He stood up to a crouch. 'I'll go,' he said. 'I'll go and get some help. You'll be all right, Taff.'

'No!' Morris bellowed at him with all his failing strength.

He grasped the young man's ankle. 'No, you're not doing that.'

Brigg stared at him in astonishment. 'But it's no distance,' he protested. 'It's yards. I'll be back in a couple of minutes.'

'No,' said Morris in a lower tone. 'Don't leave me here in the water. I'll come. I can manage it, boy. Honest I can.'

Helplessly Brigg looked into the big, sad face,

pallid under its mud mask. Morris was attempting to get to his knees. Brigg's hands went to him and he took some of the weight. 'All right, Taff,' he said tenderly. 'If you can manage it.' Morris had reached his feet, able to stand more upright because the over-growth was thinner above the stream. Brigg caught him around the waist as he swayed. 'We'll follow the stream,' he decided.

'It's bound to go through the village. They use it for washing and crapping in.'

'Done my wounds no end of good, I expect,' observed Morris. He began to cough like a consumptive. Brigg looked closely at the face and saw a thread of blood making its way down the chin from the corner of the sagging mouth. They began to move forward.

It was less than half a mile and it took them over an hour. They stumbled through the mud and water, holding on to the vegetation above them like strap-hangers on a bus. Once, with his hand around a creeper, Morris emitted a strangled gurgle. Brigg, alarmed, looked at him. 'Tarzan,' explained Morris with a terrible, blood-riven smile.

Eventually, the stream cleared the trees and ran into the Malay village. It was the night of a local festival and lights and lanterns were hanging from all the rough houses and across the clearing at their centre. The people, dressed in their best and most colourful clothes, were gathered in the centre, dancing a sedate dance to a Malayan tune from a gramophone and singing the chorus happily. There was a fire, and above the fire, suspended from a spit, were portions of wild pig.

No one noticed Brigg at first, then they all saw him together. The dancing lines broke; the singing dragged to a stop. The people, frightened, parted and in the light of the fire and the lanterns they saw the young British soldier – soaked with mud and blood, and carrying his huge comrade over his shoulder like a prize fish. Speechless, Brigg looked at them in their festive clothes. By then Morris Morris, the poof of Cardiff Docks, was dead.

18

Brigg slept that night alongside the dead Morris Morris in one of the huts. The villagers were kind but afraid, for they were caught between the jungle guerrillas and the military, living a precarious life trying to avoid or please both. They had given the bandits a hundred pairs of trousers recently, which was why they had roast pig that night. It had come as a gift. Brigg sat and ate some of the meat and drank some native beer, before crawling into the hut where Morris was lying. The villagers insisted that he stayed with his dead comrade, to prevent the ghost wandering around the kampong in the dark.

Brigg slept a night full of frightful dreams, but his weariness overcame them, although once he awoke and imagined he had heard Morris snoring.

With the morning they sent a youth on a bicycle along the track to the police post in the next kampong, and at midday a jeep from the depot came to pick up Brigg and the body of the Welshman.

'Your other blokes are all right,' said the driver as soon as he saw Brigg.

'Oh, thank Christ.'

There were two gurkhas in the back of the truck.

They put the body of Morris on the floor between the gurkhas, who never once looked down at it.

'Not the officer, though,' said the driver. 'He's missing, presumed killed.'

'He's killed,' said Brigg, without expression. 'I saw him.'

'Oh, you better tell them when you get back. Your sergeant, little big-mouthed sod, got a shoulder wound. He's gone to the hospital. Glad to get rid of him. You'd think he'd won a war.'

'And the others are okay?'

'Yeah, they're all right. The American bloke went back to Singapore this morning. He's got a posting, or something.'

'He's been waiting,' said Brigg. 'Fine bloody time to tell him.'

'Your other mucker is at the depot. They thought you'd had your chips.'

Brigg shook his head. He felt a thousand years old. 'No, he had his chips,' he said nodding backwards into the truck where Morris was stretched between the unmoving gurkhas. 'Poor old Taffy. Why didn't nobody come to look for us?'

'That officer of yours. He was supposed to leave a plan of operations, but he didn't bother. Nobody knew where you'd gone, mate, and no bugger can look behind every tree in this country. There's too many.'

It seemed a ridiculously short time before they reached the main road and then the depot. Everywhere was brazen and bright midday sun, birds were sweet among the trees, some Malay girls in coloured

341

sarongs were laughing as they swayed along the road. Brigg glanced behind at Morris Morris as if it was still a time to be anxious about him.

They turned into the main gate and Tasker, who had been squatting waiting on the step of their hut across the compound, got to his feet and ran like a schoolboy running across a playground. He and Brigg fell against each other then pulled away in embarrassment. Tasker was crying. 'Silly sod,' he snivelled at Brigg. 'We thought you'd had it.'

'I'm all right, Task,' said Brigg emotionally. 'Fucking awful, wasn't it? We've got old Taff in the back.'

Tasker turned and began walking towards the hut. 'I don't want to see him,' he said. 'I've just had enough, that's all. I don't reckon I could take any more.'

'I'd better go and report,' said Brigg. 'Tell them I'm back.'

'You'd better. They're taking us back to Panglin this afternoon. The Yank's gone already. He's going back to his own mob. He's going to Korea, poor bugger.'

'Do him good,' said Brigg sadly. 'You get too bloody soft here.'

'You ought to have seen Grainger,' said Tasker. 'It was unbelievable. He just ran straight at them firing his sten. Just like the pictures. He *must* have got three or four of them. He left us standing, Briggsy. Just standing. It was all over in a few seconds. We

342

couldn't even fire a shot because he was between us and them. He never called for us to follow, or anything; he just seemed to go mad.'

'He *was* mad,' said Brigg simply. They were in the jolting truck returning to Panglin. They left the mainland and went across the blessed causeway to the safety of Singapore Island. 'I always said he was,' he continued.

'He ought to get the VC,' said Tasker firmly. 'I've never seen anything like it. He didn't seem to care. And when they got him they turned and bunked off.'

'And you cleared off too,' said Brigg.

Tasker, hurt, glanced at him. 'What could we do? Wellbeloved was bleeding like anything and moaning about Grainger. He got a bit light-headed before we reached the kampong. He was going on about Grainger spilling that custard in his lap at Christmas. But we had to get out when we had a chance – before they came back with reinforcements or something. We had a look for you and Taffy, honest, but you know what it was like there. You could hide a battleship in that stuff. You didn't look for us, did you?'

'No,' shrugged Brigg. 'I had a search around later but, like you say, it was a bit difficult. And poor old Taff was in a bad way. It was terrible, Task, terrible.'

For something which had been so big, there seemed ridiculously little to say about it. They rode in silence, the hot road unwinding behind the truck. Eventually Brigg said: 'Twice up there and we cop it twice. Just our bloody luck.'

The truck curved into the Panglin garrison and stopped outside their familiar barrack block. 'Is this it?' called the driver.

'This is it,' said Brigg wearily. 'Home sweet home.'

They climbed down from the tailboard. On the square two platoons of newly arrived troops were drilling in the sun, their sergeant bawling at them across the white concrete. The everyday Indian ice-cream man had parked his tricycle outside the barrack block, waiting for the soldiers to come from the office. Almost from habit Brigg and Tasker, dragging their equipment by one hand, went to him and bought two vanilla cornets.

'Put them on the book, Jimmy,' said Brigg.

'On the book,' agreed the ice-cream man.

Brigg wanted to say: 'Jimmy, you know the big man, the Welshman. Well, he's dead.' But he wondered what the use would be. Morris Morris probably owed money for the ice-cream anyway. It would upset Jimmy.

Tasker and Brigg trudged up the echoing concrete stairs, on to the front balcony and then into the barrack room. All was cool and ordered in there. The familiar beds laid out with equipment and bedding. The fans working lazily. The water running noisily in the urinals at the back.

The two soldiers sat, saturated with weariness, on their beds, each licking his ice-cream like a small boy, and stared across with full, dull hearts to the bed that had been the sleeping place of Morris Morris. It was already piled with his belongings. They licked the ice-cream cornets.

'Two months, twenty-five days, twenty-two hours to do,' said Brigg.

From outside, from the sunlit square, echoed the eternal sound of soldiers drilling.

A nurse wounded look @ a private soldier!

Buy *Leslie Thomas*

Order further *Leslie Thomas* titles from your local bookshop, or have them delivered direct to your door by Bookpost

☐ The Virgin Soldiers	0 09 949003 X	£6.99
☐ Onward Virgin Soldiers	0 09 949005 6	£6.99
☐ Waiting for the Day	0 09 945719 9	£6.99
☐ The Magic Army	0 09 946917 0	£6.99
☐ The Dearest and the Best	0 09 947422 0	£6.99
☐ Dangerous in Love	0 09 947423 9	£6.99
☐ Dangerous by Moonlight	0 09 942170 4	£6.99
☐ Dangerous Davies:		
The Last Detective	0 09 943617 5	£5.99

FREE POST AND PACKING

Overseas customers allow £2 for paperback

PHONE: 01624 677237
POST: Random House Books
c/o Bookpost, PO Box 29, Douglas,
Isle of Man, IM99 1BQ

FAX: 01624 670923

EMAIL: bookshop@enterprise.net

Cheques (payable to Bookpost) and credit cards accepted

Prices and availability subject to change with notice
Allow 28 days for delivery
When placing your order, please state if you do not wish to receive any additional information

www.randomhouse.co.uk